Two Old Men's Tales

T0347757

Two Old Men's Tales

The Deformed

AND

The Admiral's Daughter

Anne Marsh Caldwell

NONSUCH

First published 1834
Copyright © in this edition 2006
Nonsuch Publishing Ltd

Nonsuch Publishing Limited
The Mill, Brimscombe Port, Stroud, Gloucestershire, GL5 2QG
www.nonsuch-publishing.com

Nonsuch Publishing Ltd is an imprint of the Tempus Publishing Group

For any comments or suggestions, please email the editor of this series at:
classics@tempus-publishing.com

British Library Cataloguing in Publication Data.
A catalogue record for this book is available from the British Library.

ISBN 1-84588-081-1

Typesetting and origination by Nonsuch Publishing Limited
Printed in Great Britain by Oaklands Book Services Limited

CONTENTS

INTRODUCTION TO THE MODERN EDITION

In the early part of 1834 Anne Marsh published her first novel, *Two Old Men's Tales*. She was forty-three years old and, while she had been schooled in poetry and literature, as befitted a young lady of means, she had never before written for anything so crass as publication. Encouragement came from two very different sources: the first was the sudden threat of financial ruin; the second, more positively, was the reaction of a friend, Harriet Martineau, who believed her work had a quality that the public would crave. Time has proved Miss Martineau to be right, as with this volume Marsh began a literary career that was to continue for another thirty-two years.

The author was born Anne Caldwell on 9 January 1791, at Newcastle-under-Lyme. Her father, James, was a partner in the firm of Sparrow & Caldwell, Attornies at Law, and a highly respected local businessman and estate-owner. The family lived at Linley Wood, a rambling Georgian mansion in some 200 acres, in Talke O'Th'Hill, Staffordshire, where the local parish church maintains to this day a plaque in James Caldwell's memory.

In 1818, on 13 July, Anne married Arthur Cuthbert Marsh, a young solicitor from a wealthy banking family who had studied with Anne's brother at Cambridge. The financial stability of the young couple was not at all in doubt, until it was entirely undone by the fraud of Henry Fauntleroy, a partner in the firm of Marsh, Stacey & Graham. The firm went bankrupt, and with this the Marshs lost the bulk of their fortune. Arthur also lost his half-brother, Michael, who took his own life as a result.

While Fauntleroy's crime led him to the gallows, it led Anne to show Harriet Martineau the manuscript of *Two Old Men's Tales*. This was a combined volume of two separate novels, *The Deformed* and *The Admiral's Daughter*. These tales of doomed love, of greed, vanity and deceit, immediately struck a chord with the reading public. As a single volume, it ran to several editions and, despite being published anonymously, contrived to make the author's name.

The *Athenaeum*, an influential London journal of the time, described Mrs Marsh as one who, while possessed of the best qualities of the writers of her time, had more ability than any to charm or terrify. 'No writer had greater powers', it said, 'of compelling tears.' Her books, however, are rare and difficult to find, as she continued to publish anonymously. This has not prevented astute critics from regarding her as part of a 'sisterhood' of writers of the age, an age which included such talents as Jane Austen and Maria Edgeworth. The 'most earnest of storytellers', Anne Marsh Caldwell remains a writer with the facility and the desire to 'plunge beneath the surface, probe the mind, and the heart', a feat which she has accomplished to great effect in the present volume.

THE DEFORMED

Un Dieu descend toujours pour dénouer le drame,
Toujours la Providence y veille et nous proclame
Cette justice occulte, et ce divin ressort
Qui fait jouer le temps, et gouverne le sort.

Lamartine

THE circumstances of life having thrown me into very close communication with a certain noble family, and made me acquainted with several events, which appeared to me remarkable, I have thought it well to record them in the best manner I am able, esteeming, as I have always done, a faithful representation of human conduct and its consequences to be the best moral lesson which can be read to youth.

I was young when I first became connected with the family of the Marquis of Brandon; I had then just succeeded to the severe toils and scanty remunerations of the medical administration of the town of Carstones and its adjoining neighbourhood—a neighbourhood, I may say, almost entirely in the dependence of the Marquis of Brandon, whose magnificent park nearly surrounded the pretty little town, in which I was to reside: indeed the principal street of Carstones served, as it would seem, but as an avenue to one of the outer gates of the castle, and was terminated by the frowning towers of what had once been the keep of the vast feudal edifice, which for centuries had been tenanted by this noble family. The town in fact owed its existence to the vicinity of the stronghold, and the castle built, as such fortresses commonly were, on a proud commanding steep, towered above the little collection of houses, inhabited by those who seemed to combine, in their relations with the great Baron of the stronghold, something of the base submission of slaves, with the affectionate dependence of children. But things were now altered; though, as

far as dependence and servility went, the present inhabitants of
the little town might have rivalled their ancestors, the outward
manifestations of such sentiments had, of course, changed their
character; and in the castle itself, the ease and luxury of modern
refinement might be perceived mingling somewhat strangely
with the harsh outlines and gloomy splendour of its ancient
architecture; round the huge dark towers, shrubberies, flower-
beds, velvet lawns, and well rolled gravel walks, might be seen;
the massive stone casements, formed rather to exclude, than to
admit, the light and air, had been succeeded in many places by
sash windows of plate glass, and on every side the contrivances
intended to promote security and defence were giving way to
those of elegance and comfort.

The vast gloomy hall, it is true, retained its ancient character
of stern magnificence. The light, penetrating the narrow gothic
windows, fell upon the waving banners, the once bright and
gorgeous armour, the shields, the lances of other days and other
manners, and the old family portraits; which displayed the fierce
countenances of the powerful Barons; at once the terror and the
protection of the domain over which they ruled; while gentle
ladies in prim cap, starched ruff, and jewelled stomacher, with the
remarkably small hand and regular oval countenance observable
in the portraits of our old English dames, still gazed demurely on
the rugged warriors frowning grimly around.

The apartments in general offered a striking picture of the
opposition between recent and ancient tastes and manners. Many
of them had been fitted up as living rooms, furnished and adorned

with all the elaborate luxury of our times, adapted, it is true, by
the skill of the presiding artist as far as possible to the genius of
the place, so that no glaring incongruity might shock the eye;
the massive carved and gilded furniture, the rich satins, damasks,
and velvets, were in harmony with the ideas of antique grandeur
inspired by the vastness of the building; but the splendid mirrors,
the extraordinary vividness of the colouring displayed upon the
walls and hangings, the splendid collection of pictures in gorgeous
frames, the thousand forms of elegance and beauty presented on
every side reminded the spectator that all was the work of recent
art. One whole side of the castle remained, however, unvisited
by modern improvement, and the long suite of its echoing
apartments still retained their character of ancient, faded, gloomy
splendour; the small pointed windows of stained glass scarcely
afforded at mid-day more than a twilight view of the ponderous,
tall-backed ebony chairs; the wide yawning chimneys with their
ample hearths, and towering mantel-pieces; the dark tapestry
which waved and moved when the opening door admitted the
air. Beds were there with testers reaching to the ceiling, from
whose heavily adorned canopies the long gloomy curtains hung
in massive folds—antique cabinets—strange, mysterious looking
chests—misshapen figures—grotesque and enormous jars—all the
treasures of rude uncivilised ages were there—arranged in the stiff,
undeviating order that had been preserved for centuries—forcibly
recalling those days when life appears to have been a system of
grave representation, where neither companionship, nor gaiety, nor
the happy domestic negligence of our times could find a place.

The towers had been long abandoned to the owls and bats; but those who chose to climb to the summit were rewarded by one of the richest and most varied landscapes to be found among the multitude which adorned this land, still, for the gaiety and luxuriance of its scenery, deserving the name of merry England. The vast domain of Brandon, acquired with all its forests, streams, chases, and rights manorial and territorial at the Conquest, by the good sword of John the Long, first Earl, stretched far on every side, intersected by a magnificent sheet of water, presenting every variety of the sweeping lawn and undulating vale and hill, interspersed with immense oaks and elms, and crowned by the waving woods which rose, in splendid profusion: through the whole extent of the park the long dark avenue might be seen extending many a mile, while glimpses of the blue and hazy distant mountains added softness to this charming picture.

The Marquis of Brandon was twice married. When I first became an inhabitant of Carstones, the mistress of this almost royal abode was a very fair and somewhat short woman, with eyes of that greyish, whitish blue which resolutely defies expression, her hair was of a hue equally uncharactered, it did not quite merit the term sandy, nor was it red, nor was it flaxen, it was a mixture of all three, or rather, a shade au juste milieu between them all—her features, however, were small and delicate, and bore an air of so much quiet and unpretending gentleness, without the slightest approach to imbecility, that it was impossible to look upon her face without being pleased and attracted: it was so with the graces of her person, she was low, insignificant, ill-grown, and, indeed, rather lame; but there was a simplicity and truth in her gestures, a tranquil composure about her movements, an absence of every thing affected or unnatural, without the slightest touch of vulgarity, so perfectly in keeping with the grave sweetness of her voice and countenance, that no one could regard her without a feeling of respect and love.

The Marquis was, on the contrary, in spite of his noble blood, rather singularly *unaristocratic* in his appearance and manners—he was handsome, but he looked rather clownish—gay, but a little vulgar—he could not be called foolish, but he was certainly rather heavy—nor rude, though he was unpolished and abrupt. He was *gauche*, in fact, both in body and mind, exactly that thing which a nobleman ought not to be; yet it is a defect from which the cares of a Sevigné herself cannot always protect the heirs of great names and great fortunes. He was, however, excessively good-natured, but this quality, in general of equivocal value, was rendered in his circumstances positively dangerous by the extreme indolence and facility of his temper—an indolence and a facility so great that, insensible to the claims of his high station, he suffered the authority and power with which he was invested to devolve on any one who chose to take the trouble of seizing them—happy if with the habit of acting for himself he could also have surrendered his responsibility—but that was impossible: he contrived, however, to shut his eyes to its importance, if not to its existence—and considered his high rank as a privilege entailing on others the necessity of labouring for him, while it exempted him from the obligation of exerting himself for others. In this alone could the sense of pride and privilege in this good-natured man be discovered. It never seemed to enter his thoughts that a thing so lofty and so rare as a Marquis of Brandon could have been created for the slightest purpose of utility. His goodness was therefore merely passive—he inflicted little pain, he was neither harsh, nor unkind, nor exacting; but he occasioned little happiness, for he had neither attention nor activity; he never intentionally wounded a single being, but he rarely would exert himself for any one's advantage. No one was injured at his hands—no one by his hand was protected from injury.

The Marquis had, like other young men of his day, made the grand tour in company with his tutor, and run the circle of London follies to a certain degree; but, as, like some other of the very great families, his family mingled less with the world in general than might have been expected from their rank and importance—he, like many other young heirs, had been kept in what has been called a state of dry-nursing from his cradle to his majority. Educated by a private tutor, a grave and rather dull young man, with him he had travelled, seeing as little, learning as little, and experiencing as little, as could be contrived in the course of visiting all the courts of Europe. On his return to London the eye of his careful lady-mother had been upon him; and having continued to reside in his father's mansion long after he was of age, the watchfulness of this busy and rather clever woman kept him a good deal in awe, and a good deal in order; therefore, when it was proposed to him to marry Miss Kirkham, the only child of the rich banker, with a fortune of 500,000l., he made no objection. He liked his ease, and he began to wish for independence: his father, in spite of his vast estates, he knew to be excessively poor—poor with the poverty of a very great man—before the wretchedness of which, the poverty of a common beggar sinks into insignificance—his is the indigence of nature—the want of a few things which the accidents of the next hour may relieve—anxieties, however pressing, which reach not beyond the present moment;—but the poverty of the great is a system of hopeless, irretrievable embarrassment—often the work of successive generations—inextricably interwoven with the web of their existence—a yoke—a burden, shackles which every successive proprietor put on at his accession to lay down only in his grave. A fortunate marriage, the acquisition by this means of one of those vast fortunes which the unfettered nature of mercantile wealth allows to descend to female heirs, alone affords the power to break this iron bondage, and shake off the accumulated load of centuries. An opportunity of this kind offered itself to the family of Brandon. The great banker, Kirkham, had one only daughter, the idol of his affections—500,000*l.* he said he should lay down—actually lay down on her wedding-day. He was himself a very old man;—this daughter was the child of his old age—the child, too, of a beloved Rachel, now no more—and it might be expected therefore that the remainder of his vast property would speedily devolve upon the fortunate man who might obtain the young lady's hand. Mr. Kirkham doted upon his daughter, who returned his affection with more than a daughter's duty. To see her happy, I should not say was the darling, it was the sole, object of his heart, and, with the error common to parents, he sought for her happiness in greatness, wealth, and power. Not that he was blindly or selfishly ambitious: had his daughter confessed a worthy preference, he would have indulged it, and sacrificed without a sigh all his airy castles: on the other hand had the most dignified in the land addressed her, wanting the recommendation of good morals, and a good reputation, his proposals would have been, without a moment's hesitation, rejected. But Jane, this beloved daughter, confessed no preference: she had been brought up by a maiden aunt, with the most exaggerated care and tenderness, suffered to associate little with those of her own age and condition, and, under the plea of ill health, denied, not only the amusements common to her years, but the opportunity of acquiring the elegant accomplishments now so universal among her sex.

Accustomed to pass her time almost entirely with her aunt and father, separated from the society of her equals in birth, by the vast distance to which fortune had lifted her above her natural connections, her pleasures were peaceful and few. With a beautiful flower garden, which she cultivated with equal taste and assiduity—a little carriage, in which she and her good aunt took their daily drive, visiting and blessing every cottager in the neighbourhood:—her school, in which the children were dressed by her purse, and often instructed by her care;—her beautiful almshouse for decayed gentlewomen, with its trim gardens, fair stone fronts, cheerful lattice windows and venerable and happy inmates;—life fleeted on in calm occupation, and unruffled tranquillity. As for love, the passion, far from having reached her heart, had scarcely even occupied her thoughts; and on marriage she had reflected as little. When the proposal of the Marquis of Brandon was laid in due form before her she perceived that her father was proud and happy—prouder—happier than she had ever beheld him in his life. She heard that the Earl of St. Germains was excellent and amiable. She saw him—he appeared to her young eyes good-tempered, lively, and pleasing, both in countenance and manner. To be the wife of one of the first nobles of England,—to belong to an ancient historic family—to share in its grave dignities, high duties, and glorious recollections.— Jane was not insensible to all this—with all her composure she wanted not imagination, and had under her gentle manner much concealed enthusiasm. She married the Earl of St. Germains—he was a very kind husband, and she was in her own way happy.

This happiness consisted in an almost unbroken residence at Brandon Castle; to which place, after a very short time passed in London, when she was presented, she retired, for her husband had come into possession shortly before the marriage was concluded. A sense of her own unfitness to adorn a town mansion, or do credit to her husband's choice, amid the glare and magnificence of fashionable life, a discovery which her very first entrance upon that stage enabled her to make, determined her, with a quiet good sense peculiarly her own, to retire to a sphere where she might find both dignity and useful occupation. Having, therefore, once appeared at court, she laid aside those diamonds which might have been the envy of Queens, and sending them to her banker's, secretly resolved never to wear them more; and having persuaded the good-natured Marquis to indulge her wish of immediately visiting Brandon Castle, there she came, and there she remained, the beneficent genius of the country.

I think I see her now, in that low garden chair, drawn by the well-known pair of demure little grey ponies—with the innocent-faced boy, who served her as a postilion, and followed by her own groom in a grey frock, visiting our little town, and stopping at my surgery door. I hear her calm but pleasing voice inquire for me; I come out and receive the gentle apologies for the trouble she is giving. There I stand, not unwilling, till minutes amount to half hours, consulting on the health and welfare of all the unfortunate around. Her good sense—the precision of her ideas—the moderation of her aims—the justness of her conceptions—the perfect purity of her intentions—the matchless goodness and kindness of her heart, still fill me with the deepest and most affectionate veneration, whenever I recall those days spent so peaceably, a blessing to herself and to all around her.

> Silent and good she steals along,
> Far from the world's gay busy throng,
> With gentle yet prevailing force,
> Intent upon her destined course;
> Graceful and useful all she does,
> Blessing and blest where'er she goes.

Beside her sits her little boy, he is not yet four years old. Alas, why should this excellent creature have been visited by so severe an affliction—the child is already deformed—and his poor little head seems pressed forwards by the unnatural curvature between the shoulders—his legs are thin, and show none of the beautiful roundness of infancy,—his fingers too are long and slender—in shape resembling those of a grown person,—his complexion is sickly and pale—but his face is beautiful, though of a strange and ominous beauty—his features are only too delicate,—his eyes are large, dark and melting, but with pupils remarkably dilated,—his hair is abundant and of a beautiful colour—there he sits by his mother, supported already by those irons which vainly strive to supply the deficiencies of nature;—there sits the future Marquis of Brandon, the heir of this immense domain, and of the vast revenue of his mother.—It may be proper to remark here that Mr. Kirkham had been very liberal in his daughter's settlements, having secured his prodigious fortune to her and her children, and in failure of them, bestowed it on the noble house to which he had allied himself—the life interest was also given to the Marquis in case of his surviving his wife.

The little Earl of St. Germains sits upon the lap of a person who must not be overlooked, Mrs. Cartwright; she is the widow of an officer, who had fallen in battle the first year of a marriage, formed under the happiest auspices, though unblest with the smiles of fortune, and who had left her unprotected, and unprovided for. Her circumstances had become known to Miss Kirkham; and she had been received into her family in the character of companion,—that most grievous of all the forms of dependence; a place of which the duties are so ill defined as to afford a constant source of tyranny and ill humour, with a salary calculated rather to compensate for the specified, than for the exacted, sacrifices. But Mrs. Cartwright had been more fortunate than is usually the case. In the well-regulated temper and perfect truth and justice of Miss Kirkham, she had found a security against half the ills of her condition; while the affectionate confidence and esteem which she speedily excited became a source if not of happiness, at least of consolation. Miss Kirkham became tenderly attached to the gentle and sensible woman whose character, in many points resembling her own, had acquired a kind of sacred elevation, by the sorrow she had known, and the fortitude and resignation she had displayed. Mrs. Cartwright had been once extremely beautiful, she was now so very pale and thin, that she had lost many of her charms; but there was something more interesting than beauty in that smooth fair brow, over which her dark hair was plainly braided, and in the delicate though faded countenance beneath; while the neatness and extreme simplicity of her attire added a peculiar character to her appearance. It was easy to see that Mrs. Cartwright was not of this world, indeed her air was that of one set apart for holy things; a sort of lay nun; a devotee in the best sense of the word; one who in the exercise of every duty, consoled by the deep mysterious influences of her religion, awaited in patience her dismissal from a scene which had no longer charms for her.

Since the Marchioness had resided at Brandon, Mrs. Cartwright had remained constantly with her, sharing in her active labours of love for all; but, more peculiarly in the incessant care and tenderness demanded by the sickly little boy, the only child that had blest the Marchioness of Brandon.

The day I have now in my mind was a sad one to me. After she had detailed all her little plans, for half a dozen of her poor people, in which I was to bear my part, the Marchioness spoke of one rarely the theme of her conversation; she spoke of herself.

"Mr. Wilson, I have not felt quite right lately, I think I had better have a little talk with you, not in the street," added she, smiling quietly. "Will you be kind enough, when you have finished all your business to-day, to come up to the castle and drink tea with me?—you will find us at tea at nine, you know; but if this is in the least inconvenient to you, pray come to-morrow—my business can wait very well."

"I will certainly wait upon you, madam, at nine, and hope to bring a good report of our patients."

"Good morning, then, Mr. Wilson."

And the little pony chair, and the sober groom, were soon out of sight.

I went at the time appointed, and had a long interview with the Marchioness. What was my grief! my anguish!—though a quiet man, I will add, my despair, to find that the painful feelings, of which she so slightly complained, were the symptoms of a dreadful internal complaint, already advanced too far to admit of the slightest hope of a cure. She saw the dismay written in my countenance, which I found it impossible to conceal, her colour heightened a little, a very little:—

"Mr. Wilson," said she, her voice just shaken, "I perceive there is more the matter here than I had imagined."

"Indeed, madam, I am sorry to confess that there is; but care and skill, I trust—"

I was running on with the usual vain flattery of my calling; she stopped me.

"Mr. Wilson, I perceive your kind wish to encourage me, but I flatter myself that you know me so well, that when I ask for the simple truth, as far as your skill enables you to discover it, you will not attempt to disguise it from me. I do ask for the truth, and you may venture to tell it me. Is my complaint dangerous?"

"I will disguise nothing, madam; it is dangerous."

"Very dangerous?"

"Very dangerous."

"Does it hold out any chance of recovery?"

"I do not choose on my single responsibility to say that it does not."

"But you think it does not?"

I paused and then said, "I confess I am ignorant of the means of arresting it, but my practice, as your ladyship knows, is not extensive, and my opportunities of improvement have been few. I trust that by consulting the first London physicians, some palliative, if not a decided remedy may be found, and your life be prolonged many years to be a blessing to us all."

My voice trembled as I concluded.

"My dear Mr. Wilson, I will not attempt to tell you how very much I feel obliged by this kind feeling, and the regard you have ever shown me; and I am not flattering you when I say, that I would rather trust my life in your hands than in those of any medical man of my acquaintance; still my life is of great importance to some, and if you believe that my chance of recovery will be in the least increased by seeing a London physician, pray let one be sent for without delay."

"I am decidedly of opinion that a physician ought to be called in."

"Then may I trouble you to write to Dr. —— for me."

I returned home, as the French expressively say, le cœur navré de douleur; for I had not myself the slightest hope that the malignant and insidious disorder, of which the symptoms were too evident, could be subdued. How I lamented that indifference to her own concerns which had made her delay so long to complain of what she looked upon as a trifling ailment—how I grieved for herself, for her unhappy child—for her husband— for all of us—for the poor child, perhaps less than for the rest. I had long considered it as a lost case, never expected that he would be reared at all, and indeed, with a hasty impatience too common to our short-sighted race, had decided within myself, that an early death would be the best thing that could happen to him.

The London physician, a man of the first eminence in his profession, arrived; his opinion justified mine, his resources were, alas! no greater: the complaint was one which had hitherto baffled human skill; it was beyond the reach of remedies whether medical or surgical.

"Mr. Wilson," said the Marchioness, "I am sorry to give you pain, and I know I do so by putting questions under my present unfortunate circumstances: you must, if you please, tell me frankly whether Dr. ——'s opinion coincides with yours."

"It does."

"And he can do no more for me than you can?"

"I greatly fear not."

"Nor can either he or you tell me how long this disease is likely to last? I will spare you the pain of telling me how it ends."

I hesitated.

"What is the longest time that a person in my condition has been known to live? What is the shortest period that life has been known to terminate in this disease? Pray tell me, [with earnestness,] consider how much I have to do, if possible, and deceive me not!"

"Two months!"

"Ah! that is short—I must not lose a moment. Mr. Wilson, will you have the kindness to consult with Dr. ——, and adopt that plan of treatment which will preserve to me the fullest possible exercise of my powers while life is granted?"

The moments of the Marchioness of Brandon had never been misapplied,

> Her virtues walked their simple round,
> And made no pause, and left no void.

But now the moments seemed doubled, and, by her admirable method, she contrived, in an incredibly short space of time, to arrange the various business for the benefit of all around, in which she had been so unceasingly and so usefully engaged, in such a manner that her plans might be carried on and brought to perfection by others, when her influence should be withdrawn.

This done, one anxiety, vast, incalculable, pressed heavily upon her heart—her little boy. I had always believed he would not live—in this her judgment differed from mine—it was her strong impression that he would. Her love partook of the calm energy of her nature, it was serious, deep, devoted,—reflective rather than imaginative— well had she weighed every detail of his unfortunate situation—well had she considered the future consequences that must arise from the strange disproportion which in his case existed between the gifts of nature and of fortune, and the still more important discrepancy was observable in the gifts of nature herself; for, niggard to the helpless and deformed frame, the mighty mother appeared to have been lavish of her compensations to the mind. The child already gave evidence of a strength of character, and a power of observation, far beyond his age; he appeared, too, to have inherited the composure of his mother's temperament, and the calm seriousness of her affection: his love for her showing itself rather in his constant preference of her society to every other pleasure, and the tenacity with which he silently kept close to her, his large speaking eyes fixed upon her face, than by bursts of tenderness, or abundance of caresses.

To watch over the development of such a mind, lodged in such a frame, had been the object which the Marchioness had proposed to herself as the future employment of her life. She had hoped by a sedulous education in some measure to avert the sufferings which threatened a being constituted like her unhappy son, and that by strengthening the higher qualities of his mind, its talents and its virtues, she might oppose a shield to the innumerable evils of his condition. She wished to develope his intellect and refine his taste to the highest degree, trusting that the pleasures thus afforded might suffice to give interest to existence, while she fondly hoped that her own devoted tenderness might afford some consolation to disappointed youth, for the loss of that more impassioned affection which forms the natural happiness of our early years, and which, she felt persuaded, no qualities he might possess would ever obtain for him.

Such had been the reflections, such the well-considered plans, of this affectionate mother; but she was to be called away, and in place of her own sedulous cares to substitute those of others, far less deeply interested in their success; warding off, as best she might, by deputy, that host of evils which hang over the head of the motherless child, even in the happiest circumstances, and which were rendered infinitely more distressing in this instance by the helpless infirmities of the unhappy boy.

That the Marquis would marry again she felt assured. Her discernment had taught her to believe that his second choice would not resemble his first; she foresaw many possible distresses and hardships for the child of her affections, but most of all, she lamented that her plans for his education might fall to the ground. She hastened to obviate as far as possible these misfortunes while yet she existed, and she wrote to the Marquis, then in London, informing him of her situation, and begging him immediately to come to her.

He arrived very much grieved and afflicted at her situation; for his affection, though not passionate, was great, and his esteem immeasurable. The influence she possessed was now all directed into one channel.

"My dear Lord, I have one or two requests to make, and I am quite sure before I make them, that they are granted—our poor little boy—"

"Alas! my dear, you need have little anxiety on his account," said the Marquis, while the tears stood in his eyes; "I fear I shall only have felt the happiness of having a son to estimate its loss."

"It is my opinion that my child will live, I would fain hope, to be a source of happiness to you and himself, but he will require more than ordinary care. Mrs. Cartwright,—you know how greatly I esteem her—is it asking too much to request that she may have the care of my son?"

"For what length of time?"

"I do not mean a tutor's, or a nurse's care, may she stand in the relation as nearly as possible of *mother* to him?"

Lord Brandon started!

"Do not misapprehend me, I cannot," with a grave smile, "wish her to stand in any nearer relation to *you*, my dear Lord, than she now does—you cannot for a moment imagine it—all I request is that, as long as it can be made comfortable to all parties, she may remain with my son, to supply my place—he will require all a mother's tenderness, poor unfortunate boy, to make existence tolerable—he will find it in her."

"My dear Lady Brandon, much less would be sufficient from you.—I hope you well know the perfect esteem I feel for you—that any recommendation of yours is sacred in my eyes. I shall be but too happy to see Mrs. Cartwright attached to my son, and a member of my family, as long as she should please to remain there."

"You allow me, then, to arrange my plans with her?"

"Indeed, I shall be relieved from great anxiety by your doing so; but alas! I fear it will be in vain."

"No, my lord, I trust it will not be in vain. I have another request to make:—my dear father, on the birth-day of my little boy, gave me 10,000*l.*; he intended it to be laid out in something by which I should ever remember him—there was no need of that—he was not likely to be forgotten by me.—I asked him a short time before he died what I should do with it; for, indeed, my dear lord, your great liberality left me nothing to wish or to want:—what I pleased, he said.—Will you allow me the same licence?"

"How can you, my dearest Lady Brandon, ask such a question? —but it is like yourself," said her husband, greatly touched.

He had, indeed, gratefully appreciated the delicacy with which, after bringing him such an immense fortune, she had behaved with respect to all money matters, and had returned it as far as lay in his power, with the most unbounded confidence.

"Only tell me what you wish—it shall be done. Is there any one you wish to provide for—anything?"

"I wish also to bestow as I please all my jewels, except the diamonds my father gave me at my presentation; those I would ask you to add to the jewels of your family, that I may leave something in your house for my father to be remembered by."

"Do in every thing as you wish—only tell me, can I in anything else obey you?"

I will not enlarge upon the tender scenes which followed. The Marquis felt—sensibly—the value of what he was about to lose. The Marchioness was grateful for his affection, and returned it with sincerity.

About a week after this she sent for me into her room, and said:—"My dear Mr. Wilson, I have perfect confidence in your honour—your integrity—your good sense.—Will you undertake a matter I have very much at heart? I have lived long enough with the great to be pretty well aware of the system of such families—so much splendour—so little comfort—such vast sums expended—so much real want of money. My little boy's situation, if he live, must be very peculiar, and he will require a thousand things which in ordinary cases would be justly thought unnecessary.—His father will marry again!"

I made a gesture of disapprobation.

"He will do right. A step-mother! Ah, Mr. Wilson, I trust it is a prejudice—in short, will you take charge of a sum of money for me,—to give to Mrs. Cartwright, or to my son—when in such portions as may be necessary? I shall take no acknowledgment of this sum—I wish it to be as completely in your power as if it were your own property—for you to make use of as you judge best for my poor boy's benefit."

"But, Madam, should I die?"

"There is no providing for all contingencies—dispose of it by will as you may think proper in that case—but if you live, as I trust in God you will, many years, keep it—you will find a use for it."

The sum was the 10,000l. All her jewels she gave me, desiring they might be sold, and the money settled upon Mrs. Cartwright—she left written directions with me to that effect; and having thus set her house in order, this excellent woman and sincere christian died with the utmost composure, and was buried, by her own desire, in the most private manner that was consistent with decorum.

The sorrow of the little boy, when he comprehended, which, in spite of all our care, he speedily did, the great misfortune which had befallen him, was, like his nature, rather deep, than full of demonstration:—he said little, but his cheek grew even paler than usual, and his weakness and emaciation increased to such a degree that it was the universal opinion that he would speedily follow his mother. Though quiet in the daytime, it was found that his pillow was wet with his infant tears, and sleep and appetite forsook him. Yet he continued to exist, almost, it would seem, without the means of existence: there was a tenacity of life about him, and he dragged on from day to day, though we concluded that every day would be his last.

I had a sister; her name was Judy; she was some years older than I was, and while I had been walking hospitals—struggling with difficulties—and seeing the world, Judy had remained stationary in the small town of Carstones, with the same prospect invariably before her eyes, till she almost believed that the world contained no other. The people of Carstones had the habit, usual with the inhabitants of small towns, of identifying their own self-love with the importance of the little place they lived in, and the dignity of the great family to which they were appended. Every thing that was done by the inhabitants of the castle—every revolution in the housekeeper's or steward's room—every mutation in the under-gardeners—every new dress, from that of the Marchioness herself, when she appeared at church, to that of the maid-servants coming down to gossip in the town;—their employments—their health—their visitors—their loves—and their hates, formed the incessant subject of conversation at our little card-tables. How the Marchioness looked, when my lord was coming down, how the little Earl had slept, &c.

Lewis XIV, in the midst of his splendour, and with all the assistance of his exquisite kingcraft, was not more a subject of excessive and indiscriminating interest to his courtiers at Versailles, than were the family of Brandon to the little people of Carstones. It is a great error to suppose that man naturally loves independence—this is only the taste of a few rarer spirits: to look upwards, to fawn, to flatter, and to lick the dust beneath the feet of riches and of power, is not only the destiny, but the taste, of the majority.

Whatever the Marquis or Marchioness chose to do, was certain to be right at Carstones—whatever Mr. Banks the steward, and

Mrs. Newsome chose to do, was in general right and proper also—they were all people of eminence and influence in their way. Not so Mrs. Cartwright: whatever she did was sure to be done wrong; she could neither look, nor speak, nor walk, nor dress as she ought to do—Mrs. Cartwright was below adoration, and within the reach of envy. What was she? a poor officer's widow. And why should she have been preferred to high places? to dine at the same table, sit by the same fire, and ride in the same pony-chaise with the Marchioness of Brandon? Not one of the numerous disengaged young ladies of five-and-thirty, at Carstones, but thought herself much better fitted to have filled the place of agreeable companion to my lady than that cold, bloodless, inanimate statue, Mrs. Cartwright. The possibility that Mrs. Cartwright might be endowed with certain hidden qualities which gave her a value, which they did not themselves possess, never once entered their imagination; for of the existence of tastes or of endowments above their own, except as far as dress and fashion and riches went, they were totally ignorant. Had they lived when magic and sorcery were believed in, Mrs. Cartwright might have stood a fair chance of being burned for a witch; as it was, she was accused of cunning, wheedling, and toadeating, the sole methods of obtaining influence with which the ladies of Carstones were acquainted.

"Really, brother, it seems very strange; so we are not to get rid of Mrs. Cartwright after all! I hear she is to stay and take care of my little Lord, poor dear little creature," said my sister Judy, taking off her bonnet and her best shawl as she came in from church.

"There she was, in the family pew, which is all hung with black cloth—twenty shillings a yard, I've no doubt—very handsome—and the pew for the steward's room—and the servants' pews all the same, and all the servants in black, and not a dry eye among them, and my Lord weeping as if his heart would break, poor dear, good man; and Mrs. Cartwright in deep black, as well she may, I understand—but not a tear in her eye, I warrant, looking as quiet! and as composed! sat as up! as if nothing had happened.—I can't bear the sight of her—so demure—and so sly—wheedling and flattering the dear Marchioness—and now!—but it will not do, I can tell her—my Lord never once looked at her all church time—to be sure he *did* hand her into his carriage—but she'll never be Marchioness of Brandon, take my word for it."

"And mine too, Judy."

"Ah, brother! you men are so easily taken in with a little affectation—but I know her—mark my words, you'll find Mrs. Cartwright a very different person from what you and the poor dear Marchioness suppose."

I said nothing, I even, for Judy was shrewd at times, resolved to watch Mrs. Cartwright narrowly. My situation, for I had been charged by the Marchioness with the medical treatment of her son, gave me good opportunities, and I resolved to use them.

I visited the little boy once, often twice a-day, but I had no fault save one to find with Mrs. Cartwright, she sadly wanted spirits, she was so grave, so still, that she was really a very unfit companion for a child. Every thing that tenderness and care, however, could do she did—her attention to his health was unremitting,—and I observed, that though cautiously avoiding dangerous excitement, against which I had warned her, she was beginning to develope his infant mind. She led, or rather carried him, into the beautiful gardens of the Castle, filled his little hands with the finest flowers, and taught him to distinguish their names and forms—he had his aviary of rare birds, which he, with her, fed and tended—his apartments were gradually filling with natural curiosities, so chosen as by their abrupt contrast, and well-marked colours and outlines, to excite the discriminating powers of children. I could not suspect Mrs. Cartwright of having studied Aristotle, or I should have supposed that from him she had learned to withhold every form that was mean or vulgar from the eye of the child; the prints with which his chambers were filled were all from drawings by great artists—the figures which adorned his shelves and mantel-pieces were casts of the most beautiful busts and statues—the servants who attended him were all remarkable for something above their condition, in air and tone of voice—no circumstance, however minute, was disregarded by Mrs. Cartwright that could serve to increase the physical strength, develope the mental powers, or form the taste and manners of her charge. The Marquis was lavish in allowing her the means of carrying her plans into execution: still I sighed over all these exertions, convinced that the delicate, suffering child could never live to profit by them.

Judy had not long to groan with apprehension lest the Marquis should fall a victim to Mrs. Cartwright's artful ways, for to a desire to please the father she would persist in ascribing all the kindness that was shown to the son. Report soon informed us that we might expect another Marchioness of Brandon.

The Marquis, with his large hereditary estates, ancient blood, and immense income, was now, it may be supposed, a very considerable prize in that great emporium for matrimony, the higher ranks of fashion. He, who, before his first marriage had been quite at a discount, had now, endowed as he was by the vast fortune of his wife, advanced to a high premium: endowed, I say, for the poor little deformed boy was of course regarded as a mere cypher in the account. That he could live was universally decided upon as impossible, and the Marquis was considered entirely as an unencumbered man, possessed of one of the finest fortunes in England. I am ashamed to say it—but I believe it to be true, that even before the first Marchioness had closed her eyes steps were being taken, on the part of many, to obtain the enviable distinction of filling her place; and no sooner did the Marquis reappear in the world than he found himself so marked an object of attention and flattery that a stronger head than his might have been turned by it. There were many competitors; the lady who carried off the prize was the daughter of the Duke of L——, the Lady Isabella Charlemont. We heard that she was the most beautiful woman in London, and belonging to a family of the very first distinction, and we all were prepared to admire and extol her; more especially as our Marquis had done us credit by marrying as he ought to have done, and had not allied himself to that odious Mrs. Cartwright.

The marriage took place the end of April, just eighteen months after the death of the first Marchioness.—In July we heard that they were coming down—in September they came. The London road lay through Carstones, and I recollect well that fine evening when they arrived—carriages and four—carriages and four—dashing through the street, and up to the great gates of the Castle. The new Marchioness, in her hat and plume of white feathers, with the Marquis by her side—and splendid equipages full of gentlemen and ladies following; with a numerous retinue of servants and attendants. Then the old walls rang with sounds to which they had for many years been strangers. Festivity in all its forms—riding, shooting, archery, in the morning—feasting, dancing, music, and a little drinking, at night. The old grey-headed servants were dazzled and bewildered; the people of Carstones, accustomed to more sober doings, knew not whether to be scandalized at, or pleased with, this new order of things. Our streets were perpetually enlivened with one gay party or other passing through: rattling carriages—prancing horses—splendid liveries—were constantly to be seen. The green shades of the park were gay with groups of elegant men and women, sketching or chatting, or reclining under the trees; the canoes and boats were in constant requisition on the water; the woods and fields resounded with the firing of the shooting parties. I can but give, a faint idea of the sort of turbillon, which succeeded to the peaceful quiet, to which we had been so long accustomed.

The Sunday after her arrival, our new Marchioness appeared at church. The black cloth, at twenty shillings a yard, had vanished, and the pew was lined with crimson velvet. The Marchioness, dressed in the first style of fashion, with her bonnet and high plume of feathers, stood by the side of her Lord, who appeared enchanted with every look and gesture. She was indeed a striking contrast to her predecessor;—her abundant dark hair hung in rich luxuriance over her piercing and haughty black eyes, which glanced restlessly around; her complexion was of the finest white and vermilion, her nose was straight and well-shaped, her lips, like the scarlet pomegranate of Solomon, disclosed her even pearl-like teeth, her figure was lofty and majestic, and the whole was set off by an air of magnificence, which formed one of the finest spectacles of the kind that I had ever seen.

The service over,—the Marquis, leading her by the hand with an air of proud exultation into the church porch, which was a sort of rendezvous for the better part of the congregation to exchange civilities, chat a little scandal, and so on, presented her, while her splendid equipage, with its four pawing horses, and elegant out-riders, waited, to such of those assembled as were worthy of the honour. Their homage—for the bows and courtsies were so low bent that they merited that appellation, was graciously received: the beauty smiled, moved, and spoke with the most amiable condescension—stooping to address even the most humble with honied words of bland courtesy. I thought them sadly too bland, and the courtesy sadly too much marked, but I was quite wrong, every one was enchanted; and one quarter of an hour of idle civility, enforced by a splendid dress and radiant smiles, had done as much to win golden opinions as whole years of benevolent exertion passed by the late Marchioness. Honied words, smiles, and haughtily courteous gestures, were all that the people of Carstones were the better for the residence of this lady at that time; for she staid only a month, and then the whirlwind passed away to some other place, and we were left to our card-parties again, and to our speculations on the health of the little Lord. The new wife had shown so much tenderness on being presented to the child, that it had melted the hearts of all present, most especially that of her husband. She kneeled down by the side of the chair, on which the little creature uneasily reclined, kissed his pale cheek, while a few pearly drops fell upon it.

"Poor, dear, interesting little fellow, you must love me very much—I am your mamma, you know."

"No," said the boy, and the tears stood in his large, melting eyes, "not mamma—don't say so—she was very little, and very pale, and very soft,—not a grand, grand, great beauty lady, like you."

"Thank you, sweet boy—what a love!—what a charming expression! My dear Mrs. Cartwright, for you must be the Mrs. Cartwright of whom I have heard so much, how happy I am to make your acquaintance—to thank you for the tender care you are taking of this dear little unfortunate—a care I hope to divide with you, while it lasts, poor little thing."

"I think he looks better, my dear Mrs. Cartwright," said my Lord.

"I would fain hope so, my Lord, but I own I see little amendment —I think he suffers less pain than he did, but that is all."

"Alas! Mrs. Cartwright, I am grieved to hear you say so; but we will hope time may do much."

The child, while this conversation was passing, had been engaged in showing one of his books to a young lady of the party, so that happily it was unheard by him.

The tender care announced by the Marchioness amounted to a visit now and then to the boy's apartments, where she always staid a very short time and would shrug her shoulders at the elaborate preparations for a finished education making by Mrs. Cartwright, which shrug meant to say,—"What nonsense, for such a poor creature!" She, however, treated Mrs. Cartwright with much civility—who, indeed, did not wear her ladyship's good feelings out by too often calling them into exercise; devoting herself to the child during the whole time the Marchioness and her party remained. I used to see his little garden chair, drawn by the old grey-headed footman, and attended by Mrs. Cartwright, creeping silently among the shrubberies, while the laugh and the song resounded from the windows of the Castle.

The next summer brought grand doings.—The Marchioness had been confined in London, and had given birth to a son. Four months afterwards she came down to Brandon, and signified her intention, in honour of his christening, to give a grand entertainment to all the neighbourhood, great and small.

It struck me as rather unnecessary to celebrate with such marked festivity the birth of a child of such slender expectations; for his mother's fortune had been extremely small, and from his father he could of course expect little—but I held my peace—Mrs. Cartwright, too, looked surprised when she first heard of it. As to the people of Carstones, who were all invited, they thought it the most natural thing in the world—and so did the tenantry, I suppose; for there was every demonstration of gladness and satisfaction— there was a grand dinner for the labourers, plenty of ale, a dance on the green, tables in the different halls for the higher order of dependants, and a ball and supper for the gentry. The beautiful infant, for I must own that in my life I never saw one more beautiful, was exhibited with a pomp of attendance almost regal; and the Marquis was congratulated on all sides, upon his promising son—*heir* was not said—but every one, it was plain, looked upon the boy as the future heir of these immense fortunes; and the mother evidently revelled in that exulting pride which a vain woman would feel on presenting a son of hers, as such, to the world.

I saw her in all the pomp of her beauty—her dark hair, and white satin robe sparkling with jewels, standing at the head of that gorgeous drawing-room, surrounded by a splendid group of noble and great personages, and placing the infant, all lace and embroidery, wrapped in a rich mantle, on the arm of the obsequious nurse, after the conclusion of those sacred and affecting rites, which ought to quell the thoughts of sin, passion, and pride, within a parent's breast, but which here, administered from a golden urn, at the hands of a right reverend bishop, with all the pomp and circumstance of an aristocratic establishment, served but to foster in their birth those venomous foes of human virtue.

The real heir, meanwhile, too unwell to leave his chamber, too much ill-treated by nature to afford pride to any one, was sitting moaning, and panting for breath, with his hand in that of Mrs. Cartwright.

"Oh, Mrs. Cartwright, I am sorry I cannot see this pretty christening—but do make them bring me my little brother. I want to look at him, and they never let me see him!"

"No, my dear—don't to-day," said Mrs. Cartwright: she felt for the boy what he was too young to feel for himself.

"Why not? he is so pretty."

He would have his own way, and the little Lord Louis, bedizoned, as I have said, with lace and satin, was carried in.

"Let me kiss him, nurse, you won't let me kiss him."

"Let him, nurse! why don't you!" said Mrs. Cartwright, somewhat impatiently, "don't you see that Lord St. Germains wants to kiss the child?"

"Oh, by no means on earth, Madam—indeed, my lady does not like me to bring my Lord Louis into these rooms at all—she thinks it vastly unwholesome—and as for kissing him, I could not take upon myself to allow it upon any account, it is as good as my place is worth, Mrs. Cartwright."

Mrs. Cartwright was silent with indignationp; she felt as if she ought to say something; but she knew not what—she was quite astounded.

"You must, I am sure, have mistaken Lady Brandon's orders," at length she articulated. "It must be her wish to encourage the affection which Lord St. Germains shows for his brother."

"Oh, as to that, Madam, it matters little, poor young gentleman, whom he shows affection for—he'll not be long, most certain, here, to show affection for any body."

"Very well, take the child away."

"The child!" repeated the nurse, as she left the room, "the child, indeed!—Lady Brandon be glad!—glad, indeed!—poor little crippled thing!—a pretty companion for you, my jewel—well, it can't last long—it will be, to be sure, a great mercy when it pleases the Lord to take him—he can't last long—that's one comfort."

"Mrs. Cartwright," said the little boy, "what does the baby's nurse mean?—why may I not kiss my brother?—I know very well why she calls me poor young gentleman!—I am indeed a poor young gentleman—I know that very well; but why may I not kiss and love my brother?—I think so about him—a great deal, indeed—I am older a vast, vast deal than he is—and I mean to be so careful of him, and I shall give him my little pony, because it is so quiet, and I shall give him my kings of England that you made me, and all my best things.—But I shall not give him two things—not this," it was his little locket, with his mother's picture and hair; "nor you, my good dear, dear Mrs. Cartwright!"

After this time my communication with the house of Brandon ceased for a while. The family went abroad, it was said, with the intention of visiting the baths of Carlsbad, to try their effect upon the Earl of St. Germains. Be that as it might, the absence lasted for several years, and eleven springs and winters had passed over our heads before the Marquis with his family returned to the Castle.

My communication with the family, I have said, ceased, but not entirely so, it was maintained in some degree by my correspondence with Mrs. Cartwright, who was punctual in writing during the whole period of their absence; she remained still attached to the young Earl in the capacity of gouvernante, for his health continued such as to require the most tender assiduity; what mortifications and contempts she received at the hands of the Marchioness, in return for her cares, I never exactly knew, for she, in no single sentence, made the slightest allusion to her own situation or feelings, except as they were connected with those of the Earl. She had made a resolution to devote herself to the child of the woman she had so much loved and honoured, and no affronts to her pride, no insults to her feelings, no vexations, no discomforts, nothing in short but an absolute dismissal, would she allow to separate her from the household of which she formed a part. I learned afterwards that she had borne all the insolences, to which her equivocal rank in the family exposed her, with the most serene and unflinching patience, appearing not to observe them wherever it was possible, and when this could not be done, opposing to every thing that imperturbable defence of a spirit that would not be ruffled.

Her letters spoke of her young élève with an affection that would have been passion in a heart less disciplined. She dwelt upon the delicacy, the sensibility, and the strength of his character, as it unfolded before her eyes. Of his thirst for knowledge—his ardent and poetic imagination—his nice discernment and his exquisite taste—his grateful and docile temper—his generous and affectionate heart—all, however, was clouded by the melancholy consideration that these bright promises would terminate in an early grave. I found that in this respect Mrs. Cartwright but shared the universal impression, that this highly-gifted youth was the victim of a mortal disease, and that in spite of all his endowments, such a deliverance from sorrow and from mortification was the greatest blessing his friends could desire for him.

"I have endeavoured unremittingly," said she, in one of her letters, "following as I best might the intentions of his wise and excellent mother, to strengthen and nerve his soul against those sufferings which I anticipate in future life, for one so exquisitely susceptible, placed under such peculiarly cruel circumstances. I believe I have succeeded in teaching him to *endure*—but, alas! how shall I deaden the sense of pain—how allay the bitterness of mortification?—it is a feeble consolation to know that he possesses the unflinching courage of the Spartan—the inexhaustible constancy of the Christian—if his life be to prove but one sad succession of anguish, physical as well as moral. Even now, young as he is, how melancholy are his days, languishing on a sick bed, or drawn in his chair round these monotonous groves and gardens," she was writing from their Italian villa, "a poor helpless cripple, while others of his age are rioting in all the enjoyments of health, and youth, and vigour. The rare brightness of his intellect, it is true, affords him, in his premature decay, some of those more sober pleasures which belong to riper years; but how forced and unnatural are these in the place of exercise and joy; how sickly and pale they appear to me, compared with the animated existence of his brother, Lord Louis, the very picture of health and beauty, springing, as I now see him, from his Arabian, on a return from an inspiring ride round this enchanting neighbourhood."

"The very fragility of Lord St. Germains' existence," she continued, "occasions serious disadvantages in other ways; he is looked upon by all as dying, and has been so ever since we left England. I have had the utmost difficulty in obtaining for him those advantages of education, to which his rank, to say no more, entitles him, and this merely by persuading the Marquis that they were necessary to his present amusement, for that he should reap any permanent advantage from them appears to all an impossibility. I confess I share in these anticipations, and should have felt my courage fail, had it been necessary to urge Lord St. Germains to mental exertion by the stimulus of the slightest severity; but all my difficulty has been to restrain this ardent and enthusiastic spirit, never weary of drinking at the wells of knowledge, emulous of every perfection, and of every accomplishment: indeed, my dear Mr. Wilson, it is difficult to express the sensations to which a reflection upon his character and circumstances gives rise, the excessive admiration, or the excessive regret, with which they inspire me."

In another letter, replying to one of mine, which contained a few cautious inquiries, she gave me to understand that Lord St. Germains lived a good deal secluded from his family, and never appeared with the Marchioness in public; that Lord Louis seemed to be considered by every one as the principal person in the family, and was treated in all respects as the heir ought to be; in short, that the Marchioness seemed so fully persuaded that the elder son would never live to be of any service, either to herself, or to her children, that she studied little to obtain his regard personally, or to cultivate the affection he seemed to wish to bestow upon his brothers and sisters.

There were now four of them, three daughters having followed Lord Louis into the world.

Thus passed, as I have said, eleven years, when orders were suddenly sent from Paris to put the castle in preparation to receive the family, and on a fine evening in July the carriages once more swept up the little street, and Brandon Castle was again alive.

This time it was not, however, peopled with a crowd of fashionable visitors, but with that swarm of—*reptiles* I had almost said—which a great family usually brings in its train after a long residence abroad. The French, and the German, and the Italian Governesses, my Lady's femme de chambre, and my young ladies' Swiss bonne—my Lord's French valet, and my Lord's French cook—my Lady's—what name ought I to give him? man of vertù, who chattered in broken English and looked after pictures—Lord Louis's foreign tutor—his mother's Albanian page—these, with grooms, footmen, couturières, and under-nurses, and a whole tribe of inferior servants, soon filled the long silent walls with noise and riot, for the household was, with all its air of pretension, ill kept and ill disciplined. Four times the necessary number of servants were retained in each department, and a certain decorum was wanting in their behaviour, when not under the immediate eye of their superiors. The foreigners were for ever quarrelling, the natives always grumbling. Jealousy, idleness, and vice, were the denizens of the stables and servants' hall; corruption and peculation of the steward's and housekeeper's rooms; how it was above I had soon the means of observing.

When I paid my respects at the Castle, I was received by the Marchioness with great apparent cordiality—she always, I cannot tell why, vied with her predecessor in marks of favour to me— and treated me as a member of the body politic of Brandon. Medical men are however frequently thus favoured by great ladies, doubtless, for good and especial reasons.

After a little conversation, she asked me whether I should not like to see the children, and opening a glass door, which led from her dressing-room, down a flight of steps, conducted me to the pleasure-ground below. It was a turfy glade hung round with large trees, and laid out with a few flower-beds, now rich with glowing colours. The first sound which attracted my attention was that of loud laughter. The laughter proceeded from a group of little girls, attended by two or three young women, whose foreign dress, airs and graces, soon showed me they must be of France or Italy. The little girls were none of them very handsome; they were pale, and cold looking—but they had skins delicate as marble, large black and haughty eyes, like their mother, eyebrows in fine dark lines, and dark silken hair. Yet, a certain stiffness, and want of expression, pervaded their features, which, though regular, gave no impression of charm or beauty to the eye; they looked extremely fashionable, but it was a foreign air of fashion, far too decidedly so, to please my English eyes, and I could not endure the womanly ways that these little creatures, of eight, nine, and ten years old assumed, nor the perfect self-possession, and finished manner, with which they received the introduction their mother gave me. They soon sat down again on the grass, and resumed their amusements and their bursts of laughter, which sounded, to me, rather affected than gay. A little way before them stood Lord Louis. I never saw so beautiful a boy—he was yet scarcely twelve, but his fine luxuriant growth, his glowing cheek—his liquid, expressive eyes—his hyacinthine locks of sunny brown, as they curled clustering round his face, his noble and manly bearing, gave him the air of one nearly two years older than he really was. He was occupied with a French poodle which he was endeavouring to train, to perform the manual exercise, when his mother, with a face beaming with pride and pleasure, presented him to me—he gave me his hand, with an air at once so frank, and so spirited, that he won my regard in a moment. It was the French poodle, I found, which was the cause of all the merriment I had heard; his tricks excited by the lively boy, who stimulated him to exhibition, were so amusing that they almost put *me* to my smiles.

After looking on this merry scene a little while, I asked for Lord St. Germains—"Ah, poor creature, where is he indeed," said my Lady—"where is Lord St. Germains, Geraldine?" addressing her eldest daughter.

"Dear mamma, how should I know?" said she carelessly, and continued her amusement.

"Don't you see him under the trees there with Lilia?" said the second daughter, Lady Isabella.

"He's ill to-day," said Lord Louis, "he won't come among us— and I suppose you'll none of you go to him."

"It's not our business to nurse him," said Lady Geraldine.

I went up towards the group of trees. There in his chair, that melancholy wheeled chair, sat, or rather lay, my unfortunate young friend.—He had leaned back, and his eyes were closed— and his expression was of that painful cast which rests upon the countenance when severe bodily anguish has at length abated. His finely chiselled features were pale and exhausted—a wanness, rather than a delicacy, was upon his temples, over which hung his raven hair in dark heavy masses—his mouth was in the least open—but round it breathed the expression of that repose which succeeds to acute pain.

"Hush!" whispered a gentle voice.

I looked down—on the footstool of his chair sat a little girl, about nine years of age—the most beautiful little being that I had ever beheld, her sweet childlike face was moulded in the most exquisite form and tinted with the richest roses; her hair, of a fine auburn, threaded with gold, and slightly confined over her brow by a narrow blue fillet, fell in abundance of waves and curls over her lovely cheeks, and soft and waxen neck and shoulders. The prettiest dimpled finger in the world was laid on lips like two parted cherries, while her large brilliant eyes of that clear dark grey, which reflects every feeling of the soul, fringed by long silken lashes, were fixed on mine with an expression of the most speaking earnestness. She had a book open upon her lap, and seemed to have been occupied in reading while she watched by his side.

I approached very softly—"Is he asleep?" I whispered.

"Ah oui—mais il a tant souffert—tant souffert, mais il dort, il dort enfin—hist—hist,"—and rising from her seat, she regarded him—her little features working with compassion, and the tears standing in her lovely large eyes.

"Does he then suffer so much pain?" I replied.

"Hélas, oui beaucoup, beaucoup,—mais qu'il est bon—qu'il est doux."

"And who are you, may I ask, my pretty little lady, who seem so kindly watching him? are you one of his sisters?"

"Hélas, non, je suis Lilia."

"And may I ask why you are here instead of being with the rest? hark, how they are laughing."

"I know it," said she, "they have got the dog; but I can't bear to leave him in his pain all alone. Oh, I am so sorry for him, such pain! and all by himself too—*si triste—si triste*. I like better to take care of him than to hear them laugh."

"Are you then such great friends?"

"Ah yes! he is so good to me, he teaches me every thing almost; and when Mademoiselle is very cross" (with the prettiest air of confidence in the world), "I creep, creep away to him—and though he is sometimes in such pain—such pain—he says all sorts of kind things to me—and comforts me—and tells me to be patient and quiet—and when I am passionate and naughty, he speaks so gently and so kindly, that I am ready to die with sorrow and shame."

"Then you *are* sometimes naughty?"

"To be sure I am—every body is naughty but him. Ah never! never!—he is never the least tiny bit naughty."

This little whispering conversation was interrupted by a slight movement in the sleeper.

"Ah, he is waking," cried the little creature—and, flying to his side, she put her face close to his; "You are better, are not you?"

"Yes, my dear," in a low and languid voice. "Have you been with me all this time?"

"Oh yes, and have read all that long piece—I can say it now very well."

"Not at present—how they are laughing! go to them, my dear little girl. I can do very well by myself now."

"I would rather stay by you."

"But you have been by me all this afternoon—and this dear little tongue must be sadly tired of being so still—*n'est ce pas, ma très jolie petite Lilia?*"

"But I may chatter to you now, you know:—but I forgot, here is a gentleman."

I advanced from behind the chair. "I fear, my Lord, you must have quite forgotten Mr. Wilson."

"That I shall never do," with the most polite air in the world. "Mr. Wilson, I am very happy indeed to see you again—Will you excuse me rising?—I am almost a prisoner—still in this self-same chair, though I fill it somewhat better than I once did."

"Your Lordship is indeed very much grown, and I hope improved in health and strength since I had the honour of seeing you last."

"I cannot boast much of that.—Existence is to me still an effort and a pain … That I exist at all, I believe, astonishes all the world, and no one more than myself—but having struggled so long, I begin to think that I am to live; and, much as I sometimes endure, I assure you the expectation is an agreeable one. Now, my sweet little Lilia, you must go and tell some one to bring a chair here for Mr. Wilson—for if he has a little leisure I mean to keep him by me for a space. I live, sir," turning to me, "in the open air, and I too well remember the kindness you used to show me not to feel sure that you will sit by me, and indulge me with your company here."

"I need not assure your Lordship of my great pleasure in doing so," said I, struck and affected by all I saw, and gratified to find myself so cordially welcomed by one in whom I took so deep an interest. The little Lilia fluttered away like a butterfly, pausing from flower to flower.—His eyes followed her.

"What a very sweet and pretty child!" I said.

"The sweetest, dearest little being in the universe!—how charming some children are, Mr. Wilson,—what affectionate hearts and tender feelings!—Would you believe it? this dear little thing, from the moment she first came into this family, has attached herself to me, evidently from the purest sentiments of compassion.—She sees my isolated situation;—and forsakes every pleasure, and neglects every amusement, to flutter round me, like a little cherub … This very day has that creature held my hand for nearly an hour, while I was very ill—and then when I sleep, she sinks down at my feet, and sits the very picture of silence. 'More patient than the brooding dove, when that her golden couplets are disclosed.' Though when I am well, it is the merriest, wildest little spirit—"

"She must be a great amusement to you."

"Ah! she is much more than that—I am unfortunately," with a slight sigh, "very fond of children, and am not, as you know, a very engaging companion for such volatile beings.—The affection and company of this little girl are a consolation for some disappointments—carry a sweetness with them.—Besides, I think, pretty creature, I can be of use to *her*—that is gratifying to one who longs to be busy, as I unluckily do.—I endeavour to repeat some of the excellent things Mrs. Cartwright has laboured to teach me, to this far softer and more docile mind—and I really think my little pupil will do me credit;" smiling, "though Nature has been so prodigal, I almost fear to meddle with her handy work."

The little lady now came flying back, followed by a footman carrying a chair. I sat down by Lord St. Germains' side.

"Now, dear little Lilia, you must gather Mr. Wilson a nosegay as large as your head."

Away she flew over the grass, her white frock fluttering, like the wings of a swan, behind her; and we continued our conversation.

I think there must be something in me which invites confidence; for, young as Lord St. Germains had been when we last met, I was treated by him as an old friend the moment we met again, though certainly there were many subjects which he did not enter upon till some time afterwards. He began to speak of his travels, of the various countries he had visited, displaying the most ardent enthusiasm for the beauties of nature, and the most refined taste in those of art. Probably because I was a medical man, he talked more openly to me than he would otherwise have done of the effect produced by his peculiar situation upon all his views and sentiments—for he seldom alluded to himself except in confidential conversations with a very few of his friends.

"I am aware," he said, "and I think to their full extent, of the disadvantages under which I lie—to be deformed is a heavy misfortune, the bitterness of which I have only, perhaps, begun to taste.—The time for that is not yet fully come—but I should have found it more easy to reconcile myself to being a sort of monster in the eyes of the world, if I could have hoped to win approbation and regard by acts of energy and of virtue. Unhappily, the miserable helplessness of my condition renders that very difficult, and seems to condemn me to a woman's obscurity, without her usefulness. Reflections such as these might have driven me, as they have sometimes well nigh driven me, to despair,—had not the wisdom of Mrs. Cartwright rescued me. She has taught me to look upon life with different, and, I hope, purer eyes,—as a theatre of duty rather than of success;—and where the first duty is obedience,—the second, not to bury, in fretful impatience, the *single talent* in a napkin. She has stimulated me to endeavour to improve my small one to its full extent—and in this endeavour I have found peace, and, since this darling child came amongst us—happiness. I hope to live now to be of some service to my fellow-creatures.—It will be something, at least, to show that personal defects, however great, need not irretrievably blast the career of a resolute man. And the hunch-back Lord, miserable cripple as he is, may, perhaps, leave some worthy evidence of his existence behind him, when he closes it."

He was interrupted by Lilia, who flew to him, her face streaming with tears.

"My Lilia, what is it?"

"They will not let me get any flowers—and the Marchioness is angry with me for touching her roses.—I said they were for you, but she is very, very angry, and bade me take care how I presumed to gather her flowers—and they are all very cross with me—and oh! where shall I get flowers for you? sweet flowers—such as I used to gather for you at Fontainebleau—orange-flowers, and carnations, and roses, that you loved so—and I drest your room all over with them when you were ill!"

"Never mind, little girl, we—" kissing the tears from her glowing cheeks and brimming eyes—"we must not touch other people's things, you know—no one likes that.—I did not know they were in the Marchioness's garden when I sent you. We must have a pretty little garden of our own in some nook or other; and then my Lilia shall bury me in roses, if she likes. But don't cry—it is wrong and weak to cry—and I would rather never touch a rose more than that my Lilia should do what is wrong or weak."

"But it is so hard!" said the little one, indignantly sobbing, "they take every thing themselves, and they give you nothing.—

Lady Geraldine has a lap full of roses—and you, who are so good, and so ill …"

"My dear, roses are more proper things for Lady Geraldine than for me. You know I am quite a man now, and roses are for ladies."

"But you like them, though."

"I like them, my Lilia, when you bring them. But if you will fill your frock with daisies, it will do as well—I saw some under the trees. Go and gather me a load of them."

Away went Lilia again. I was silent, and looked surprised and heated.

"Mr. Wilson, may I ask of you one great favour?—I hope to see very much of you while I am here. Will you be so kind as to endeavour not to see *for* me some few things which I desire to be blind to myself?"

I soon after rose to take my leave; Lord St. Germains first exacting a promise that I would visit him very frequently.

"You loved my mother, Mr. Wilson.—May her unfortunate son presume upon that regard, and look upon you as his friend? Helpless as I am—it is absolutely necessary for me to have some one whom I can trust with implicit confidence, and make, in short, a second self—one who will have the benevolence, and the patience, to assist a feeble being in its efforts at action.—Will you be this friend, Mr. Wilson? You may perhaps wonder at, or rather despise me, for showing so much forwardness and confidence— but I feel as if I knew you very well—your kindness to me, before I left England, made a strong impression on my childish feelings, and your correspondence with Mrs. Cartwright has increased my respect for you. Besides, are you not my guardian? Are you not the friend selected by my mother to be mine in the hour of my need?"

It is unnecessary to add that I was much touched by all this; he could not for a moment doubt the interest I took in him. He felt it, and took my hand.

"Mr. Wilson, you are the man I have been in search of. I thank God he has granted me what I so much wanted."

On my return home I found Judy in an ecstasy. The Marchioness had been into town, with that beautiful Lord Louis on horseback. "She stopped at Mr. Derne's for some writing-paper, looking so charmingly—and Lord Louis ordered I don't know how many things at Mr. Blore's for his dog-kennel—he has a hundred and fifty dogs, I do believe—and there was following him such a King Charles! black and tan, with such ears, and the sweetest little head! and last of all, brother, they called here—for the little darling had hurt his foot, and they thought to find you at home. So, when I saw who it was, though you know I *never* go into the shop under any circumstances—yet I would not leave them to the boy, so I just popped my best bonnet over my cap and put on my new black apron, and looked very tidy, I assure you, and I went down to the door, and I said—'I am most concerned, my lady, that my brother is not at home. What is the matter with the sweet little darling—your ladyship's dog?' and then she said, 'Not my ladyship's, but Lord Louis's dog, Miss Wilson—this is Lord Louis,' looking proudly up at him—and then he lifted up his head like an archangel, as he is, all glowing with his ride, and said—'I can't imagine what the deuce is in Fanfan, mamma—she certainly runs lame, and I can see nothing the matter with her foot.' And then I said, 'May I presume, my lord'—and sure enough, there was a thorn, which I extracted—and my lady said, 'Thank you, Miss Wilson;' and my lord said—'Off with you, Fanfan,' and away they cantered to the castle. —Ah, he is a noble boy, and will well become his great estate."

"His great estate! Judy, what are you talking of?"

"Oh, I had forgot; it's not his estate just yet, to be sure—but sure it will be, for they say the poor cripple can't last long."

I turned from her, and I felt it was of no use to be angry. I thought it a sort of profanation to discuss Lord St. Germains' circumstances in such a conversation as this.

A few days afterwards, I paid a second visit to the castle—I then saw my friend Mrs. Cartwright—I found her occupying the ancient part of the castle—Lord St. Germains and herself having retired to these deserted chambers—where they had formed a sort of establishment of their own, removed from the noise and hurry of the other apartments. She seemed gratified by the impression her pupil had made upon me. She told me that the little Lilia was a humble connection of the Marchioness, and had been received into the family with a view to her talking French with the little girls; that her education had been entirely neglected, and was not likely much to have advanced, under the care of her cousins' governesses—much too fine, and much too indolent, to throw away their labours upon a being so insignificant: that the child had early attached herself to Lord St. Germains, evidently from the most generous feeling of compassion; and that he, much touched by her sensibility, and interested by her situation, had, in a manner, adopted her as his own: that he had carefully instructed her in every thing which she was capable of at present acquiring, of which her progress in English was some proof—to say nothing of music, in which she was already a proficient for her age: but that he was still more intent upon forming her mind and character, so as to prepare her to endure the numerous ills of her situation, without mean subservience, or impatient irritation.

"These two unfortunate young creatures,"—said she, "unfortunate in circumstances so exactly opposed, yet coloured with the same character of mortification, seem to have been drawn by a secret sympathy towards each other, and the little Lilia is to Lord St. Germains every thing he could desire in an affectionate sister; while he is a father and protector to her. You see our apartments are distinct from those of the rest of the family—and our presence in the general circle appears little desired; so that our life is solitary enough at times—but it is enlivened by this sweet little being, and she is so glad, I believe, to escape from the haughty governesses, and from her cousins, who love her little, that she is for ever with us; and, being not much wanted, and not much missed, is seldom inquired for. They are now together very busy, making a garden."

Mrs. Cartwright was not fond of gossiping.—She never, but to me, I believe, mentioned any circumstance that passed in the family—but she gave me to understand that the Marquis, easy and indolent, left every thing to the Marchioness—that she, imperious, self-willed, and cold-hearted, governed with little regard to justice, or an equitable attention to the respective rights of the members of her family—and that no expense was spared upon Lord Louis: that his pleasure or advantage was consulted at the expense of every other consideration—he being the idol of his mother's heart, who evidently still looked upon him as his father's future heir. He had his dog-kennels, and his stables already, and, though a mere boy, had the tastes and habits of an expensive man.—His sisters were somewhat differently treated.—To make them fashionable—elegant—accomplished—distinguished—was the mother's sole aim—little regard being paid to any other consideration. Health might be a little attended to—but the morals—the temper—all that forms the disposition and character, were totally and entirely overlooked. Abandoned to interested governesses, the little girls were flattered into pride—tempted to meanness—and initiated even thus early, into those arts which are thought so useful in the great world. Dress, accomplishments, and personal attractions were the incessant theme of their conversation, and the objects of their thoughts and wishes; and these ill-conditioned French women were not ashamed to propose to creatures so very young, the consideration of making excellent matches, like their mother, as the motive for all their exertions.

In the meantime, every thing was denied to Lord St. Germains—or, I ought rather to say, would have been denied, had he not, with a simplicity in unison, and a firmness and a pertinacity which seemed scarcely consistent with the usual gentleness—even softness—of his demeanour, persisted in asking for, and in obtaining, all he thought necessary for his own improvement and rational well-being—at the same time that a murmur never passed his lips at all that was done for the others; and he sedulously abstained from interfering with the proceedings of the Marchioness, in the slightest degree.

"He gave an example of this yesterday.—You were present when poor little Lilia was repulsed while gathering a few roses.— He took no notice whatever of the affront; but soon afterwards he went to the Marchioness, and petitioned for a particular spot, about a quarter of an acre, which lies in a remote part of the shrubberies, quite neglected; and asked to be allowed to have it for a garden.—She seems quite to dislike granting him the smallest indulgence—as if it were a concession to rights she would fain never acknowledge; but the request was made with so much respectful plainness, that she could not refuse—so Lilia and he are very busy there this morning."

There I went, and there I found them—and who so proud or so busy as little Lilia?—The young Lord was in his chair, as usual, with a small table before him, covered with plans, which he was explaining to the happy child.—His design was to make a sort of botanic garden of this spot: but he was promising to the tiny fairy, a world of roses, carnations, and orange-flowers. Several workmen were employed preparing the ground: and Lilia, all animation, was receiving orders, measuring, chatting, and running about. Their books lay upon a bench near, and Lilia's work-basket.—Her book was the *Robinson Suisse*—his, a volume of Wordsworth's Poems.

After the first salutations were over, "I find you bestowing much happiness, my Lord!" was my remark.

"And receiving it," was his reply. "What a sweet and calm afternoon!—how soft is the air!—how soothing the various sounds that reach us in this quiet corner!—the hum of the insects—the distant lowing of the herds—the very sound of the mattocks and spades, as my labourers ply their work in my little Lilia's behalf … How beautiful an opening into that glade, where the deer are reposing, their glossy coats tinted by the mellow sunbeam!—how dark the foliage of the noble trees that hang around us!—and that sweet child, what a brightness her fluttering gestures and playful smiles give to this little landscape!—It is indeed a glorious world, Mr. Wilson, and I feel that heavenly moments are granted to us here—which make it a privilege even to exist—poor miserable creatures as we too often call ourselves."

I said I had often experienced what he was now feeling, and that I rejoiced from my soul that he had so disciplined his mind as to be capable of tasting the enjoyments offered to him, without blighting them by repining or discontent.

"Mrs. Cartwright has taken great pains with me, and has endeavoured to impress upon my mind that it is better to face inevitable calamity at once with courage, and gratefully accept such alleviations as the nature of the case allows—than to endeavour, by a feeble self-flattery, to delude the imagination, by concealing the reality and the extent of an evil. I think I have considered my situation in all its bearings—and have endeavoured to estimate it justly.—Doubtless, the disadvantages I endure are very great—but they may be supported by a proper resolution; and the better parts of human life, I may still consider mine—ennobling thoughts, efforts at virtue—the simple pleasures of nature—and I hope, in some degree, of affection—the love of that little darling! … but I am weak there.—How it has raised me in my own self-estimation!—yet that is but a reed to lean upon," with a gentle shake of the head, "and I have other, and I trust, more stable supports. Do you know this book?"—pointing to the one lying before him—"It is to poets such as Wordsworth, that minds like mine lie under everlasting obligations." He opened at the Excursion.

"What an admirable poem!—replete with wisdom and with consolation. I have endeavoured (but you will smile at my simplicity) to form myself in some measure upon thoughts such as these—so well becoming a solitary—for such, alas! I am,—and to rest my philosophy upon the noble foundations which are here pointed out:

> Alas! the endowment of immortal power
> Is matched unequally with custom, time,
> And domineering faculties of sense,
> In all.—In most with superadded foes,
> Idle temptations, countless, still renewed,
> Ephemeral offspring of the unblushing world.

And in the private regions of the mind,
Ill govern'd passions, ranklings of despite,
Immoderate wishes, pining discontent,
Distress and care.—What then remains?—to seek
Those helps for his occasions ever near,
Who lacks not will to use them—Vows renew'd
On the first motion of a holy thought,
Vigils of contemplation, praise, and prayer,—
A stream, which, from the fountain of the heart,
Flowing however feebly, never flows
Without access of unexpected strength—
But, above all, the victory is most sure,
For him who, seeking faith by virtue, strives
To yield entire submission to the law
Of conscience—Conscience reverenced and obey'd,
As God's most intimate presence in the soul,
And his most perfect image in the world—
Endeavour thus to live—these rules regard—
These helps solicit—"

He paused—his pale and sickly countenance was illuminated for an instant—then, as if ashamed of all he had been saying, he began once more to apologise, and to attribute to his sickness, and to his infirmity, this tincture of romance, as he called it, in his temper—"And you will not forget, Mr. Wilson, that I have lived little with *men* at present—and that I have, till now, wanted the advantage of having my ways of thinking corrected by communication with minds more masculine than my own—But now I will have done talking of myself—for really, if you have time, I have so much important business to speak upon—that I scarcely know where to begin."

He then asked me what funds I had which he might call his own—"The income I mean." I explained to him that it amounted at this time to 600l. a year; for which, or for any part of the principal, he could draw upon me as he wanted it.

"I shall want it directly for my child and myself," said he, laughing; "and it will not be half enough; so I mean to get my father to pay for my own education—while I provide for that of others—like a true enthusiast, you know, who always overlooks his most natural wants and duties."

He then told me that he must immediately have a tutor, who must be a gentleman in his manners; but, above all, a profound scholar—"I wish to be a scholar myself. And dear Mrs. Cartwright, with all her pains, has never been able to obtain for me the means. I must obtain them *now* for myself. If my father cannot afford me that indulgence, I shall pay for it; but I think he will not refuse."

"It is impossible he should," cried I.

"I am sure he will not, if he can help it: but his is an expensive family. In his rank, it is lamentable how much apparent extravagance and real poverty there is."

"His very mother's remark," thought I.

"Mr. Wilson, I know you will find me what I want. For my lovely one," added he, "much is not yet necessary, and my education will be finished before hers begins: but an education she *shall* have."

"I should have thought," I said, " that the means were already provided in the young ladies' school room."

"No," replied he, "not for Lilia," and dropped the subject.

Lord St. Germains then proceeded to ask me several questions relating to the old dependents of the family, and the situation of the poor upon the estate; and made me explain in detail what had been his mother's arrangements to secure the welfare of the cottagers. Her benevolent plans had been sadly neglected during the long absence of the family; and want, vice and disorder had succeeded to comfort, industry, and regularity. He lamented with me this change, and promised to spare no exertions to restore things to their former situation; a promise he amply redeemed. Young as he was—and helpless as he was—the energies of his mind triumphed over his situation; and, from the corner of his chamber, he contrived to regulate these matters so well, that in a few years, from the most idle, poaching, squalid peasantry in the country, our cottagers became remarkable for respectability and good conduct.

As we were thus discoursing, we were interrupted by the joyous cries of Lilia.

"Oh, they are coming—they are coming."

And several men, wheeling barrows full of plants and flowers, entered the garden. Lord St. Germains now devoted himself to his little friend—pointing out to her, on the plan before him, the place each plant was to occupy, and explaining, in words suitable to her childish understanding, the reasons of his arrangement. She was charming—now fixing her large eyes so seriously on his face—now clapping her dimpled hands and springing for joy, as she understood his ideas.

"*Oui, mais il sera charmant—charmant—notre petit jardin*! Ah, St. Germains! good St. Germains! nice St. Germains. *Que vous êtes aimable!—aimable—*"

I was as busy as she was, assisting and talking, and laughing, when a noise was heard in the thicket.—First rushed in two beautiful setters, whose appearance sent Lilia screaming and flying to the chair of her protector.—They were followed in a moment by Lord Louis, glowing with exercise—a noble figure.—He carried his light gun in his hand, but threw it down, as he approached, with an air of vexation.

"How are you, brother? What a charming spot you have found for you and your pretty, sweet, lovely little pet!—but Lilia, why do you cry, and run away from my dogs?—they will not hurt you, you foolish little thing."

"Indeed, Louis, we must excuse her: they came upon her so unexpectedly; but she will be wiser in time—won't you, Lilia?"

"I don't like such great horrid creatures," said Lilia.

"You don't like them! why did you ever in your life, you foolish, confoundedly pretty creature, see such a couple of noble animals? Only look at them, St. Germains—*you* have the eye of a painter.—Are they not quite a study?"

"Noble dogs—where did you get them?"

"Oh, Pitson got them from Lord Clare's keeper—broke on purpose for me—a hundred guineas the pair—well worth a hundred and fifty."

I looked down—so did Lord St. Germains. He only laughed, and said:—"You are a clever fellow, Louis—I shall think you a cleverer when you see your *one* hundred again."

"And now," cried Lord Louis, "what the devil bewitches my mother, I cannot guess; but a crotchet is come into her head— that I am too young—too young! heaven help her! to be trusted with a gun. Not use my gun!" added he, petulantly. "One might as well be dead, as submit to this tyranny.—I'd rather be dead, if I mayn't have my pleasure—a thousand tines rather be dead."

"Ah, how silly you are, Lord Louis;" said Lilia, "how very— very silly;—what! be dead because you may not shoot—you who have horses, and Fanfans, and pheasants, and guinea and rabbits—all of your own—own—own."

"You know nothing about it at all, you silly little exquisite charming darling; so give me a kiss, and don't lecture *me*."

"No, I shan't," said Lilia, "I have made a vow—"

"You a vow!"

"I shan't kiss any one in this house, but Mrs. Cartwright."

"Nonsense! that piece of grey marble!"

"She's not a piece of grey marble," said Lilia, firing up, "and you are a very, very naughty boy to call her so.—She's very good— she's very clever—she's very kind. And if she *is* pale, that's prettier than great red cheeks, like yours." And hers were crimson.

"Softly, my Lilia," said St. Germains, "defend your friends, but don't abuse your adversaries."

"Oh, let her abuse me, the pretty little vixen, but I *will* have a kiss."

"No, brother, not now, you will vex the child. Shall I speak to the Marchioness about your gun?"

"That was what I was just going to ask you, St. Germains; I really shall be prodigiously obliged to you—it is monstrously absurd, is it not?"

"We must remember," said St. Germains, " she is a woman and a mother—and a doating mother.—So much love as you receive will bring its inconveniences."

"I wish she would give me a little less of both then," was the undutiful answer; "however, do see what you can make of her.— She minds you a good deal, I can tell you, when you speak in the proper way."

"But I am afraid I shall not be able to speak in the proper way, in this case," said St. Germains, laughing, "that is, according to your ideas of the proper way—very decisively—for you are her own son, and she has a right—"

"Don't talk of rights, bothering.—Will you do it or not?"

"I will try—but I will not speak in a manner that you ought not to wish me to do—that is to say, imperiously, decisively, as you call it."

"Well, well, manage it any way, but let me have my gun—and Lilia, I will shoot you a dove!"

"Don't," said Lilia, "I don't want a dove shot, I'm sure."

"Why, you simpleton, I thought you loved birds!"

"I don't love to have them shot—and I don't love you for shooting them!"

"Don't you? but you must—for I cannot live without shooting—nor without sweet pretty Lilia loving me: and so, good bye—for you are so cross—I'd better be off;" and he left us, whistling away his dogs.

We were all silent for a short space.—At last, "He is a fine boy, is he not, Sir?" said St. Germains.

"It is somewhat of a pity he is indulged so far," I ventured to say.

"I don't know," was the generous answer. "I hope it will do him no serious harm, and it must be so pleasant to be adored by a mother, that I cannot regret it."

For myself, I found it difficult to sympathise with this generosity. I stood pondering upon the unjust partiality which, while it denied to one son the means of accomplishing the noblest purposes, lavished money without reserve upon the most idle tastes of the other. The summer passed on. In the course of it, I procured for Lord St. Germains the attendance of a gentleman of my acquaintance, an excellent scholar, under whose instruction he soon made an astonishing proficiency in those branches of learning which, whether justly or not, are considered by us as essential to the character of an accomplished gentleman. He at the same time commenced those schemes for ameliorating the condition of the peasantry which, as I have before stated, produced in a few years such excellent results. Little Lilia, under his fostering and gentle care, continued to expand in loveliness; her gay smiles and heart-cheering laughter, her winning frolics and caressing ways, compensating to him for many hours of suffering and despondency.

Lord Louis went to Eton, where he was speedily distinguished as the handsomest and cleverest boy in the school, and also for a reckless wantonness of expense which, even in that seminary renowned for fashion and for folly, not to say vice, made him quite remarkable; but his fine talents and generous temper endeared him to all, in spite of his faults, and appeared in some manner to justify the excessive fondness of his mother.

So time rolled away, and years passed over our heads, bringing with them few changes, except as regarded the growth of all these young creatures. Lord St. Germains slowly ripened from the tender and sensitive youth to a manhood of deep and powerful feeling. His understanding strengthened with his years, and acquired a firmness and an expansion truly wonderful, considering the life he had led; but his health amended little.— He appeared still hovering upon the edge of the grave, visited at intervals by cruel pains—a cripple, walking and moving with difficulty, and his deformity, though somewhat less apparent to the eye, still rendering him remarkable wherever he went. He came of age during this interval, and, by his own desire, the day was marked by feasts and gifts to all the poor upon the estate, and by dinners to the tenants and to the gentlemen of Carstones; but he came not down to Brandon, his sense of his appearance being chiefly shown in a somewhat studious anxiety to avoid representation of every sort.

Lord Louis went from Eton to Oxford, where he continued his career of splendid extravagance, mingled, however, with rather less of vice than might have been expected: the example of his brother acted upon him certainly in the most salutary manner; he loved and he respected St. Germains, and though often careless, and sometimes rude, treated him with deference, and with something almost like tenderness.

Some summers were passed at other country seats, and I lost sight of them all, once more, for a year or two.

It was early in June of the year 18—, that the family came down once more to Brandon Castle to spend the summer—a summer, how eventful!—Seven years have elapsed since last I presented them to my readers. They are all much changed in appearance. Lord St. Germains has acquired a brow of stronger character, an eye of deeper expression, he is become a man—thoughtful—energetic—and with profound sensibility. No one can look upon his very striking countenance without being assured of this.

The form of Lord Louis has expanded into a grace and beauty which render him pre-eminent, even among the handsomest race upon earth, the aristocracy of England.—His countenance glows with animation—his brow is clear and open—his eye sparkling, his lips haughtily curling, yet endowed with a smile of ineffable sweetness—his figure tall, symmetrical, with an elegance, and yet energy of gesture and action, singularly beautiful. His mother, on whom years have laid an unkind hand, gazes on him with a restless, anxious, uneasy love; her eye is become hard, her complexion withered—her countenance unquiet—unsatisfied longings—uneasy fears, and the dark passions—rankling jealousy—evil discontent—bitter envy—have on it marked their lines.

The young ladies are just what one should expect from their education—fashionable, haughty, and cold—polite in their manners —ill regulated in their tempers—accomplished, without taste or imagination, worldly wise, with much real folly—over-taught, with much real ignorance—"seeming—seeming—seeming …"

Mrs. Cartwright is grown greyer and paler than ever. She is much in her own apartments, or rather in those of Lord St. Germains; for they still preserve the custom of having one sitting-room together.

But Lilia! how lovely is Lilia! she is just sixteen, and has ripened into something so sweet, that though it may be possible for others to conceive, it is out of my power to describe her.—She is formed, not like the Venus we love to paint, but, if possible, she is still more charming. That cherub face on which glows radiance scarcely of this world, a glory of youth, health, and innocence—those large, speaking, melting eyes—that round and dimpled cheek—that mouth of dewy roses—that form so soft, so light, so childlike still— those torrents of shining brown ringlets of hair which defy control, and fall over the ivory neck and shoulders, shading that fair brow and that sweet smiling countenance … Then she sings—from those parted lips pour dwelling floods of enchanting notes, flowing "like a stream of rich perfume upon the air," and filling as with a volume of sound all those lonely, echoing, ancient apartments, where Lord St. Germains and Mrs. Cartwright are.

… He was reading, as usual, when I came into the room, placed in the deep embrasure of one of the old Gothic windows, the sun pouring through the stained glass, and transparent foliage of a vine which mantled over the rich stone work, a gleam of purple and golden light into the room. At the remote end of it Lilia sat at her pianoforte, giving the full melody of her voice to one of those delightful songs by German or Italian masters, the beauty of which I first learned from her to appreciate.—Mrs. Cartwright sat at her work, at a small table not far from Lord St. Germains.

I approached the window unperceived by Lilia, who was occupied with her instrument. On seeing Lord St. Germains, I was immediately struck with the very great improvement which had taken place in his appearance.—The hue of health had succeeded to the paleness of disease on his countenance— his frame had acquired strength and firmness—he looked, in short, quite well. He received me with the utmost cordiality. I complimented him on his appearance, and said I had never seen him look in such good health in my life.

"I believe," said he, "it is impossible not to be well, when one is happy.—It will give you pleasure; my dear Mr. Wilson, as my oldest friend, to hear that I am *quite* happy. My painful disorder seems to have subsided—all my wishes are gratified … I look upon myself as the happiest man upon the face of the earth … But I must present you to my pupil—Lilia, my dear, here is Mr. Wilson—" going up to her.

She came forward, holding by his hand,—he with an air of pride and pleasure, mingled—she with a sweet blush as he presented her to me. I was quite astonished at her beauty, and for a moment could not speak for admiration.

"Mr. Wilson," with the softest tone in the world, "how very glad I am to see you again I—I hope you have not forgotten little Lilia?"

"Impossible to forget her—yet you are so much grown, the sweet little plaything is become—you must excuse me, such a very lovely young lady."

"Oh! Mr. Wilson, fie! you are on forbidden ground—you must not flatter—my guardian here does not allow any one to say the least civil thing in the world to me,—do you, St. Germains?—He pays me the compliment to think me quite vain and headstrong enough already, without any encouragement. But I hope you will ever keep your partiality for your little friend—I have the greatest value for it, I assure you.—But how do you think St. Germains is looking?"

"Most remarkably well."

"Oh! how glad I am to hear you say so! He has no pain now—no suffering; and we are *so* happy."

The eyes of Lord St. Germains were bent upon her, as she spoke, with the most touching expression.

"Ah, Lilia!" they seemed to say, "who would not be the happy object of so sweet, so innocent an affection!"

I staid chatting some time with them … Lilia gay and joyous as ever—the same wild petulant creature she had been as a child—with the same warm generous heart. I saw they were the best friends in the world, and they treated each other with an affectionate familiarity which set my mind quite at ease: for I had begun to fear, that the lovely Lilia might prove rather a dangerous companion for my young friend.

Whenever I saw them together, (and they seemed almost inseparable,) he appeared still the kind considerate tutor, she the willing, though rather unmanageable, élève. Provided he was well, she, content and playful as a wild fawn, sported about the woods and bowers, blest in her own existence—unvexed by care—untroubled with reflection.—She left all that to him— and tenderly did he watch over her. The others meanwhile treated her with a contemptuous neglect, which I thought had something in it of envy. The Marchioness affected to lament her dependant condition—the sisters to speak of her as one of a caste different from their own, and as *poor* Lilia. Little did Lilia regard all this; she returned their neglect with indifference— their contempt with a little saucy pouting now and then, and bestowed as little of her company upon them as possible, and lavishing her time, all her gaiety, all her sparkling merriment and innocent caresses, upon Mrs. Cartwright and her guardian, as she called him.

How often did we sit together in the little garden, now a perfect paradise. He, busied with his various concerns—for, well knowing the lamentable indolence of his father's temper, and appreciating the evils thus occasioned to his tenantry and dependants, he was indefatigable in endeavouring to obviate them, and in fulfilling the important duties connected with large possessions. While Lilia would be there at her little table, in a sort of rustic bower they had made, reading, writing, drawing—then starting from her labours to frolic among the bowers, and by a thousand gay wiles endeavour to overset the gravity of her friend; it being evidently the triumph of her malice to make him laugh, when he wanted to be serious, and smile, when he was trying hard to frown. The French term *folâtre,* which I often heard them use, I thought was invented for this bewitching creature.—Then she could be so charming with Mrs. Cartwright, so gentle, and so grave, as if she feared to oppress her spirits by too wild a gaiety—while Mrs. Cartwright returned her attentions with a fondness I thought it scarcely in her nature to feel.

I never saw any being so perfectly in the possession of supreme happiness as Lord St. Germains appeared to be, at this time; his eyes and his countenance spoke the fullness of his heart, which indeed his lips often, in confidence, expressed to me; describing the charms of an existence, replete, to use his own words, with the most exquisite enjoyment.

Little did he think, little did I imagine,—for wise as we considered ourselves upon some subjects, we were sad novices upon others—little did we suspect where the magic lay, which lent such a charm to every object.

A short time, and our eyes were opened.

I have spoken of Lord Louis, as if he had come down with the rest of the family.—It was not so, however.—He arrived about a month after the rest, and his appearance was made the signal for a ball, which his sisters were wild to give; so cards were sent out, and every one was invited, far and near.

Should Lilia be at this ball? The ladies at once decided in the negative. The Marchioness said drily, that, at all events, she was too young—besides that it was cruel, improper, to give a poor young creature, circumstanced as she was, a taste for pleasures not belonging to her situation. The young ladies all declared it would be absurd to think of such a thing—besides that, she had no dress suitable for the occasion—a full-dress ball it was to be—and Lilia was allowed to wear nothing but white muslin frocks.

Poor Lilia had depended upon this pleasure, as her cousins of the same age were to be allowed to appear. Mrs. Cartwright, who, with all her gravity, was the advocate of every innocent enjoyment, and who hated to see a cloud upon a countenance that she loved, was quite disconcerted.

"My dear Mrs. Cartwright," said Lord St. Germains, "what is the matter? *Your Serenity*," for so he would call her in play, "appears this morning in that extraordinary state for you—quite out of humour."

"And indeed so I am, my Lord.—Poor little Lilia! they do not mean to let her appear at this ball."

"And why not?"

"Oh, there are abundance of reasons, if that would do any good.—But not one of them contents me—much less the sweet thing herself, whose little heart has been in a flutter of expectation.—Ever since she heard Lady Mary, who is one year younger than herself; was to be there, she took it for granted she should appear also—but it is decided otherwise—and, poor little girl, she is terribly disappointed.—She is but a shabby philosopher, my Lord, in spite of all your excellent teaching."

"Alas! sweet Lilia, her heart beats too fast and too warmly for my discipline.—I think she would not much mind the amusement, but she will feel the slight keenly.—This must not be."

"What must be done? Will *you* speak—will Jove descend and interfere? I have said all I could venture upon."

"To be sure I will, if it be necessary, rather than my little girl should suffer a cutting mortification. I will go directly and speak to the Marchioness about it."

He went immediately.

"I am come, madam, as usual, with a petition."

"Every petition of yours, Lord St. Germains, is granted, before it is even made."

"'Tis for Lilia."

"Oh, you are excessively indulgent to the poor girl—but what now?"

"This ball! Is it not a pity to deprive her of the pleasure of dancing at it?"

"I think she would be very much out of her place there—and that it is time she should be taught the difference between herself and *my* daughters—a difference perhaps too long forgotten. I think this a good occasion for making her feel it."

"Alas! poor little Lilia, she must feel that early enough—may we not safely leave it to an ill-natured world to instruct her, without taking upon ourselves the odium of the lesson?"

"I think not—it is, in my opinion, the kinder part to educate young women, in her circumstances, in habits of humility."

"But this one ball, my dear madam.—Indulge me—she is still a mere child—spare her the disappointment of being left out— she is too young yet to bear it."

"I very much disapprove of her appearing in a place so unfitted for her."

"I am truly sorry to persist, after hearing you say so—but out of indulgence to *me*—consent this once to act against your judgment.—I must entreat that Lilia may appear."

"As usual, my Lord, your will is to be my law—do as you please:— I hold myself absolved from all the consequences of a mode of breeding her up which I never have—nor ever can approve."

With this ungracious permission St. Germains was forced to be contented: "I am as weak as an old doating grandfather," said he to me—"I absolutely cannot bear to disappoint the child; I want resolution to see that innocent and affectionate countenance clouded in the slightest degree."

I hinted that she might meet with mortifications at the assembly, being the object of so much ill-will.

"I have thought of that," said he, "and I mean to go myself.—It will be the first thing of the kind at which I was ever present— but I must learn to conquer this weakness of mine—I shall make the very best of my appearance, and walk about and take care that nobody affronts my little girl—for with the gentleness of the lamb she has an indignant spirit—and will fire up at insolence—I am very much afraid."

"Oh you dear, sweet St. Germains!" said Lilia, in raptures at the boon he had obtained, and too young and too heedless to dwell upon the mortification of its having been at first refused.—"What a charming, charming, wise man you are! to mind my folly so much—but indeed, indeed, Mr. Wilson, I did think—when I should hear the band, and perhaps the very footsteps of the dancers—and be moping about all by myself—that it would quite, quite drive me melancholy mad.—Poor little Lilia! I sometimes think, what a desolate creature you are—but then I remember St. Germains, and I feel safe: oh! you are the dearest, most delightful St. Germains, that ever has existed, for the thousands and thousands of years, that they tell me there have been St. Germains in this old castle."

The Marchioness and the young ladies were, however, in excessive ill humour at their defeat. No preparations were made for Lilia's toilette—a plain white muslin frock was all she was to be allowed to wear; and when Mrs. Cartwright remonstrated with the young ladies' maids, she was told that it was the positive order of Lady Brandon that a muslin frock was what Miss Lilia was to have, "in order to teach her to know her place."

"In order to make her feel like the dependant she is," said Mrs. Cartwright, quite angry again, to Lord St. Germains.

"Never mind, my dear Mrs. Cartwright, there is a remedy for that; we will take means to make the muslin frock appear rather a measure of taste than a mark of caste—you cannot deny that with a few roses in her dark hair, our little girl will look very pretty."

The eventful day arrived, and Lilia came down to Lord St. Germains' drawing-room, to join Mrs. Cartwright, who had promised to go with her to the ball-rooms. I was there. She entered, fluttering, and blushing, and laughing—her colour and eyes still brighter than ever—her hair seemed more glossy, more wavy, more rich; a few crimson roses were in it—her dress, of the purest white, adorned with a profusion of falling lace, set off the charming contour of her figure.—Her little foot glanced in its shoe of satin—as she stepped with the lightness of a fairy over the carpet—smiling at her own hurry.

"And now the night *is* come—I am so silly I don't quite like it so much—I feel so shy, and so afraid—but there will be a great many people, and I shall not be much seen. Oh, Mr. Wilson, have you been in the ball-room—is it not beautiful?—I stole down to see it.—Shall I do, dear Mrs. Cartwright?"—figuring gaily before her. "Shall I do, St. Germains?"—he was gazing at her with an expression I had never seen before—his colour went and came.

"Very nicely indeed, my dear," said Mrs. Cartwright, fondly.

"Shall I do, I say, St. Germains?—why don't you speak?—something is wrong in me, I am sure," rather anxiously.

"Do!" said he, starting. "Do?"

"What do you mean?—how you look!"

"Oh, forgive me, Lilia,"—rousing himself; "you want something to complete your dress for this splendid occasion."

"Ah, yes, I want a thousand things," said she, laughing: "a diamond necklace, for instance."

"Such as this?" said he, opening an etui which was in his hand—and taking out a simple chain of diamonds, to which was suspended a locket, small, but set with jewels of very great value.

"Will this do, Lilia? to hold your dear Mrs. Cartwright's hair and to remind you of one who only lives to see you happy?"

"Oh, St. Germains, this for *me*—it is not fit for me—did you? —" and her sweet eyes, literally swimming with feeling, were lifted to his face. "Did you? were you so kind? with all your wisdom and all your philosophy—and all your contempt for show and grandeur—to think of my dress and my appearance—and the vanities of this foolish, foolish heart?"

She took the diamonds he presented, and kissed them—and one tear, bright as the gems she held, fell upon her hand.

"'Tis not the diamonds.—Oh, no—no—it is your goodness—and your kindness—and your consideration—I understand it all—but, indeed, these are too good for me!"

"No, my dearest Lilia, nothing is too good for you. It is the first present I ever made you—keep them for my sake."

"Is your hair there?" asked she.

"No, my dear!"

"Then let me have some—let me have the hair of my two only friends together;" her scissors were out in a moment. Mrs. Cartwright severed from Lord St. Germains' head one of his beautiful ebon curls, it was placed with her own silvered sable among the diamonds; she then clasped the necklace round Lilia's neck.

All had been moved by this little scene—when Lilia began to smile as usual again, Lord St. Germains said it must be time to go into the drawing-room.—He took my arm—Lilia hung upon that of Mrs. Cartwright.

We found the Marchioness and her daughters sitting at the head of the long suite of apartments. None of the company had yet arrived; Lord Louis, who had come down from London just in time to dress, was with them, chattering an exuberance of nonsense to a young French lady—a sort of companion to the Ladies Brandon, the most affected coquette it ever was my fortune to behold.

The Marchioness quite started, when she saw St. Germains.— She turned pale, and looked like one who had received a sudden shock—but she came forward, and thanked him graciously for the unexpected pleasure of his presence. Lord Louis turned his face from the French lady, and, seeing his brother, came up with his usual animation, shook hands heartily, and expressed his pleasure at seeing him looking so well. My turn came next—then it was:—

"Ah, Mrs. Cartwright, are you really, too, come down from the hermitage—and are you become one of the wicked, like the rest of us?"

"I hope not very wicked," said she, "I merely came to conduct Miss De V—— and to pay my devoirs."

"Oh, Lilia! I missed you, but they told me you were coming." As he spoke, his eye glanced rapidly towards her. "Is this Lilia?— why I left you the most darling little romp in the universe—and I find you—no matter—no matter—will you dance the two first dances with me?"

Lilia blushed, and looked pleased—I believe she had not felt very sure that any one would ask her.

"If you please."

"If *I please*?"—looking at her with the most radiant expression, —"then you are not engaged, and you will."

Lilia moved forward to her cousins.

"Oh, St. Germains! what an exquisite creature she is become! what a lovely, bewitching girl! what a change in one short year— how different from my sisters! how graceful! how winning! how arch! how soft!—only look at her!"

And he was following her in a moment,—and at her side, talking to her in the most animated manner. She was laughing, and seemed to be coquetting with him—an innocent coquetry I mean—quite innocent—a little more gaiety, and still more softness, ever than usual, in her looks and attitudes.

I heard Lord St. Germains sigh.

The room now began to fill with company, and I was soon separated by the crowd from the family party. When the quadrilles began, I again saw Lilia.—She was dancing with Lord Louis, with equal grace and animation, and certainly made a most distinguished figure, in her white dress and the brilliant necklace which adorned it. Her dancing was exquisite, and her beauty excited the admiration of the whole room. Every one was crowding round the Marchioness, inquiring who Miss De V—— was. The Marchioness was in a wretched humour—for, while Miss DeV—— was attracting all the attention from her own daughters—she had the mortification to see Lord Louis completely eclipsed by his elder brother. Lord St. Germains, on this his first public appearance, if it may be so called, was greeted by the whole neighbourhood with equal respect and pleasure. Every one seemed desirous to pay court and attention to a man, who, though little seen, had made himself, by this time, pretty well known by his actions.

Lord Louis, for the first time in his life, now found his just level, and, instead of being treated as had hitherto been the case, as the heir apparent of the titles and possessions of his house, he sank at once into the insignificant place of a younger brother.—As for him, he cared little about it, and, with his usual thoughtlessness, devoted himself to Lilia—equally disregarding his mother's mortification, and what was due at such a moment to the world in general. The Marchioness therefore looked very cross, and, turning to St. Germains, said:—"I wish, Lord St. Germains, it were possible to divert Louis from this nonsensical trifling with Lilia, and make him attend to others.—Will you be good enough to speak to him?"

Lord St. Germains had been talking to a knot of gentlemen; but at this he turned—his eye glanced hastily towards his brother—Lord Louis was whispering—Lilia was blushing, scarlet. I saw it all, as I thought, in a moment. St. Germains turned quite white; but he took my arm, and said:

"Let us do as she says."

We went up to them.

"Louis," said St. Germains, "your mother wishes you to disperse your attentions a little more, and not limit them to those of your own family."

"Upon my honour, I *am* behaving like a bear—I'll go and ask the Lady Carltons to dance, shall I?—Lilia—mind you dance the supper dances with me."—

"You had better not,"—said Lord St. Germains. "His attentions may be wanted elsewhere."

"She had better *so*—for I engaged her—I will go now, and do my duty; but nothing on earth shall prevent me dancing those dances with her—mind Lilia!"

"Oh, to be sure," said Lady Geraldine, who stood by. "*Mind*, Lilia—don't let the crowd, who will be pressing for the honour, lead you to break your promise—break it to *better* advantage, my dear," with a sneer.

"Lilia," said Lord St. Germains, "don't dance the supper dances with Louis—he is in one of his thoughtless humours to-night—we must remember the claims of others."—And he walked away.

"*Now*," said Lady Geraldine, "you'll not dance with Louis, I'll engage—no—no—we understand our own interests, with all our innocent looks—we have begun with *diamonds*—the next lead shall be in *hearts*—we are not such very good children for nothing, it seems!—Virtue is its own reward.—Mind your good guardian, child—and it shall have something still better next time—who knows!"

Lilia's cheeks were all on fire at this speech—she stood quite still, however, and answered nothing—she seemed reflecting upon something which had struck her for the first time—presently she, too, moved away.

I saw Lady Geraldine and the sisters addressing her, in a sneering way, as I thought once or twice—and, to my surprise, most certainly the supper dances were danced with Lord Louis, and by his side at supper she sat—and he, as if in defiance, was paying her every sort of attention, which she seemed to me to receive with a conscious shyness which she endeavoured vainly to throw off.

I saw Lord St. Germains—for he did not sit down to supper, not having danced—standing in one corner of the room—he was looking at them with a countenance in which anxiety and distress were so strongly painted, that I was afraid it might be observed.—I went up to him, and touched his elbow.

"My Lord, pray excuse me—but the eyes of fifty gossips may be upon you."

"Thank you, Mr. Wilson—it is very kind in you to take an interest in one so utterly and irremediably miserable—so lost!— so lost!"

I was quite shocked!—he who was usually so calm—"This is no time for explanation—wretch that I am! I have discovered the secret of my heart in the moment of its bitterest despair—take no notice—I want courage to fly—I want strength to remain— miserable that I am—I hate and abhor my brother—yes—" as his eyes once more turned to Lord Louis, in all his glorious beauty of countenance, literally speaking with his eyes to Lilia, whose averted face, and dropping lids concealed from us the expression of her features.—"I envy him—and I hate him—I am become detestable to myself—and contemptible to all the world—little! little! did I anticipate the snare I was weaving for my soul—I thought, till this moment, that it was as a father—as a brother, that I doated—Alas! alas!—it was with a passion for ever forbidden to me!"

He paused, for they began to rise from the table, and the loud music of the band once more called together the giddy dancers.—Lord Louis and Lilia passed close by us, he had hold of her hand, she did not now withdraw it.

"Lilia!" said St. Germains, timidly.

She looked up in his face, with a wistful, uncertain expression; but Lady Isabella followed, and as soon as she heard her voice she turned to Lord Louis, and began bantering and laughing, with a freedom far from pleasing, and so they went away.

At the end of the evening, I saw this beautiful young creature—weary, jaded and pale, preparing to leave the room.—

"Good night," said she, "Mr Wilson," very sweetly, but with a melancholy voice.

"I hope you have enjoyed yourself, Miss De V—— ," I said, rather drily.

"Oh, yes, a charming evening!"

"I fear Lord St. Gerinains will be tired," added I—

"Do you think so.—Oh, I hope not! he fancies himself weaker than he is."

This from you—thought I, and so soon!—I turned away thoroughly disgusted.

"It was such an evening," said Judy, who, in crimson satin, trimmed with huge beads, her flaxen wig surmounted by a large turban, had taken part in its festivity—"Every thing so splendid, and so well appointed—and the Marchioness looking the picture of happiness, with her lovely family around her—and those very sweet young ladies Brandon, in those lovely pink dresses—but

I cannot think where Miss Lilia got that diamond necklace, if they were diamonds—and surely it was very bad taste to put it on her—it looked quite preposterous, I must say—and I heard, indeed, the young ladies Brandon say as much—that diamonds on such a child were quite out of place; and that it was very ridiculous of Lord St. Germains to allow her to wear them—poor creature, without one farthing,—they seem quite vexed about it—and they were very right. And for my part I could not help being sorry when I saw Lord Louis, to think he would never be Marquis of Brandon—such a fine young man! And poor Lord St. Germains, he looked mighty well for *him*, to be sure—and is really wonderful considering—but *he* to be the heir;—it certainly is a very great pity—and must vex poor Lady Brandon most extremely."

"I should not wonder if it did," said I.

Never did scene of festivity produce such disastrous consequences as this unlucky ball.

To begin with the Marchioness herself. It was but too true, what Judy said; the idea that Lord Louis, her adored, idolized son, would never be anything but a mere younger brother, did vex her most bitterly.

The appearance of Lord St. Germains in public, as the acknowledged head of his family, had given, as it were, the lie to all her ambitious hopes—and opened her eyes to the fallacy of that expectation which she had so long obstinately cherished, that the poor deformed boy would never live to obscure his brother's prospects. When he appeared however acting, moving, and speaking, just like the rest—the instant conviction struck her, that his life was just, to use a business expression, as *good*.

The conduct of Lord Louis had increased her mortification.— He, for whom she had laboured with such cutting anxieties, had taken his just place, as easily, and as good humouredly, as if no other destiny had ever been anticipated for him, and, absorbed by a foolish admiration for Lilia, had devoted to her all his attention, all the flower of his extreme personal beauty and lively talents, on this his first public appearance in his native county.

To these causes of vexation were added others still more pressing.—The excessive and wanton extravagance with which the establishment of the family was kept up had already rendered the Marquis somewhat of an embarrassed man; to this must now be added the weight to Lord Louis's debts.—He had lavishly spent, but he had done more—he had played. Educated to deny himself no indulgence, and already smitten with that feeling of satiety, which drives the man of pleasure to vice; he had played—he had played high, and his mother, the confidante of all his distresses, was haunted by the perplexity of having debts to discharge, of which the apparent health of Lord St. Germains showed her the impropriety. Even *she* could not help feeling that, as a second son, Lord Louis had been indulged too far. Still her haughty spirit revolted from acquiescing in what her reason told her was a just view of the subject; she flattered herself that at least it was impossible, or highly improbable, that St. Germains should ever marry—and lulled her uneasiness, as well as she could, with this flattering unction.

The Marchioness had been made unhappy by the events of the evening—but *she* had been unhappy before.—Its baleful effects were more discernible on one blest with the peace and tranquillity of a virtuous and well-regulated spirit—on one whose tranquillity and peace that evening had utterly destroyed.—Lord St. Germains, awakened suddenly from his dream of happiness, and made aware of the fatal secret of his heart, abandoned himself at first to a grief and despair, quite terrible in one hitherto so self-governed.

I was a sorrowing witness of some of those bursts of uncontrollable feeling, to which he became a prey.

"Oh! Wilson, what a change! what a fatal discovery! my Lilia! my sweet innocent—how little did we, either of us imagine, that the monster—to whom you had tendered, in spite of his deformity, your sweet, guileless affection, could nourish in his heart a passion, that would render him for ever odious and detestable in your eyes,—I, who, even as a son and as a brother, have found myself loathsome and hateful—to dare to cast a wish that way.—All, all is over—my happiness—but that is a trifle—my life—the very spring of action, is stopped—a heavy curse is upon me—I cannot—no, it is in vain—I cannot recover that blessed ignorance with which I delighted myself in her sunny smiles—her celestial, her adorable beauty.—Now all is become poison for me—when she comes before me, my very heart aches with her sweetness,—her softness—all her thousand—thousand enchantments, till breath and sense seem leaving me—would to God they had left me, and for ever."

"Alas! my Lord," I said, "do not abandon yourself to this frightful despondency.—Be more just to your own merits.—Why should not you too endeavour to win—as thousands of others have done before you,—consider the many advantages you enjoy!"

"Don't speak of them, Wilson—don't tempt me with the cruel thought—yes, there *are* moments—when I feel I could buy her—when I could try to persuade her to barter her loveliness to my doating self, for gold—horrible temptation! never—never;—gratitude might do much,—ambition and vanity might do something—she is not quite an angel—but God forbid—God forbid—Oh! Louis!—Louis—how I envy you!—but do you think she loves him, Wilson?"

I could not tell the truth—I said, I thought not.—He seemed relieved.—"I am spared that pain—thank God—she is but sixteen—time enough for her to begin the dreadful dream of passion—yet a few years, if this wretched heart would have allowed—I might have still owned her as mine, and satisfied the affections of her innocent nature—time enough to have died—when the light had been for ever extinguished—but now even this is denied me—these few years of peace are forbidden—my torments have begun before their time."

I have said that I dared not hint to Lord St. Germains that Lilia loved Lord Louis; but what could I think?—from the evening of that fatal ball she, too, had been entirely changed—clouds hung upon that once serene and open brow—her eyes would suddenly fill with tears, which she strove impatiently to hide—and often have I caught her wandering in the woods by herself, the very picture of melancholy despondency.—Was this love?—and was it the love of Lord Louis?

He had remained but three days at the castle, and, during those three days, she had been the object of his open admiration and most pointed attention. He swore to his sisters that she was the most beautiful and enchanting being that the world contained,—that they did not approach her by thousands of leagues—and that her softness and melancholy were more attractive than all her sportive graces had been.—In short, his raptures were as extravagant as they were undisguised; indeed they were so thoroughly undisguised that even the Marchioness, to whom it might have been expected they would have occasioned some uneasiness, was quite indifferent upon the subject. She simply offered no opposition, when he proposed returning to town—vowing that the intolerable old castle was only fit for the antediluvians, or, the same thing, his ancestors at the time of the Roses.

He left us therefore at the end of about three days; and after he was gone, the depression of Lilia certainly increased, so as to be remarkable to every one.—Her manner, too, to Lord St. Germains was altered—a shyness, a constraint had succeeded to her former artless familiarity. She never now went up to his chair with a caressing, almost fond, manner, to show him her flowers, her drawings, her birds, or to make him laugh at her nonsense, or sympathise in her admiration of some exquisite passage in her book. She was little indeed in his room, less with

Mrs. Cartwright even, and much with the young ladies. Was it that she had instinctively discovered his feelings, and that, in spite of her better self, they filled her with disgust? Was it that her partiality for the other brother attracted her to the society of his sisters? The first was the interpretation that Lord St. Germains put upon it, and it completed his distress.

"It is betrayed," said he to me. "I have betrayed myself—and the sweet thing flies me with disgust and terror—how should she otherwise, poor little creature?—She is driven from her last asylum, by a horrible monster, that terrifies her young imagination like a strange vision.—Oh, my Lilia! my lovely! Lovely Lilia! why cannot I be your brother and your guardian still?—but no, she has learned to detest me—she fears me—she hates me—she, who once sought all her joy and happiness in my presence—my selfish passion has deserved such a return."

Thoughts like these fastened on his mind: in vain he strove to master them, and made heroic efforts to conquer his sensibilities. The struggle was too mighty for his delicate frame, and with anguish I saw the foundations of being about to give away—a disease more painful, more hopeless than that of his mother had fastened upon his frame, and was rapidly consuming the springs of life—the disease of hopeless love in all its bitterness—aggravated by the perpetual presence of its object—such a situation, happily for human nature, is a rare incident in life—many circumstances must combine to produce it—they were all united here.

I saw his cheek grow paler and paler, his eyes acquire a ghastly brightness,—while his voice lost its clear and sweet intonation, and broke hollow on the ear—I watched these symptoms with an aching heart—I told him of his danger—I conjured him to let me try what could be done.—

"Not for the universe," was his reply.—"I will not, even *attempt* to succeed—where success must prove a curse to *her*.—Shall I take advantage of her youth—her inexperience—and wed her to this hateful mass—this heap of miserable infirmity?—she could not even know herself how detestable I might become to her. No—no—let me be—my good friend, I shall recover—or I shall not—'tis no great matter."—

Did Lilia perceive all this?—the time had been when so rapid a decay would have called forth the sweetest attentions, the most lively expressions of anxiety. Now all was changed. She would indeed start forward, as in former times, to move a footstool, or to place a pillow—but then, shrinking back, would leave the kind office unperformed. He noticed to me this decline in her attentions, with a sigh; "and yet," added he, "it is better as it is."—I had observed him, indeed, once or twice gently repulse her, as she attempted to perform some of these little personal services.

"Vous me faites mal, Lilia," would he say, "leave it, my dear, to Mrs. Cartwright."

Then she would retreat—colour like crimson—after a little while, make an excuse to leave the room—and not, perhaps, return for the whole evening. He would sigh, turn over his books, ask for his pencils—and then beg Mrs. Cartwright to play a game at chess—making apologies for his dullness and inattention.

Between this lady and myself no confidence was exchanged: the deep gravity which hung over her countenance alone betrayed her conviction that all the prayers of his mother—all her own efforts, had been vain—and that he was perishing, the miserable victim of that passion, from whose power they had so fondly hoped to shield him.

It is difficult to conceive circumstances better calculated to increase his fatal disorder than those under which Lord St. Germains found himself—or to imagine the extent to which Lilia had become necessary to his happiness. Mortified in all his affections, with a heart formed for tenderness—ever since she had entered the family and attached herself spontaneously to him, a new spring of life had appeared to animate his existence. Gratified by the devotion of the warm-hearted little child, his disappointed heart had adopted her as his own—and in protecting her happiness, and providing for her instruction and improvement, he had found a delightful interest for his lonely hours—while her gaiety and her petulance, the lively spirit discernible in every thing she said and did, sweetened and cheered his once melancholy existence.—As elder brother and as little sister, how perfectly happy they had been!—His improved health, his animated looks, his life of cheerful action, bore testimony to his felicity. But now all this was over, a passion the most intense, long nourished unknown to himself, had been manifested by the bitter pangs of jealousy—and, bursting at once upon his astonished soul, reversed every circumstance of his condition.—She whom he had guided and controlled as a sister—as a mistress, only inspired him with feelings of fear and of humiliation—the innocent affection he had been proud to display, and she to receive, had been exchanged for a sentiment which he believed, if known, would inspire her with horror—and cover him with derision in the eyes of the world. Her very presence became a source of anguish—though when she was absent he seemed scarcely to breathe.

It was plain to me that the life of Lord St. Germains was threatened with a rapid decline.

What the Marchioness thought I do not pretend to say; but I never saw so great a change in any human being.—She seemed, as it were, to breathe again, her countenance resumed its colour—her step its elasticity—all the restless anxiety that had darkened her brow disappeared. She lavished expressions of interest upon the situation of Lord St. Germains—inquired after his progress with the greatest anxiety—and omitted no mark of affectionate attention—in short, she played the part of tender mother to perfection.

"She is truly angelic," said Judy, "I think it is quite affecting to see her—she came down herself to day to speak to me about the asses' milk—Mr. Deane has an ass, as I told you, brother."

"My dear Judy, you need not tell me—Lord St. Germains won't drink asses' milk."

"Oh! how can you say so!—The Marchioness said to me so condescendingly, and in her sweet manner, 'It is the *very* and the only thing for him—don't you think so, Miss Wilson?—I am excessively concerned about him,' said she, 'and I think of writing to his father—he is in very great danger—does not Mr. Wilson think so?'—I said I did not know what *you* thought—but for my part I knew he must die—then the tear came into her eye—and she said—'What a loss he would be to his family—and to the neighbourhood, and to herself in particular—for you know,' says she, 'he has shown me more than the duty of a son—and I have loved him with more than the affection of a mother:'—how generous of her! when all the time, poor creature, he has been keeping her own beautiful son out of the estate!"

"I wish to God, Judy," said I, out of all patience at last, "you would make an end of this everlasting theme. What do you mean by keeping him out of an estate which never was *his*—and if there be power in medicine never *shall* be?"

I went up that night again to the Castle. Lord St. Germains was very ill.—He was grown so feeble that he could scarcely walk across the room—he was, for the first time I had ever seen him, in tears—he was reading a little torn book when I entered, he put it hastily behind the cushion of his chair, and passed his hand across his eyes.

"You are not so well this evening, I fear," said I.

"Not worse—not worse—but moved—melted—cut to the soul. What is there about you, Wilson—that I confess to you every thing—weaknesses that would disgrace a child?—is all of manhood utterly lost?—You will wonder," after a pause, "what has thus touched me—it is one of *her* books—I recollect giving it to her when she was quite a little child—it has been read and re-

read, and is now all torn and tattered—so like her, little careless thing—I never read the story before—it is very pathetic."

He took the book and showed me the title. It was the little Fairy tale of *Zemire and Azor*, or of the Beauty and the Beast.

"Ah! if those days could return! and I—under the mask of my deformity, were sensible that I concealed the power to charm and to delight—how would I too humble myself to implore—and to kneel—and to sue—like the subject of that touching tale.—Alas! alas! my tortures at times exceed my strength."—

He was much agitated—and his frame shook under the struggle to repress his emotion—after a time nature sank, and he fell back into his chair in an uneasy slumber—his hand hung listlessly over the arm of his chair—he looked the picture of extenuation.—I was hidden by one of the deep windows, and watched him, my heart torn with grief and regret—when the door slowly opened, and Lilia glided into the room—she had a bunch of roses in her hand—they were the first specimens of some plants Lord St Germains had procured for her from Normandy.—She came softly forward—and, perceiving he was asleep, and imagining him to be alone, she laid the roses softly beside his book, and then stood long gazing upon him. I could not see her countenance—but I did see her sink upon her knees, and imprint one rapid kiss upon the pale and wasted hand which hung suspended.—He moved,—she started, and suddenly left the room.

I was struck with her flushed face, but attributed it to the heat of the weather.

I staid all that night by Lord St. Germains. I did not tell him what I had seen, thinking it best not to agitate him either by pleasure or by pain.

The next day I was forced to announce in form to the Marchioness that I thought him in very great danger, and almost despaired of his life. She received this intelligence in her boudoir.

A vast heap of bills were lying before her, and a letter from Lord Louis—it contained, as I afterwards learned, an account of his embarrassments, of his large debts, and of the impossibility of his making head against them. He, who had literally nothing, either in possession or in expectation,—he expressed his apprehensions that he must quit the kingdom.

She looked up anxiously from her employment as I entered the room. I never saw a countenance in which mortification—harass—perplexity—were more visibly expressed.

"Well, Mr. Wilson, to what am I indebted for this visit?"

"Madam, I am the unwilling bearer of very painful intelligence."

"What!—what!"—with a faint cry—"what more!—my son!—Lord Louis—"

"Madam is well, for anything I know to the contrary: but Lord St. Germains—"

"Oh! what of him?"—peevishly.

"He is very ill."

"Oh, as usual, I suppose,—one of his tiresome lingering attacks, which render him a burden to himself—" and *to others*, —I mentally added for her.

"I am afraid, Madam, he is worse than usual—worse than I have ever seen him."

"You don't say so—What's the matter?"

"A more general decline of the powers of life than I have ever before witnessed—I think it right to make your Ladyship acquainted with the truth.—Will it be impertinent to add that I think the Marquis, his father, should be informed that his life is in danger?—A few months—perhaps a few weeks—perhaps a few days—may end it," said I in a broken voice—for his mother was then before me; and I imagined I saw the anguish she would have felt, painted on her gentle countenance.

The Marchioness heard me in perfect silence.—Her eyes were bent on the papers before her—then gradually the clouds rolled away from her anxious countenance—and with a sigh, or rather a deep drawing of her breath, like one relieved from an intolerable burden, she began slowly to refold the papers before her, and, having put them carefully into her writing she seemed suddenly to recollect herself, and, turning to me with as much concern in her face as she could throw over it, she said,

"This is very afflicting news, Mr. Wilson, and will grieve us all deeply—I will write to my Lord."—

I made my bow, and withdrew.

Three days after, the Marquis arrived.—His son was by this time worse, but at the sight of his father he seemed to rally a little: at least the unaffected grief which the Marquis testified at his situation, roused his interest, and softened the bitterness of his feelings.

"I had not thought that I had made any part of my father's happiness—such a constant source of mortification as I must have been to him.—I feel grateful for such an affection, and would fain live a little longer to show my sense of it—but it will not be."

The apartments of Lord St. Germains, now that his life was despaired of, were crowded by his friends. His step-mother—his sisters—even the French governesses, were busy proffering their attentions. He received them all with patience, and even with a sort of gratitude—but found little in them of consolation. As for Lilia, she appeared lost in the bustle, overlooked by every one, rarely addressed even by St. Germains. She moped about, looking wretched, when no one appeared to observe her; but preserving, in public, her spirits in a wonderful manner.

I was astonished that no one surmised the cause of Lord St. Germains' illness. I could not be sure of Lilia—but the others never appeared to suspect it in the slightest degree;—so blind are we to what lies directly before us. They had probably never read the story of Antiochus. I had—and I saw the symptoms described by the historian all represented in this unfortunate young man. Lilia never entered the room, but the crimson mounted to his temples; and it was evident his heart beat 'till he could scarcely breathe. His voice faltered when she approached him, and was almost inarticulate when he addressed her.—Though when she spoke, he would often seem to turn away inattentive or indifferent—Lilia came less and less into his room—at last she did not come for a whole day.

The next evening I was called to see her—she was ill—very ill, and in bed. A neglected cold had generated a pleurisy—she was soon in imminent danger.

I have said, that I had been much estranged from this lovely young creature: unjustly, I own—was she to blame that she preferred one brother to the other? Was she to blame that she shrunk from a passion she could never return? I had, indeed, been unjust—but I could be so no longer. Her softness, her patience, her gentleness, her piety on her sick and lonely bed, were worthy of her teacher. He had made this sweet and playful girl, a being of magnanimity and power—a being worthy of himself.—Oh! how I grieved over his misfortune, as I witnessed every hour fresh proofs of excellence, which justified his idolatry and his despair. She never once mentioned him to me, or to Mrs. Cartwright, who was her constant friend and nurse, and devoted herself to her as much as was possible, consistently with the attentions necessary to Lord St. Germains; and to keep the secret of Lilia's danger from him, which, without exchanging confidence, we tacitly agreed to do—persuaded that to hear of it would have killed him at once.

Poor lovely Lilia—she grew worse and worse—with her, too, anguish of mind appeared to add poignancy to physical suffering. I thought her in very great danger, and my heart bled over the young creature, whose blossom had been so suddenly and unexpectedly blighted. I visited her day and night, and watched her like a child of my own—but my skill was unavailing, she appeared to me to be sinking.

One evening I was sitting in her room—the hour I shall never forget—the moon was rising with calm solemn brightness, on a clear, still night, over the distant woods—the fall of waters, the song of one solitary nightingale were the only sounds heard. The moon-beams fell on the massy stone frame-work of the antique window now half opened—and thence in large bright masses on the bed and floor—I thought she slept, and, fearful to the light might disturb her, rose softly let down the curtain.

I found she was awake and leaning on her arm—gazing with her large effulgent eyes upon the landscape; while one or two big tears stood upon her cheeks. Something was in her hand which was pressed closely to her heart—she heard me move—and looked up at me wistfully—hesitatingly—"Mr. Wilson—it is a hard question for one so young—must I die?"

"I trust not, my dear young lady."

"But am I likely to die?—Am I in danger? I feel very, very weak. And then—" and the tears rolled rapidly down—"And then I am *so* unhappy."

"You so unhappy!—sweet Miss De V——: what can make you so unhappy?"

"Are we quite alone?"

"Quite."

"Then I will do it now—while I have breath.—Pray come near me, dear Mr. Wilson."

I approached, and sat down by the bed-side.

She opened the hand that had been pressed to her heart.

"You remember it?" said she.

It was the diamond locket with Lord St. Germains' hair.

"You were there, when it was given to me on that fatal, fatal night. Oh, Mr. Wilson, why was he so good?—why was he so kind? and all to—"

"To what, my dear young lady?"

"To make me so wretched—so wretched."

"My dear Miss De V——, what should have made *you* so wretched?"

"Alas! Alas!" and her cheeks—temples—very hands—were dyed with a sudden crimson. "Did you not see it?—they told me all the world did see it—would see it—and that I was degraded for ever in *his* eyes. But now I am going to die—now, at least, I may tell him—without suspicion of mean, hateful, interested views.—Oh, how little they knew me!—I may tell him on my death-bed—how I honoured him—how I blessed him—how I prayed for him—how I thanked him—how I—Oh, Mr. Wilson, you are good and gentle, like himself, and I am not afraid—don't tell him that his unkindness has cut me to the soul—don't tell him how bitterly I repented that *one* act of disobedience—don't tell him all that his cruel, cruel sisters said—but when I am gone, give it to him—this locket I mean—let me hold it in my hand till I die—and place but this lock of his own hair— the last indulgence he ever granted me, was to cut it from his head—lay it with me in my coffin—that is—that is—if it is not wrong—"

"He!—whom do you speak of?—Lord Louis? you surely wander—"

"Lord Louis? what do you mean?—Ah, he has been kind too—but I am not thinking of *him* on my *death-bed*."

I was struck dumb—was it possible?—was she ignorant of the passion she had inspired? Were her young affections still his in all their first purity—But what if she were made aware of the nature of his feelings—would disgust and dislike take their place? And, alas! alas! was it not all too late for both?

I was for a moment or two silent and ruminating, when I looked again—the colour had faded to deadly pale. Shame and grief were painted on her countenance.

"Alas! even *you*," she said, with a tone of tender reproach, "even *you* despise me.—Oh! that I had carried my secret with me to my grave.—Yet to leave him without one word of explanation—without one word of gratitude—after all my neglects—and after all my coldness."

"My dearest, dearest young lady—for Heaven's sake—for *his* sake be comforted—take this draught—save yourself—save yourself for him."

"Alas, no!—he loves his poor Lilia no longer. I was very wrong to disobey him—very, very wrong—but they sneered so at me—I could not—I dared not. Oh, I was very weak—and he has turned off his little Lilia, and he loves her no more."

"Ah, Miss De V——, if you knew how well!—too well for his own peace."

She coloured again like a rose, her eyes fell.

"Ah, Lilia, is it possible that your gratitude, that your affection—can stand the test? Is it possible, Miss De V——, that you have not seen—what he is dying in agony to overcome?"

"It is then as his sisters said—he does not wish to disgrace himself," said she in a hollow tone.

"Disgrace himself!—what can you mean?"

She was much confused, and stammered out—"I mean—they said—Oh, Mr. Wilson!" and the ingenuous frankness of her childhood shone once more upon her brow. "They made me ashamed—his sisters I mean—of my affection—of my regard—they told me it would disgrace him in the eyes of the whole world, if he thought of me for a moment; and for me—Oh, the horrible—horrible accusation that I honoured him for his wealth—and flattered him for his gifts—and would sell myself for his gold!"

The idea of him, then, as a lover *had* then been presented. It certainly was not that suspicion which caused this estrangement.—A flattering, sweet hope rose in my heart.

Had I been the lover himself, I vow I could not have been more interested.

"But there would not be a shadow of degradation in Lord St. Germains thinking of you, my dear Miss De V——. Your family is as good as his own—and, were it not, is he the man to regard such absurdities? Alas! if no other obstacle presented itself, he might yet be blest—he might yet live."

"Live!" repeated she. "Oh, Mr. Wilson, tell me—tell me!—is it—can it—?" She suddenly covered her face in her pillow.

"My dear Miss De V——, is it possible that you have not seen —may he—dare he plead for himself—, and ask your affection in the name of a dearer sentiment than gratitude—than regard? May I tell him—can you give him hope?"

"Tell him nothing—he would despise me! No—no! let my secret die with me—let him not scorn my folly and my weakness."

This was enough. I read in her ingenuous confusion—in her radiant eyes—in her endeavours to hide the smiles that stole to the corners of that mouth, the happiness of my friend. I could have kneeled down, and thanked Heaven aloud. But then the thought of their mutual danger, the dread that the boon came too late, agitated me to a distraction that quite unworthy of my temper and years.

Having explained as softly as I could to Miss De V—— the situation of Lord St. Germains, and added assurance that what I had to tell him would call him back even from the very gates of death, I entreated her for his sake to endeavour to compose herself. She took the draught I gave her, and, with the docility and confidence of a happy child, laid her head upon her pillow, and in five minutes was fast asleep.

As she slumbered, I seemed to see health visibly returning to her countenance. Quiet and rest I now believed would save her. I never moved from my chair that night. Luckily she was almost forgotten. Mrs. Cartwright had once softly opened the door—I had signed to her to allow no one to come in till I rang.

Lilia slept all that night. About six in the morning she moved and sighed, looked at me, and her cheek suddenly crimsoned again.

"My dear Miss De V——, you are better—you will live."

"Shall I?—ah, keep my secret!"

"Most carefully—God bless you—now for your breakfast," said I, almost beside myself with joy.

Her attendants came—I left with Mrs. Cartwright such directions for care upon care, that she was quite amazed.

"Oh, she is of value inestimable," I whispered. "She will save him."

I now left the apartment, and flew, rather than walked, to my other patient.

When I entered the room, which I did very softly, he opened his curtain.

"I am not asleep, Wilson. My night has been tedious enough. I am quite glad you are come—what brings you here so early?"

"Why, my lord, I have got a new medicine, which I think—"

He sighed, and shook his head.

"A famous new medicine, my lord—one that saved the life of the son of Seleucus—please Heaven, it shall do as much for you!"

"Wilson," said he, gravely, "I do not understand you. This is a strange hour—is it possible? a man so temperate—"

"I beg your pardon, my lord. I believe I am intoxicated; but it is with hope—not wine. Hope for the man I most love upon earth! My lord, can you find fortitude to hear tidings that will render this world for you a paradise?—Can you hear that Lilia—yes— *your* Lilia—Oh, my lord, how shall I find words delicate enough to tell you? Your heart has found its echo in hers!"

He rose suddenly in his bed, then sunk back upon his pillow, so pale, that I thought for a moment he was gone.

"No, no," said he, in a voice of utter despondency. "Her compassion—her noble, generous heart has betrayed her. It is impossible. You have urged her, Wilson—I see it too well."

"As I hope to live, my lord, I have done nothing—said nothing. The whole has been to me most unequivocally and most unexpectedly betrayed."

"Tell me all."

He lay quite still while I related to him what had passed—adding what Lilia had told me: that the unfortunate diamond necklace—I suppose by exciting the jealousy of the young ladies—had drawn upon her a most unprovoked attack from the sisters, who had declared that they thought, and every body else thought, that she was only flattering Lord St. Germains for what she could get; and perhaps hoped to entangle him in a marriage that would be an everlasting disgrace to him. The secret of her heart had been thus rudely betrayed to Lilia—and agonised by the discovery which she believed all the world had made, and which she supposed would excite the contempt of Lord St. Germains—she had taken refuge in coldness—absence—flight, like a timid fawn, springing at any risk from the danger she feared.

The idea of Lord St. Germains' passion had never crossed her mind. She saw only coldness and estrangement in his altered manner, and their timidity had only served to confirm their mutual mistakes.

As a conviction of the truth slowly took possession of Lord St. Germains' mind, the glorious spectacle of his countenance was such that I shall never forget it while I live—hope—happiness—rapture—intense gratitude—as those eyes, literally of more than earthly beauty, were raised in inward prayer.

"Mr. Wilson, I shall live," he said, at last—"I shall live to thank her, and to bless her—and, GOD of heaven!—to make her happy! My Lilia—my Lilia—my sweet enchanting one—darling of my pride—idol of my heart. Yes—yes—I ought to have known it—our hearts were made for each other. Was it possible that what agitated every pulse of my being should find no answering chord in yours? Oh, Wilson," turning to me with a sweet luminous smile, "what a world of nonsense I am talking! Forgive me, and feel my wrist."

I did so; and the blood which had been hurrying in dreadful agitation through his veins now flowed with the even current of perfect health.

Three more days, and I had the inexpressible satisfaction of announcing to these two tender beings that they might meet. Over that meeting I draw a veil: it was a scene too sacred to be exposed to vulgar eyes, when two lovers, rescued by their mutual truth and goodness from the very jaws of death, met to open upon a promise of happiness rivalling the joys of heaven. Lilia, transformed at once from the thoughtless child, to the feeling, blushing woman. He, rendered almost beautiful, by the charm his felicity shed around him.

Happy, happy lovers! Three weeks of sweet, unclouded joy were theirs, while they remained with Mrs. Cartwright, a good deal secluded in the large suite of apartments which had been appropriated by Lord St. Germains; recovering, by gentle degrees, the strength which their sufferings had so much impaired.

Lord St. Germains told me, that as soon as he was well he should at once disclose his secret to his father, and ask his consent to an immediate marriage, with permission to occupy one of his country seats. And, with his usual mental activity, he was already planning to make his abode a blessing to all around, and to begin, with Lilia, to discharge the cheerful duties of a useful life. She, moulded by his hand, and virtuous, reasonable, and good, with all her playfulness, entered into his views, and shared his feelings: showing in every look and tone such a sweet, confiding, perfect love for him, and every thing about him, as might have made the vainest and handsomest coxcomb proud and happy. What ineffable sweetness was it then to him, whose whole life had been one struggle with mortification, to find himself the object of such an affection—the possessor of such a heart! But I talk like a doting old man—the recollection is still too much for me. I have often left them to hide my tears of joy; for I loved him like a son, and honoured him like a superior nature. I was, however, forced to quit this scene of happiness for about a week, so of what passed in that interval I can only speak by hearsay.

As soon as Lord St. Germains was able to quit his apartments, he proceeded to inform his father that he had fixed his affections upon Miss De V——; that he had been so fortunate as to meet with a return, and that he prayed his consent to an immediate union. His father, a kind-hearted, plain man, immediately signified his satisfaction at his son's happiness, and his readiness to make all the proper arrangements. He expressed to Mrs. Cartwright his joy that Lord St. Germains had found *one* woman capable of appreciating his excellent qualities. He visited Lilia, kissed her affectionately, calling her his beloved daughter; and then, in the fullness and simplicity of his heart, went down to communicate the agreeable intelligence to the Marchioness.

What passed between them I never knew. I had watched her narrowly.—I had seen the clouds, which she vainly strove to dispel, gathering again over her brow, as the intelligence of Lord St. Germains' convalescence reached her. Darker and darker they gathered over that haughty countenance.

When, however, it was communicated to her that an event so wholly unexpected as Lord St. Germains' marriage was about to take place, an event which entirely closed all prospect of that ultimate succession for Lord Louis, of which she had allowed herself to make sure, her rage and disappointment at last burst all the bounds of decency, though, I believe, she did manage to conceal the real origin of her violence from the undiscerning eyes of her husband, by affecting to cloak it under indignation at what she called the *mésalliance*, the degradation of his son by a marriage with a mere dependant, a child of charity, a child of shame; for so she scrupled not to declare the unfortunate Lilia to be.

Accustomed to yield to her influence in all things, and to evade rather than to oppose her wishes, when they did not coincide with his own, the Marquis was quite unfit to make head against the storm. As usual, he began to think that there must be much reason, where there were so many words—to waver in his judgment—to see things in a new light—and finally to be persuaded totally to alter his opinion—and to agree that the match was a monstrous piece of imprudence, impropriety, and so forth. He concluded by declaring it must be thought of no more—a determination to which he appeared resolved to adhere, with that stubborn obstinacy in which infirm minds love to take refuge.

Lilia was assailed with a torrent of abuse by the Marchioness and by the young ladies—abuse, which it may be hard to believe, can pass from right honourable lips—but so, alas! it is—Passion, the passion excited by the sudden overthrow of selfish hopes, can be as violent, can be as rude, in these mechanically regulated children of false refinement as in the basest vulgar.

They threatened to turn her out of the house—to expose her to shame—to drive her friendless on the world!

The unhappy Lilia, almost terrified out of her senses at the storm, was sinking, almost fainting, on the floor in the Marchioness's dressing-room, where this scene of violence passed—when the door opened, and Lord St. Germains entered.

No longer slow or halting in his gait, but as if inspired by a sudden energy—he walked firmly across the room to where Lilia stood, looking as if she could stand no longer.

"Silence, young ladies," in a voice of thunder. "Have done with this disgraceful noise: has all decency quitted the earth? And is the betrothed wife of your eldest brother a fit subject for your outrageous contempt?"

"Your *wife*, my lord," said the Marchioness, bitterly—"Yes, when she *is* your wife—we must all learn to mock her with idle ceremony—while she remains my dependant—as the forgotten child of my brother's youthful errors—I shall treat her as her disgusting treachery deserves. But she is not your wife yet. Your father has empowered me to say that he forbids this marriage—this degrading marriage, under pain of his eternal malediction."

Lilia clasped her hands, shuddered, and, with a faint cry, sank upon her knees, exclaiming "Ah! no—no—no."

"My dear Lilia," said Lord St. Germains with great composure, "this is no place for you: can you walk?—Go to Mrs. Cartwright, I will be with you soon."—He handed Lilia to the door, and then, returning, placed himself before the Marchioness, who, exhausted with passion, had sunk upon a chair.

"What am I to understand, madam, by the threat of my father's malediction, if I persevere in an engagement, for which I have this very morning received his hearty congratulations? I ask you, have you presumed to interfere between me and my father? I have borne much, perhaps too much.—There are things, madam, you had better not attempt to make me endure."

"I have said what I thought proper," said the Marchioness, more than ever enraged by his firmness. "I have said he was disgracing his house by so weak a compliance—I say so still.—Your marriage!—Have you yet to learn what you are? I am ashamed of you, my lord! What!—purchase a wife with your gold?"

The colour flew up to his temples—his passion mastered him.

"Madam, you shall find—there are words—never forgiven and never forgotten!" and he left the room.

He went straight to his father, and at once declared that no power on earth should separate him from Lilia—that if his father refused, as he threatened, a provision, he would live upon what remained of the money his mother had provided for him—for that his resolution was unalterable—Lilia should be his wife. All this was said with great respect, but with an air of determination which could not fail to have its effect on the Marquis.—He veered once more—again declared himself satisfied with the match—and, having done so, as the shortest way of avoiding further contention, he ordered his carriage and left the house for London.

The rage of the Marchioness, when she found that he was gone, leaving the marriage irrevocably decided upon—seconded by the jealous vexation of her daughters—and the envious exclamations of the governesses, it would be difficult to describe. The noise, the ferment, the tumult, can be judged of only by those who have had the misfortune to live in families—unprincipled, selfish, and violent. In the midst of the confusion, Lord Louis unexpectedly arrived.

His mother's eyes sparkled with exultation when he was announced—a champion when most wanted. She trusted to his vehemence to aid her cause, and triumph over his brother's. Hearing his mother was in her dressing-room, he ran lightly up stairs; but, when he opened the door, he was shocked at the disorder in which he found her with his sisters.

"My dearest mother, what can have happened?"

"Oh, Louis! Louis!—my pride!—my joy!—welcome to your miserable mother!"

"Miserable! who has dared? Mother, who has dared?

"St. Germains."

"St. Germains!—impossible!—he never would—he never could—he is too sensible, and too good.—Mother what is this?"

"Oh! Louis, he is going to marry."

"To marry! impossible!—how! to whom?"

"Yes," cried his sisters at once, "to Lilia."

"To Lilia!—what a sacrifice!"

"Oh! far from that," cried Lady Geraldine, sneering. "Oh! quite a love match, I assure you. Lilia is desperately over head and ears in love.—We've had such a scene."

"No! you don't say so—Lilia love him!—is it possible?—Does she really, sincerely, love him?—value him, as she ought to do?—and at her age too!—God bless her honest, affectionate heart! Oh! the sweet child!—I always said she was the best and dearest creature in the world—I must run and congratulate St. Germains immediately, for he is a happy fellow, and well he deserves it.—How heartily glad I am!" and he was gone in a minute, with his usual impatience, totally unheeding the effect his words produced upon his mother.

He passed quickly through the long galleries which separated the apartments of St. Germains from those of the rest of the family, leaving the Marchioness, as I have since heard, in a state which defies description. The human heart is strangely constructed, and it is difficult to calculate what may be the effect of a sudden impression. The manner in which Lord Louis had received the intelligence of what his mother had worked herself up to consider as the most disastrous, cruel, and overwhelming event that ever befell a human creature, seems to have operated upon her in the most sinister and extraordinary manner.—Disappointed in her expectations of support and sympathy—mortified to the very quick, to see her own son, the efficient cause of all the bitter feelings she experienced, rejoicing openly and unfeignedly in that which she had reprobated so loudly—her countenance, they say, took a hue so dark, that even her usually careless daughters observed it.

"He triumphs every way," she was heard to mutter. "Yes, even Louis—even Louis. Let it be—let it be—a second son—a poor dependent, second son—obeyed by every one—ruling every thing—his father—my children—myself—my son—Lilia—children—honours—fortune."

I can only very imperfectly relate what followed on that eventful night.

The Marchioness had, as her private attendant, one of those venomous reptiles whom the pen of our great poet has, in its overflowing gall, cursed with an eternal celebrity:—

> Skill'd by a touch to deepen scandal's tints
> With all the kind mendacity of hints;
> While mingling truth with falsehood, sneers with smiles—

A thread of candour with a web of wiles.
A plain blunt show of briefly spoken seeming—
To hide her bloodless heart's soul-harden'd scheming.
A lip of lies—a face form'd to conceal,
And, without feeling, mock at all who feel—
What marvel that this hag of hatred works
Eternal evil—latent as she lurks—
To make a pandemonium where she dwells,
And reign, the Hecate of domestic hells!

Mrs. Grace Holdfast was one of those which pride and a haughty contempt of others, when based not upon power and energy, but upon weakness and vanity, selects as a confidante, for the violent and bitter feelings of a heart too feeble to endure, unsupported, its own vehement emotions. Such was the Marchioness—violent, without force—rash, without courage—proud, without dignity—haughty, without self-dependence—contradictions which are the very cradle of wickedness. She wanted, at once, a flatterer and a master—to encourage her where she was failing—to urge her forward where she hesitated. She found both in Mrs. Grace Holdfast.

Holdfast was, in her sphere, such as we may suppose to have been that servant, at once illustrious and base, who ruled to evil the destinies of a regent, and a queen. Possessing, under a servile and vulgar exterior, a mind of masculine daring, and of fiend-like ambition—to govern her mistress—and through her the fortunes of a noble and powerful house, was the secret pride on which she fed. She had, too, identified herself so completely with the Marchioness, that she had in a manner adopted all her passions:—she, too, had long looked upon Lord Louis as the proper heir of Brandon—and with bitter contempt and hatred upon St. Germains, as a poor, miserable, diseased being—"a mildewed ear, blighting his fairer brother." She, too, shared, and more than shared, in the stinging envy with which the elevation of Lilia was contemplated throughout the family—and anticipated, with an imagination of unusual strength, all the change of feeling and circumstance which must, sooner or later, ensue—when Lilia and St. Germains, at the head of a rising family and immense fortune, should dole out their kindness and their assistance to the fallen, impoverished, and dependent members of the second house.

The rest of that evening the Marchioness spent alone with Mrs. Holdfast in her dressing-room. Lord Louis, having found his brother, and congratulated him with his usual warmth and frankness, had begun, for the first time, to understand that something was amiss—and, having learned that it arose from the violent opposition offered by the Marchioness to the marriage, and having, in spite of his carelessness, in some way divined the disappointment which lay at the bottom of all this ebullition of feeling, he felt mortified, and very angry; for he had a good and right heart, with all his faults, a heart from which jealousy and envy were as distant as one pole from the other. He was vexed at his mother, and he spent the rest of the evening with St. Germains, Mrs. Cartwright, and Lilia.

They had all been disturbed, more especially Lilia, by what had passed in the morning—her cheeks were yet flushed, and her eyes sad and heavy—but Lord Louis, all gaiety and affection, soon restored the smiles to her innocent countenance. St. Germains appeared consoled by the generous conduct of his brother for the pain and mortification he had experienced. He was evidently, as Mrs. Cartwright told me, much gratified by the behaviour of Lord Louis, whom he had always loved with the tenderest affection— gratified not only for his own sake, but in finding the bosom of the son unstained by the selfishness and meanness of the mother.

He had been strangely ruffled, but his usual composure was now restored. "He sat," said she, "in that antique window (which I so well remember)—in his large chair, looking tranquilly on the declining sun, whose broad red orb was sinking behind the horizon—while a glow of the richest crimson, gold and purple, illumined the sky. At his feet on a low stool was Lilia—the last rays of the evening gleaming upon the vines. and twisted plants that ornamented the apartment, and falling softened upon that hair, of which it is impossible not to think whenever one is imaging her—so peculiar was the charm it added to her beauty—so rich its floating folds, so unspeakably graceful all its affluence of curls, waves, and ringlets. By her side was Lord Louis, on the ground, amusing himself by whispering in her ear a thousand innocent malicious trifles—which sent the crimson into her cheeks in glowing streaks, bright as the heavens they were looking on—and," said Mrs. Cartwright, "I thought she resembled one of those inhabitants of heaven with their sweet cherubic faces, that the old masters love to represent—leaning from the clouds of the sky amid the angelic host—happiness, love, tenderness, beamed upon that ruby lip and smiled in that eye, investing her with a sort of radiance of feeling and purity. Lord Louis, too—I was so much pleased with him and all his ways, that I thought he looked something almost too beautiful, and too good, for this world. I sat, half shaded by the curtain, myself regarding them. It was a moment, Mr. Wilson, that paid me for many pains—I saw the eyes of St. Germains raised, as if to Heaven, once or twice. He was offering the thanks of his righteous and grateful spirit to the Being he worshipped in the depths of his inmost soul. He looked round, and seeing where I was—without moving so as to disturb the two whisperers at his feet—he held out his hand—took mine and pressed it—I understood him well."

The Marchioness, while this scene of peace was passing at one end of the Castle, remained as I have said, in her own room: she was heard to pace the floor with vehemence—her voice was elevated, so as even to penetrate the well fitted doors of these splendid apartments:—she was evidently talking and gesticulating with violence. After a while, however, all this ceased, and Mrs. Holdfast was seen to go down stairs, and, contrary to her usual custom, at that time of the evening, to leave the house.

It was autumn, and the day was closing in—but no candles were ordered into the Marchioness's dressing room. The young ladies were assembled as usual in the saloon, but the lady mother did not appear. The daughters were not in the habit of attending her when she was indisposed, either in body or mind. Such care always devolved upon Mrs. Holdfast. So they spent the evening, dawdling about the room with their French governesses—playing now and then a few notes on their pianoforte—humming opera airs—hanging over the fire—and so on. They were all sad and dull, after the excitement of the morning.

At length, says one, "I suppose mamma won't come down again, and as for Louis, it is too bad, he has been in St. Germains' room all the evening; I never thought he would have taken *that* side."

"So foolish, and so ill-natured!" said another. "But I shall go to bed, for I don't know what's amiss, but I never felt so uncomfortable in my life."

"Ah! c'est que vous avez tant de sensibilité!" said one of the French ladies: "et moi aussi, je n'en puis plus."

Lady Geraldine, the picture of gloomy discontent, now rose to go. As they went to their rooms, they stumbled upon Holdfast.

"Holdfast, how's mamma?—Why! what in the name of Heaven is the matter with you, Holdfast? You are as white as a sheet."

"What she never was before, and never will be again," said one.

"But are you as silent, as well as pale as a ghost?" said Lady Geraldine. "Can't you say what's the matter, woman?"

Holdfast had all this time been endeavouring to pass on without answering. She was accustomed to treat the young ladies at all times in her own way. She now, however, stopped.

"Matter!—what do you mean by matter? nothing's the matter—what do you mean?"

"Nay! what do *you* mean, you grumpy old thing!" said Lady Mary. "You look in the *oddest* way."

"I suppose, I may look as I please without troubling you," said she roughly, "and I want to go to bed."

"Off with you then, old crab!" said the girl.

The young ladies had been in bed about two hours, when Lady Mary started up.

"Something is the matter, indeed," said she. "Good God, what a cry!"

They were all at once raised from their pillows. There was a cry—such a cry!—a wail, so wild, so clear, so shrill, that the very flesh seemed to creep upon their bones. It rang through the still immensity of that building with a piercing unearthly vehemence. "Again! and again!" said Lady Geraldine. "God of heaven, what is the matter?"

"Au nom de Dieu, qu'est-ce que c'est?" said the French governess, rushing into the room.

The door was now wide open—hurried steps were heard—the whole household seemed roused—there was a rapid opening and shutting of doors—murmuring voices—stifled calls—a low-toned noise of confusion, if I may so express myself—above which, at intervals, were heard the loud clear shrieks of one in agony.

"Where shall we go? what can it be?" cried all three together. "Oh! it is impossible to stay here. Let us run to my mother's room."

Dressing gowns were hurriedly cast on—they were at the Marchioness's door—the horror of the moment, overpowering every old habit and custom, they were flying, like frightened birds, to their mother's wing. "Mamma! Mamma! Holdfast! let us in—let us in," as the shrieks, quicker and quicker, more and more piercing, reverberated through the apartments.

Holdfast came to the door. She only half opened it.

"Let us in! let us in!" cried the terrified girls, rushing forward. She was forced back, and they ran, with one impulse, into the room.

"Mamma! mamma!" but to look at her was enough—they shrunk back appalled. She was standing bolt upright, stiffened, in the middle of the apartment, as perfectly white and almost as rigid as if she had been dead. Her eyes were fixed and staring, and she seemed to be drinking in the horrid sounds, insensible to every other perception.

"Mother! mother! mother!"

The sound roused her, but it was to fury.

"Go away! get away! what are you here for? how dare you come here? get away from me—fly my eyes!—hide yourselves from my sight!—take them away—Good God!—Holdfast are you mad?"

The terrified girls shrunk to the door, alike afraid to remain, or to depart.

The door was rudely opened again. It was Lord Louis.

"Almighty God! it is all over—he is dead—he is gone!"

The mother sank down flat on the floor—Holdfast flew to her—bent her head over her, and was busy, endeavouring to relieve her—while the sisters gathered round Lord Louis.

He paced the room with an air of distraction.

"Only four hours ago, and he was as well as I am—and now he is dead!—Four hours ago, and he was the happiest and the best of human beings—and now he is nothing!—now he is nothing—and Lilia—poor—poor—poor Lilia—"

"Dead!—what? who?" exclaimed they, breathless.

"Why, your brother? our brother!—the best and dearest friend and brother that ever man possessed! St. Germains—the best—the kindest—the worthiest fellow that ever walked God's earth—"and, covering his face with his hands, he sank into a chair, and shed a torrent of tears.

The Marchioness was by this time sitting on the floor, supported by Holdfast, who was soothing and composing her. Her eyes were fixed intently on her son—but at these last words—and when he burst into tears, as if some secret sympathy had rent the cold ice of her soul—she fell into violent hysterics, and her shrieks, laughter, sobs, and ravings, were horrible—were appalling.—Holdfast, the resolute Holdfast, trembled and shook like a wretch in a fever—the young ladies screamed aloud.

"Mother, have done!"—said Lord Louis, rising fiercely. "Have done!—It is impossible to bear this—Control yourself—hold her hands, Mrs. Grace:—have done, mother, with this screaming—all the shrieks of hell will not awaken him. He is as dead as *that*," dashing on the floor a piece of marble, which stood near. "Have done, mother, and let them put you to bed."

"For the love of Heaven, young ladies," said Mrs. Holdfast, in a tone of entreaty, which she had never before been known to use, "call for some help—I *cannot* bear it any longer"—and she gnashed her teeth in an agony of horror.

It was all too true—St. Germains was dead. Four hours ago, he was in the full enjoyment of his vast intellect—a thinking, powerful being—and now he was a lump of miserable clay! His servant, whom accident had brought into his room, had discovered that something more than usual was amiss. Mrs. Cartwright had been called—Lilia had followed. Hers were the shrieks, as his lips fell in the last ghastly agony—as his eyes rolled on her, without sense or sentiment—hers were the shrieks which had filled those vast vaulted chambers. Well might they fill those vaulted chambers with their miserable outcry! They were the shrieks of a heart broken in the full energy of its feelings—the cries of the soul, bursting its youthful tenement—the agonies of death, by mortal sorrow. That young, affectionate heart was not left to mourn the being so devotedly loved and worshipped. The beautiful tresses of Lilia swept over the bosom of her lover—and on his heart that faithful, head was laid like a cropped flower.

> Peace to thy broken heart, and virgin grave!
> Ah!—happy!—but of life to lose the worst!
> That grief—though deep—though fatal, was thy first!
> Thrice happy!—ne'er to feel, or fear the force,
> Of absence, shame, pride, hate, revenge, remorse,
> And that dread pang, where more than madness lies;
> The worm that will not sleep—and never dies;
> That winds around and tears the quiv'ring heart!
> Ah! wherefore not consume it and depart?

They were buried together: something strange, hasty, and mysterious involved the whole business. A private examination was made, but the precarious state in which Lord St. Germains had been known to exist, ever since his earliest childhood, seemed to afford sufficient grounds to account for this sudden catastrophe; particularly when the agitation of the preceding day was recollected. The funeral took place quite privately—the Marquis coming down from London to attend it.

It was a fine morning in autumn, when I returned home from my journey:—a misty grey morning. The sun was just beginning to penetrate the soft haze, and to beam gladly upon the trees, calling out the songs of those few birds which made that season still cheerful by their warblings. I journeyed pleasantly along, enjoying the agreeable tranquillity of spirits, which my habit of early rising usually procures me—but when I entered Carstones, and rode up the well-known street, I was struck with the air of gloom which pervaded it. Looking round me, I perceived that the shops were all shut—that the children, usually at their noisy plays in the market-place, were hushed. There were few passengers, but many people were standing at their open doors—and many faces were at the windows. Suddenly the bell of the church, which stood at a little distance on a green eminence above the town, began to toll. The tolling of a funeral bell is always a most mournful and heavy sound to me—but now it struck me with more than usual melancholy. I hastily rode up to my own door—and throwing the rein of my horse to my boy, who came out, asked what was the matter.

"What has happened? why are all the shops shut up?"

"Lord St. Germains is buried to-day."

I thought I should have fallen on the pavement.

"Lord St. Germains! what can you mean, Richard?"

"He is to be buried to-day—and Miss Lilia, too—and sure they say it will be a mortal fine sight—but we shall none of us have the heart to look on it. A better man never went to his grave than he who goes there this day." And he brushed his eyes with the back of his hand.

I hurried into the house—Judy was not as usual to be seen fidgeting here, there, and every where: she was up stairs in our sitting-room.

"Why, Judy!" I cried, "what are they saying?—what has happened?"

"Oh! brother, such a thing!"

"They tell me—but it is impossible. The Marquis he means—but he cannot be dead—and I never to have heard of it!"

"No, not the Marquis—Lord St. Germains—and Lord Louis came down here—his own self—bless him, to ask when you would be back. He wanted you to be at the funeral—He takes on so, poor young gentleman—as if for the world, there never was such another as his brother." She was running on, but I begged her to tell me all—and then I learned, with many interruptions, much of what I have related.

I am not writing my own history—I have no wish to dwell on what I felt.

I attended the funeral of the two beings I most loved and honoured upon earth—I saw the long train descend the Castle hill, and sweep mournfully up the street of Carstones—the waving plumes—the mourning crowds—I see them still—I saw Lord St. Germains laid in the tomb of his ancestors—with his faithful little Lilia by his side—Lord Louis would have it so. Never shall I forget him, as he stood in his long black velvet cloak— bowing his beauteous head over the coffin of his brother—as sobs became groans—and groans ended in passionate tears, while he called upon St. Germains and Lilia:—he was knit to my soul from that hour.

The poor Marquis was likewise much afflicted: and he showed his grief with an honest, homely sincerity which moved the hearts of every one.

As for the neighbourhood in general, few deaths ever excited so much sensation. Lord St. Germains was deeply and universally regretted, both by poor and rich. Short as had been his career, the power of his active intelligence was generally felt and appreciated, and the prospect of seeing him, at some future period, lord of this great domain, and head, as it were, of the county—had been every where contemplated with satisfaction.

It seemed for some time as if nothing could console Lord Louis (for so I shall continue to call him). He had loved and honoured St. Germains more than any other human being; and, insensible to the splendid prospect now opening before him, he showed, without affectation, that he valued such a man, and such a brother, more than castles or estates, tenement or bank bills. He soon went away from Brandon, seeming to feel nothing but pain in every thing connected with the place.

Wave, however, succeeds to wave:—the waters of oblivion speedily cover the grave of the wisest, the most honoured, and the best. The sensation which the sudden death of Lord St. Germains had excited, the pity which dwelt upon the tomb of the young and lovely Lilia, died away, and, in a few months, every thing appeared to have resumed its wonted course.

The Marchioness had been long in recovering from the violent agitation into which she had been thrown, on the tremendous night of Lord St. Germains' death: for some weeks she was quite unfit to appear, or to mingle in the ordinary society of her own family. Her appearance was entirely changed. She became pale, and complained that even the sudden shutting of a door made her tremble and turn faint. I saw her about three weeks after Lord St. Germains' death; and I thought her nervous system, I must say, in a most deplorable state, recollecting her, as I did, so haughty—so dignified—so cold. I could not remark without great compassion, the change which had taken place. She was tremulous and terrified, could not sleep by night, nor rest by day—in short, was suffering under what appeared to me a regular nervous seizure.

Holdfast, whom I never liked, was grown, as I thought, more disagreeable than ever—her assiduous, and almost servile, attentions to her lady were changed in their character. Assiduous she was, indeed, more than ever; but her attentions rather resembled those of a cross yet careful nurse, to a troublesome child, than the respectful attendance of a servant upon a noble mistress.

Time, however, as I have said, wore away. Month rolled on after month—the disorder of the Marchioness gradually subsided, and by the end of the year she was haughtier and prouder and colder than ever. She began at last to take an open pride in the great expectations of her son; for at first she seemed so insensible to gratification of every sort, that even this appeared to afford her but a feeble pleasure. She assumed a wider authority than she had ever done before, and acted still more completely than ever the part of grand lady and a grand princess.

Eighteen months had now elapsed, and the day approached when Lord Louis was to come of age. He had never entered so fully as one might have expected, into the pleasure of his inheritance, though that he was indifferent to its advantages I do not pretend to say—and he told his mother that he had no wish that his coming of age should be signalised in any very remarkable manner. But her love of splendour, of representation, of magnificence, was all alive again, and her idolatry of her son greater than ever. She declared she would have his majority celebrated as it ought to be for one so magnificently endowed—so highly gifted—and at Brandon Castle; for that, being by far the most princely domain belonging to the family, there alone could its heir, with due propriety, be honoured.

Brandon Castle was become to me a place of gloom and shadow. All that old side of it which Lord St. Germains used to inhabit was shut up, and totally abandoned. I never could tell why; but I observed that not a servant in the Castle would enter it even by daylight, if it were possible to avoid so doing.

As for me, I fled from all that could remind me of a loss so deeply lamented—a feeling which was united in my mind with a painful distrust—a sort of formless disagreeable suspicion. I never saw Mrs. Holdfast without a kind of creeping of the flesh. Her looks, indeed, were more offensive to me than ever—I caught something almost fiendish in her expression, at times. But, as I intended to say, all that side of the Castle was utterly deserted— for Mrs. Cartwright, it is needless to relate, had left Brandon immediately after the funeral of those alone dear to her, and had betaken herself to a distant retreat, where she waited in patience, as she told me, her dismissal from a world in which she could no longer occupy a post of usefulness.

Lord Louis, as I have said, appeared to share my feelings:—he came very little to the place, and seemed to dislike particularly the idea of revelry in such a scene. But the Marchioness was determined; and the 10th of July was appointed for rejoicings on a scale of magnificence unknown even in the annals of this splendid family.

The tables were laid for five hundred people on that magnificent lawn, which those who know Brandon will recollect is surrounded by an amphitheatre of woods, and crowned at its extremity by the lofty towers and grand front of the feudal castle or palace; call it which you will, for it was both. The first board was on this occasion for the nobler guests; and from this, as in the olden time, a continued succession of tables was set, for every one, even to the poorest tenant, and meanest retainer of the family. The tables were covered with plate, of gold and silver, loaded with viands, adorned with the most beautiful fruits and flowers, brilliant with the abundance of shining ornaments of glass, china, and marble, that were glittering in profusion on every side.

The company was splendid, and distinguished crowds of gaily-dressed people were gathered among the trees, or surrounded the tables. Loud sounded the triumphant music of the several bands. The clear notes of the trumpet rang shrilly through the woods, a signal to the revellers to come to the feast. The day was superb, gleaming under one of those bright, glowing suns which, when breaking out upon our scenery, before long heats have destroyed the verdure of the groves, and the brilliant emerald of the grass, produces such a shining effect to the eye.

What a scene!—There stood the Marchioness in a robe whose magnificence exceeded all I had ever before imagined; a circlet of jewels sparkling like a crown in her dark hair. She looked splendidly beautiful. Her daughters, a showy group, stood round her—her husband was by her side—her son, the noble—the beautiful Lord Louis!—I see him now;—but my thoughts were far away—they were resting on that grave where so much goodness and excellence lay buried, forgotten by all but me.

I thought of the good Marchioness—her career of benevolence, so soon closed. I thought of all the unjust and selfish and ungenerous feelings and actions of her, who now reigned triumphant in her stead. There she sat as upon a throne, receiving the homage of multitudes for that son of her pride—all her vain and wicked aspirations gratified, and the favourite established in his brother's place.

But, while I was gazing, the scene of triumph suddenly changed its aspect. Dark, heavy, lurid clouds began to gather round the horizon—low rolling thunder was distantly heard—a sudden silence in the woods succeeded to the noise and stir of life among the bird and insects, and the distant herds might be seen creeping to cover. A universal stillness was in the air, over which, shadows, dark as night, were slowly stealing:—a stillness every where, save round the immediate scene of revelry.

The dinner had, in the mean time, proceeded. The wine had freely circulated, the hum became louder and louder—the noise of the instruments appeared, to my senses, more triumphant. I looked on the sky: all was dark, threatening horror—on the tables, all exulting joy.

On a sudden, there was a general ringing of glasses—a general rise—a general shout—they were drinking health and happiness to the heir. Hip! hip! hip! Hurrah!!

I saw Lord Louis, his head bending in proud and graceful acknowledgment of the honour he received. One ray of the sun shot between the dark clouds, and illuminated his face. The next moment—a crash of thunder—loud—terrible—rattled through the sky, and one bright flash penetrated, for a second, the horrible gloom. One flash—and a cry, a universal cry, rent the air—Lord Louis! Lord Louis!—the thunder bolt had fallen—and struck him dead at his mother's feet.

The confusion that ensued—for a deluge of rain followed immediately the fatal flash—rain—as if the very windows of heaven were once more opened, pouring their torrents upon a world of sin—prevented me from seeing clearly, or remembering much that came after.

I saw the Marchioness, her hair and clothes all drenched and dabbled with wet, carried shrieking past me, through a darkness almost like that of midnight.—I saw Mrs. Holdfast holding her, quivering, shaking, trembling—the daughters flying on the wings of fear for shelter. The splendid crowd at once dispersed—while the wind was bending the trees to the very earth, the rain streaming from the clouds, the hoarse thunder howling, rattling, and clattering through the sky.

Last of all, I saw the dead body of Lord Louis.—Four young men, dressed in the extreme of fashionable elegance, with countenances pale with horror, and hair matted over their bare heads, were carrying the lifeless form between them. His head, yet beautiful, leaned on his shoulder, perfectly senseless—perfectly still.

The whole scene had literally stupified me, and passed before me like a dream. Nor did I move till I heard my name loudly called.—"Mr. Wilson!—Where is Mr. Wilson?—Can nothing be done?"

They came to me, and hurried me into the Castle. Nothing could, indeed, be done for Lord Louis. The lightning had penetrated his breast, and the flash had scorched and slightly blackened his face—this was all—but life was utterly extinct.

The daughters were standing in the corridor, all pride, all ceremony over—shrieking, "Mr. Wilson! Mr. Wilson! come to mamma! come to mamma!"

I ran up stairs. I entered the room of the Marchioness.—She appeared to me raving mad. She was screaming with all her might, and tearing off her raven hair in locks. Her eyes were distended with horror.—"Yes! I see him!—I see him!—he is there still!—He came, like the mighty archangel, in the storm—he rode upon the blast. They have struck me in the soul:—all is over at last.—Louis! Louis! Louis!—you for whom I have perilled salvation!—offended God—called up his mighty rolling thunders—where, where are you?—Gone—gone—gone.—Is it you at feet?—My life! my pride! my son!"

As the thunder rolled and crackled round windows, her horror and distraction increased.

"Another blast for me? I come!—I come! Mighty God!—Hide me—hide me from His rage. Ha!" with a shriek, the most terrible I ever heard—and she seized Holdfast firmly by the arm, till her fingers seemed to meet in the flesh—"Devil! are you here?—seize her!—take her!—She bought the poison!—she mixed the cup!—I saw her smile—the she devil!—I saw her smile while she did it!—the tempting wily serpent! Seize her!—take her!—rack her!—she has murdered us all!—she has damned my immortal soul!"

Mrs. Holdfast looked aghast at this address. Unable to release herself—deserted by her usual presence of mind, she stared stupidly at the Marchioness, as if paralysed—but I went up to her.

"Mrs. Holdfast, this is a serious accusation," said I.—"There is something here more than common—Lady Mary, may I entreat you to call for help?"

"What do you mean, Sir?" said Mrs. Holdfast at last, angrily—"Let me go, if you please."

But I still detained her, while the Marchioness, whose senses were evidently gone, continued to rave in the most incoherent manner.

So she continued to rave for many, many years; the slightest ray of intellect never visited her more.

Mrs. Holdfast was arraigned, tried, and executed. It was proved that she had been down to my surgery that very evening, and bought the poison from Judy. Judy confessed it, after much circumlocution.

Brandon Castle was absolutely deserted. It has been shut up ever since. I do not know what has become of the young ladies. I have heard that these dreadful scenes were not profitless to them. The old Marquis is still alive.

This is all I now recollect of this history—the latter pages of which I have written with so much pain, that, I begin to think I was very foolish to attempt to write it at all.

THE ADMIRAL'S DAUGHTER

Ye gentle pow'rs, that, day by day, unseen,
Where souls, unanimous and link'd in love,
In sober converse spend the vacant hour,
And give the hasty minutes as they pass
Unwonted fragrance—come and aid my song.
In that clear fountain of eternal love
Which flows for aye at the right hand of Him,
The great Incomprehensible, ye serve—
Dip my advent'rous pen, that nothing vile,
Of the pure eye or ear unworthy, may
In this my early song be seen or heard.

Hurdis

I

At the end of the village of Middleton, on the western borders of Wiltshire, stands a handsome, though rather ancient, red-brick house, adorned with stone facings round the windows, doors, and at the angles of the walls, and with urns and balustrades of the same material at the top.

This style of architecture has something handsome and imposing about it—the large ornamented door—the flight of stone steps—the profusion of long narrow windows—the excellence of the brick-work—the fine freestone by which it is relieved. The apparent stability of such edifices conveys an impression of equal stability in the station, fortune, and habits of those to whom they belong, which does not exactly attach to the more classical elevations of cast iron, and cement, which characterise the present era of our architecture.

These impressions of stability, in situations somewhat remote from the metropolis, are not yet altogether illusory. Even in this age of restless changes, of fleeting attachments, of ever-varying schemes and plans of life, some few may be found who, whether wisely or not, preserve their local attachments undiminished—

still cling with a mixture of reverence and fondness to the abode of their forefathers, the cradle of their own infancy—still honour with a hallowed sentiment the antique apartments where parents once presided with a grave dignity, well becoming those grey hairs of which they were not ashamed. For them the genius of the place still haunts the smooth walk, the trim hedges, the formal parterres, even the very walls and elaborate iron gates, which enclose the ancient courts—and they deprecate and resist that spirit of change, under the name of improvement, which would sacrifice all the recollections of the past to the comforts and conveniences of the present—holding light by our more spiritual, in comparison with our more sensual, enjoyments.

The individual mansion which I am about to describe was a remarkably well preserved specimen of its kind. It stood surrounded by a large garden, court, and shrubberies, where all the features of a different age and different manners were carefully preserved. In the front was the court, bordered on each side by lofty elms, where a rookery had for more than a century subsisted, whose cheerful, noisy inhabitants had successively, from generation to generation, annoyed the gardeners, and diverted the children, belonging to the mansion. This court was separated by a broad straight gravel walk, which, though intended to admit horses and carriages to the house, was kept so scrupulously, and exactly smooth, that to bring horse or carriage upon it appeared almost like a profanation. On either side were plat bands of green turf, mowed, rolled, and swept, till every well disciplined blade of grass was as exactly of the size and height of its brother as the pile upon a piece of velvet: even the rooks, which swung on the high branches of the spreading elms above, appeared to respect the delicacy below—or the ever-active hand of the gardener removed, as it fell, every twig and leaf which those busy citizens might let drop; for certain it is, the perfect neatness of the place was never impaired for a moment.

A wall surrounded the court, ornamented, like the house, with white freestone, and boasting, like it, urns of the same material at the angles, while, on either side the gate, frowned in stone, as erst the grim bears of Bradwardine, two fierce leopards, the crest of the family who now here resided. A gravel road ran entirely round the court, separating the grass from the wall, while exactly opposite the entrance rose a flight of fair stone steps leading to the massive doorway and handsome ponderous oaken door of the house itself—the front of which stretched on either side, magnificently adorned by a long succession of windows, inserted before taxation had taught us economy of light, among a thousand other good and bad economies.

The back of the house was, however, what pleased me the most:—there lay the garden, of a kind I have always delighted in—it reminded me of a description which I found in an old book I often read, called the Spectator—such a wilderness of walks, and hedges, and fruit trees, and flower borders—arbours, summer houses, strawberry beds, rose bushes, vines and apricot trees, treillages, fountains, and canals;—and those pretty basins of water, transparent as crystal, with the trees dropping over them their flowery branches, as if, like the beautiful Narcissus,

enamoured of their own image. Here were often to be seen,
disporting themselves, little fairy water fowl with tiny-webbed
scarlet feet and downy breasts; and that beautiful, but long
forgotten, favourite, the mellow carp, its scales more shining than
the burnished gold, would come to the bank, and open his yellow,
leathery mouth, to receive the food dropped into the water by a
pair of the fairest hands that ever were ungloved to feed a pet.

In addition to the other charms of the place, this delightful
wilderness was absolutely peopled with birds of every hue and
song. There, when the cherry was one sheet of white blossoms,
might that delight of my eyes, little Bully, with his crimson
breast and velvet cap, be seen, busily hunting for his prey; while
the smaller yellow wren glanced round the blushing boughs
of the perfumed apple tree, in rapid and incessant motion.
Robin would be hopping pertly in the walk; the blue titmouse,
chattering among the lilacs—while the thrushes, blackbirds, and
that complicated musician, the nightingale, filled the green leaves
with their varied *ramage*—as I think I have heard my young lady
call it, in a language which she loved too well.

I am a garrulous old man—and, before I go on with my story,
let me please myself with the recollection of those bright clear
mornings, when I would be stirring, and all the household, save
the gardeners, in their berths—when the lilacs in full blossom
were bending under their rich clusters of flowers, which the
clusters of the purple vine alone can rival in beauty—the
shrubberies gleaming, like sheeted gold with laburnums—the
gueldre-roses throwing up their snowy foam into the air, as

that sweet poet Cowper has it—every plant, herb, and flower, glistening with dew—the thrushes echoing to one another from the topmost branches—hailing, as it were, the glorious sun—as in his great majesty he rolled up the shining sky. I often thought of an engraving that hung in the small parlour, from a picture by one Guido, I believe, where the God of day, glowing with youth, health, and vigour, is represented guiding forwards his rushing steeds—while the rosy light-vested hours come dancing round his car, and the fair Goddess Aurora scatters the sweetest of flowers before them—those *were* days, days of peace, of goodness, of happiness:—why am I left alone to tread these silent walks? to remember what *was*—to recall the fleeting shadows of the past—and from my recollection and the recollection of others, try to compose a tale?

This, to me, delightful old place, belonged, when I knew it so well, to Rear-Admiral Thornhaugh: he lived at it with his only daughter (for he had long been a widower)—his only daughter—the charming—the most lovely Iñez!

I often used to say to myself that I did not know whether the old Admiral or his fair daughter was most in character with, or most adorned, the place. He, with his lofty and manly figure, stern, weather-beaten, and battle-riven countenance, set off by his venerable hair, white as the driven snow: or she, with that light, elastic form, that face of delicate-speaking features, those large piercing black eyes, that hair than which no raven's wing was ever more dark or glossy; those smiles—

Which went, and came, and disappear'd
Like glancing sun-beams on the dimpled water,
Shaded by trees;—

those bewitching gestures—that sweet musical voice—that little saucy laugh—those wilful naughty ways. Miss Thornhaugh was not like an English young lady—indeed her mother was of Spain;—a most beautiful Spanish lady, whom the Admiral married at Valencia, or at Seville, and she came with him to England, where she shortly afterwards died. Her daughter, every one said, was very like her:—certainly she wanted that rare pink and white which adorn our beauties—there was a tint of olive some might not like; but then her skin was smooth and polished as the finest marble, and her figure had a waviness and delicacy which I cannot describe—a sort of graceful pliancy about it that I never saw in any other. Her feet and hands were so extremely beautiful, it scarcely looked natural—they seemed modelled by art. I once saw her, like that beautiful Dorothea we read of in Don Quixote, with those lovely feet bare, shining through the transparent water of one of the little canals. I believe it was after one of her favourite carp which looked sick that she had gone in, with her usual prompt way of doing what she pleased; be that as it may, I certainly never beheld the work of any artist so exquisitely formed as those feet of marble then appeared. She used to dress, too, in a way of her own:—she rarely wore colours, but was always in black or white; and her dresses were not trimmed and sticking so oddly out and about as those of the best dressed young ladies we visited; one did not know how they were made. They used to flow like a drapery round her limbs, confined by a band round her waist, where usually would be a clasp of very rich jewels and gold. On her arms she sometimes wore a rich bracelet or so, and a splendid gold chain now and then round her neck; but never any thing in her hair, which was braided about her head in a manner quite her own, which I used to think very charming; and she had a way of wrapping a great mantle of delicate lace, at times, about her that was very striking. I was told she had it from her mother, as well as the pattern of her black satin shoe, which certainly was most prettily fancied.

Miss Thornhaugh was all gaiety and good humour—but as wild and as wanton as a bird. She never much heeded what other people thought or did, but went her own way, perhaps one should say, wilfully—but it was such a pretty wilfulness that I, for one, could not quarrel with it. I never knew any living creature wounded by her: she was, in spite of all her sprightly carelessness, the kindest of beings to those who wanted kindness. An angry or harsh tone never passed on those beautiful lips, the many years that I knew her. Some found fault with her for being a sad coquette; but I think it was mere envy; she certainly did smile, and laugh, and talk with the young gentlemen; but all she said and did was so innocently gay, I never thought there was too much of it; and I am sure they did not. Then she had such a warm heart:—how she loved the old Admiral, her father! and as for him, he adored her—he loved her as the apple of his eye:—she was the light of his footsteps—the fountain of joy to his soul. She was to the stern old seaman, after all the dark and rugged passages of his life, like some strain of wild and sweet music filling the intervals of the storm. His features, on which the severity of the quarter-deck had traced those lines—firm to rigidity—almost harsh in their stern dignity, would relax and soften, at her approach, to a sweetness quite remarkable; and his voice, which, when a little raised, we could none of us hear without an undefinable sensation, would melt to her into the modulations of a lover. As for denying her any thing in the world that she wished for, or thinking any thing she chose to say or do could be amiss, that never entered into his head. She played with all his fancies, which were some of them whimsical and obstinate enough:—she smiled him out of his anger, for when there was reason he could be very angry. She coaxed him to follow her ways—when others found it impossible to bias him. She prattled—she caressed—she made him do all she wished and liked, just as I have sometimes seen a pretty little delicate girl tease, and caress, and fondle, and tyrannise over, an immense, dignified, and rather surly, dog, that no one else much cared to speak to. The comparison is irreverent, but it seems so just.

II

THUS they lived together at the large house at Middleton, visiting and giving dinners to the gentlemen and ladies of the neighbourhood—Miss Thornhaugh dancing at all the balls, and shooting at all the archery meetings—till I believe she might be about nineteen—and then the change came which I was always expecting—and Miss Thornhaugh was engaged to be married. There was a young naval officer who was a prodigious favourite with the Admiral, and he had indeed told me once or twice, that Harry Vivian, and none but he, should have his darling daughter. Harry was a man after his own heart—an honest, open-hearted, sensible fellow—brave as a lion, and the best officer in his Majesty's service: and Harry, and none but he, should be his son-in-law. These things, I thought, seldom turn out as planned; and I felt as if the above-mentioned recommendations might not be those most exactly fitted to engage the heart of so elegant a young lady. Luckily, the good Admiral had the prudence to keep his schemes to himself, so that the perverseness of the beauty was not awakened to oppose his design; and when Captain Harry Vivian actually made his appearance, he really was so charming a young man that I began to hope that my old master would not be disappointed.

Captain Vivian was all the Admiral said—an excellent and able officer—open-hearted, sensible, and spirited—and possessing that frank off-hand manner which I think so becoming in our naval men. But the days are gone by when such qualities were alloyed by a certain unpolished roughness, that women of refined taste could not have liked. Captain Vivian was a perfect gentleman— no fine coxcomb of the Guards, or of the Blues, could be nicer in his dress, or more scrupulously refined in his manners. Yet was the sea man's native gallantry not lost, under these modern refinements. Nor could the somewhat elaborate elegance of the exterior conceal the honest simplicity of the most affectionate and direct character I ever met with. Disguise, pretension, art, or calculation, were alike strangers to Harry Vivian. A clear and plain understanding, a warm and upright heart, spoke in the expression of these fair blue eyes—might be listened to in the tones of the most agreeable voice in the world—might be read, as it were, in the very waves of that light brown hair which blew so pleasantly round his open sunny countenance.

He came down to Middleton to visit his late father, Admiral Vivian's dearest and oldest friend:—need it be told that he fell deeply, passionately in love with Miss Thornhaugh? I do not like the word (passionately) which I have used to express the character of this attachment—passion seems to me always to have something selfish in it; the attachment of this young seaman was too fervid, too devoted, too vehement to be expressed by the term affection—yet possessed much of the generous purity of that hallowed sentiment.

It showed itself little by those jealousies, whims, and mutual tormentings, which I have been taught to believe distinguish the passion of love in its most excellent degree—it was a tenderness like that our immortal bard has painted in his tragedy of Hamlet— a tenderness that forbade even the very winds of heaven to visit its idol too rudely—and enshrined its object amid sacred and precious deposits—as a thing too exquisite and celestial for the touch and uses of baser life.

Had such sacrifices been necessary, Vivian would have toiled his life out to have furnished her with luxuries—would have exposed himself bareheaded to all the intemperance of nature to have pillowed her head on down—would have met danger, pain, death, unshrinking, to have shielded her from the slightest sorrow. His was the devoted attachment of a most sincere and feeling heart, enhanced by that peculiar sentiment of mingled admiration and reverence with which the seaman regards an elegant, refined, and beautiful woman.

Miss Thornhaugh was not insensible to all this. She seemed soon to like him very much: they were for ever together in that sweet garden. He, as might be supposed, never weary of tracing her steps amid her flowers and birds; and she, nothing loth, smiling, and laughing, and rallying, and coaxing—as she was wont to do with her father—but more wilfully, more naughtily, more sweetly. She would have wiled the heart out of the coldest philosopher breathing—his was at her feet.

I well remember, one fine summer afternoon—the sky blue and clear over head, and the sun shining with a splendour rather brilliant than oppressive—coming down the long gravel walk in the flower garden, bordered with the yew hedge on this side, on the other with the roses all in full blow—a beautiful sight it was—I met the party; the Admiral walking rather loftily and stately, as was his wont, (for he was a tall, large man,) and his daughter, her veil floating round her, gliding with those dainty mincing feet by his side, prattling and smiling, and coquetting so prettily; and that elegant young man, not much above her own height, his hat off, his fair brown hair blowing lightly round his face—those beautiful blue eyes fixed on hers!

I thought what a charming couple they would make—and that day I believe it was all settled. The Admiral was called away by the gardener, and then Harry took that lily hand within his, and led her within the treillage, now thickly shaded by the luxuriant vines, whose flowers perfumed the air—and there he told his tale of love. There, while her beautiful cheeks were dyed with crimson, with a faltering voice and trembling gesture, did he confess his passion—a passion which alone justified his supplications to so much beauty, and to worth so far above his own. He, the child of the ocean—untutored in the arts and ways of men—unschooled—unpolished—he had but his adoration and the poor offer of his life and soul to make—(he might have added, and of a very handsome fortune also). She was too much confused to answer him: but her countenance was enough; and he soon ended by thanking her in raptures for what had never been pronounced in words.

I do not imagine that Miss Thornhaugh was precisely what ought to be called in love with Captain Vivian—but though she was very fanciful, she was not foolishly romantic—and, gratified by the devotion of such a heart, she consented with satisfaction to an engagement which was to introduce her to the realities of life under auspices so flattering. Certainly she had known little of such realities at present—yet few possessed a riper understanding for their years than she. There was nothing about her of that silly nonsense apt to attach to girls brought up as she had been—her mind, on the contrary, though imaginative, was remarkable for its vigour and energy. Her father had infused a most happy touch of his own character into her disposition.

When Miss Thornhaugh was engaged to be married, there were no nervous headaches—no depressions—no anxieties—no would and would not proceedings:—she had no vain anticipations of life—either as a paradise of passion—or a wilderness of disappointment. She did not suppose that even the sedulous affection of Captain Vivian could preserve her from her due share of its sorrows and its cares—but, so protected, she was ready to engage with them courageously. She expected much felicity in his attachment—much happiness in his society—but ecstasies were out of her head.

As for him, he was less reasonable. His love was of that kind which, when not justified by the charms of his object, we regard as insanity—and than which insanity itself cannot be more foreign to the usual habits of the mind. But I will not attempt to describe his raptures at the idea of possessing this charming being. He loved as another loved before him, "not wisely but too well." His passion interfered with his modes of action—affected his very tone and manners—gave at times an awkwardness, a *niaiserie,* as the French have it, to his expression and gestures. These infallible signs of a genuine attachment provoked Miss Thornhaugh, sometimes, to exercise her powers of tormenting, in a way I was sorry to see. She, who was good nature and kindness itself to every living being, was a little too hard sometimes upon this devoted lover—but this never occurred before her father. The Admiral was so fond of Captain Vivian, that even the love he bore his daughter seemed weak in comparison; and I am quite sure that had he detected her in the commission of any of her little acts of tyranny, she would, darling as she was, have paid dear for it.

Well! The engagement soon became matter of public discourse—settlements were being prepared. Captain Vivian made frequent visits at Middleton. That is to say, he made very brief absences. After one of these, he came, but not alone—he came, by the Admiral's desire, accompanied by his particular friend Mr. Laurence Hervey.

Laurence and Captain Vivian had been attached from boyhood. Their parents, now all dead, had been connected by ties of the closest friendship, and the sentiment seemed to have descended with, if possible, added intensity upon their sons. The children had, as long as circumstances would admit, been educated together; and when the decided taste Harry showed for the sea, with the equal repugnance manifested to it by Laurence, at length separated them—as in parting of brothers—distance seemed to do nothing in diminution of affection, and they felt united by a tie too peculiar to themselves to be weakened by competition with newer attachments. Accustomed to share every thought and feeling with Laurence, Harry was all impatience to introduce him to his charming betrothed; and the Admiral, discerning his wishes, had begged the pleasure of a visit from Mr. Hervey.

Nothing could be more unlike in appearance than the two friends. I should imagine the contrast might have been carried through every feature of their dispositions, habits, views, and feelings. Captain Vivian, formed for activity, with light and animated gestures, and speaking, glowing, rather ruddy countenance;—Laurence, tall, pale, with an air of languor, amounting almost to extenuation—features of delicate outline, but strongly defined character—a brow of reflection, almost of melancholy—dark hair shading it, though not heavily— eyes remarkably still, yet sufficiently expressive when he was speaking—a very sweet voice—and a calm smile that was both soft and feeling. I remarked, too, the extreme beauty of his hand— the delicacy and whiteness of which, though the fingers were rather too long, added in a singular manner to the gracefulness of his appearance; for though less fashionable and complete, if one may say so, in his dress and manners, than Captain Vivian, he was perhaps as elegant in his way. There certainly was something in the unaffected repose, amounting almost to indifference, which characterised his face and deportment—still more refined than the carriage of a finished man of the world, which, after all, he might be said to want.

I have said their mental were as strongly contrasted as their physical qualities. One was all life and action—the other all reflection and inquiry. While one pursued a brilliant profession with ardour, the other had chosen no profession at all; preferring the gratification of his taste for study and speculation to all the temptations of avarice or ambition. The one, quick and prompt, with a native vigour and good sense which taught him, as it were by instinct, how to proceed, reflected little, read less, and did much, the other, endowed with an acute and discerning mind, examined much, read immensely, and did nothing. Yet in some things they closely resembled each other. They were alike free from all that was narrow, selfish, or interested, in their notions, and alike exempt from those irregular habits too common with men of the world.

They came in late—the candles were already lighted in the drawing-room—the fire blazing bright, and crackling—the Admiral always would have a good fire of an evening in September.

I thought Miss Thornhaugh looked beautifully shy; and yet there was the suspicion of a smile in the corners of her mouth as Captain Vivian, with a little too much fuss, and a little too much hurry, (for, as I have remarked, honest true love does not make us graceful,) presented to her his long-limbed friend, who looked very quiet, but excessively shy too. The Admiral, who happily saw nothing at all of these little awkwardnesses, welcomed Mr. Hervey with his usual cordiality, while I, who was always stupid, stirred the fire, and made the room so hot that Miss Thornhaugh could scarcely endure it.

"And now, my dear creature," said she in her usual lively way, "as you have made my cheeks an admirable colour, may I trouble you to give me a screen, and let me obscure that noble blaze a little. Mr. Hervey, if I do not mistake, you will be glad to find another within your reach, and not sorry for tea in this torrid zone. Captain Vivian, will you oblige me so far as to ring that bell? How far have you come to-day?"

"From town—and with four horses," said Laurence, quietly.

"No doubt," said the Admiral; "Harry is not a fellow to loiter in the chase—all sails set, eh? how many knots an hour?"

"Indeed, sir, I kept no reckoning."

"Ten to twelve miles an hour," said Laurence. "Captain Vivian had the wand of the enchanter; and the horses flew, as if their impatience equalled his own."

"I cannot conceive why you will be in such a prodigious hurry, Captain Vivian," said the young lady. "How vastly wise was he who said a man of sense may be in a haste, but never—" but her father was there, and she pursed up her pretty mouth, dropped her eyes, and looked as innocent as a lamb.

Tea came in, and was handed about—Miss Thornhaugh never made tea—I think that was a pity. I like the tea board, and the hissing urn, and the people gathering round; but every thing that looked in the least like being useful was quite out of character with her. She idled away her whole time. The Admiral was too good a disciplinarian to render female interference necessary in his household; and Miss Thornhaugh, though she presided at his table and his drawing-room, took no part in his housekeeping. To tell the truth, that was partly my doing—I had been the Admiral's secretary; and when his friendship made me a sharer of his fireside, my old habits made me love to be useful, and I became in fact the *maitre d'hôtel*.

While she was sipping her tea, how light and gay was her attitude, how playful her smiles, as she turned from her father to her lover, from her lover to his friend! for she had soon recovered her self-possession, and was all airy trifling.

Captain Vivian looked as if he could not take his eyes from her face; and this seemed to make her at times impatient; and if their eyes met, she would turn hers almost haughtily away:—his adoration was too undisguised, it is true, and it perhaps offended her taste and delicacy before a stranger.

As for that stranger, he watched her also with looks of great, I might say, deep interest: but what surprised me extremely, I did not think he appeared to admire her very much. He was the first man I had ever seen who had the air of considering her with a critical eye:—every one, in general, was so fascinated by her charms, that even to investigate their source seemed impossible—far less, to discern the slightest defect in them. When she spoke saucily, as she did once or twice to Captain Vivian, Laurence looked displeased; and when she addressed himself, with an insinuating politeness which I should have thought no mortal could have resisted, answered drily.

III

THE next morning, Mr. Hervey was walking much in the garden by himself—musingly—as I thought—and when Captain Vivian reproached him for his stoicism, that he could for a moment absent himself from the society of so charming a creature, he smiled in his quiet way, and said,—

"Nay, Harry, don't desire me to be intoxicated, too:—the spectacle of one man thus deprived of reason is surely enough at a time: you have emptied the cup yourself, and left no poison for your friend. But, indeed," as Harry's brow darkened, "she is a most beautiful and charming creature, and furnishes the very best excuse a man could find for what—I beg your pardon—but really I cannot help it—does seem to me a strange infatuation. You lovers appear to us sober men as the dancers do when I close my ears in a ball-room—one is at a loss to conceive what causes all this excitement and hurry; but don't be angry, Harry," for Captain Vivian looked heated: "no, if I spoke truly, I should rather pity you, and could wish you did not love so well."

"Perhaps," said Captain Vivian, with a sigh, "perhaps I do love too well—at least it is utterly out of the question that such a fellow as I should meet with an equal return—but then she is an angel—and to adore her without reason or measure appears to me all that is most reasonable in the world. Confess, Laurence, confess she is an angel."

"An enchantress, without doubt," said Laurence.

"But can you see a defect in that lovely face—that faultless form?—Don't laugh at me, Laurence. We are not accustomed to pass our days among such beings. We cannot imitate you landsmen—you philosophers, in a heartless indifference, which I envy as little as you do me my devoted—my happy passion."

Laurence smiled again; but his friend did not see it. They were joined by the Admiral and his daughter. Captain Vivian was at her side—his arm was offered, with a look too submissive:—it provoked her, and she would not take the arm.

"No, no—not yet—let me enjoy my charming liberty while I may:—for the love of Heaven, don't let us anticipate!—Mr. Hervey, I do hope you like my garden—I do hope you admire the taste with which I have arranged all these parterres, and the knowledge of botany I have displayed. You are a botanist, I conclude:—Captain Vivian assures me that you know of every thing upon the earth—and above the earth—and under the earth, too, if he is to be credited. You know we seamen are a wee bit superstitious, and whistle for a wind, and see flying Dutchmen—and are apt to fancy science is art-magic—Eh, Captain Vivian?"

Captain Vivian looked annoyed:—he was not exempt from trifling weaknesses of this sort; and she had taught him to be ashamed of them.

"If you arranged this flower garden, Miss Thornhaugh," said Laurence, to turn the conversation, "I may safely compliment you on your scientific knowledge, whatever my own may be—it is remarkably well done."

"Pooh!" said the Admiral—"She arrange it! She knows nothing about it. I should be sorry to see her poring over musty books, tormenting my ears with long names—or soiling her dainty hands with pottering in a garden. She knows a rose from a cabbage:—that is enough for a sailor's daughter."

"Alas! Mr. Hervey—all too true:—there is no knowledge in me—I have at least abstained from that tree, if such there be in the garden. I believe," laughing, "because it never was pointed out to me. I never was bid not—so I scarcely know one tree from another, except by its beauty. I do think roses, and lilacs, and honey-suckles, most delightful creatures; but I abhor their clever names."

"Then you have disposed them in those charming arbours?" persisted Laurence.

"Too idle for that—no, I have left all to the gardener—that old Adam—do you see him there, Mr. Hervey?—he loves this garden as if it were his child—his own creation:—it is not that—for you may be sure those yew hedges with peacocks at the corners are of the taste of our revered ancestors:—no, I never give an order—it would break his heart if I did."

"Then what *do* you do?"

"Oh, I flutter about as idle and useless as a butterfly—some think as ornamental," looking at her father—"some as *volage* and as trifling;" and she glanced at Laurence—then at Vivian. He was still looking out of countenance. "Ah, Captain Vivian, why do you not come to my support, as usual? Why will you not give your voice with me for the *bella cosa far niente?* Confess we both of us delight in it—confess we are content to worship the exquisiteness of nature, without analysing—and dissecting—and examining—and losing all the charm, in accounting for it—like *philosophers!*"

"So you literally do nothing," continued Laurence, amused.

"So I literally do nothing—and I never mean to do more. I think business the most ugly body in the world—ever since I read in "Evenings at Home" how she was dressed in a grey stuff, and her sash stuck with knitting needles—scissors—bodkins and crisping irons. Acknowledge, Mr. Hervey, that is not very attractive—except to the very wise."

Her arm was in Captain Vivian's by this time. He had taken it on her addressing him, and held her hand in his:—she looked pleased and happy, as he did. "We have a weakness for the lady with the wreath of roses, have we not, Captain Vivian?" The we gained a squeeze for the hand that he was holding.

"I believe if you had on the stuff gown knitting needles— crisping irons—and all—I should think even that enchanting— but I prefer the roses."

"I am sure *I* do," said Laurence, "and I hope they last for ever, that is all."

"They would not be so sweet if they did," said she.

Laurence looked pleased with her now. As he afterwards said, there was no resisting her on Captain Vivian's arm—she had such

a gay sweetness in her eyes—looked so happy—and made him
so exquisitely so! Yet he confessed he could not entirely like the
situation of his friend. "He should love her less—if he would
insure his felicity. She ought to be controlled:—she has been too
long idolised. Her lover should exercise a certain authority over
her—she would love him the better if he did:—Harry might
make her every thing one could wish—if he were not so foolishly
in love. How can a man of his sense surrender himself so blindly
to a wayward, wilful girl? Marriage is a grave business—a man
should not enter upon it as if he were beginning a romance. She
must be the mistress of his family, the mother of his children.
Why does he indulge every whim, and flatter every caprice?—
But it is of no use reasoning with one in a dream—indeed it only
vexes him;—yet I do wish he would make her a little more afraid
of him—respect him a little more."

Laurence felt acutely whenever he saw Captain Vivian out of
countenance at her raillery. He confessed that she was sprightly, but
that her wit had scarcely sufficient poignancy to put a man of spirit
out of countenance. His pride seemed offended for his friend—
though, had he been in Harry's place, he would himself little have
heeded Miss Thornhaugh's playful impertinence; but he could not
endure to see Captain Vivian's mortified, crest-fallen look before
her. It sometimes made him so irritable that he became really
unjust, and took that amiss in her which, on any other occasion, he
would have thought the most innocent malice in the world.

"I confess, honestly," said he to her, with some asperity, one
day, after a little scene had passed of the nature I have alluded to,

"I would cut and run if I were Harry:—I never will believe that a woman esteems the man she dares to trifle with in this manner; and if you do not esteem him, and that immeasurably, allow me to say, you want a discernment into character common to all the rest of the world."

"I flatter myself I can discriminate as justly as some infinitely wiser, and all that, than myself—and know how to appreciate these characters of immeasurable perfection; but if Captain Vivian expects to have me in a perpetual attitude of adoration, at his ineffable qualities, I tell his friend, and I am ready to tell himself, that he is mistaken."

"He is very much mistaken in putting himself into that attitude with respect to yours."

"No doubt:—others are more measured in their sentiments—but I know you don't like me, Mr. Hervey—and I can't think why."

"To be sure," said Laurence, and he could not help smiling:—"it is difficult to find a why, for not adoring a being so faultless."

"I don't fancy myself without faults, whatever you may think—but I do detest being told of them. My father never tells me of them—Captain Vivian I believe really likes me all the better for them—so it would be quite a pity to correct them merely for a whim of yours."

"A great pity, certainly—faults are delightful things:—unfortunately they are a sort of thing of which the charm has a trick of escaping. Men sometimes get weary of being tormented—and their feelings refuse, after a certain period, to accept carelessness for kindness, and indifference for affection."

"Indifference!"

"Yes, Miss Thornhaugh, indifference. If I were a woman—if I were you—I think I should adore Harry—I love him well now—but to be his chosen, his beloved—to have excited all the passion of that honest heart—to have melted such a high-spirited temper to very girlish softness—not because he is weak, but because his feelings are so strong:—would I, if I were a woman, trifle with such a heart?— No, I should love deeply, seriously, earnestly—as he ought—as he deserves to be loved. Knowing how infinitely my nature and qualities were inferior to his—I would not childishly endeavour to lower him to my standard—no—I would try to merit the partiality I had inspired—to do credit to the choice he had made."

"Vastly fine:—you know very much about the matter. I shall be content with studying to *please* him:—whatever my ignorance in other matters may be, I do confess I understand that. I don't think he hates me yet—do you?—Do you think he ever will? And do you really believe if I were to go moping about—striving to be excellent—and deserving, and worthy of such a paragon— which Heaven knows I never shall be—that he would like it? Pooh! you are a child in these matters—all wise, and grave, and most melancholily disapproving as you now look. We shall do very well, if you will let us alone. I am breaking him in:—he will go beautifully in harness by and by—you yourself shall confess it:—I *am* more fit to drive than he—you know I am, and—"

"And he is a great fool," said Laurence, bitterly.

"And what are you, Mr. Hervey?—Can you possibly be so very absurd?"

"I see you don't care for him:—you could not, if you did, use him as you do."

"Don't I? So much the worse for him:—we shall see whether any one will care more for you. Fine as you are, Mr. Hervey, you may be glad if you are ever loved like Harry Vivian."

And so she left him, rather hastily; and away she went to Harry, whom she found somewhat sulky in the drawing-room; and lavished on him such a thousand pretty smiles and wiles, that they were the best friends in the world before Laurence, in his indolent, lounging manner, had reached the house.

When he entered, he was convinced that all was forgiven— that half-a-dozen soft words had dissipated all Captain Vivian's indignation, and that Harry was more a slave than ever. He sighed and he smiled. She looked up at him, as he entered the room, with a sort of triumphant "you see how it is" air—and then glanced with a little saucy smile at Captain Vivian—Laurence felt angry again—"She is deceiving him," he thought.

Laurence was greatly mistaken; but, unfortunately, he had a bad opinion of women; he thought them for the most part shallow in their understandings, volatile in their feelings, and capricious in their tempers; he believed every woman, at heart, a coquette, taking pleasure in exercising an empire over men, by playing with their best affections, which she recompensed with very little return of her own. He had lived much in the great world, and had taken his ideas of the sex from what he witnessed in the haunts of fashion and dissipation. In truth, he was little a believer in virtue of any sort, for he had seen so much cant, pretence, and hypocrisy, that he always distrusted appearances. He ought with this temper to have placed some confidence in the reality of Miss Thornhaugh's good qualities, because she was so far at least from affecting any—but he looked upon her with a jaundiced eye; he almost would not be pleased. He could not tolerate the empire she exercised over his friend, especially as he believed, and justly, that it was of a nature that wedlock would not destroy: he thought Harry was bewitched to see so many virtues, as well as so many charms, in his idol—he never suspected how he might himself be bewitched and bear an eye distorted by prejudice. Miss Thornhaugh was, in fact, much more resembling the faultless image in Harry's heart than the idle trifler of his own imagination.

IV

So things went on, Miss Thornhaugh little diverted from her amusement by the grave looks of the philosopher—who, indeed, to tell the truth, was no very great favourite with any of us. We had our own ways of proceeding, may-be not the wisest in the world, and we looked with little kindness upon the man who appeared, if not absolutely to disapprove, at least not much to relish them. Captain Vivian, I could see, leaned to our side of the question, and was in some measure less entirely one with Mr. Hervey than he had been; Laurence perhaps perceived this, and attributing it to the increasing influence of Miss Thornhaugh, it was not likely to augment his satisfaction in that influence. All these different feelings at play produced scenes lively and entertaining enough to the observer of human character, as I, from that chair on the lower side of the fire, which it was my privilege to occupy just opposite the Admiral's, used to be.

Miss Thornhaugh caught a cold. This cold was so very becoming, that I half suspected it was only a manœuvre of coquetry. Her face tied up with an elegant lace handkerchief, contrasting delicately with her jetty hair—two eyes looking most provokingly bright and saucy above all the wrappings of an invalid—half-a-dozen cachemeres, as it is now the fashion to call them, about her, hung on her shoulders, or over her arms, forming the most charming draperies around her beautiful figure, or thrown with happy negligence upon half the chairs and couches in the room. Surely never sickness was more captivating. Captain Vivian was happy—tending her, as only seamen, of all men on earth, know how. He was so gentle a nurse, it was a pity there was not more real occasion for his services. Mr. Hervey seemed more out of humour than ever—especially when, after she had been reposing on the sofa covered up to the nose whispering and chatting with Harry, who sat close by the head of the couch—a wave of the curtain might give a glance of a charming moonlight, and she would be up in an instant, and on the shining gravel walk,—may-be with a shawl, may-be without, just as it happened.

Could Captain Vivian, who followed her, to assist her in gathering her bunches of roses and geraniums, and who attended her through all the mazes of the garden, object to such imprudence? He remonstrated, as much as he thought it his duty, and was but too happy to have his remonstrances disregarded. The Admiral never troubled his head with precautions, nor with fears; he did not believe, I think, that there was such a thing as sickness in the world—his lovely daughter had given him no experience of it. Her maladies were usually of this light nature, and she was accustomed to manage them as best pleased herself.

She came in again with a colour like a rose, coughing furiously.

"A delightful evening, Mr. Hervey. Only conceive, Captain Vivian—here is your friend with that very book which he has had in his hand these three days. There, read away;" and she threw an immense heap of flowers over it.

"Even this, Miss Thornhaugh," looking up gravely, "shall not tempt me to seem the thing that is not—nor to say that you are wise to go out this evening—nor that Harry is wise to allow you. How you cough!"

"Well, I confess that I do cough: but I am certain this charming air can only do me good, for this room is insufferably hot;" and she threw up the window, and stood with her shawl thrown negligently over her, just before it.

"Well, Miss Thornhaugh, it is no affair of mine. But I do wonder, Admiral—I do wonder, Harry.—Why, Vivian! she will be in a fever to-morrow."

She coughed again.

"My dear Miss Thornhaugh," said Captain Vivian, and he made a gesture to shut the window.

"No," said she obstinately enough, but in a low voice; "not to please *him*. Captain Vivian, if you are his slave, I am not. I will do nothing at *his* bidding."

"Not even when he is right?"

"Not even when he is right—but he never is right—except when he is *right* cross."

"Then for my sake, Iñez, do be persuaded; it is so very cold."

"For your sake! ah, that is prettily said—I do not mean expressed, every one *says* that. But, Harry, you are sure you don't ask me, because he bids you?—I hate tyrants. Shut the window."

And she came back, shivering and looking as pale as she before had looked red. Laurence now spoke out. He certainly was a strange kind of person, with all his air of quiet languor—he could be so authoritative—yet he never even raised his voice; and every body minded what he said, though he spoke so low and carelessly, as it were.

"Miss Thornhaugh, I may be a tyrant—I wish I were absolute here, and I would send you to bed. Captain Vivian, you don't understand coughs—I do—and tell you that if this goes on long—"

"To bed, indeed!" said she, "like a scolded child! I shall do no such thing."

"You had better."

"Indeed, Miss Thornhaugh, you are ill—do confess it for once," said Captain Vivian pleadingly.

"Go to bed," said Laurence.

"Then I won't," said she, provoked at his interference. "I wonder how in the name of Heaven we existed before Mr. Laurence Hervey came among us—such a set of foolish, ignorant, children! It is a merciful thing we got on at all. I wonder whether I am to be allowed, most wise signor, to get up in the morning—if, like a chidden child, I go to bed now?"

"No!"

"You will be very glad of that for one,"—a violent fit of coughing, and her hand at her side.

"Why don't you go to bed?" reiterated Laurence.

"Why, you had better, my dear," said the Admiral, lifting his head from a book of charts, which he was studying. "I never heard you cough so before: what Mr. Laurence says is really very wise—bed is the proper place for you. Don't go on coughing in that way."

"Oh! to be sure—now I must go. Harry, the longest day I live, I never will forgive you for making a master of that tiresome man. Any more orders?" courtesying to him with a vexed ironical air, as she took the candle Captain Vivian presented.

"No more," said Laurence, rising and looking as if he would not be provoked. "I wish you a very good night, Miss Thornhaugh—and that you may not find cause, before morning, to be less angry with me than you are now."

Cause enough she had, at least, to acknowledge the wisdom of his advice. We did not see her again in the drawing-room for three weeks. Mr. Hervey had often proposed to leave us during this time, but the distress of Captain Vivian was so excessive, at the danger into which Miss Thornhaugh had been thrown by his and her imprudence, that he was easily persuaded to remain near him. I must say he was very kind on this occasion, showing his friendship by a series of affectionate attentions, which quite surprised me, from a person of so indifferent a temper.

Miss Thornhaugh at length appeared again, looking pale and thin, but not one whit subdued in spirit. She was, if possible, more wilful than ever, and seemed determined to make the best of the short time allowed her, to torment her lover and his friend.

I say short time—and her malice was perhaps increased by that circumstance. Captain Vivian had during her convalescence, been pleading hard for shortening the period of his probation. She had resisted, and expostulated, and refused—but a "Pooh, pooh, nonsense!" from her father had settled the matter at once:—a month, and they were to be married.

Well—she came down, as I said, not quite in humour at this, and with a spirit which seemed only to have gathered strength with what might have quelled that of another. There happened to be a lady sitting in the drawing-room, who had called upon her; and among other female chat, the lady began to lament that Miss Thornhaugh could not be present at the hunt-ball, which was to take place in a few days.

"Not be present!—My dear Mrs. Grandison—what could possibly put so strange a notion into your head?—I shall most certainly be there."

"You!" said Captain Vivian.

Laurence was standing in a corner of the room:—he only lifted up his eyes with a significant "Whew!"

She was provoked at this, for she saw it:—she gave him a hasty, angry glance, and turned her head quickly away. It was to vex him that she said,—

"Yes, Mrs. Grandison. I shall most certainly go—Lord Edward Beauchamp is steward. I would not miss it for the universe."

"Oh no!" said Mrs. Grandison, who was a silly woman enough—laughing affectedly—"I remember, my dear, that he was a great admirer of yours:—in gratitude you ought to go. You will break his heart if you don't."

"And there will be a coxcomb the less," said the Admiral, gruffly.

"A coxcomb!" said Mrs. Grandison—"La! Admiral, how can you say so? He's a most elegant creature—is he not, Miss Thornhaugh?"

"I always thought so," was the answer;—"but here, we can relish nothing but quarter-deck manners."

I felt sorry she said that—very sorry—so was she, when the Admiral spoke:—"Miss Thornhaugh, that is the first speech of yours I ever wished unsaid."

"Then I wish my tongue had been bitten off before I had said it, dearest papa," was the sweet-tempered reply, going up to him and smiling so gently; but her eyes flashed as she added —"Let no one else take it as an apology."

Captain Vivian coloured and looked down:—his face, when his feelings were wounded, took so sweet and melancholy an expression, I wondered she could resist it.

"Too bad," said Laurence aloud, and left the room.

Mrs. Grandison took leave, and we felt more uncomfortable after she was gone.

At last, Captain Vivian raised his head, and with a gravity and authority I had never seen him assume before, though it became him well, advanced and said,—"Perhaps the time is not yet come when I am warranted in making a request—almost amounting to a command!"

"A command!—No, indeed!"

"*I* have not forgotten—if you have—what I suffered in consequence of my weak acquiescence in former imprudence—may I *beg* that it may not be repeated?"

"Sturdy begging, sir!—I always refuse such petitioners!"

"You will not refuse me, Iñez?"

"I shall, Captain Vivian."

"I am very sorry for it," looking hurt, but not abashed as usual.

"You cannot possibly suppose, that I shall give up going to a ball, when a very old and valued friend is steward merely. Lord Edward would be excessively surprised that I, of all people, should stay away."

"And what in the devil's name," thundered the Admiral—(she had quite forgotten that he was present) "does it signify, what ten thousand perfumed puppies, like Lord Edward, think, or don't think? If Harry says you had better not go—why you had better not go"—and so saying he went out of the drawing-room.

"No," said Captain Vivian in the low tone of deeply-wounded feeling. "I beg leave to retract my interference—if my wishes," with softness again—"if my anxious wishes—if my past sufferings, all plead in vain. Iñez, if they plead in vain—why—I have no desire to exercise an influence that requires a father's command to enforce it. I beg your pardon, Miss Thornhaugh—I have presumed upon my happiness too far—I see it in your eyes—I had presumed—fool!—puppy!—that my wishes—my peace—my—"

His eyes were speaking volumes of tender eloquence—hers were beginning to melt—she was evidently relenting. I was about to leave the room, when, unluckily, Mr. Hervey re-entered.

The change was curious:—her figure bending to catch the whispering accents of her lover, who spoke low, and with his head bent down—her veiled eyes seeking the ground—the softened expression of her countenance—all changed like a charm:—she was erect in an instant—her eye sparkling—her lip curling and—

"Upon my word, Captain Vivian, you require vastly too much," was her reply.

"I am answered," said he, and retreated a few paces.

She ran on, as people sometimes do, who wish to be contradicted—"So strange, to oppose in this obstinate manner a trifling pleasure on which I had set my heart—the last pleasure of the sort I shall ever enjoy. Adieu all such things for me, in a week or two—a mere caprice on your part—a mere exercise of tyranny—to which you have been urged, I make no doubt, by that most expert regulator of young ladies' affairs, that delicate censor of female proprieties, Mr. Laurence Hervey. I know his creed well enough:—we are to be restrained, and controlled, and guided, even in the most insignificant matters. No exercise of discretion even in trifles for us:—we are not gifted—at least, some of us, it would seem, with good sense, or good taste enough to decide for ourselves. But he has mistaken his game—or your game—if he thinks to rule me! I detest tyranny—I abhor jealous tyrants, and all their caprices—and to show I detest them, here I vow!—"

"Oh, Miss Thornhaugh!" cried I, quite forgetting how improper it was in me to interfere.

"Even you!" said she, turning quickly round. "This is too bad:—what a combination!—Poor Captain Vivian!—What, do you require so much support to make your part good? I am sorry, sir, that we cannot discuss our trifling disagreements without taking the whole world into our confidence," looking at us all with sovereign contempt. "Lord Edward Beauchamp, I'll engage for it, retains no advocates."

"Perhaps not," said Captain Vivian. "He is happier in that than I am."

"He ought to be:—he can manage his affairs of the heart without being backed by his friends."

"If all this tirade be directed against me, Miss Thornhaugh," said Laurence, at length, "you may spare yourself the trouble of continuing it. I beg to say that so ridiculous an idea as that of supporting Captain Vivian's cause with you never entered into my head. I confess, I have taken the liberty once or twice to remonstrate with you, because I own it did appear to me that I was the only creature in the whole circle of your acquaintance sufficiently insensible to your fascinations to possess the power of doing it with any effect. I may have been romantic enough to conceive that truth, when pointed out, might have been admitted by a mind so candid as I *once* thought yours. I believed, too, as the friend of Captain Vivian, what I might have to offer would have been received with an indulgence it otherwise had not merited. I—"

"No," interrupted Harry, "not as my friend—that is the last claim you should prefer, to the indulgence of Iñez:—she is right—she despises a passion too humble—too uncontrolled:—she condemns the possession of a heart that has, in its excess of devotion, perhaps forgotten to respect itself. To be a subject for capricious tormenting has been the highest excitement I have been able to afford her;—to be led captive to adorn the triumph of another is perhaps the best reward she destines for my infatuation;—but *that* I have still sense enough left to resist. She shall not risk a life too precious, in order to indulge in that pleasure:—*she* may go to this hunt-ball—I will not." He turned away, for his voice faltered—he was evidently deeply wounded.

She looked up at Laurence—his eyes were fixed on the ground—he seemed very sorry—fortunately she could not read the marked disapprobation in them which always drove her to defiance. So she turned to Captain Vivian, who had walked to a window, evidently struggling for that victory over himself which he felt that he ought to achieve. She hesitated a moment—then rapidly crossed the room.

"Harry Vivian, I beg your pardon—I have behaved in a very silly and unworthy manner to you before these witnesses. It is right they should hear me acknowledge it. I do acknowledge that I have trifled with your good opinion in a manner that merits the severe punishment of losing it for ever; but restore it to me this once—I will not forfeit it again. I will certainly not go to this hunt-ball, as you think I ought not."

"Mr. Hervey!" The softness with which she had spoken to, and looked at, Captain Vivian, giving way before her native spirit, as she turned with a sparkling determination to him: "Mr. Hervey! be pleased to believe this apology has no reference to your interference, and that I can perform my duty to Captain Vivian without assistance of yours."

"I never doubted it," was his quiet answer; "and I own, I think you have at last acted—(I beg your pardon) as you ought at first to have done!"

It was my turn to feel angry then. The tears were in my old foolish eyes at what I thought so generous a submission:—I knew how much such a condescension must have cost her; and while Captain Vivian took her hand and raised it to his lips, kissing it, I was bidding God bless them from the bottom of my heart. What Mr. Hervey said, sounded strangely cold and hard to my ears; but she did not seem to care about it. He went away the next morning, and this was the last of the lovers' quarrels.

Miss Thornhaugh from this time did seem subdued—that is to say, there was a tenderness and softness about her, which might somewhat impair those brilliant flashes of wit, whims and gaiety, than which, I used to think, nothing on earth could be more enchanting; but her softness proved more bewitching still. It is a comparison often made—perhaps stale and commonplace—but so I have seen the silver moon, on a clear still night, tinting that sweet garden with a trembling pallid lustre; bestowing a staid and sober radiance on the wilderness of bowers and thickets, a tender brilliancy on those pleasant waters—and then I have been led to think that hours there are, yet more beautiful, yet more impressive, than even those of the glorious, shining, beaming day.

V

THEY were married.

Bright shone the sun through the azure sky—merrily rang the bells from our tall church steeple, which rose behind a grove of trees, at the opposite end of the town from Middleton Court, as the Admiral's house was called. Captain Vivian's elegant carriage and four, the Admiral's chariot of sober green, and the carriages of one or two of the neighbouring gentlemen whose daughters were invited to the wedding, filled the court-yard, with an unusual air of hurry and bustle—while the little town wore an appearance of festivity and gaiety, which reminded me of things I had seen in foreign Catholic countries, where they have a custom of adorning their houses, on occasion of their many processions, with pieces of tapestry of gaudy colours suspended from their windows.

As had been the custom in the town of Middleton, from time immemorial, on occasion of the marriage of any member of the family of the Court—the streets were garlanded with flowers, the windows and doors of the houses bedecked with evergreens and roses, and filled with faces awaiting in joyous expectation the approach of the gay procession.

Down from her chamber at length came the lovely bride—the transcendently lovely bride—I must use a big word. She was attired in a white dress; her raven hair, her dark piercing eyes, softened by the delicate veil that hung over—as one may have seen on a fine moonlight night the brilliant orb softened, but not concealed, by shadowy vapour. Those animated features composed by modesty and by sentiment; those lips wont to be parted by such flashing smiles, if I may use so strange an expression, now closed with a pensiveness that was more captivating than any thing I had ever before, or have ever since, seen.

She came down the ancient massive mahogany staircase, surrounded by the young ladies, her friends, who were to officiate as bride's maids, looking like a tall virgin-lily among the other flowers, tripping softly, half reluctantly, forward, that small and delicate foot relieved by the dark stair she was treading.

There we stood to receive her—the Admiral and I, his faithful Achates, on one side—Captain Vivian, the picture of graceful gallantry, as I thought, on the other—behind him his friend Mr. Hervey.

I will only say of Captain Vivian that I never saw a more charming countenance, one more full of manly joy and tenderness, await a bride, as he leaned eagerly forward on the first appearance of the group at the head of the stairs. The Admiral was as erect as ever—perhaps more erect than ever; his countenance beaming with pride and exultation—an honest parent's best of pride—at the approach of his lovely daughter. As for me, my old eyes were, as usual, filling—I cannot look upon any thing very beautiful without being touched by this contemptible weakness. The eyes of Mr. Hervey never moved from Miss Thornhaugh; and I thought, at last, he did regard her with something like the admiration she merited.

The Admiral handed his daughter, for the last time, to his own carriage; the rest of us followed as we might, and we were soon dashing through the town.

I ought not to omit that among the ladies assembled on this occasion was Miss Dorothea—or, I should rather say, Miss Vivian. She was a sister of Captain Harry—but, as I have heard, above twenty years older than himself. He said she had been very handsome in her youth. Every body declared that she was a most excellent and superior woman. As for her beauty, that was rather an old story—all that remained of it now was a long thin face—with large, hard-looking eyes—a slight regularly formed nose—and lips thin and compressed. She carried her lofty figure perfectly erect, never bending her head except for a sort of stiff bow, which she intended as the extreme of courtesy. Her immovable frigidity formed, certainly, a remarkably perfect contrast with the flexible figure and ever-varying countenance of Miss Thornhaugh.

Possibly she might be very good: at least, she said a great deal about goodness; never went to any public amusements, was always employed in governing and advising the poor—distributing good books—presiding at societies, schools, and so on:—I cannot think what made me find her so disagreeable.

I don't know why she was invited to Captain Vivian's wedding. She looked strangely grim and out of place among all those merry young people at the wedding breakfast—like death's head at a feast, as they say—and she had a certain dignified air of disapprobation at times on her countenance, when she looked at my dear, sweet Miss Thornhaugh, which made me hate her.— Such a contrast to her brother!

What a pretty breakfast it was—that wedding breakfast! The Admiral would put the bride and bridegroom side by side. She resisted, in her playful way, and said she hated such old-fashioned doings and should sit by her husband's friend, Mr. Hervey. Laurence did not look as if he cared enough about the privilege to be so indulged—she had been amusing herself the day before by bantering him, and he did not like it. So I was glad to see her set by one who prized her, and doted on her, and idolised her—even more than her fond, fond father, or her more fond, and more foolish old friend.

She took me aside after breakfast, and giving me a small box which contained a plain ring with a stone of great value, begged me to wear it for her sake.

"I need not recommend my dearest, dearest father to you, Mr. Roper.—You love him as well as I can do. You have served him better far. But if ever you for a moment feel coldness creeping on between you and your old friend, look upon this talisman— remember the daughter far away, who loves *you* dearly—but would *die* for him."

Tears were in her radiant eyes as she spoke—tears that affected me much: they rarely were seen from Miss Thornhaugh. But though she bore up courageously, they fell in streams as she flung her arms round the old Admiral's neck; and pressed kiss after kiss on his rugged countenance, bidding him farewell, and answering his blessings by her prayers.

But the leave-taking was over—Harry Vivian placed his bride in the carriage; the horses, which had been pawing and prancing, and tearing up the gravel walk in a shocking manner, dashed forward, and away they flew.

How dull every one feels when a wedding is over, and the young couple gone! all the excitement and interest of the story at an end, the book closed, and every body dimissed to common life once more;—to that common life, so irksome to our natures, to our high imaginative natures, that we are all incessantly striving, though almost unknown to ourselves, to escape its monotony—some by action, some by romantic reverie, some by virtuous exertion for others, some by vicious indulgence of themselves—striving to excite those high powers which seem to lie undisclosed within the heart of man. But love! alas! it seems to me that love is the only passion which thoroughly and entirely possesses this hidden power; and I am inclined to think that it is to this, and to this alone, that that divinity owes his hold upon minds of the best and fairest order. He comes under so seducing an aspect—with visions so beautiful though so false—with promises so sweet, yet so vain … but where am I straying? I have not the wit to moralise—and though I think a good deal, how should I put down my thoughts in a form to be useful to others? I who have lived upon the stormy roaring waters, listening to the hoarse voice of the seaman, submitting to the stern laws of naval discipline;

where should I find skill to speak of the softer passions?—of that softest, most treacherous of passions—whose voice, like that of the fabled syrens, mentioned in Mr. Pope's Odyssey, so enchanted men—that when they heard—though the cruel rocks, whitened with the bones of the betrayed, stood gloomily warning before their eyes,—they could not, they would not, but listen—they could not, they would not, but be lost.

We stood all of us some time on the steps. The wind had risen a little, and those large old elms were rocking to and fro, and the rooks waving on their branches. The Admiral was looking up, as it seemed, towards them—I, rather troubled at the state in which our beautiful gravel walk appeared, was treading up and down, with my hands in my pockets, endeavouring to repair the damage with my feet. Mr. Hervey, in a deep reverie, was walking to and fro beneath the trees—the ladies sauntering under the portico. Nobody had much to say, until Miss Vivian courteously approached the Admiral, and begged to order her carriage. A signal for the young ladies to order theirs.

At this little stir, Mr. Hervey came up, with—"And it is time, Admiral, I should order mine."

"Yours! why you are not going to leave us yet, Mr. Hervey? I and my old friend here shall be lost by ourselves—where are you for."

"For the Continent," said Laurence. "For Paris."

"Sorry for it," said the Admiral, who never could, or indeed had tried, to conquer the antigallican prejudices of the days of naval victories and bumpers of port. "What the devil must all you youngsters go to Paris for, now-a-days? What will you learn there—except to make a palaver and strike your colours?"

"Much worse than that," said Miss Vivian, gravely. "He will learn to read Voltaire, and deny his Maker."

"It is not necessary to go to Paris to do the first," said Laurence. "Nor is the second an inevitable consequence of such a proceeding."

"As for Voltaire, and Rousseau," said the Admiral, "and a heap of infidel French jacobins, who pestered the world when I was your age, Mr. Laurence; I don't suppose there's much in their rubbish to hurt such a head as yours—but I hate Paris—I hate the French, and all their ways—their coxcomb airs—their kickshaws—their congees—their high flying, nonsensical, republican trash—"

"Their irreligion," again interrupted Miss Vivian, "their horrid infidelity—their licentious profligacy—their contempt of all the laws of morality and decency."

"Really, Miss Vivian," said Laurence, "you give the second, if not the first, nation in the world rather hard measure."

"I give them what they deserve," said she angrily, "and I wonder at—and I always shall wonder at—and regret too, Mr. Hervey, your partiality for a nation so odious and so dangerous. I know what I say has never the slightest influence with you—but I shall live to see you repent of your contempt for all that is sacred and respectable—and your foolish *engouement*—I hate to use a French word—for this blasphemous and licentious nation."

"Indeed, Miss Vivian," said Laurence drily, "I don't know where you learnt so much about their licentiousness and profligacy. It cannot be that you have stolen a march upon us, and made a little actual experience at Paris. I am very much afraid you must have been reading wicked French novels."

"French novels!—no indeed!—but without polluting the mind with such reading, or disgusting one's nicer sense by visiting Paris, one may, if one chooses to observe, form a judgment of the ways of thinking peculiar to a nation, and draw an inference as to their probable consequences. I know what I say—I abhor utterly French irreligion, French indelicacy, French gallantry. No son of mine, nor daughter of mine—had I been a mother—should have been contaminated by communication with a nation—which I look upon as that monster typified in the sacred, mysterious, yet unsealed book—as making many nations drunk with the cup of her iniquities; as the mother of blasphemies, the great mystical head of abominations. No! no, Mr. Laurence—no son nor daughter of mine should ever go there. So I used to say to your poor mother, when Mr. Hervey would send you abroad to complete your education—I knew what would come—I know what will and must come of it."

"Indeed! my dear madam—I hope that the greatest harm that ever has, or will, come of it is, that I prefer a French *nécessaire* to an English shaving-box—and an *andouille de cochon* to a pork-pie."

"Well, well, I have done."

I have observed that people of a cold temper, and no great range of ideas frequently see particular objects with a justice more brilliant wits might envy; but they have too often such a disagreeable dictatorial way of expressing themselves, that they force one, mistaking excess of right for wrong, to believe that what is so positively announced must have been hastily determined upon, and what so passionately advocated be doubtless exaggerated—I felt at this moment that nothing upon earth could be so absurdly prejudiced as Miss Vivian—nothing so reasonable as Laurence—I found cause to alter my opinion.

Miss Vivian's warnings, whether just or not, had, however, no effect at this time.

Mr. Hervey went immediately abroad, where he remained, and chiefly at Paris, during several years.

Captain Vivian and his lady finished the happiest honey-moon that ever was passed, and went to reside at a very pleasant, though not very large, house, which he took in Spring Gardens. He had, as I have said, a handsome fortune, but as he did not in the least intend to abandon his profession, he made no purchase.

Here they lived in elegant mediocrity, neither mingling in the dissipations of the regularly fashionable world, nor abstaining from the society of those of their own rank and fortune. Mrs. Vivian, in spite of all her professions of idleness and indifference, managed her family, and those affairs of her husband which fell properly under her cognisance, as I always hoped and expected she would. Without losing her sprightly gaiety, she conducted all with order and prudence—and, abating not one whit of her elegant carelessness, contrived to be both useful and good. Two sweet little girls were born to them during this period. They were neither abandoned to interested nursery maids, nor did

the charming mother forget that she was a wife, to become a
nursery maid herself.—A system of judicious superintendence
effected all that was desirable. The children were healthy, active,
and intelligent—graceful, lovely, beautiful—how could they fail
to be with such parents?

Can any one forget that sweet sketch, drawn by Sir Thomas
Lawrence, of Mr. Calmady's children? I remember, the first time
I saw the engraving in the shops, I thought it was intended for
Captain Vivian's little girls. The eldest, Miss Florence (she was
called after the Captain's mother), had just that dark brown hair,
curling in natural ringlets, those shining eyes, that sweet pensive
smile, which adorn the elder child in that charming drawing. The
other little darling, Miss Georgy, had those flaxen curls, like her
father when a boy, those large eyes, that open sensible forehead,
and well defined small steady mouth, which one observes in the
other portrait.

I never could tell which I loved the best. I used to sit with
one on each knee, by the side of the ample, lofty fire-place in
the drawing room at Middleton Court, while the wind might
be raving outside the house, and a cheerful fire blazing within—
filling their little hearts with stories of a sailor's toils and a sailor's
dangers, teaching them to love an honest sailor; breeding each, as
I fondly hoped, like their sweet mother, to make a sailor happy.
Then as I repeated some piteous story, the tears would roll,
silent and slow, down the cheek of the eldest darling—while the
little one would kindle up, and be all alive at a tale of strife and
danger.

Captain Vivian and his lady spent most of the summer, and great part of the winter, with the Admiral. He never could bear to part with them or the children, and was always begging them to come back again. He loved the young ones more fondly, if possible, than he had loved their mother.

How often have I seen him walking up and down his garden, a little prattler in each hand, chatting and laughing like a child himself, while the Captain and my sweet young lady, arm in arm, were sauntering carelessly and happily along, at peace with each other and all the world—and certainly Mrs. Vivian's countenance did then acquire a gentleness and sweetness of expression (I thought it arose from her constant habit of smiling on her husband and children) which some might have thought it had wanted before.

But let me pause—let me pause to weep. Where are ye all?— sweet innocents!—blessed beings!—where are ye?—my pen refuses its office. The task I have undertaken surpasses my force …

★　　　★　　　★　　　★　　　★

VI

It was a fine morning in April—two gentlemen met suddenly in St. James's Street.

"Ha, Harry!"

"Laurence, my dear fellow!—is it you?—How long have you been in town? Why did you not send to me? Glad to see you once more, with all my heart!"

"I am come from Paris," said Laurence—"I was making my way to you. In Spring Gardens still, I suppose? How are Mrs. Vivian and the children?"

"Perfectly well, I assure you, as I hope you will acknowledge when you see them.—Ah, Laurence! you were but a sorry prophet—an ill-omened augur—I am the happiest fellow on the face of the earth."

"I doubt it not, my good fellow. And why I ever should have doubted it I am at a loss to conceive. I must have had strange fantastical notions, before I went abroad—but *vive Paris* for curing one of all nonsense. I am come back prepared to believe you not quite the very most miserable of men, because you have married the very most beautiful of women."

"Come and see for yourself. We dine at seven. I hope you conclude there is a cover for you as long as you stay in town— and may that be for ever! But don't wait till seven—|come now, and see Iñez and the children."

Mr. Hervey accompanied his friend home. They were shown up stairs, the door opened, and before him he once more beheld Miss Thornhaugh—Iñez—Mrs. Vivian.

She was sitting on a low footstool, with her youngest child in her lap. The little creature had just stolen the golden comb from her mother's hair, and was holding it in triumph above her head; the raven locks of softest silk were rolling in a profusion of dark clouds over a face and neck pure as alabaster, and now rather thrown back, as those eyes, so exquisitely beautiful, were turned upwards, to the cherub hands of the child. No picture ever designed by the hand of any master, no imagination of any poet, could surpass the loveliness of the one presented. She rose hastily, as the gentlemen entered the room—on which the hair, "in hyacinthine flow," literally swept her delicate feet. Gathering it hastily round her head, with her little child in her hand, she stepped forward to welcome her husband, and the stranger—Laurence!

Laurence was actually startled at her beauty when he first saw her. He seemed to have forgotten how very beautiful she was, or perhaps he had never *very* much admired her before; but now his countenance, usually so indifferent when regarding persons or things, became animated with surprise and pleasure.

As soon as she was aware who it was, her little confusion at being thus surprised by a stranger, gave way to the most cordial affability. Her hand was stretched out with a "Mr. Hervey! I am unaffectedly glad to see you."

"Are you, indeed?" said Laurence, all his former asperities rushing into his memory—"Are you really so good?"

"Indeed I am. But now I recollect it *is* very good of me. You did your best to quarrel with me, ages ago—and to put Harry out of humour with me too. But as I triumphed in spite of you—so I bear you no ill will. You only enhanced the glory of my victory."

"That was well," replied he: "otherwise, to vanquish, with means like yours, would have been but a contemptible proof of skill."

"The same fellow still," said Vivian, "always half unintelligible to me. What the deuce can you mean by that."

"Oh, he means a very pretty compliment," said Iñez. "I can't agree with Miss Vivian at all—I think Paris *has* improved Mr. Hervey vastly."

"I think London must have done the same by you; for I cannot recollect that Miss Thornhaugh—"

"Exactly the same. But you seem to have lost, it must be confessed—a little—a little touch of cynicism—and hate-all-not-just-according-to-my-own-model whims. Is it not so? But I beg your pardon.—As poor Harry is irretrievably lost, we need not renew old disputes. You can no longer serve him by abusing me now—and as I shall not fear, perhaps I shall not hate you. And now what do you say to Harry's little girl?"

Laurence did not like children, but this was a charming little creature. He took it in his arms, and kissed it heartily. Mrs. Vivian

looked pleased, Captain Vivian gratified, to see himself once
more united to the man he loved; and to find that he appeared
at last inclined to sympathise in his admiration of his almost
faultless wife.

They sat down to chat, and were immediately as confidential
and as much at ease as if they had parted but the day before.

Laurence talked of all he had seen, and was excessively agreeable.
He, whom she had used to think dry and critical, was now so
droll in his remarks, so acute in his observations, so brilliant in his
descriptions, so caustic, yet so full of good humour, that both his
friends thought they saw him for the first time, and were quite
delighted with him. He appeared as much pleased with them.

They dined together without other company. It was one of
those well appointed little repasts, where a few elegantly arranged
and exquisitely cooked dishes succeed one another in silent order;
where nothing is superfluous, and nothing is wanting. Servants
of respectable demeanour, well mannered and adroit, without
puppyism or forwardness, bore evidence of the good sense which
regulated the mansion. After dinner, the children appeared for
one short half hour, attended by a nurse, neither fine nor vulgar,
but respectable, sensible, gentle—to take her glass of wine from
her master, and courtesy round with grave precision. The little
ones were, as they have been described, lovely children, simple,
and unspoiled either by flattery or unseasonable reproof. They
were neither shy nor obtrusive. Laurence was delighted, and
the more so when he found the charming mistress of the scene
altered in some points which he had wished amended.

At Middleton Court, to say a book was never seen, would be untrue—for the *shelves* of the library at least were full—but to see a book opened, or to hear a book even mentioned, was a rare occurrence; and Mr. Hervey's insatiable love of reading, so far from meeting with sympathy, had excited against him something a little approaching to a prejudice.

Miss Thornhaugh had openly and undisguisedly expressed her most sincere abhorrence of every thing that could be called study, greatly to the annoyance of Laurence. He had always regretted that Captain Vivian was not, what could be called, a reading man. Harry was not ignorant; he had received a good education; and, possessing a remarkably quick perception united to a fund of sound good sense, he had observed and learned much of the varied world in which he had lived; still, Laurence, like other men of deep and various reading, acutely felt, in conversing with Vivian, the want of a more diversified knowledge than mere personal observation will ever supply. Sensible of the vast advantages which intellectual cultivation now offers to a man—be his sphere of life what it may—he had lamented that the talents of the friend he loved should want the assistance of solicitous cultivation. He had, therefore, felt sorry that the young lady selected by Captain Vivian should be considerably deficient in these respects herself, and he was disposed to be angry when, far from being ashamed of such deficiency, she openly gloried in it, satirised the professors of science and the sons of literature, and ridiculed, without the slightest mercy, every pretension of the kind in those of her own sex.

But time had opened the eyes of Iñez upon this subject. Endowed with an excellent natural understanding, she, on her first entrance into general society, had discovered her own deficiency, and had not been slow in endeavouring to correct it. As a woman of the world she wished to possess those acquirements which all around her possessed. As a mother, she wished to direct the minds of her children. She had abundance of time at her command, and, since her marriage, had devoted much both to reading and thinking. Her drawing-room table was littered with books; and her powers of conversation had extended to a degree which at once surprised and delighted Laurence. And not only did she speak well herself, but she had become capable of fully appreciating his remarkable powers of thinking and speaking— and to be so appreciated by an intelligent and beautiful woman is perhaps the climax of success to an intellectual man.

It would be hard to say which of the three friends was the best pleased with this happy day of re-union, The hours seemed to have wings—and, before they parted at two o'clock, for so long did the conversation, which seemed as if it could not find an end, continue, Laurence had promised to breakfast and to dine in Spring Gardens the next day—to dine, &c. &c. &c.

Mrs. Vivian was not found to be less lovely on the morrow. So sweetly gay and cheerful over her breakfast table!

After breakfast, Captain Vivian went out, as was his custom. Laurence remained sitting over the drawing-room fire—a book in his hand, into which he never looked—his eyes engaged in watching the movements of his hostess—how first she played and frolicked with the children—how next she wrote and folded all her tiny notes and billets—how last she, too, came to the fire, buried herself in a crimson-cushioned chair, and took her book.

"You are become quite studious since I went away," he began.

"Not much of that: but I was so egregiously ignorant, it really would not do—I have been forced to read Bingley's animal biography, that I may know a Walrus from a Camelopard—and Mrs. Markham's History of England, to learn whether the Pretender or the Conqueror was beaten at Culloden."

Laurence smiled, not, as formerly, with a sort of contemptuous compassion—"and what book have you got now?"

"Oh, I am ashamed to tell you—you will think me so ridiculous—I know you of old, Mr. Hervey," putting down the book, and looking sweetly, yet archly in his face; "you will be as ready to accuse me of pretension as you used to be of ignorant negligence. Indeed, I can scarcely myself believe what pleasure the attempt to cultivate my slender faculties has given me."

"Don't speak of old times:—what a bear I was!"

"Not quite that—yet to call you amiable, would be rather flattering—however, you seem resolved to make amends now."

"I can never forgive my own stupid folly. Is it possible, Miss Thornhaugh I mean Mrs. Vivian—that you can ever look upon me as any thing but the most conceited pragmatical puppy that ever walked the earth!"

"I shall always look upon you as Harry's oldest and dearest friend," said she warmly:—"a recommendation sufficient for me, if you were that rugged bear or Hyrcane tiger you describe yourself—I am not, as I told you, afraid of you now—I am past that."

"Indeed you may say so:—Harry is the happiest man on earth, and he is fully aware of it."

"I believe it—I believe it—that is—he acts as if he were—never woman—" she stopped and looked shy at being thus about to eulogise her husband.

"You need not be afraid of me, Miss Thornhaugh. I am his oldest friend—you know how I love him."

"Do you? then don't call me Miss Thornhaugh again, if you can help it:—I am not ashamed of his name, and would rather, if you please, bear it."

"I beg your pardon a thousand times, Miss Thornhaugh—but really those days return in so lively a manner."

"Again!"

"No—did I call you so again?—well, I must ask your pardon again—will you grant it?"

"Will you mind what you are about, if I do?"

"I won't promise that."

"Then how can I excuse you? But here he comes—are you for us?—He is going with me to look at a new carriage for my father. Will you come?—oh! I forgot, you are too lazy—stay here by the fire according to the good old custom, while we silly ones do all the business of the world—Harry, I will be ready in one moment!" and as Vivian opened the door, she flew up stairs for her hat.

The hat was very pretty, with a plume of white feathers in it; and, muffled up in her cloak, Mrs. Vivian looked more attractive than ever.

"My dearest Iñez," said Vivian, "it is cold. Don't walk, I have ordered the carriage."

"Oh, pray don't for me—you said you wished it not to go out this morning—a horse was sick or sorry, or the coachman had a pain, in his temper, perhaps—but, dear Harry, it is only a fresh gale—you will make me ashamed by your care—we shall have the schoolmaster abroad again, if you are not more prudent—I am half sure, Mr. Hervey, you think he is much too tender of me still."

"I don't quite think he can be," said Laurence.

"Well, that is comfortable—but do you come or no?"

"He!" said Vivian, "he must be strangely altered if he puts down his book to see the best carriage that was ever built—he does not know a phaeton from a dog-cart; and how should he? Let him enjoy his fire and his chair till we come back, and then you may take him into the Park if you like."

"No—I am coming!" said Laurence, rising lazily.

Why did Laurence, when the door closed after them, pause, before he offered Mrs. Vivian his arm?—Captain Vivian however bade her take it, and between the two friends, gaily laughing and chatting, she walked up Pall Mall and St. James's Street, the admiration of all the world. Many were the eyes fixed upon her, many the heads turned round for yet one other gaze, as she passed lightly forward with an ease and grace of motion peculiarly her own, her countenance playing with bewitching smiles, and her conversation, at once careless and pointed, fascinating the attention of her guest. The husband was, as husbands are apt to be, less sensible to charms that were for ever before him; and, if truth must be spoken, he was at that moment thinking more of the Admiral's carriage than of his own enchanting wife, while she naturally directed her conversation rather to his friend than to himself.

Laurence had passed five years in Paris—they had not been without their effect.

VII

THAT day, and the next day, and the next, and a succession of days, were passed in this manner together. Laurence usually breakfasted in Spring Gardens. Captain Vivian as usually went out immediately afterwards, and was occupied abroad, the greater part of the day. He had been just appointed to the command of the Sybile, one of the finest ships in the navy.—She was at this time lying in the river at Woolwich; and he was occupied, as naval men under such circumstances, are, in superintending her outfitting—without much expectation, however, of being called into actual service.

These were the days when war languished—and a few contests on the outskirts of civilised society excited little attention among men, earnestly intent upon that grand debate, which had arisen between the things that *were*, and the things that were to be.

His friend, who had little to do with the actual business of life, under any of its various forms, remained with Mrs. Vivian and the children, lounging, in the old way, over a book by the fire; but not, in the old way, devouring its pages with the avidity of one who draws all his pleasures from the intellect. His eyes were usually wandering or abstracted, following the beautiful form of Iñez about the room, or fixed upon the page unmeaningly. Feelings, to which he had hitherto been a stranger, began to melt his heart with a seductive sweetness—feelings, of which he rendered to himself no account, began to make that arm-chair like what the fabled chair of the enchanter has been described—a place from which he found it impossible to move. Life, which, till now, might have been called, to him, a simple succession of ideas, assumed a new character—it became a succession of sensations—of sensations only—or rather, it appeared a succession of sensations no more—*one* sensation, the most intoxicating—the most engrossing—the influence of one predominant passion, seemed to have over-powered every other sentiment, idea, and feeling—and the charm appeared fatally attached to a certain arm-chair in Captain Vivian's drawing-room.

Iñez, innocent as a child, was, like a guileless child, entirely ignorant of the mischief she was doing; and Laurence, unaccustomed to self-examination and self-responsibility—in the habit of yielding to the present influence—of passing away his days in doing what was most agreeable, without calling himself to any account for the use of his time or his talents, abandoned himself to the indulgence of his present sensations without examining into their source, or questioning their propriety.

Laurence Hervey was no profligate—he abhorred profligacy— it disgusted his taste, and offended his moral sense: but a sceptic in religion; a questioner of all those common-place rules of order and morals which have, under one form or other, been reverenced by the mass of mankind, since civilised society first was constituted. An enemy on system to all which bore the character of rigidity or constraint in social intercourse; the indulgence he was ever ready to extend to others, he fatally permitted in himself.

That his sentiments were assuming a form which might militate against his own future happiness, was a reflection which, if it had occurred, would have been dismissed with contempt;— that they could possibly interfere with the happiness of others, would have been scouted as ridiculous. For what passed within the secret recesses of his own breast, he held himself accountable to no being in existence. He had rejected the teaching of that Master who said—"From within, out of the heart of man," &c. &c. Why should he not delight himself in the cup presented to his lips? What if the draught did intoxicate his senses, did dim his perceptions, did drown his reason in flattering delights—what was that to any one but himself?

Iñez had, as we have said, become a reader. She had failed to inspire her husband with the same taste. The delight with which her imagination, naturally powerful, had collected the brilliant images of poetry, the pleasure with which her intellect had unclosed to the perception of philosophy and truth, had been of necessity confined to her own bosom. Her gratification, therefore, may be imagined, when, in the fine taste and accomplished mind of Laurence she found, what she had sought in vain—sympathy in all her new pleasures, and the power to guide and assist her dawning faculties in their new-born efforts.

She might now be seen, the docile pupil, sitting on a low chair by the side of Laurence's sanctuary, reading to him, or with him—questioning him—listening to him—laying all the confusion of her struggling thoughts, springing as it were into life, before him. Did the voice of the teacher falter, as he busied himself in giving some order to the brilliant incoherency of her ideas? Did the eye of the teacher beam a too soft approbation, as with a glowing countenance and voice, which was melody itself, she read some of the sweetest snatches of poetry? If they did, the unsuspecting Iñez never, for one instant perceived it. Secure in the purity of her own heart, the dangerous infection of passion was here without power. That Laurence liked her now so much better than he used to do, pleased her, for Harry's sake, and for her own. She fancied she must be very much altered, for the better, when Mr. Hervey approved. She had been long accustomed to look upon him as one whose decisions were undoubtedly right.

"But how you do sigh, Mr. Hervey, this morning, over this Italian lesson? Is it too stupid an operation to expound Petrarch to me? I confess he is often tedious—yet, do you know, in spite of all his conceits, his verses have an air of truth which interests me. I have heard many ridicule the idea of his constancy and fervour; they say his passion was the mere indulgence of his imaginative vein—that the heart had nothing to do with it. I don't feel it so; I think I read a history of deep and genuine feeling in these verses. Here is none of that self-gratulation which the mere poet would feel in the indulgence of his fancy; these are the regrets and self-questionings of one, enslaved in his own despite, who is wasting powers, which he felt were entrusted for better things, in vain aspirations—in forbidden wanderings;—but you are silent—you don't think so?" She had been running on, with her eyes fixed upon her footstool more as if she were thinking aloud, than addressing him. His eyes—he was sitting a little behind her—had not moved from her face. "You are not one who can compassionate such a state of weakness—one from whom he might hope to find '*sperar trovar pietà non che perdona.*'"

"Why do you think that?" was the quiet answer.

"Oh, I am in the habit of supposing you proof against these sort of follies; I have an impression that you very wise men (you know it is the fashion here to consider you of this order) are not susceptible of such weaknesses."

"But was not Petrarch a *very* wise man?"

"Yes, but then he was a man of imagination."

"Which I certainly am not. You are quite right in what you say"—and he sighed again.

"We will have done with him now, however," said she, cheerfully, "for you sigh, just as poor little Georgy does over her lesson:—really, Mr. Hervey, it never struck me before, but I think you are very good-natured. All this must weary you to death; you must hate my new wisdom even more than you did my old folly, only it would look so common-place to own it. I can conceive nothing more tiresome to an accomplished mind than talking over subjects like these with such a mere beginner as myself—you really are very good-natured."

"That is not quite the proper term to use," said he again, with great sweetness. "It is possible that there may exist other charms for me besides those of erudition—candour and ingenuous good sense, for example."

"Yes, I might have been sure of that—you are now as easily pleased as you were formerly impossible to please. Did you learn that happy art at Paris, Mr. Hervey? Doubtless it was worth while to spend five years in the acquisition."

"I have not acquired it—I am more hard to be pleased than ever. Nothing pleases me in the whole world, I think, but sitting in this chair and playing with your children."

"Truth will out—the reading is a bore, then."

"I am sure I never said that—I don't profess to live in the palace of truth, but I could not be so egregious a liar as to say that the sweetest occupation in the world was a bore," said he, more warmly than usual.

Iñez coloured a little; "I am glad of it," rallying her spirits; "I do own that reading with so accomplished a tutor is a great assistance to my scanty wits. By the time my children are old enough to be the better for it, I hope I shall be as dry, and as horrid, and as wise, and as every thing, as any she professor of them all."

"How you do talk!—may Heaven avert such a consequence! One would rather all the books in the world were burned—but I see no danger."

"Nor I neither," laughing; "I am an inveterate dunce—well, so be it. There is one will not care—that's my dearest Harry. There's another will not break her heart about it— that's myself. There is a third," turning playfully to him, "must reconcile it to himself as well as he can. There is no remedy; we cannot either of us come up to your ideal of perfection, Mr. Hervey; but we expect you to love us nevertheless."

The eyes of Laurence had an unusual expression.

"I will do any thing, however impossible, if you will only not call me Mr. Hervey. Why am I not *Laurence* to you?—Miss Vivian calls me Laurence—I am Laurence to every one but you—let me hear you call me Laurence," in an earnest manner.

"Laurence!"—as if considering it carelessly—but however carelessly, the syllables thrilled through his veins. "No, I can't do it—you know in former days you inspired me with such profound respect and awe—I should as soon think of calling my father by his proper name."

"Your father!" with an air of excessive provocation—"your father!—do you look upon me as a father?—good heavens! how provokingly you speak!"

"And, good heavens, how easily provoked you are! No, indeed —Laurence—will that do? I did not mean to offend you—I don't mean, with all your wisdom, that you look exactly as venerable as my father, though, truth to tell, I imagined you too great a philosopher to care how you looked—mistaken there, it seems. Oh, men—men—but really you have taken such pains to impose yourself upon us for one of the wise, that in my simplicity I really did respect you; but if you are so unaccountable you may rely upon it that I shall not continue in that error."

"I hate respect."

"You hate respect! Oh, monstrous! well I do think you the most susceptible person to *disrespects*, that ever made such a confession."

"What do you mean by that?"

"Oh, upon my word—I have done," rising: "you look so angry—I will not say one word more—indeed, Mr. Hervey, your temper—"

"Angry!—Temper!—Am I angry?—Do you care one atom whether I am in the most fiendish temper in the world?—Can any thing connected with me give you one instant's uneasiness? If I thought one being on earth cared for me or my humours, I would soon correct them. If I thought my irritation a matter of the slightest regard to any one, I could be as a lamb," rising and following to where she stood by the fire.

"I wish you would, then, be like a lamb, Mr. Hervey, for really—"

"You called me Laurence, just now."

"Did I? Well, that put you in a passion—so I will not do it again."

"A passion! How cruel!—but 'tis no matter—I made you hate me at the beginning of our acquaintance—you always did—you always must, hate me—*secretly*, though your kindness makes you endeavour to hide it—but I detest concealments, if you do hate me, tell me so at once—I am gone."

"How you misconceive me! How can you suppose that I ever intend to offend you?—How can you suppose that I bear malice for what I have always honoured in you, as a mark of your genuine friendship for Harry? Don't renew those days of misunderstanding—you know how Harry values you—how, I value you for his sake:—do not indulge the only fault you have—this odd, capricious way of misconceiving things. I am sure I don't know what I said, but you know I did not mean to say what should hurt you; believe me that I have corrected in myself the love of being provoking—believe—"

"Don't ask me to believe any thing—don't go on, generous Iñez—don't trouble yourself about me.—Every thing you do, every thing you say, every thing you look, is perfect in its excellence. Forgive me, I am capricious—I am unreasonable—it is my infirmity—forgive me—"

She looked surprised, yet she felt pleased; she had always misdoubted his regard before, and her innocent heart rejoiced in this proof that she was dear to him.

"There is nothing to forgive—it would be strange if I could not tolerate a little singularity, in one so singularly dear to Harry," his countenance fell—she answered it, as it were by instinct, without comprehending its expression exactly—"So very kind to myself, and for whom I have so true a regard—but indeed I never intend to try your temper," looking up so sweetly in his face, that Laurence felt as if his heart were choking him.

The door opened, and Captain Vivian came in.

"Have you got me a box?" was the first question of Iñez, turning to him with the most perfect and frank composure; while Laurence turned *his* face to the mantel-piece, and for a moment seemed busy considering the china vase thereon.

"Yes, my love—but you will excuse my attendance at this German Opera—an Italian affair is as much as I can well digest, you know—and I want to dine at the Club with an old friend or two—but Laurence, you are a capital fellow, you delight in all this unintelligible stuff—I am sure you will dine with Iñez, and attend her—you are a fanatico, you know, and can be immured in an Opera box a whole evening without a complaint, to hear Haitzinger—will you do duty to-night? Iñez has set her heart upon going—will you take care of her?"

A guilty pleasure throbbed at the heart of Laurence, as, now lifting up his head, he spoke thickly enough. "I shall be very glad to be of service," was all he said.

"I am very sorry, my dear Iñez," said Captain Vivian, "that I have not been able to get you a box that you will like, I went about it sadly too late, and could only find one in the third tier— you will be out of the way, but as you go chiefly for the music, you will not much care, I hope."

"Oh! not in the least—I will take little Julia Sullivan with me, as I promised—and then I need not imprison Mr. Hervey. You can leave me without compunction (turning gaily to him) when you are tired of me."

The heart of Laurence was beating fast—beating in a way that ought to have alarmed himself—but self-distrust was a lesson this philosopher had yet to learn.

He dared not utter the words that were rising to his lips, so affected not to hear her.

"Why, Laurence," said Captain Vivian, "you look quite out of sorts—you are the strangest fellow in the world. If it really will plague you to go to-night why not say so at once?"

"Do I look as though it would plague me?" said Laurence, recovering himself; "I am sure I did not intend it. I am sure it will give me the greatest pleasure to attend Mrs. Vivian, and I will now go home to dress, for it is late," and he left the room.

"I am afraid," said Iñez, "that you have trespassed too much upon his complaisance, Harry—he is evidently out of humour. I had better give it up."

"He out of humour! what in the name of Heaven does it matter if he is? You shall do no such thing. Surely he may make a little sacrifice of his whims for your amusement. I am very sorry, my dear, I can't go with you in his place, but I have entangled myself with an engagement I cannot well break; never doubting that Hervey intended to go. Take little Julia, and then he can leave the box when he is weary—which he is of every thing on earth sooner than any man I know."

And after this Captain Vivian and his wife sauntered away the remaining hour until dressing-time, with their little children—happy in perfect confidence, in sincere affection, in cheerful interests, neither requiring nor desirous of extraordinary excitement; content with the peaceful joys of their placid and innocent existence.

Laurence, meanwhile, walked to his lodgings in a tumult of pleasure. He neither asked himself why nor wherefore. His mind dwelt intensely on the delight of passing one evening alone— alone, to all intents and purposes, with Iñez; for Julia was but a child of eleven years old. To enjoy the society of this charming woman exclusively was all he allowed himself to wish, and the great addition which the absence of the husband gave to his prospect of enjoyment seemed to escape his observation.

VIII

As the clock struck six, Laurence, dressed with an elegance and care not usual with him, though it became him well, entered Captain Vivian's drawing-room.

Iñez was already there, looking more beautiful than ever, as if to complete his satisfaction. A dress of white crape gave a peculiar delicacy and grace to her figure; her dark hair was a little more studiously arranged than usual, and a few jewels were shining there. Captain Vivian, hat in hand, was taking leave. It would have been difficult to say which of the three made the most charming appearance—Laurence, as with languid elegance he leaned against the marble chimney-piece, his eyes fixed upon Mrs. Vivian or she, in her beautiful white drapery, making a playful adieu to her husband; as he, with that delightful union of refined polish and naval frankness, which distinguished him, even among the most attractive members of his profession, was taking his leave. The door closed, and he was gone—and Laurence—

He sat down in his accustomed chair as Iñez placed herself by the fire in a state of enjoyment so perfect, that he neither spoke nor wished to speak, moved nor wished to move—and to have remained thus passive for ages, without change, or desire of change, appeared to him natural, nay, delightful. A state some mystics have vainly endeavoured to render possible to the human soul, when engaged in contemplating the divine perfection of its Creator, was attained at once by the witchery of human passion, by the witchery of that passion so mysterious in all its influences.

Iñez, who, far from divining his feelings, imagined him still a little out of humour, took her embroidery, and amused herself with a thousand trifling thoughts that passed through her cheerful imagination—while Laurence might be said not even to think, so entirely was he absorbed in sensation.

Dinner was announced.

"Come, Mr. Hervey! Must I awaken you!—From what distant region must I recall your thoughts? Have you been 'unsphering the spirit of Plato?' or what? But philosophers must dine, like other mortals, and we shall be late—I have a wish to hear the Overture."

He rose and gave her his arm, still without saying a word; but when, with a look of unfeigned astonishment, not unmingled with vexation, she said, "What can be the matter, Mr. Hervey? If you really are indisposed to go, be candid and say so—I am sure I wish to be a trouble to no one." He again rallied.

"Not indisposed—perhaps out of spirits: mine are capricious, wretched to myself and others, like every thing about me. No— music to-night is, I believe, almost the only thing I could endure; it will charm this vile temper out of me. Have patience with me, sweet Iñez—I beg your pardon, Mrs. Vivian—I really don't know what I say—I will behave better after dinner."

Iñez was again surprised.—Something seemed reversed in her situation; she could not understand it. He of whom she stood formerly in awe—the severe censor of all she did and said—the unimpeachable arbiter of all that was right or wrong—the cool, impassible Laurence—the man neither to be influenced by her smiles, nor moved by her caprices, seemed all at once to have renounced his character for superiority and wisdom, to be as fanciful, capricious, and wayward as she could have been in her best days, and to acknowledge his folly, and solicit her indulgence, with an humility utterly foreign to his nature.

At a loss to account for all this, she felt compelled unwillingly to admit that Laurence, like the rest of his sex, could have his moments of caprice and unreasonableness; and though she, perhaps, reverenced him a little the less for the discovery, she liked him the better, and felt interested in what appeared to her. a state of suffering.

So all dinner time, she attempted by every sweet attention, and by the most engaging cheerfulness, to restore his spirits—and Laurence, after a few glasses of Madeira, began to appear better at ease, and to converse in his usual easy agreeable manner.

The children appeared at dessert. While one occupied Mrs. Vivian's knee, Laurence took the other—the illusion was complete. He fancied himself the master of that table at the lower end of which he sat, the father of the child he held in his arms, the husband of the adorable being who presided. It is not too much to affirm that he actually felt as if he were all this. Passion is a brief insanity; its illusions are often literally as perfect and complete. Under this momentary hallucination Laurence felt perfectly happy. All his turbulent emotions subsided into the calmness of satisfaction; and had he been the husband of her youth, he could scarcely have more gaily adjusted Mrs. Vivian's cloak, or handed her to her carriage, or sprung to her side, with a more frank appearance of satisfaction.

The intelligent author of Stello has observed, that even the closing or unclosing of the eyes is sufficient to break the chain of thought, and to introduce a perfectly new series of associations. This is far more, certainly, with respect to change of place and scene. No sooner had Laurence entered the carriage than the vain illusion vanished from his imagination—thoughts of a far different hue succeeded—a gloom black as night gathered round his brow—and he again appeared a prey to the most tormenting ruminations.

Iñez looked at him with terror, almost with dislike. His manner had suddenly become as cold, harsh, and distant as it had been, ten minutes before, cordial and agreeable: she was glad when they stopped at Admiral Sullivan's door, and her little friend, in ecstasy at the thoughts of her first opera, sprung into the carriage, with a "Dearest Mrs. Vivian, how very good of you!" Mrs. Vivian, relieved by her presence, and pleased with her delight, began to talk immediately to her. There was much to say between them, and not a word for the silent Laurence, who, now really out of humour, hung back in a corner of the carriage, and uttered not one syllable.

When they alighted, however, he seized Mrs. Vivian's arm, almost rudely, in the press, and, without speaking, took her to her box. Here little Julia, being placed in the best situation for seeing the stage, Mrs. Vivian took the shaded seat on the other side, and Laurence, drawing his chair behind hers, leaned his arm with a sort of desperate defiance of his conscience on the back of it; and, thus concealed from general observation, remained motionless and silent, in the dangerous contemplation of a beauty and sweetness which already produced an effect upon his senses more enervating than intoxication.

He strove to swallow down the sighs that struggled from his overloaded heart, lest they should, as they once before had done, excite her attention. He strove to repress every external sign of the feelings which overpowered him, while he abandoned his inner self, without resistance, to their seductions. He thought himself a man of honour; for the universe he would not have wronged his friend, not by a word: but thought was his own, into that region his scruples extended not. To adore the wife thus confided to his care, was no injury, so long as that adoration was confined to his own bosom—to share in these sweet influences no crime, while their effects were hidden from every eye—nay, even to desire to possess in some degree a peculiar place in her affections, if such might be his most fortunate distinction, no sinful ambition, while no syllable of his passionate attachment was breathed to her ear. Why should he deny himself that which, if evil, could hurt no one but himself?—He would delight himself with the charm of his present existence, so long as that charm might be enjoyed in security; when it was withdrawn, why then—*alors comme alors*. Such were Mr. Hervey's ideas of his duty to his friend and to himself—such the knowledge this accomplished philosopher possessed of human nature, and of his own heart.

The idea of accountableness to any tribunal but that of his own reason, never once crossed his mind. A sceptic upon principle—he would have rejected the idea, with disdain, as the most superstitious weakness. Nay, would have despised himself, had he believed that his virtue required those ordinary incitements of hope and terror, which govern the vulgar of mankind.

Mrs. Vivian was absorbed by the music, to which she listened, and was some time without noticing Laurence. At last she turned suddenly round:—"Mr. Hervey, have you been asleep?"

"Yes, I believe I have," with a smile.

"Or is this a mere pretence?—you must have listened to that last song—that delightful song: I thought you loved music."

"I do like music, exceedingly."

"Then listen, again!" as the voices of Schroeder and Haitzinger made vocal those notes which the very muse herself whispered to the author of Fidelio.

"You feel that," said Laurence.

"I do, indeed."

"You could be that page?"

"Oh, yes, I could—for Harry."

"Happy Harry!" rather sighed than uttered.

"You think so, then, at last," with sudden animation; "you do, at last, believe him happy?"

"Happy!—Good heavens!—To be so loved, Iñez, for one second—I would wear the poisoned shirt of Dejanira—I would be content to be torn limb from limb by wild horses. But for one moment to be so blest!"—she looked astonished. "But no woman will ever love me," said he, checking himself with a forced laugh.

"Nor would I advise them. You are so odd that you would plague the life out of a woman that loved you."

"No one will ever care enough for me. Even *you,* though I am Captain Vivian's friend—almost his brother—even you, if I were to die to-morrow, would smile the next day just as sweetly as you do now."

"You are very unjust to say so," said she, much hurt. "Why is it your pleasure to suppose me the most heartless creature breathing?"

"Did I say so?—You heartless?—I think you all heart—all tenderness—all feeling. I only presumed to believe myself not worth a thought. Forgive me—you cannot tell—*you,* gifted with the ceaseless sunshine of a happy heart—you cannot even surmise what it is to be the victim of morbid thoughts that eat into one's very being. Forgive me, I did not mean to offend you, Heaven knows; but—but—I have been in an execrable humour all this evening. I will shake it off;"—and he rose from his chair precipitately, and left the box.

She felt sorry for him—half angry with him—interested by him—wished to know what preyed upon his mind—thought she would tell Harry—she would do all she could to cheer him.

He came back, looking more composed.

"That is right.—Come Mr. Hervey, and sit by me. Don't give way to these fancies. You used to school me—let me return the good office. It is indeed unworthy a man like you, a man so gifted, to be the sport of melancholy fancies. 'Tis true you have few natural relations, but is not Harry your brother?—Am not I almost your sister?—Are not our children your's? Don't say no one loves you; you know how we love you—*en attendant mieux*," smiling, "be content. And now look round this brilliant circle of beauties, and fall in love for yourself as fast as you can: that will be the true remedy. I confess, I should have a malicious pleasure in seeing you caught."

"Well, give me your opera-glass, and let me try."

She held it out—he took it—looked round the house with it a second or two, and then put it in his pocket. After this he resumed his cheerfulness, and regarded her with the sweet and calm expression which she loved to see in his eyes.

She went home relieved about him, and satisfied with herself, to sleep in innocence and waken in peace.—He to roll restless from side to side, feebly endeavouring to repel the thick coming fancies that swarmed around his pillow.

IX

THE next morning when Mr. Hervey entered the house in Spring Gardens, he became aware that something more than common was the matter. An air of hurry and confusion pervaded the usually well-ordered mansion. He opened the dining-room door, no one was there: presently, Mrs. Vivian appeared; her face was beaming with excitement, yet her eyes were red, and her cheeks blistered with tears:—"Oh, Laurence!—Oh, Mr. Hervey!"

"What is the matter, my dearest Mrs. Vivian?"

"I ought to rejoice—Heaven knows I do"—and she burst into tears.

"What is it, sweetest Mrs. Vivian?—what can have happened?"— He spoke warmly, for he felt innocently—sympathy in her distress was the uppermost sensation of the moment. His vagrant and sinful fancies had vanished with the wholesome light of day, as the bad and evil spirits are fabled to "slip to their several graves," before the rising dawn. He felt then as he ought always to have done.

"What is it?—tell me. Has any thing happened to Harry? Can I be of the slightest service?"

"I ought to rejoice.—It is very honourable to him. But, oh, Mr. Hervey! how can a wife! You will despise me; but, ah, how can I!—how can I exult as he does, in a service of honourable danger?"

"What service? what do you mean?"

"He is appointed to the command of the secret expedition about to sail from Portsmouth. He was apprised of it last night. Little did I think, as I sat in vain security—little did I think that I was losing the last hours of his society in idle dissipation!"

"To the command of the expedition!" said Laurence; "this is honourable. My dear Mrs. Vivian—do forgive me—you a sailor's wife, you must not weep at this," taking her hand and pressing it affectionately. "It must gratify Harry so excessively. It must gratify every one who loves him."

"Believe me it does, it does gratify me; but ah, Heaven! it is the first time." And again the tears rained down her cheeks.

Laurence was himself now. A circumstance of interest, belonging to the events of real life, dispels, like a charm, the illusions of the imagination. Her genuine distress, the honourable distinction shown to his friend, interest in Harry's danger, in Harry's success, honest and affectionate interest, drove the hateful intoxication from his mind, as a sudden shock will sober the brain, disordered by the grosser intoxication of wine.

"My dearest Mrs. Vivian, weep with me. Be certain I honour these tears. But recollect you are a sailor's wife; consider how Harry adores you; repress this weakness before him; show him that you are worthy to share the destiny of so honourable a man.

You must not enfeeble his resolution by your sorrow, you must not exhaust his energy in striving with your distress."

"You are right.—Oh, you are right!—as you always are. No, my Harry, I will not pain you by a look of regret. I will bid you go in God's name—and never cease to pray God for you till you return."

A tear twinkled in the philosopher's eyes—those eyes which never wept.—He pressed her hand—"God will preserve him, to bless you."

Captain Vivian had been out, his hasty knock was heard at the door, he came in quickly—"Laurence, my dear fellow I am glad you are come—you will congratulate me heartily—which this foolish girl," putting his arm round her waist, and pressing her fondly to his bosom, "cannot find heart to do."

She lifted up her face, and smiled in his, "I will try though, my dearest, dearest Harry—I will try to rejoice in what rejoices you, as well as Mr. Hervey.—But when must you go?"

"To-night."

"To-night!—Good Heavens," with a sort of cry.

"I must be off for Portsmouth to-night, but it will be some days before I sail. What say you to running down there, and giving your benediction to my charming Sybile before she sails? Will you, my love?—will you start with me to-night? Laurence will run down with us, I am sure, and bring you safe back to town. Laurence, I *do* take a friend's freedom with your time."

Laurence was at that moment cursing himself for the thoughts of the past night, and vowing to his own soul, that, if entrusted

with the care of Iñez he would guard her with the jealous care of
a father; he would justify the unsuspecting reliance of his friend;
he would not even *think* what ought by possibility to offend him.
The purity of his sentiments seemed as by a miracle restored; he
answered cheerfully and without hesitation:

"My dear Harry, you will really offend me if you speak in that
way.—You know I only live to be of service to you, Mrs. Vivian,
and the children. Employ me in any way, every way, my good
fellow; you know how happy you make me."

"I was quite sure you would say and feel so, Mr. Hervey,"
said Iñez, giving him her hand, with the sweetest expression of
countenance. "Ah, Harry! I shall like to go with you—to see your
ship to see you sail. Ah, Heaven!" and again she burst into tears.

"My dearest Iñez!"

"Oh! forgive me—this is the first day—I have not had time to
rally I shall be very well behaved in a little while—I won't cry
at Portsmouth—but one must have it out once. My dear, dear
Harry, don't be ashamed of me, if I cannot bear it just at first—I
shall be better soon,"—and she ran out of the room, flew to her
children, and, having deluged them with her tears, washed her
eyelids, and composed her appearance, she came down into the
dining-room once more with a gentle serenity settled on her
countenance.

Harry had in the meanwhile been detailing to Laurence all
the particulars of the appointment: the Sybile had gone round
to Portsmouth a week or two before, and in her Captain Vivian
was to sail, to take the command of an expedition, of which the

object was as yet a secret. All he knew was, that he was to sail immediately, and with sealed orders. He explained as briefly as he could the situation of his private affairs—told Laurence that, in case any thing should happen to him, he had appointed him executor to his will, and guardian of his children—commended the little ones to his tenderness and care—and, above all, entreated him to watch over and protect his Iñez.

"You understand her as well, perhaps better, than I do—you see what a heart she has. Neither her father, nor Miss Vivian, the only two near connections we either of us possess, would be capable of supporting and consoling her under an infliction such as, Heaven bless her! she would feel for a poor fellow like me if I never came back again. Be kind to her, Laurence. Even you have been sometimes harsh and unjust with her—she does not deserve it. If ever there was an angel on this earth, it is she. Be tender to her for my sake."

The heart of Laurence responded to the generous confidence of the husband—"As there is a God in heaven,"—the most habitual sceptics, in their solemn moments, appeal in spite of themselves to a higher power—"As there is a God in heaven—I will be every thing to her that you can wish—I will guard her as the apple of my eye—protect her as the honour of my mother—defend her and keep her as my own soul."

"Thank you, Laurence—I know I can trust you—here she comes—Heaven bless her!—how sweetly quiet she looks."

The rest of the day was passed in busy preparations, in which Laurence was engaged like a member of the family; and if at times his admiration of the conduct of Iñez might appear too excessive, no busy throbbings at the heart reminded him that it might be criminal.

At ten o'clock in the evening they started with four horses in Captain Vivian's carriage, for Portsmouth.—Laurence insisted upon travelling outside—he would not intrude upon the last moments of tender sorrow. He would allow Harry the opportunity for being as weak and as womanly as he pleased—and Captain Vivian, it must be confessed, took advantage of the occasion— and Iñez and he, weeping in each other's arms—exchanging vows and blessings, and endearments, and prayers—passed that night of sorrow in all the hallowed sweetness of sincere affection.

Two days they spent at Portsmouth; two beautiful days of fine shining weather: the radiant sun and clear blue heavens reflected on the bosom of the glittering ocean, studded with vessels of every description. The beautiful Sybile lying gracefully on the water, her light spars and lofty masts rising in the air, and tracing their graceful lines upon the sky. Long, and often, and tenderly, and painfully, did Iñez gaze upon that vessel which was to bear away her husband; often did she walk, silently listening to the low beating of the waves, summoning courage for that parting, which she found it almost impossible to endure. There was much to be done, and she was necessarily a good deal alone; those moments were not wasted, they were spent in that best exercise, the fortifying of the heart by reflection to meet approaching evil.

The hour, the fatal hour, at last arrived; Captain Vivian's boat lay at the sally-port—the carriage of Iñez stood ready at the inn door. Vivian had arranged with Laurence that he should not accompany him from shore, but placing Iñez in her carriage the moment the parting was over, should instantly return with her to town, and to her children.

She stands with a beating heart in the inn parlour listening to the returning footsteps of her husband—returning, it might be, for the last time. The colour flutters in her cheek—now streaks it with a sudden crimson—now, as the blood retreats to the heart, a deadly paleness succeeds. Still she struggles for composure to support this dread parting as she ought to do. Quick footsteps are on the stairs—she presses her hands tightly upon her bosom, to still the almost insupportable beating within—the two friends enter—Harry, hurried, agitated, catches her in his arms—his fervent kisses are on her brow—her lips—his "God bless my Iñez—God in heaven bless and keep my Iñez," faltering, in broken accents, from his tongue. She has her arms folded round his neck—she answers his caresses by her low inarticulate murmurs she cannot speak—she falters—she reels—her head swims round—one last, fervent embrace. He must be gone—he places her in the arms of Laurence, with "Heaven bless you—take care of her"—and Harry Vivian has left all he loves best upon earth, and is hurrying down the High-street, dashing, as he goes along, the signs of tenderness from his manly cheek.

Was Laurence worthy to receive this pledge of confidence? was he worthy to be entrusted with the sacred treasure thus deposited under the guardianship of his honour? Alas! he who has indulged in sinful longings, in unjustifiable wishes, he who has forfeited the inner purity of the heart, may vow to himself that his actions shall be squared by the rule precise of rectitude—that no temptation shall allure him from the path direct of truth and honour—he may vow sincerely, but he vows in vain. Hasty, though honest, resolutions, where corruption, unresisted, nestles in the bosom, feebly resist the force of rising passion. Sin is within. "Blessed are the pure in heart, for they shall *see* God;" but cursed are they who nourish a secret wickedness—they *see* God in his evidence, a clear, discerning conscience, no more. Their eyes are darkened, their perception of things impaired. To their distorted apprehension, right becomes wrong, and wrong right, evil good, and good evil, till crime, arrayed in those flattering colours with which the perverted imagination loves to adorn her, displaces the image of virtue in the soul. This is true of most crimes, which seldom utterly possess a man until his moral vision has been impaired by corrupt secret contemplations, and he becomes, at last, in great measure, the victim of his own blindness. It is most especially true of those sins which bear a relation to the softer passions, those insidious betrayers, so deceitful in all their influences.

Iñez had not fainted, but she could not at first stand, and Laurence continued to hold her in his arms, though it was with difficulty he could stand himself. He supported her to the window, and threw it open. As the fresh air blew over her face, the colour returned, and, with a few convulsive sobs, the breath of life revisited her bosom.

"Is he really gone?"—were her first words.

"He is, indeed—for his sake, be comforted."

"I am—I shall be—thank you, Mr. Hervey; you are very kind. My dear Harry—Heaven bless him,"—and then the tears ran fast and silently down her cheeks.

Laurence, who had expected a storm, was relieved by this gentleness, and melted by her soft and patient air.

"What will you do?" said he.

"Oh! go to my children—take me to my children—I shall be better when I have seen them. Ah! Mr. Hervey, how little one thinks what the word *parting* means!"

"Your carriage is waiting."

"I am ready."

Laurence soon placed her within, sprang to her side; every thing was prepared, the carriage started immediately, and Portsmouth was speedily left behind.

Laurence sat silent and immovable in one corner of the carriage, while Iñez, her face covered with her handkerchief, sank into the other, silently weeping over all her fond recollections.

His sensations it would be difficult to describe as, alone with the only woman he had ever found it possible to love, in a carriage, that most perfect of solitudes, he seemed severed from the universe, and only existing in her. She, who was innocence itself, however, never even felt the *alone*, so inexpressibly precious to him; and after having wept for some time, till calmed and relieved, her tears ceased of themselves, she wiped her eyes; and, having looked out of the window, as a sort of preliminary, anxious to show her sense of his sympathy and kindness, she addressed him with an air of reliance and confidence, as if certain of finding support and comfort in his friendship and his wisdom. He was not insensible to the appeal, and exerted himself to talk in his usually agreeable manner. They talked of her future plans—of her children—of how she would occupy herself till Harry's return—Iñez with the cheerful readiness of a healthy mind, having already imagined a thousand schemes for cheating the weary hours. Soon the smiles of hope revisited her lips, as her sanguine imagination passed hastily over the space that was to intervene before her husband should be restored to her arms. While Laurence, though his tones were unusually soft, and his eyes bent too pensively upon her, preserved, with some effort, that appearance of tranquillity which he had rigidly enjoined to himself.

X

THE travellers reached London before tea-time, and were received in Spring Gardens by the stately Miss Vivian, whom Harry had requested to give her company to his wife during his absence. Not that either of the two very much liked Miss Vivian, for the precision of her manners and the formality of her ideas suited ill with their own cheerful *insouciance*; but they both felt instinctively that Iñez was too young, and too beautiful, to be left absolutely without protection, and agreed under that convenient form, "it will be better," to invite her to pass the time in Spring Gardens. Iñez, indeed, might have gone to Middleton Court; but, besides that she wished to remain in London, where she should be on the spot to receive the speediest intelligence of her husband, the Admiral and his faithful Pylades, Mr. Roper, had done a most unusual thing for them—they had gone a long journey into Ireland, to visit an old naval friend of the Admiral's, and were to be absent some weeks.

Miss Vivian lived in a very lovely cottage on that beautiful range of hills rising from the Thames and terminating in the village of Roehampton. There she had converted a few acres of ground, by her persevering gardening, into a perfect paradise; in the centre of which stood her little villa, built, as it is the pleasure of some to prefer them, with a number of low rooms, and surrounded by a roofed verandah, which, invented to repel the piercing beams of an Italian sun, effectually excludes the cheerful light and agreeable heat of an English one. The rooms were small and inconvenient, as if contrived to show the power of elegant furniture and tasteful arrangement to triumph over these defects of proportion. Neatness, elegance, order, and propriety are excellent things, and without them life speedily degenerates into a brutal and intolerable affair; but there is a neatness, order, and propriety, so still, so cold, so passionless, that both the heart and imagination receive a sudden chill on entering where they reside. It was so at Bellevue, the drawing-room so purely fair, as if that moment fresh from the hands of the painter—the furniture so perfectly, yet so immovably, arranged, that it appeared like presumption to move a chair out of its place—the book-shelves stored with elegantly bound volumes, too elegant to be handled or to be read—the cold, composed mistress of the house, not a fold of her dress, not a curl of her hair, but in the most perfect order, as if passion, hurry, and emotion were alike strangers to her bosom and to her household.—Captain Vivian and Iñez never visited Bellevue but they felt the day insupportably long: Iñez endeavoured to be cheerful and pleasant, but her pretty mouth was distorted by inward yawns, and, in her efforts to avoid an uncivil silence, she perpetually made blunders and uttered platitudes, which Miss Vivian was certain to take up in her composed manner, and show off to the best advantage; while Captain Vivian played with the children—talked to Miss Vivian's large, solemn looking dog—walked to the window—strolled into the garden—and hugged Iñez for joy at their release, when they were shut up in the carriage to go home.

Iñez could not even now help considering Miss Vivian's visit as a necessary evil, but trusted its continuance would be rendered less irksome to all parties by the incessant business in which she was usually engaged. For this lady was eminently a committee woman, a member of societies, a drawer up, and reader of reports, a frequenter of meetings where great lords and gentlemen play at business and affect eloquence to please busy single women of much time and much money. She was a busy inspector of the poor, an enemy to all indiscriminate charity, an especial enemy to all Sunday relaxation, to all idleness, all carelessness, all extravagance. She was one indeed whose activity would have been invaluable had it been united with that "love," that gentle indulgent spirit of love, which He who knew the heart declared to be the foundation of all social virtue; but, animated by no such sentiment, she walked, a cold and spectral image of charity, serving too often to disgust those who wished to do good with the means of doing it—and to reconcile those whose good works were the accidental effect of impulse alone, to their own negligent and careless good-nature.

The effect she had produced upon the mind of Iñez had been certainly hurtful as far as it extended. Miss Vivian, who appeared to her so unamiable and tiresome, she knew to be reputed an excellent person, and she was tempted too hastily to conclude that she owed somewhat of her unamiableness to her excellencies. The mistake is common with young and ardent minds, and the soberer virtues are too often despised because associated in idea with that coldness and insensibility of character which render their exercise so easy.

Miss Vivian was somewhat shocked when the door opened and Mrs. Vivian and Laurence made their appearance:—it had not struck her before, but she, who wanted that charity which thinketh no evil, immediately reflected how much more proper it would have been, if the charge of Iñez from Portsmouth had been committed to herself.

Mrs. Vivian gave her a hasty welcome and ran up stairs to her nursery. Laurence walked into the room: he felt not sorry to find Miss Vivian there; the continual restraint he had put upon his feelings during the long *tête-à-tête* was beginning to become wearisome—and he felt relieved by the presence of a third person from that dangerous charge of himself which every hour rendered more dangerous—from that irksome effort at indifferent conversation which every hour rendered more irksome.

He was glad to take possession of his accustomed chair, and indulge in silent languor those dangerous contemplations which were again fast corrupting the integrity of his thoughts.

The fire was blazing cheerfully, and tea was waiting for the travellers. Iñez soon appeared, her younger child in her arms, crowing and screaming with delight, patting her cheeks with its little hands, and loading her with caresses; the elder one, silent and tender, hanging on her gown, as if afraid again to lose her; she sat down on her chair, close to that occupied by Laurence. He took the eldest in his lap, she placed the other in hers; the little ones laughed, played, and chatted with their mother, and Laurence talked to them in that quiet joking manner, which made him a vast favourite with children. Miss Vivian sat making tea behind the hissing urn:—it was a comfortable family party.

When Laurence went to his lodgings that night, he drew his chair to the hearth, and having placed, as he was wont (like most bachelors and some married men) a foot on each hob, engrossing the whole fire, he began to reflect upon the events of the day, and for the first time seriously to ask himself the question, what were his feelings, what were his views, and what, under his circumstances, he ought to do? In spite of his self-delusion, he found it difficult to allay certain fears to which the various emotions of the last few hours had given rise, and could not divest himself of a doubt whether he were, all things considered, exactly the fittest and safest guardian to whom his friend could have entrusted his wife. He could not help asking himself whether, if Harry had suspected the intense sensation with which the deposit had been received, he would, with so much satisfaction, have left his treasure almost in his arms; and whether to live in the perpetual presence of one whose distant voice or footstep sent the blood hurrying through his veins, yet one on whom it was treachery even to cast a wish, was exactly what was most prudent and wise. Should he fly while it was

yet in his power? Was not that a measure due to his own peace
of mind, and to the faith pledged to his friend? To fly while it
was yet in his power?—but was it in his power? The very idea
was already insupportable. To live in perpetual self-restraint, to
deny himself the pleasure of looking at, or of almost speaking
to her—to feign coldness, indifference, injustice, every thing
was easy—but to leave her altogether—to suffer her to forget
him—to endeavour to forget her—it seemed to him, under the
infatuation of his fatal disorder, that to be cured—to learn to
forget—to be restored to his usual state of insensibility, would
be, of all results, the most to be deprecated; it would be to pass
from life to death; from warm, animated existence, to dreary,
pale, monotony: and why? why should such an exchange be
made? By what law was he required to annihilate feelings so
exquisite?—trample out as it were the flame that animated and
exalted his heart? What! because his secret feelings, which no
power on earth should ever tempt him to disclose, might, by
this incomparable creature be somewhat excited, so as to pass
that line which frigid moralists have laid down as the proper
limit of sentiment in his circumstances, was it necessary that he,
like a tutored school-boy, should renounce the delights of the
most generous of passions? and for what? What was this absurd
monopoly which, under the name of public order, would forbid
those secret aspirations of the heart, with which public order has
nothing to do?—would restrict the influence of these matchless
perfections to one probably rendered insensible by too long and
too secure a possession? Was he to be the dupe of all this old-

world cant?—and, after all, if he felt in any real danger, it would then be time enough to run away.

And with this conclusion, he laid his head upon his pillow, and with this conclusion he rose in the morning, resolving to be cautious—and avoid even the shadow of evil in action, and confine every tempestuous emotion to his own bosom; and in this conclusion he began the most dangerous system of intercourse that ever beguiled man or woman.

XI

Miss Vivian, we have said, was unfortunately no companion for Iñez , who had indeed—fortunately or unfortunately—for that is as it may prove—no very intimate female friend. She never had possessed much taste for the sort of thing; indeed Captain Vivian had, since her marriage, stood so entirely in the relation of friend to her, their union and confidence had been so complete—that had she been blest with a treasure of this nature—it is more than probable she would have, before this, fallen under the reproach of most young and happy wives, and have been somewhat negligent in the performance of the duties exacted by that connexion.

After her husband's departure, though she neither pined nor fretted, yet she certainly felt her spirits saddened below their usual level, and she was therefore little inclined to mix in general society. One only person possessed the art of charming her attention, and beguiling the hours, otherwise so tedious, of her widowhood; and he, having vowed to himself to taste temperately of the forbidden cup—to visit in Spring Gardens only occasionally and moderately, with due intervals, &c.—ended by passing there nearly the whole of his time.

Miss Vivian was, as we have said, a woman of business. Her mornings were occupied with meetings and committees, her evenings in drawing up and correcting reports. Laurence and Iñez were left almost completely to themselves and to the children, who, playing on the carpet at their feet, just sufficiently broke the continual *tête-à-tête* so as to render it less alarming, and perhaps more dangerous. The books were resumed, and were again, as erst to those unhappy victims of passion who met the wanderer at the gates of Hades, inseparable in their melancholy immortality—the food of dangerous tempting thought. Again, the study of those poets was resumed, where Laurence found reflected all that was passing in his own bosom—again, as the sounds came softened from those beautiful lips, while with her dark and braided hair, her brow of antique mould and purest marble, she bent over the book, would he suffer his eye unchastened to fasten upon her countenance, till his very heart sickened within his breast— "*Galëotto fù il librò e chi lo scrisse.*"

Many weeks passed in this manner—Laurence engaged in a contest in which every day he felt himself losing ground; yet still his resolution was preserved, and not the slightest expression of his feelings had as yet passed, at least beyond his eyes—but his frame, not built to endure the struggles of a passion, the more destructive because not in union with his usual system of being, began at length to yield under days and nights of passionate and hopeless excitement; his brow assumed an air of delicacy—the blue veins were visible on his transparent temples—his frame looked extenuated—his breath came and went with difficulty—his eyes burned with a gloomy concentrated fire. She noticed these changes with concern, but without the slightest suspicion of their cause.

"How pale you are grown, Mr. Hervey," said she: "what ails you? Something, I am quite sure, is the matter. Something weighs on your spirits—I do not mean to intrude upon your confidence—yet—"

"You *never* call me Laurence. Why that odious formality?"

"You cannot mean to answer me in that ridiculous manner. I ask you whether you are ill or unhappy, and you answer, 'You never call me Laurence.' Does that make you ill and unhappy?"

"Yes."

"Yes!" moving the chair a few paces from his, while she looked, wondering, in his face—"What are you thinking of?"

"Don't move your chair away—in pity—in pity, Iñez."

"In pity!" very much surprised.

"I am weary of restraint—I can bear these tortures no longer," he cried vehemently, as if some mighty barrier opposed to his feelings had all at once given way. "Human nature can endure them no longer—I must—I will—Iñez," imperiously—"sit down where you were before—sit down by me—" with the most pathetic earnestness—"sit down by me, or kill me at once."

"Good heavens! Mr. Hervey," said she, shocked and astonished, yet still without an idea of his meaning—"what can you mean? what is the matter? Have you any thing to tell me?—any thing of Harry?"

"Pooh, nonsense," peevishly—"I beg your pardon. Sit down where you were before—only do that."

"And why should I?"—drawing her chair some paces farther away. "You are more inconceivable than ever this morning—and I think scarcely deserve that I should endeavour to understand you. If you did not look so deadly pale—and wretchedly thin—I should be very angry with this—*nonsense* I will call it."

"Do I look pale?—do I look thin?—Iñez—Iñez—you see it then at last—I am a dying man."

"You—oh, Laurence, don't say so. Surely you are not in earnest," approaching him with affectionate solicitude. "Tell me nothing is really the matter. No, you are only frightening me— nothing is really the matter—yet how *very* ill you look! what ails you? do you suffer?"

"Suffer!—good God—ah, Iñez, the bitterest tortures that ever racked the wretch expiring on the wheel are ecstasy to mine.— Suffer!—merciful heaven!—Give me your hand."

She held it out—he took it in his—his, so thin, burning, and wasted—she thought, with fever.—Alas! little did she suspect what fever was consuming his veins. For a moment he pressed her fingers, with an almost spasmodic contraction—then, recollecting himself, was contented with holding them in his— while the colour faintly revisited his wasted cheek.

"Iñez, let me—let me—it does me good"—as she strove to withdraw her hand. "Sit down where you were before—I suffer—"

She obeyed—melted and alarmed at once by an expression of excessive pain, which she now observed, as she had once or twice done before, cross his countenance.

"Iñez, could you—if I were indeed dying—could you have the patience to sit so by me?—Will you—could you—would you—pity me?"

"I could sit by you for ever, if that would do you good, Laurence," said she, melting into tears; "but tell me—tell me—where—how do you suffer?—Ah! why have you concealed it so long?—I see how ill you are—but surely you will take advice. A remedy must be found."

"There is no remedy," cried he passionately. "Earth affords no remedy—heaven no cure. The grave—sleep—everlasting annihilation, is all I hope for—and all I deserve. Don't ask me questions, but sit by me—that soothes me. Let me hold your hand—that allays my burning torture. Oh! Iñez, look at me—I forget myself!—I am lost!"

Even yet it seemed that she did not in the least understand his meaning—so unsuspecting is perfect innocence. Yet she endeavoured to withdraw her hand—he would not relinquish it. She felt very awkward at first—but ended by letting it remain as it was.

Then he began again, in that sweet persuasive voice so seductive to her ears, to converse in his usual delightful manner—pouring his ideas, like a flood, into her mind—charming her every faculty by his eloquence, his sensibility, his intelligence. At length, though still he abstained from alluding to his own peculiar feelings, he began to speak of *love*—that dangerous theme. He painted the passion as Iñez had imagined, but never yet witnessed its power. He spoke with an eloquence and enthusiasm rare, even in him— but he had abandoned himself, in reckless despair, to the tide of his feelings, suffering them to bear him where they would.

The lock of the door was heard to move. Laurence started, and let drop the hand. Iñez drew her chair a yard or two away—she felt the colour rising to her cheek—the first faint signal of approaching danger. She heeded it not—that is, she thrust from her mind a thought that intruded—she would not admit it for an instant. Laurence promised himself to be more cautious; he had promised himself to *fly*; but he could no longer exist separated from the object of his passion. Death—dishonour—perdition—had he believed in such a thing, he would rather have dared all. "To cast out his right eye—to sever his right hand"—he had not been taught in that school.

The next day the agitation was not confined to him alone. Iñez!— thoughts had at last entered that, till then, pure and innocent mind—thoughts not rejected with the indignation of a virtue all in arms—thoughts seductive to her vanity—flattering, must it be said, to her heart! Was it possible?—a man so highly gifted—he who had held so lightly by her—he—could it be? had she a power?—She dismissed the idea—she would not for a moment entertain it—it was nonsense—but the idea was obstinate—it would recur. And when, the next day, as a matter of course, he took her hand, and held it, while she faintly strove to withdraw it—and he, his pleading eyes fixed upon hers—his lips pale—his countenance wasted—said, "Let it be, Iñez—it is an innocent indulgence—I shall not ask it long." Did she withdraw it?—No.

Laurence was not adept in seduction—but had he possessed, in perfection, all the secrets of that black and villainous art, he could scarcely have practised them with effects so fatal as those which flowed from his own infirmity of purpose. He struggled—but he struggled imperfectly. He strove with half a wish. He would, like Macbeth—"not have played false—and yet unfairly won." He would have indulged a culpable passion—yet leave unstained his friend's honour and his own. He shrank from the path which alone could guide to security—he persisted in treading, though with faltering, irresolute steps, that which must inevitably lead astray.

Meanwhile this irresolution—his efforts to conceal the passion he would not master—to resist temptations to which he ought never to have exposed himself—his torments—his emotions—his internal struggles—his despair—acted fatally on the imagination of his victim—the effect he would once have deprecated ensued—Iñez began to watch with pity—with interest—with tenderness—the alteration of feelings which never took a form that could offend her.

Harry was far away, pursuing his arduous profession on the stormy ocean—week after week elapsed—and no letter, no tidings, reminded her of the absent wanderer, or diverted her attention from the agonies of him, adoring and dying at her feet.

To separate from Laurence—heedless and confident in herself, she never surmised the possibility of her own frailty—or that evil could lurk where the high-souled, gifted Laurence was concerned—she was imprudent, unreflecting, unschooled, compassionate, and generous—he, the slave of a passion the more intense, as it was the very first that ever had mastered him.—Shall we follow, step by step, the advances of guilt? Shall we disclose the vain delusions, the false reasonings, with which the mind disguises to itself its own turpitude? Shall we betray all the miserable weakness of human nature under temptation? Suffice it to say, the consequences were such as those who venture to walk in forbidden paths, relying on their own strength, ought to anticipate …

Her grief, her anguish, her self-reproaches, her despair, mock description—yet, like the poor bird, fascinated by the bright glittering eye of the serpent—where did she fly for support, for consolation, but to that bosom which had so cruelly betrayed her trust?—to him she had so long regarded as all that was wise and right—him the image of virtue in her mind? Her very guilt—the strange and false position in which the innocent find themselves placed by their first crime—formed a tie to bind her more closely to her deceiver:—she seemed to exist to breathe— but in that presence which had been her destruction.

Oh! that we had the pen of the great master of human passion—that, like him, with some few faithful touches it were given to us to portray the real horrors of guilt—the fall from innocence to vice.—To paint that dark cloud, which settles over the bright unsullied temple of the thoughts—the miserable weight hanging on the heart—the feverish, hasty joy—the bitter self-loathing revulsion—the disorder of the ideas—the diseased and corrupted affections—all the harmony of life turned to foul discord—

Like sweet bells jangled, out of tune and time—

and worse—the meannesses, and the basenesses, the subterfuges and the deceits, which, linked in fatal consequence, drearily attend upon crime. Truth and purity, and self-esteem, and honest dignity, and generous regard for others—and that sweet confidence of a living God, testified by the whispers of conscience—exchanged for confusion, and selfishness, and fear! Such a picture, had we but the power to paint it—would scare the soul from the very first thought or suspicion of wrong—would strip the flattering veil from guilty excitement—rob passion of its flatteries—pleasure of her delusions—investing purity and rectitude, and fidelity and honour, with their own bright and unparalleled attractions.

Alas! for the unfortunate Iñez! She was formed to taste, in its full extent, the bitterness of the exchange she had made. She awakened as it were from a dream—an illusion—a delirium—to an anguish the more touching, as it was unmingled with one word of reproach to her seducer. Often, in the dead of the night, did she leave her sleepless pillow—driven by tumultuous thoughts (those relentless furies), and, pacing her room—seek vainly for refuge—for relief from her distraction. After a night of sleepless despair, would she wait, divided between hope and remorse, till he came—till that step was heard upon the stairs—till he entered unannounced that fatal drawing-room—till, like a child on its mother's bosom, her forehead bent upon his arm, she would sob and weep herself to rest.

The effect produced upon Laurence by this intense—this agonising sensibility—this childlike confidence—this artless, though guilty, attachment, baffles the power of words: the common expressions of idolatry of adoration, words—rendered vulgar by their application

to transient and capricious feelings—are utterly insignificant here
—suffice it to say, his whole soul was absorbed by her. For once, the
usual consequence of success did not ensue—satiety—indifference—
contempt—those bitter precursors of still bitterer retribution. Let it
not be deemed an immoral softening of the picture to acknowledge
that, for once, though woman was frail, man was not ungrateful—
and Iñez escaped a consequence which would have terminated the
tragedy by breaking her heart. But let no woman flatter herself that
such poor exemption may be her own fate—Iñez fell—but it was
as the victim of no selfish vanity—no secret corruption. She fell—
and angels might have wept her ruin. Laurence felt and knew this,
and he doated upon his victim to an excess with which even his
former feelings could not be compared. To devote every hour of
his existence so her—to soothe—to console—to make himself the
veriest slave that ever trod the earth, cost this man, once so proud in
his independence, nothing:—he lived but for her—and in her:—he
had not a view—not a wish—not an idea, that centered not in her—
he had no time for remorse—no moment for self-reproaches—she
was his—it was enough—and could he once have reconciled her
to herself—or could—would the winds and the waves restore the
virtue, the peace of mind that was lost? Would the elements, the
servants of nature, interfere to protect the victims of her powers?
He dared not form a wish—he dared not whisper the dark, the
guilty hope, even to his inmost heart—but how did that spoiler's
heart beat—when the image of Iñez—his Iñez—released from other
ties—restored to herself—his, by all the laws of society—his beyond
the power of fate—his *for ever*—crossed his mind.—Cain!—Cain!

XII

Captain Vivian did not return. No letter—no sign of existence, reminded Iñez that he lived—time rolled on—and still the husband was silent.

Miss Vivian had been absent the first unhappy week which completed the downfall of Iñez:—she had remained long enough away for the guilty pair to recover from the first violent excitement of their new situation:—the arguments—the soothing cares—of Laurence had, before her return, produced their effect on the plastic mind of Iñez. She began to yield to those sophistries, which every man knows how to make use of on such an occasion; and who better than Laurence? whose ideas of morals were all vague and undefined—and who had been a too willing disciple of that school which prefers pleasure, liberty, taste, and refinement, to severe virtue and rigid right.

He intended not to corrupt—but was it likely that, imbued with principles such as his, he should not use arguments, convincing to himself, to blind that clear searching eye of rectitude which still too plainly estimated the evil in its full enormity?

Iñez, gradually lulled by those opiates of the conscience—those slow poisons of the soul—sank into a state which, though it could not be said to be happy, might be called, in comparison, easy—and it was now only at intervals that the sharp poignard of recollection would stab her to the heart—when her children—her blooming, innocent children—when little Georgy, with her fair hair, the image of her father—threw her chubby, infantine arms round her neck, covering her with sweet kisses—then would she press the child wildly to her bosom—set her rapidly down—sink on her knees before a chair—and, burying her face within her arms—and her arms in all the wild superfluity of her hair, cry as if her heart were breaking.

Miss Vivian was slow of perception, though reputed a remarkably clever woman. Like other characters of her frigid class, she had little sympathy with, and very little knowledge of, what passed in the bosoms of others. As Laurence was rather more cautious in timing his visits than he had been before her departure—those little vague suspicions, which had played about her mind, that Mr. Hervey came too much to the house, were allayed; she marked not the hesitating start, the rising colour, the shaking hand of Iñez, as one brief knock struck on the house door—she marked not those eyes bent to the ground as Laurence entered—that averted face, as he took her hand. Laurence had always some good reason for coming—now a book—now a picture—now a piece of music—now a lesson to the little Florence—for with, what might seem, a strange inconsistency, he seemed to endeavour to atone to the child for the injury he had done, by devoting himself to her improvement in the most sedulous manner—he, who had hated exertion of every sort, now patiently pursued the wearying task of instruction, with a gentleness and perseverance that ensured the rapid advance of his pupil, while it engaged all her childish affections. The little ones were for ever on his knees, fondling him as if he had been their father.

"Really, Mr. Laurence," said Miss Vivian, one day, when Mrs. Vivian was out of the room; "you quite surprise me, by the pains you take with that dear child. You are quite a singularity—you who used to hate trouble so heartily—I am sure Captain Vivian is very much obliged to you."

The blood did then mount to the temples of Laurence, as he bent over the little girl's exercise.—He affected not to hear.

"I say, Mr. Laurence, that Captain Vivian is under great obligations to you, I am sure; for that child, what between Harry's negligence and Mrs. Vivian's weak indulgence, was on the very point of being utterly ruined. But is it not strange that we hear nothing of him?—I called at the Admiralty as I came this morning. No despatches. Pray Heaven, he may be safe." Laurence still kept his head bent to the little hand he was directing.

"I must own, I think Mrs. Vivian looks very anxious, though she never says a word to me on the subject. She strikes me as looking worried and nervous; but she is so reserved, I can make nothing of her."

"It is natural that she should be anxious," at length articulated Laurence.

"She is certainly a very charming young lady," continued Miss Vivian; "yet I used to think Harry might have done better."

"Why so?" said Laurence, hastily.

"My heart long misgave me about that marriage. The first time I saw Miss Thornhaugh there was something airy, and flighty, and fanciful about her manner I did not quite like. I think indeed you said something of the kind yourself; but I own my opinion is changed—I think she is devoted to him now—indeed, I never saw a happier couple, except that he was hardly the *husband* enough—you understand me—a *little* too indulgent; but she evidently frets about him now—I only wish she were a little less reserved. That hidden anxiety is a slow poison, Mr. Hervey."

Laurence started, for Iñez entered the room. He gazed to see what ravages that slow poison had already made in the form he idolised; but, except the languor of a melancholy softness, he saw no trace of poison there.

The next day was Sunday.

"Have you ordered your carriage, my dear?" said Miss Vivian. "In that case I will beg a seat. My horses don't come out of a Sunday, you know."

"I am not going to church," said Iñez, in a low tone.

"Why not, my dear? it is a beautiful day. Excuse me, Mrs. Vivian—but such duties—I am an old-fashioned woman—such duties had better not be neglected. I hope, Mr. Laurence," turning to him, "you are not putting any of your notions into Mrs. Vivian's head. I *never* knew her neglect church before. If your carriage is not ordered, let us walk."

"Will you not go to church?" said Laurence, in a low tone. "You had better."

"No," said Iñez.

"Very strange," said Miss Vivian, rising to prepare herself. "I am afraid you cannot be well."

"I am not well," said Iñez, with forced composure.

"What is the matter?" said Miss Vivian, now hastily returning. "Oh, my dear Mrs. Vivian, I have thought you not looking well ever since my return. Do send for Dr. L——. What is the matter?"

"Nothing—nothing! only I don't wish to go out to-day."

"I am sorry," said the other lady, again in a tone of reproof, "that you don't choose to go to church—where, I think, once a day at least—"

"Indeed," said Laurence, "I am no great advocate for these things; but, if you are pretty well, Mrs. Vivian, had you not better go?"

He was always in an agony for her reputation, and on the watch to guard it from the breath of suspicion.

"Do *you* bid me go?" said Iñez, with a look of melancholy reproach.

"And why should he not?" interrupted Miss Vivian. "I am sure it gives me great pleasure to hear you, Laurence, for once advocating such things. I trust yet to see you alter your opinion upon some points. Indeed, I think you improved since I knew you. I little thought to hear you persuading Mrs. Vivian to her religious duties."

It will be perceived that Miss Vivian was one who did not dislike to exercise the office of censor in her domestic circle, and who exercised it without any extraordinary delicacy.

"I am glad you think me improved in any way," said Laurence. "Do go, Iñez," in a very low tone, as Miss Vivian left the room. "Do go, Iñez."

"Go!—Can you ask me?"

"Yes, my beloved Iñez—Miss Vivian—she will be surprised."

"Don't think, Mr. Hervey," hastily, "that if I stay at home *you* stay—but not, even to fly from you, will I pollute the house of God—Almighty God!—*Father*—no more!" lifting up her arms in an attitude of adoration. "Not yet so utterly a wretch am I become—I will not blaspheme before thy holy altar—I will not double dye my soul in guilt by black hypocrisy. No, Laurence—God—Heaven—all that is pure and good, I have forsaken for you—for your sake—be content. Ask me not to do a thing so abhorrent. The house of God I enter no more."

"My Iñez," said Laurence, deeply affected, "my Iñez—forgive me—forgive me! Oh, when, when shall I be like thee!—thou angel! When will my gross—base—wretched nature rise to thine! Yet, believe it not.—The God of nature . . ."

"Stop, Laurence—blaspheme not. Because we are sinners, let us not darken the light of our own souls. *He* sees me—He sees me as I am. He sees that, prostrate in the dust—imploring his mercy—I cannot—I cannot tear thee from my heart. He sees that I am *thine*—not his—that perdition—with thee—alas! Alas! But I will not mock the God I have forsaken."

When Laurence now and then heard words such as these, and saw the deep impression which, in spite of all his efforts, was made upon her mind, a dark anticipation of future retribution would suddenly come over him,—a pain short, yet so acute, would oppress him, that he would turn deadly pale in an instant. Then Iñez forgot herself—her remorse,—and was again all softness—all tender anxiety. Every thing was forgotten, while she strove to soothe an anguish, so little in proportion with her own.—But such is woman.

Iñez adhered to her resolution, and joined in religious services no more. "Sinning," says one who knew well what he was about, "will make us leave off praying, or praying will make us leave off sinning." Having once confessed that her lover was dearer to her than her Creator—having once owned the infatuation which would have made her insensible to the call even of one risen from the dead—Iñez not only refused to mingle in public prayer—she ceased to pray in private. How dare she, more and more wedded to her sin—more obstinately devoted day by day to her guilty passion,—how dared she pray for mercies she refused to earn—for the Holy Spirit which she had grieved—for the salvation she had rejected! Every day took something from the sharpness of her remorse—something from the purity of her mind—as, at length deadened by habit, her better thoughts were laid in fatal slumber, and Iñez began to feel that careless indifference—that reckless insensibility to wrong, creep over her.—Fatal refuge from the intense, but healing, agonies she had experienced.

Men are not nice discriminators of the delicate shades by which the female mind becomes gradually darkened and depraved; and Laurence, who would have mourned the degradation in tears of blood, had he been aware of it, saw only a fresh proof of her devotion in the smiles which, though faintly and rarely, began to illumine her countenance. Every change, indeed, only added fuel to his passion. He had loved her penitence and her tears—he loved her composure and her smiles yet more.

So passed the time—Iñez became more a companion for Miss Vivian than she had hitherto been; for as every moment of Laurence's absence was insupportably irksome, she endeavoured to beguile the time by interesting herself in Miss Vivian's charitable persuits; she was led, too, by that very common feeling, that very common error, of endeavouring by the scrupulous and almost excessive discharge of one duty to make amends for the persevering breach of another.

She would fain have made atonement for her guilt by any sacrifice but *one*—that *one*—the cherished sin that was beyond her strength—but any thing that it might please Heaven to require. So she, too, attended meetings, and subscribed, visited, and was busy and stirring, and did good, as she hoped; and Miss Vivian began to grow quite fond of her, for she was not insensible to the vanity of carrying such a coadjutor along with her. And when Iñez had lavished her guineas, and been received with gratitude by the poor and wretched she had helped to raise, she returned to sit by the accustomed *fauteuil* with something almost like her early cheerfulness—and Laurence resumed his looks, and the whole house recovered a certain air of domestic comfort.

Miss Vivian, flattered and in good humour, was now ever ready to make one in various little excursions proposed by Laurence in the neighbourhood of London. The summer was now pretty far advanced, the weather charming, and, with a view of dissipating thought, and indulging refined luxury of enjoying fine scenery and a summer's sky under the enchantment of an adored society, he was every day proposing some new scheme or other, which his delightful powers of conversation rendered but too attractive to Iñez.

It was the end of August. A glorious morning gave promise of a day of unusual heat. Laurence came to breakfast, and proposed to the two ladies an excursion up the river to Richmond: to go by water, and let the carriages meet them by land, as he feared Mrs. Vivian might be wearied by the double passage. She looked wearied already, as if she had passed a restless night, and his eyes followed her anxiously, to ask her what was the matter? A look of melancholy sweetness was the only answer, and a sigh—which touched him the more, because it was evidently suppressed.

"It will refresh you—the sweet breeze on the water," said Laurence. "I have been out already. It is delicious. Let us take the children."

"Ay, let us take the children, nurse," said Iñez. "Give me a load of shawls. You may trust them with us—we will not let them get into mischief. Will you go, sweet little ones?"

The little things were delighted.

"Florence shall be mamma's share to day," said Hervey; "and I will take you, naughty little Georgy—for else you will jump out of the boat."

"Very well, Mr. Laurence," said Georgy, "I shall be so naughty you won't know what to do with me."

"And I'll be so good," whispered the gentle Florence, "if I may be your child, mamma."

"Will you," stooping down, and kissing her, while a tear was in her eye, "*always* be good?"

"Always good—*so* good—as good as you!"

Mrs. Vivian hastily walked to the window.

"I do wonder when papa will come home," said Georgy, heaving a great sigh. "He used always to take us on the water."

"Hush, my dear," whispered Miss Vivian, hastily. "It makes mamma unhappy. Don't speak of him, my dear."

"Does it make *you* unhappy too, Mr. Laurence? What is mamma crying for?—I do wish he were at home."

"And so do I," whispered Florence.

"Very right of you, my dears—you ought to wish for him. But don't talk of him just now."

Laurence, while Miss Vivian said this, had put the child very coldly on the ground, and, taking up the newspaper, began to read it busily.

Breakfast was soon over, and they went down to the boat. Laurence had provided an excellent one. He seemed resolved to enjoy this day with all the refinements of pleasure. The white awning softened the rays of the sun, and the size of the boat allowed of a cushioned and luxurious seat; while the glittering waters, the soft wafting breeze, the coolness, the tranquillity, filled the soul with delicious languor. Miss Vivian sat at the end of the boat—Iñez by her side—Laurence and the two children lay at her feet. He had a book, and, from time to time, read from it some of those impassioned verses, of which, alas! she had been too fond—Miss Vivian understood no Italian.

Iñez perhaps this day, for the first time, yielded herself without remorse to the seductive enjoyment of the moment. Her eyes were bent downwards, but he could read them—he could read her smile. That day was the first in which, unreproved, they had seemed to taste that felicity which love promises For those few hours he might be said to keep his faith. But they shall not be described here—nor the walk in Richmond Park, where, hanging upon his arm—Miss Vivian on the other—she wandered through the shades—nor the return home in a sweet, clear evening—the nightingales making the groves and hedges vocal.

It was agreed that Laurence should be dropped in Pall-Pall—go to his own lodging, where he was to dress, and return to dinner with the ladies. It was about five o'clock when the carriage stopped in Spring Gardens—Iñez hurried up stairs. The guilty intoxication was complete. She had no thought but of the dinner; and, having hastily consigned the children to the nurse, hurried up stairs to choose the pure white she knew he loved, and adorn herself to please *those eyes*. She was impatient to dress to meet again.

She ran to her dressing table. A letter lay there. She snatched it desperately up—tore it open—and read—

Portsmouth.

My beloved Iñez,

I leave to newspapers the task of communicating the result of our harassing expedition, content to thank God that I am landed alive, to fly to your arms, and bury in your bosom all my cares—all my troubles. I shall leave this as soon as possible, and be with you all, my darlings, at eight this evening.

HARRY VIVIAN

Kiss our children ten thousand times over for me.

The heart of Iñez suddenly stopped, and she became not pale, but of a cold blue clay colour. She did not fall—she stood rooted to the spot, like one on whom the curse of God had suddenly fallen. One instant—one single instant had sufficed to open her eyes. It was as if scales had fallen from before them. She saw herself as she was—the guilt—the inexcusable infatuation—the pollution—the degradation. As the picture of former happiness, love, and innocence rose suddenly to her fancy, with all the brightness of the clearest perception; as her husband—wronged, insulted, betrayed—stood, as it were, in all the honesty of his devoted affection—his cheerful tenderness—his generous confidence, living before her eyes. She said nothing—she laid the letter open upon the table. Her hat was yet on—she wrapped herself in a large cloak, and slid softly down stairs.

"I am come!" said she, as she opened the door of the room in the Albany, where Laurence, ready dressed to go out, was sitting: "I am come! to claim my place at last! I am come—a guilty, degraded, blasted being—to claim my place by your fire-side."

"Good God, Iñez! what is the matter?" cried he, struck by the hollow tones of her voice—still more by the spectral hue of her countenance. "My Iñez, what is it?"

"*Your* Iñez?—Yes, indeed! my husband is come home."

"Vivian!"

"He is come!—yes!" flinging herself prostrate on the floor, while her long black hair fell over her to her very feet, as she lay like a crushed worm—contracted together, as though she would bury her forehead in the earth. "Yes! he is come home. By this time he is come! He has found his trust betrayed!—his hearth defiled!—his faith—his heart, broken! Yes! he is come—his children are in his arms—their tears are on his cheek—their hands are in his neck—they are all calling for the mother."

And, at these words, such a tempest of groans, and sobs, and tears, rushed forth, that Laurence thought she would have been suffocated.

He fell on the floor by her side, but she pushed him from her—rude—violent—for the first and only time. "Touch me not, Laurence—pollute not my first honest tears. Serpent! mingle not your insidious poison with my groans. Oh, Harry! Harry! receive me back once more. Take back your wife to your bosom! Forgive me, Harry!—forgive me, Harry!—I have been mad—but I am mad no longer. It was a dream—it was all a horrid, wicked dream—nothing but a dream. Why am I not at home?" starting suddenly up. "What am I about?—Why am I not at home? Mr. Hervey, do take me home! He is coming,—where am *I*?"

"Will you go home, my dear Mrs. Vivian?" said Laurence, repressing with a violent effort his own emotions. "Will you go home? Indeed you had better. Let me call a coach."

But the transient delirium was already over. "You would take me *home*, then," with a look of withering contempt. "You would take the empty casket back to your friend. Offer him the worthless withered rose that you have rifled;—a fit present for an honourable man. You would take me *home*?"

"Alas! Iñez, what is it you say? I would do anything, everything—I would die at your feet—I would endure every torture that the ingenuity of barbarity could devise—I would be torn to pieces—only, my Iñez, to serve you, and to help you."

"Would you, Laurence?—I know you would. Forgive me—I spoke in my agony—I never intended to reproach you. Forgive me!"

Laurence burst into tears.

"That is right. Yes, let us sit down in the dust and weep. Yes, let us fall down on the earth—let him trample us under his feet—Harry!—Harry!"

She sat down on the ground, and Laurence by her side: and there, like that guilty pair, who opened the gates of sin and death on this dark world, sat those two creatures formed for excellence and for light—cowering on the earth, their faces buried in their hands, weeping and groaning aloud.

XIII

Eight o'clock was striking on St. Margaret's as Captain Vivian's carriage-and-four dashed up Whitehall. The horses seemed to participate in the impatience of the traveller. They turn sharply—they stop, foaming and smoking at the well-known door. He flung open the carriage, ran up his steps, knocked with his own brief sharp knock. His heart was beating—his action hurried—his dress dusted and disordered by his rapid journey— heat, and toil, and weariness were in his aspect—his beautiful hair was matted about his temples. The door opens.

"Well, John! How's all at home?"

And without waiting for an answer, or casting a look upon the servant, he sprang up stairs and entered the drawing-room hastily.

"My Iñez!"

But no Iñez replied; the cold formal figure of Miss Vivian presented itself, with that solemn, gloomy air of woe, that dark funereal aspect which, at the first glance, "foretells the nature of a tragic volume."

He was so struck with consternation that he almost fell, as, stumbling forwards, he hastily exclaimed,—

"My sister!"

"*Your sister*, Harry," said she, in grave accents.

"And Iñez,"—glancing round the room with an eye of horror—"and Iñez—Almighty God—tell me the worst at once!"

"She is not here."

"Tell me the worst," seizing both her hands and looking in her face. "What is it? Your countenance is dreadful—but your clothes," glancing rapidly downwards. "I thank my God," with a loud cry, "she is not *dead*!"

Miss Vivian turned away her head—she wept.

"Tell me, sister—she is not dead—ill—very ill—dying—anything but dead. Let me only see her—kiss her—hear her speak once more. I'll bear it all like a man. Only say she is not dead."

"She is not dead," faltered Miss Vivian; "but, oh, brother! think of her no more"—all her virtuous severity returning to her bosom, and hardening even to the very tones of her voice. "You must think of her no more."

"What, in the name of God, do you mean? Think of her no more!—May Heaven blast me when I forget her!"

"You must—you must."

"Must—must—must. Speak out! What horrible ideas do you mean me to entertain? Is she mad? Is she lost? In the name of every thing in heaven—and in *hell*—speak out, speak out."

"Oh, Harry! Harry!"

"Mad!—is she mad?"

"Mad—alas! mad indeed—infatuated, lost! Harry, she has left you—left this house—she is no longer yours—she is gone—she is dishonoured—she is another's." There was time for no more—

Captain Vivian uttered a sharp cry, sprang from the earth as if a musket-shot had entered his heart, and fell down senseless on the floor.

At six o'clock, when dinner had been served, a vain search had been made for Mrs. Vivian. She was not in her own room. She was sought in the nursery—in every corner of the house—in vain. The open letter which lay upon her dressing-table was at length brought into the drawing-room, by nurse, a grave respectable woman, between forty and fifty.

"Where can your mistress be, nurse?"

"Madam, this letter was lying open upon the dressing-table."

"Good Heavens!" looking at the letter, "my brother will be here in two hours. Where can she be gone to? Did she say she was going out—and not to know. She is gone out to the Sullivans, I dare say—and Harry will be back. How provoking that she did not get the letter!"

"Madam, she did get the letter—it is *open*," said nurse, expressively.

"It is impossible. How could she leave the house? She cannot be so wild as to be gone to meet him."

"Not to *meet* him," said the nurse, with emphasis.

"Nurse," said Miss Vivian—now for the first time looking up, and perceiving in the servant's face a look which said, *question me*,—"Nurse, do you know where your mistress is?"

"I can't pretend to say, madam—but I fear. Oh! Miss Vivian"—and the poor woman, turning away, covered her face with her apron—"I am not fit to be put upon to tell you, ma'am, but we have all had our suspicions some time. It is not fit for such as us to judge our betters—but servants are not stocks and stones. We must see—we cannot help seeing—oh! if it had pleased the Almighty first to darken my eyes."

"Good heavens," said Miss Vivian, shaking from head to foot, "what do you mean?"

"Mr. Hervey—ma'am—he came too much to this house." Miss Vivian was frigid—but she was not, as poor nurse said, a stock or a stone. She turned very sick at this, and fell into a chair, almost fainting. At last she articulated:

"Take care what you say."

"Ah, madam," said nurse, the tears rolling fast down her cheeks, "such a sweet young lady!—and my poor—poor master."

"Sweet young lady!" with indignation—"such an abominable wretch—such a cold blooded—vile hypocrite.—Your poor master!—poor, indeed!—but tell me what you suspect?" Nurse then, in broken accents, told her story—that oft-repeated tale of domestic guilt, which, concealed from every other eye, is detected by those important though secondary personages in the human drama, who, standing somewhat aloof from the game their superiors are playing—discern its bearings and its progress with so just a penetration!

"And we are afraid, madam," she added, sobbing—"that my master's return it is, has driven my mistress from her blessed home—poor creature—poor creature!"

"Where to?"

"To the Albany—to Mr. Hervey's, John supposes—but he said he would step and see, to make sure for, good Lord Almighty! if we wrong her!"

"God grant it!"

At this moment John entered the room—he looked pale—he was out of breath—"*She is there*," was all he said—and hastily shutting the door, he ran down stairs, and, locking himself into his pantry, cried as if his heart would break.

Far were these honest servants from showing the malignant, envious triumph of inferiors in their mistress's fall. Though their servile situation—though their too often base acquaintances—though their innumerable temptations have a tendency morally to degrade this class of society, beyond any other removed from the most abject want—yet, in worthy and honourable families, servants will be found to be generous in their feelings, and with a certain dignity of behaviour which becomes them well.

The servants of Harry and his Iñez had seen nothing in their superiors, before the last fatal weeks, but uprightness, sincerity, truth, and honour;—had experienced nothing but gentle restraint and unvarying kindness. They doted on their master and mistress, and took each a dependant's honest pride in their graces, their charms, and their virtues:—they had deplored unfeignedly the errors they suspected—and, with something of the grossness of their rank, had most fervently hoped they would never be found out—and even now, the aim of the good nurse—her last hope— was that scandal might be avoided, and Mrs. Vivian recovered, before her husband should return.

"You see how it is, ma'am," said she. "She is there: but if you would please to let me call a coach, and just put yourself and little darling Miss Georgy in, I think she would hear reason and come back, may-be—and all would be well again."

"Hear reason—and all be well again!" said Miss Vivian, the coldness of injured pride now overpowering all softer emotions. "No, nurse—she has chosen to leave my brother's roof—where she has taken refuge, there let her remain—I, at least, will not enhance his dishonour by endeavouring to conceal it from him."

"Yet, madam—"

"Not a word more—you may leave the room now—take care the children do not come down till I have seen my brother first, alone;" and she sat down in dignified silence, to await his coming.

Long was it before the injured husband recovered to a sense of his miseries—long, like one dead, did he lie stretched on the sofa, while his faithful servants, their eyes streaming with tears, endeavoured vainly to recall him to life. Nurse held his pale head, bathing his temples: the man-servant chafed his hands—Miss Vivian stood by, gazing like one half stupid, half vexed. The very excess of his grief irritated her—she thought it a tribute too great to be paid to the fallen Iñez.

At last he opened his eyes with a glazed, staring look, and fixed them on the swollen countenance of nurse:—

"Nurse—where's your mistress?"

"Oh, sir! oh, my poor dear master!"

"Where's your mistress?—where's my Iñez—my own—my Iñez?—my—"

"Nay, brother," said Miss Vivian, coming forwards, "not before them all.—Nurse, you may go—John, I'll ring—your master is better now."

The compassionate servants left the room.

"My brother, disgrace yourself not before your servants:—indignation is the only sentiment worthy of a man of sense and virtue, in such a crisis. She is beneath your regrets—you must forget her—forget her very existence—she is a vile—degraded—"

"Hold, for God's sake, Miss Vivian," cried her brother, for the torture of such words was insupportable—"I shall bear my affliction, I trust, like a man—but don't abuse her—don't blame her—don't—don't—my dear Isabella," and he covered his face with his hands.

Miss Vivian stood cold and silent by. Characters of her stamp never know what to do when feelings burst those conventional bounds of ordinary propriety, in which their own are content for ever to dwell—the poignant grief of Captain Vivian excited her surprise and anger. That he ought to be entirely absorbed in indignation and contempt—that he ought to dismiss such a wanton from his heart and thoughts at once—and never suffer himself once to regret the inconstant—was reason enough with her for expecting that he would; and when she found that he did not—but that his anguish at his loss mocked consolation—she found herself quite at fault:—all the common places of consolation, she felt instinctively, would be of no use here—and she knew of no other—while he felt wounded by her manner, and almost irritated by her presence.

At length, after several efforts, he began to put questions, with a sort of desperate hope that he might discover some reason to think that Miss Vivian had been deceived. She answered in that dry clear manner which, while it left no doubt upon his mind, drove him almost to distraction.

"And who?" at length he said—"You have not named him yet—who has robbed me of my treasure?"

"Who but one—but the man you so imprudently trusted—that accomplished French philosopher and sceptic—Mr. Hervey—"

"Mr. who?"

"Laurence Hervey."

"God in heaven!" He had not fainted this time, though he fell back—and as she stepped forward to assist him, he motioned her away.—"Thank you, sister—I think I shall be better left to myself a little.—Will you go to the nursery—and, when I ring, tell nurse to bring my—my—children? Don't come yourself—let me see them alone—don't be displeased, dear Isabella, don't be angry," as she walked rather cold out of the room, chilled by that barbarous self-love which in the awful presence of extreme misery can still be personal—full of the virtue of its own attentions—offended when they are not acknowledged with gratitude—and expecting consideration and respect amid the rackings of agony.—"Don't be angry with me—" How humble, how gentle, is extreme sorrow!

In ten minutes the drawing-room bell rang—the door opened—nurse put the children into the room, and instantly retired, leaving them alone with their father.

"Papa!—papa! dear, sweet papa!—are you come home?"

"My little ones!—my little ones!"

Their arms were round his neck. "Where's mamma?—where's mamma?" cried the youngest—"She wants you so—where's mamma?"

"My child—my child—don't—don't—she's gone—she's gone for ever.—Oh God!"—and clasping his children to his bosom, tears at last gushed forth, wetting their little innocent bosoms, while they loaded him with their affectionate caresses.

"Don't cry—she'll come back—she's only just gone—she'll come back, I am sure," said the little one, endeavouring to console him, in her usual busy way.

But Florence buried her face in her father's breast, and her tears mingled fast and silently with his; while her beautiful hair fell over the arm which pressed her to his aching heart.

It was past nine o'clock before Captain Vivian had recovered sufficient composure to reflect upon his situation. The children having left him, he remained alone, and his steps might be heard, with melancholy cadence, pacing his deserted drawing-rooms—those apartments which had been to him as the shrine of a divinity, and as the temple of happiness, the abode of perennial, never-fading joy—now dark and solitary—the walls, once brilliant with the abundant evening lights, and echoing to the cheerful prattle of his lovely wife and joyous children—now silent and gloomily overshadowed by the closing evening which fell ominous, heavy, and cloudy, after the bright splendours of the preceding day. Large masses of shade lay on the walls, as twilight gradually deepened into night, wrapping that scene of former joy in silent gloom;—but Captain Vivian called for no lights:—the uncertain gleams from the lamps, as successively lighting, they shed their twinkling fires—or the flashing light of some rapidly passing carriage, fell upon that figure traversing the gloom, with folded arms and head bent upon the breast, the very image of despondency.

He was reflecting upon what he ought to do. In the excess of his grief, there was scarcely a place left for indignation—genuine sorrow is a gentle, a humbling feeling.

Harry Vivian had in secret always cherished that sense of his own want of merit, which attends upon the most refined and feeling minds—a mark, at once, of the purity and of the delicate perceptions of a taste too refined to acquiesce in those imperfections which attend upon all—but which most are too gross, or too vain to perceive in themselves. He felt no wounded pride, no exasperating sense of ill usage. He was utterly absorbed in grief over the ruin of so much innocence and happiness. Yet, with the feelings habitual to him as a gentleman and a military man, almost the first defined idea that presented itself, after the first paroxysm of grief had subsided, was that of demanding such satisfaction as the code of honour requires for injuries of this nature;—and to call Laurence to an account appeared to him but as the natural, inevitable consequence of what had been done—a consequence to which it was not necessary to be led by any extraordinary feeling of rage or indignation.

The treachery of Laurence, in truth, excited but a slight feeling in his mind. Had he loved him as he once had done, no doubt there would have been more violence of exasperation in his sensations;—but it must be confessed that the devoted passion inspired by Iñez, had, in some measure, weakened the force of earlier attachments.

At length the drawing-room bell was heard to ring through that house of mourning, where all had been, for some time, silent as death.

"Bring me a candle," said Captain Vivian, as the door opened, "and, John, go and find out where Captain Sullivan is—you will learn at the Admiral's. Ask him to come to me—tell him I could not write"—putting his hand to his head, and clearing from his brow and jaded countenance that hair which once blew so lightly round it, and which already hung in the dingy faded masses of sickness and neglect.

The servant soon returned with a candle, as his master had desired, and putting it on the table, where its faint glimmers served only to enhance the lonely melancholy of the apartment, departed on his mission.

Captain Vivian glanced once round, and then, with a deep sigh, sat down to write. What he had to do was soon finished: he folded his letter without reading it over, and, with a slight shudder, wrote the address—"Laurence Hervey, Esquire."

This was just done when the light step of Captain Sullivan was heard on the stair—he hastily opened the door. This was no moment for conventional greetings:—Vivian rose to meet him—the friends were in each other's arms.

"My dear fellow," was all that Sullivan could say, for his heart was too full for words.

Vivian pressed his hand without speaking, and sat down to recover himself.—At length—"You know what has happened?"

"I do."

"And why I sent for you to-night?"

"I suppose so."

"I am very unfit to act for myself, Sullivan," passing his hand languidly across his eyes:—"you will arrange things for me— time—place—it is all indifferent to me—the sooner the better, that is all.—Will you go there to-night?"

"Most certainly I will (The damned scoundrel)," aside.— "Have you written?"

"Yes, here it is—will you take it, or send it?"

"I'll call with it, and send it up—so think no more about *that*—I'll settle it all for you—but Vivian—good God, how ill you look! You had better go to bed and rest yourself for a few hours—indeed you had better, before morning."

"No, I would rather be here," pressing his hand again upon his forehead—"I shall recover in a few hours.—The shock," and his manly lips trembled, "the shock has been great, Sullivan—but I shall be more composed by and by when all this is done—it will be a relief:—will you go then?"

"Yes, directly—but can I do nothing more for you first?"

"No—come back as soon as you can, my good fellow."

Captain Sullivan was gone.

XIV

THE servant opened the door of the room where Laurence and Iñez were still sitting, in that sort of stupid disconsolate gloom which succeeds to passionate anguish, exhausted, but not relieved by its own vehemence.

"Here is a note, sir, for you—and a gentleman waits."

Laurence took it; but when the address met his eye, he became very pale—the colour fled even from his lips—an universal shiver ran through his frame—his hands trembled—he could scarcely open the letter.

Iñez saw his emotion and guessed its cause, and rising hastily from her chair she crossed the room—grasped the quivering hands of Laurence earnestly in hers—fixing her eyes wildly on his face.

"You never will meet him," she said in a shrill and ghastly tone—"you will not—you dare not—you cannot come to me covered with his blood—with Harry's blood—I am not like that wicked woman you once told me of, am I? will you come to me covered with his blood?"

"My Iñez, what is it you say?—his blood!"—shuddering.

"No, no, you will not meet him—you will not—you could not—you dare not—say you will not—say you will not."

"Alas! my Iñez—you know I must."

"Must! Good Heavens!" casting his hands suddenly away—"You will dare to look him in the face?—you will dare to point a pistol at his heart? that heart!—monster!"

"Oh, Iñez, some pity even for me! Some pity for a wretch, a lost, damned, miserable wretch," cried Laurence, writhing with agony. "You do not think—you cannot think me, such an accursed rascal.—If you do!—Oh, eternal Judge, strike me dead at her feet now! I am punished enough."

"Then you will not meet him," again advancing eagerly—"you will not heap injury on injury—tell me you will not, Laurence."

"Laurence! … I will not if you bid me not—I will be trampled upon—spit upon—shamed—disgraced—scouted—abhorred of men, as reprobate of God—I will do all you tell me:—yet, consider, Iñez—it is a satisfaction that I owe him—it is the last atonement I can make:—he ought to have the poor amends of aiming at this miserable breast—but, may I perish eternally, if I could point at his—No, let me meet him—if he strike me, all the better for every one—I shall not return his fire.—Could you, Iñez—utterly as you despise me—for one moment believe that I would?"

She turned away, melted at this—"You are right, Laurence. I see you ought to go."

He went down stairs without saying more, and found Sullivan in the dining-room, waiting for him.

The cold, distant politeness—the icy ceremony—with which that young officer received him, did more to sink Laurence in his own opinion than all which had yet passed. Though properly more a man of science than a man of the world, and belonging to that division of society which dwells rather in the regions of speculation and philosophic inquiry, than of action and manly communication—he felt acutely the censure which the manner of the usually frank and thoughtless seaman conveyed. That he had offended the laws of morals, and despised those of religion, might perhaps have sat lightly on them both;—but he had betrayed confidence—he had outraged those rules of honour, by which men of honour are governed—and his eye quailed before that of one, whom, a few weeks before, he would have considered his inferior in every respect.

It is common with moralists to disparage this sense of honour, perhaps without sufficient reflection. The law of honour is, after all, a noble rule of action in that exact regard to obligations enforced by no other power, in that detestation of all that is mean, treacherous, and designing—and, in the generous contempt of life, which it demands, it lays hold of, and cherishes some of the best principles of our nature; and it may be questioned whether the cold injunctions of what may be thought a more reasonable system be so favourable to the growth of energetic and generous sentiment, as this wilder, and more heroic law.

Captain Sullivan drily and briefly explained the purport of his visit; and, expressing Captain Vivian's desire that the meeting might take place as soon as possible, proposed early in

the morning of that day, now rapidly approaching, and asked
Laurence to name some friend with whom preliminaries might
be arranged. Laurence named a Mr. Trevor, to whom he instantly
despatched a note; and having, in a nervous, agitated manner,
signified his acquiescence in Captain Vivian's desire of an early
meeting, the gentlemen separated.

"A coward as well as a rascal," muttered Sullivan to himself, as
he left the Albany. But there he was mistaken. Laurence, though
he wanted energy, was insensible to fear. It was the conscience
within—that voice which, sooner or later, will make itself
heard—which vanquished him.

XV

WHEN Captain Sullivan had departed, Laurence, exhausted by all that had passed, remained in that state, vulgarly, but expressively, denoted by the term, more dead than alive. A kind of stupid insensibility had succeeded to that rapid succession of feelings so unusual to him. The sudden catastrophe—the rapidity with which all seemed hurrying to a conclusion—the confusion of various sensations—the shame, the remorse, the pity, and the love, which agitated him by turns—produced a hurry of thought foreign to his usual habits of analysis and reflection. He did not return to the room where he had left Iñez, but remained in gloomy abstraction, awaiting the arrival of Mr. Trevor, who at last made his appearance.

Mr. Trevor was a tall dark man, with that sort of lengthened grave countenance, which seems incapable of reflecting the expression of joy or pleasure; yet, though its character was severe and ascetic, it was neither harsh nor stern; and, with no follies nor vices of his own to regret or blush for, Trevor knew what it was to pity the infirmities of others. His connection with Laurence had been rather that of an intimate acquaintance than of a friend; for Laurence was, as is usual with refined and fastidious characters, slow in forming attachments, and perhaps had never in his life loved, warmly, any friend, but Captain Vivian: he had applied to Trevor as the man he most esteemed amongst his intimates, and now received him without any of that embarrassing sense of disgrace which had marked his meeting with Captain Sullivan.

We all feel that there is something in reflection and experience which, though it does not abate the detestation of sin, very considerably increases compassion for sinners. Those who know, and think, and observe much, find in their own hearts, and in the conduct of those around them, but too many reasons for pitying, as human frailties, the excesses of human passions—learning to regard the errors of their fellow-men with melancholy, rather than with anger; while in the direct open abhorrence of more simple minds, the culpable seem to see some slight reflection of that purer eye—that eye too pure to behold evil—and tremble at the prospect of their own deformities.

Mr. Trevor, however, looked extremely grave, though kind, when he entered the room, and shook Laurence by the hand, with little of his usual cordiality.

"I relied upon your kindness," said Laurence, "and I applied to you, as the only man I know, who, while he condemns me as he ought, can still feel for my situation.—This is no common case, to excite a smile on the face of a man of the world. My guilt has been great. I have betrayed confidence, double confidence— nor should I have asked you to go out with me, except as one desirous to make the only expiation in his power. You will of course conclude I mean to stand his fire, and not return it."

"I concluded so. Under the circumstances, I agree with you—it is the only thing to be done. Who is this second?"

"Sullivan. Will you go to him?—And will you provide me with pistols?—I am so little used to the sort of thing—I scarcely know whether I ever had a pistol in my hand since I left Harrow. I never was engaged in an affair of this kind, either as second or principal. I am ignorant of all the etiquette of these matters. You will confer a very *serious*—I was going to say, *lasting*—(with a faint laugh) obligation upon me, if you will instruct me, and arrange for me—so that the last act of a worthless and useless life shall at least not be disgraceful."

"Certainly. Leave it all to me. Will you have a surgeon?—and who?"

"No, it is not any wish when I fall to have the dying embers of life excited to a momentary sensibility by professional tricks. The sooner all is over with me, the better—the better for me—the better for all."

"The better for *you!*" said Trevor very gravely.—"Excuse me—you know I am what is called a serious man. The better for *you!* —I perhaps exceed my province in trespassing on such matters—but you remember what the father of Hamlet laments as the most fearful circumstance of his sudden departure—Unhouselled—unanointed—unannealed—and sent to his account …"

"Oh, as to that I must take my chance."

Mr. Trevor shook his head. "It is an awful chance, Hervey—and permit me to wonder that a man of reflection like yourself can consider it so lightly."

"I have, indeed," cried Laurence, with sudden energy of manner, "miserably wasted the existence that the unknown Power has bestowed. If I am an accountable being—a miserable account have I to render;—if there be a Judge—a wretched criminal must I appear at his bar. I have wasted intellect in vain speculations;—I have dreamed away health in indolent self-indulgence—I have abused power, for vicious purposes:—the only one I loved, I have ruined—those who loved and trusted me, I have betrayed. I have been more wily than the serpent—more cruel than the beast of prey. I have glided into the chamber of peace, to poison and to destroy. I have entered the fold of the lamb to despoil and to devour. If there be a hell—it is peopled with such as I am! If there be an evil spirit—I am his."

"Yet," said Mr. Trevor, shocked, though affected—"despair is twin brother with blasphemy. The Author of our being has held out the means—a sinner called even at the eleventh hour—repentance—the grace of his Spirit—a change of the inner nature—confidence in a Redeemer—it is never too late."

"It is too soon with me," said Laurence. "I am not old enough—weak enough—doting enough, for all that. Such mystical dogmas are too high for me: if I am worthless, it will please, I presume, the Being who created me, to resume the existence he gave, to restore me to that nothingness whence I sprang. If it please him to continue me in existence, his mercy is surely sufficient—I want none to mediate—I am what I am. No mystical washing can whiten me."

He spoke bitterly—and Mr. Trevor's countenance assumed more than its usual seriousness, tempered however with much gentleness, as he said,—"I have been long convinced, both by reflection and observation, that these things are deep mysteries to a participation in which it pleases our Creator to call some, while he excludes others; else why should the same subject present itself under an aspect so totally different, to men of equally sound minds, and abilities about upon a par?—I thank God I am not of that despairing creed which confines extension of mercy to extension of light. I believe there may be life where there is darkness—I am sorry you cannot think as I do; but I have done. I will now go to Admiral Sullivan's. You will have something to do while I am away. Doubtless there are matters relative to your fortune that should not be neglected; there is an unfortunate person concerned, who may be dependent upon your forethought for a provision. I do not know how that may be—but it should be thought of. You should also get a little sleep; for your looks are so haggard that, without some refreshment of that sort, I doubt whether you will be able to walk to your ground. I remember you at Rome—you were no Hercules."

"Thank you," said Laurence. "If I lay down, I should not sleep—I have done with that, I believe—unless I find it where I hope to find it. I will attend to your other suggestion. Strange it should not have occurred to me before! but, really, the action of this tragedy is so crowded, it admits no time for thought. When will you be back?"

"At four, at latest—we must be early these fine mornings, to escape interruption. Order your carriage at half-past four—but I wish you would try a little rest."

"I shall have it by this time to-morrow. Good night!"

Laurence employed himself in writing till nearly three o'clock; and the only gleam of consolation that soothed his spirit on that dread evening was while thus employed. While endeavouring to provide for the comfort of her he was about to leave, he felt a sweetness mingling with his sorrow. To act for her benefit—to care for—to provide for—to be still in some measure the protector of, Iñez—carried with it a balm to his wounds. Having provided for her in his will, mentioning her in terms the most distant and respectful, he took, for the last time, pen and paper, and, in a farewell letter, poured forth, with that touching and simple eloquence of which he was so fatally the master, the last adieus of a heart, whose devotion exceeded all common powers of description. He exhausted every topic of encouragement and consolation, to reconcile her to an existence of which he himself was weary—to revive her hopes and energies, though himself the victim of hopeless despair. All that reason, tenderness—nay, sophistry—could urge, was exhausted, to reconcile to peace that heart which he had set at so cruel variance with itself.

Having somewhat composed his thoughts by this occupation, his feelings took an unexpected turn, and he began to reflect, for the first time, with remorse, and with a return of his former partial affection, upon his injured friend. Harry, in all the ingenuous simplicity, the generous confidence, of his nature, rose before him, and tears gushed over the paper on which he confessed his injuries, and asked a late forgiveness:—those first honest tears of repentance and humility—the first which ever had fallen from his eyes, seemed to open the frozen springs of grace within his heart. Softened and humbled, the pride of reasoning intellect at length gave way; and, as Laurence called upon God to bless his friend, and compensate him for all the misery he himself had occasioned, he felt that there was a God—he trembled and he adored.

A calm now succeeded to the paroxysms of anguish. He rose to prepare for his departure; and, having arranged his dress, and placed his hat and gloves ready, with that sort of slow deliberation with which we sometimes retard a moment ardently desired—he opened the door to take a last parting look at Iñez.

He stole slowly up stairs. All was still as death through the apartments. His servant had been long abed; and only the click of his time-piece, on the stairs, was to be heard through that strange silence of universal repose which wraps the Great Babylon at that hour. He opened the door very softly, hoping to find her asleep—he was not disappointed. Exhausted by suffering, and still retaining so much of her blissful infancy, as to find sleep a refuge from acute distress, the unhappy Iñez lay stretched upon a very low couch that stood at the end of the room. Her cloak was wrapt in large folds round her form, but her hat had fallen on the ground beside her, and her dark raven hair fell, dishevelled and disordered, over her face and shoulders. Her cheeks were pale, soiled, and blistered with her tears—her long eye lashes, yet wet and matted—her arms, thrown in the negligent despondency of one who, having flung herself down in despair, has, weary with weeping, been surprised by slumber; and so had it been—the idea of the duel had stupified the remaining senses of lñez.

The first desperate agony with which the idea of her husband's danger had been contemplated, having yielded to the assurances of Laurence, had been succeeded by a sort of confused horror, as the thought of his own probable fate rose to her mind. Death, pale and ghastly, mingled its shadows with her other cruel reflections:—yet, looking upon this as a sort of sacrifice and atonement for their mutual sin, she contemplated it rather with melancholy awe than with bitterness. Her mind was in that state which seems to demand a victim as compensation for a heavy crime; and her own misery, and the probable fate of her deceiver, appeared to her natural, just, and right.

Yet the weight of that sentence, against which she presumed not to murmur, sank heavily upon her frame; and with that weariness of body, in which the unhappy often find a temporary relief from mental agony, she had stretched herself upon the couch, and heavy with abundant weeping, had fallen asleep.

Laurence, shading the candle with his hand, entered the room, in which there was no light, save what the moon threw in broad masses on the carpet and walls. He scarcely breathed, lest he should disturb her repose; as long, in bitter contemplation, he stood gazing upon this lovely ruin, and learned by cruel experience to know—what are the ravages of sin.

She slept so deeply that he soon became aware that there was no danger of awakening her; and, placing the candle upon the table, he softly let down the curtain to shelter her head from the window, and to shade her eyes from the bright moon-beams that fell in bars of light and darkness over her face, giving a something flickering and unearthly to her features. Then the thought that she might awaken, and find him gone, and feel deserted and perplexed, distressed him; and, taking a scrap of paper that lay on the table, he wrote these few words:—

"Farewell. My friend Trevor will be with you by nine o'clock, at latest. Before that time, you may be able to think without guilt of one, who, guilty or guiltless, living or dying, will never cease to adore you."

He laid the paper near her, where it must inevitably catch her eye on awakening, and then, after many a wistful gaze, many a heavy sigh, many a retreat, and many a return, he summoned all his resolution, and, without looking back, hastily left the room.

XVI

MR. TREVOR was in the dining-room at half-past three, and telling Laurence that it was time to be off, and that he would make him acquainted with the trifling arrangements necessary as they went along. The two gentlemen entered Laurence's cab; and, Trevor taking the reins, they left town by Cumberland Street, and, passing through several cross lanes, found themselves in that lonely part of the way lying between West End and Hampstead, now crossed by the new Finchley road, but then quiet, still, and secluded.

Here, leaving the cab in charge of the boy, Mr. Trevor, taking the pistols out of the carriage, led Laurence, through what were then a few lonely fields, to one, protected from observation by the sudden rising of the bank, surmounted by a wild pear tree, and sheltered on the other side by a high hedge, at this season rendered impervious to the eye by the tangled bushes of wild roses and woodbine that rose, straggling and fantastic, almost to the height of the trees.

The place was at present solitary, and the sacred silence of the rising morning as yet unbroken, save by the busy rustling noise

which the birds, those stirring housewives, make in every bush
and tree, at that sweet hour of prime. The dew lay on the grass
and herbs; and the soft misty veil, which gives earnest in England
of a brilliant day, hung over that magnificent landscape, on which
Laurence, as if taking a last farewell of a world so beautiful, fixed
his melancholy eye.

Beneath him stretched the glorious plain, rich with woods,
and hills, and champaigns, and groves, the magnificence of
nature enhanced by the splendours of that vast and gorgeous
city, which now spread to the glittering beams of the rising sun
its innumerable fanes, and towers, and domes, and sparkling lines
of snow-white palaces; that vast hive of living creatures, each
so minute, so feeble in his form, yet in his world of sensations
and of thoughts so vast, so important, so infinite. But now the
restless tumult of human passion within the pulses of that mighty
heart was still—at rest after the vain agitations of the day—all
still—save the speck, the atom, the worm, now crawling on the
extreme verge of existence, hesitating, speculating, marvelling;
such was the reverie of Laurence, as with folded arms he stood,
calmly waiting the moment of his fate, while Mr. Trevor, with an
air of deep concern, remained watching the path by which he
expected Captain Vivian to approach.

"I see them coming," at last, he said.

But at those few syllables, all the calmness of Laurence forsook
him in an instant—the blood rushed to his heart—the colour
flew into his face—he trembled—he shook—he could scarcely
stand—the reality of actual presence—to see!—to face!—Harry!—

Vivian!—the man he had loved—the man he had betrayed—to meet him—to confront him!—It is impossible to calculate the effect which the sudden appearance of one we have wronged, suddenly presented, will produce. Few dare attempt the ordeal—all fly instinctively from the face of those they have injured—but so to meet a friend!—All the circumstances of their last parting—Harry's wringing hand and faltering voice—the tender accents in which he confided his all, to the faith of his friend:—the looks—the words—his own solemn oaths—his own faltering purposes—rushed to his mind with that dreadful force with which we may imagine our forgotten sins, our obliterated acts of wrong—our carelessly atoned for errors—crowding in confusion on the memory, as we stand in trembling agitation before the awful bar of final judgment.

Harry approached steadily and calmly:—his eye was serene, serious, yet mild—his face pale:—a sudden hectic passed over it, as he first looked upon Laurence, but as suddenly subsided. He came forward, followed by Captain Sullivan; and, having exchanged salutes with Mr. Trevor, remained without suffering himself to be mastered by any external sign of emotion, while the seconds arranged the few necessary preliminaries.

Not so Laurence—he had turned away.

> He could not endure the sight to see,
> Of the man he had loved so fervently.

His heart was indeed wrung—and great was his difficulty, so far to retain his self-possession as to forbear from groaning aloud:—all the softness of the mother melting in his bosom, he longed to fling himself upon the earth, to kneel before his friend, confess his fault, and implore his pardon;—he longed to crawl in the dust, and kiss his feet with all the abjectness of remorse and shame.

He stood thus—his breast heaving, as if it would burst—his breath thickening—his frame shaking, when Mr. Trevor touched him on the shoulder, and, presenting the pistol, told him to turn and face his adversary.

"The dropping of my handkerchief is the signal," said he; but Laurence listened as though he heard not:—his eyes were dizzy—his head swam—he fumbled with his pistol instead of holding it as he ought to have done.

"This way," said Trevor. Laurence turned, as it were, mechanically—his knees knocked together—his hands, as if in a spasm, suddenly contracted: the pistol was a hair trigger, and, as he raised his arm convulsively, it exploded … a loud report … and Vivian dropped senseless on the grass at his feet.

Laurence clapped his hands over his forehead, and with a shriek that rang through the heavens, fell down upon his knees, and thence tumbling forwards, rolled over towards the hedge, while Trevor and Sullivan sprang forwards to assist the wounded man.

The face was one mass of blood—the head seemed shattered in pieces:—the two young men, almost insensible with horror, could at first only kneel down simultaneously on each side of the body. Captain Vivian was, to all appearance, dead. He lay extended on the turf—his hat off—his fair hair scattering on the ground—a miserable, mangled spectacle.

Sullivan's tears streamed warm over the insensible countenance of his friend; while Trevor, more composed, though not less affected, lifted the hand which lay by his side, and began to feel for a pulse.

"He breathes yet," said he, at length. "He is not dead!"

"What a cursed thing we have no surgeon!" said Sullivan. "What must be done?"

"Fetch some water in your hat: there is a stream in the next field—and then run for help!"

When the water was thrown in the unhappy Vivian's face, he uttered a low groan, like one in mortal pain, who is insensible to every other sensation. Trevor, then, with a fortitude which vanquished the repugnance of nature, endeavoured to ascertain the extent of the injury. The eyes, and upper part of the face, presented nothing but a disfigured mass; and the blood was welling fast from the ghastly wound.

"We must send for a surgeon before we move him.—Hampstead is not far.—Leave him with me, while I endeavour to stanch the blood, and keep life in.—You fly for help."

Sullivan was off instantly, while Trevor, placing himself on the grass, endeavoured to abate the flow of blood, as best he might. He was thus engaged, when, lifting up his head, a spectre suddenly confronted his sight. Haggard—stiffened—his hair erect—stood the form of Laurence Hervey.

"Is he dead?" said he, in a hollow tone.

"No," said Trevor. "Hervey, I saw it all. You are the most unhappy wretch that ever the Almighty has been pleased to create—but for this you are not to blame. What do you intend to do?—you must not stay here."

"Why not?"

"There is no knowing—this is an ugly business:—it would drive you mad to be confined for weeks, like a wild beast, in a cage, waiting the decision of nature—gnawing your own heart-strings. Be guided by me—return to that place—wait till I can tell you some thing more certain of the result of this most cruel affair—I will come to you!"

"I don't know," said Laurence, in a stupid, confused tone, "what it is you want me to do. I don't clearly see what all this is about," and looking as if he were rooted to the spot, while he turned his head in a strange unmeaning manner from one side to the other.

"You must go, and sit down there," said Trevor, with authority, pointing to a corner of the field, "and wait till I come to you."

"Yes," said Laurence, "I understand;" and, seeming to obey the external impulse, something in the manner of a sleep-walker, he returned to the hedge-bank, and, sitting down, buried his face in his knees, in a stupid, idiotical manner.

The surgeon soon arrived. He found the unfortunate Captain Vivian apparently recovering some little sensibility; for he shrank, and gave signs of suffering, on his wounds being touched. After a careful examination, the surgeon gave it as his opinion, that, though presenting a very alarming appearance, none of the

wounds were of necessity mortal. The pistol had exploded, as
Captain Vivian, in the act of turning, presented a side face to
Hervey's fire, and the ball, which otherwise must have penetrated
the brain, had shattered the cheek-bones and brow, leaving the
vital parts untouched. The total destruction of the eyes appeared,
however, to be the probable consequence of the injury; but on
this it was impossible yet to decide.

The first thing to be done was to convey Captain Vivian,
nearly exhausted through loss of blood, as quietly as possible to
the nearest place where he could be put to bed;—and Sullivan,
having summoned the servants from the carriages, and made a
sort of litter of the cushions, with the help of Trevor, assisted the
men to lift him from the earth; and, followed by the surgeon, the
melancholy procession set forward, towards West End.

But before he left the ground, Trevor, the moment the surgeon
had pronounced the wounds not to be mortal, had stepped to the
place where the wretched Laurence still sat, his face buried in his
hands; and having informed him that he trusted no irremediable
injury had been sustained, he, with the greatest kindness,
endeavoured to soothe the agitated mind of his friend, for whose
reason he began to entertain the most serious apprehensions.

Laurence, who had somewhat recovered from the distracting
confusion of thought into which be had at first been thrown,
listened to his remonstrances, and, endeavouring to collect his
scattered senses, suffered himself at length to be put into his cab;
and Trevor, having written an address and a few lines on the
back of a letter, and enclosed his card, gave it to the servant,

desiring him to drive, without stopping, to town, and, by the least frequented streets, carry his master to the place designated.

"You will find a very old acquaintance of mine there—and at his house you will lie *perdu* a short time, till we see a little better before us:—I will come to you as soon as I possibly can."

Laurence grasped his hand, put his face close to his ear, and whispered:—"Iñez."

"I understand you—I will go to her the instant I return to town—I will take care of her."

"God bless you!" said Laurence, fervently, and throwing himself back in the cab, he shut his eyes, and passively allowed himself to be guided at the discretion of his servant.

XVII

WHEN Trevor returned to the field, he found the surgeon arranging the cushions for his patient's departure—and he directed the gentlemen and servants so to place their arms as to form a sort of bier; but, in spite of every precaution, it was impossible to move Vivian without apparently occasioning the most intolerable agony. His groans were terrible, for he had not yet sufficiently recovered his senses to master or conceal these symptoms of pain; he, however, was carried down into West End: but here his sufferings were so great, and the flow of blood, bursting out afresh, so alarming, that they laid him down in utter despair, where the different roads meet.

It was still so early, that no one appeared to be stirring in the neighbouring houses: but as they hesitated whether to summon some of the inhabitants, and ask to be taken in, or what other course to pursue, the green gate of a small garden opened, and an elderly gentleman, whose formal, old-fashioned, air designated the retired tradesman, stepped out, and in a voice where more of the clear treble than of the manly base predominated, and a manner of simpering, and somewhat conceited interest, begged to know whether he could be of any service.

"It appears to me, gentlemen, that you are in distress:—I have been looking at you all the way, as you descended the hill, for I am an early riser, and have been employed in my garden more than an hour. I think there is a wounded gentleman among you."

"Indeed, sir," said Sullivan, "you may well say we are in distress. It is impossible to be in greater: this gentleman can proceed no farther."

"Oh, my stars above! what an awful sight!" exclaimed the old gentleman, approaching nearer. "A very dreadful spectacle—and one never beheld by these eyes afore.—Gentlemen, this poor young man, sadly wounded, as I am alive, is in a desperate condition."

As he slowly dragged out these expressions of commiseration, Sullivan, in his endeavours to do something for his friend, pushed the old man impatiently on one side; but Trevor, looking at a countenance in which he, penetrating and benevolent, could trace lines unremarked by the somewhat exclusive young officer, said,— "Indeed, sir, we are in great distress. This unfortunate gentleman can proceed no farther.—Is there any inn?—public house?"

"No, sir. The inn is a low noisy place, at the corner there—very noisy, dirty, and disorderly, as such places in the vicinage of Lunnun too frequently are;—but I was just going to suggest—when that young gentleman—a very young gentleman, I believe, pushed me so rudely away—but that was, perhaps, not ill-meant—he was in haste;—I was just going to suggest—there is my own house, gentlemen—the garden and all quite quiet, and surrounded as you see, and at a great distance from the road.—I have a well-aired bed in my best chintz room—and if the gentleman could make himself easy there—why he is very welcome to all my poor little matters."

Trevor glanced rapidly at the cold, precise, yet kind and worthy countenance, of the old-fashioned citizen, then at the surgeon.

"By all means on earth," said Mr. Hart. "There is no other chance of life."

"Sir," said Sullivan, turning round suddenly, and taking the old man's hand, "I thank you as if you had saved my own life—and honour you as my father.—Pray let us not lose a moment of time, but get my unfortunate friend to thy chintz bed—thou worthy good Samaritan."

"This way, gentlemen," with an air of most patronising self-consequence—"through this small gate—stay, there is a coach road. Let me undo my great gates, as I call them.—Plenty of room, as you see, gentlemen—though carriages seldom enter, on account of my gravel walk. One likes to see a place a little in order. Pray, gentlemen, walk in. Is it to the chintz room you would wish to go? Stay till I have ordered Biddy to lay on sheets.—Quite right, sir—not wait—this way—up stairs—somewhat narrow for a villa of this respectability. That will do—lay him down. Pray don't regard soiling the counterpane. What's a counterpane in a matter of life and death? Do you think he will be well here, sir?" to the surgeon, who, busily employed about his patient, heeded not his loquacious host, to whom Trevor took upon himself to reply.

"We cannot be better:—it is impossible to express our sense of your hospitality.—If it be possible to save his life, you have done it, sir."

And Sullivan—"God bless you, sir—God bless you, sir;" while the old man bridled, and looked modest.

It was well he had been so magnanimous about his counterpane, which was soon soaked with blood, large drops of which had fallen upon the carpet of pink and green roses. This last mischief, the old gentleman, stooping down, endeavoured to remedy with his pocket handkerchief; but, finding he only made things worse, he straightened himself again with a generous "No matter," and then, on hospitable thoughts intent, bustled out of the room to commune with Biddy on the subject of breakfast.

The gentlemen now busied themselves with arranging their patient in all the comforts which a capital down bed, well stuffed mattresses and pillows, could afford. Biddy soon appeared with sheets. The curtains, flaunting with the gaudiest colours, were arranged; the blind of the bow-window let down, and the chamber assumed an air of perfect comfort and quietness.

It was now decided that while the surgeon and Sullivan remained at West End, Trevor should proceed with all possible haste to town, and summon that distinguished surgeon, Mr. X., to attend upon Captain Vivian; his injuries, it was plain, being of a nature to require the assistance of the most consummate skill and experience.

As Trevor entered the little lobby, he was met by his host:—

"Well, sir, what news of our patient? Does he find himself somewhat more comfortable?—And shall you gentlemen be ready for breakfast? I think you must be impatient for something. I suppose you are more than usual early this morning. You fashionable gentlemen seldom are out of your beds before one or two o'clock, I am told. I fear it was for no good you were out at this time. A *jewel* (duel) I guess, or rencounter of that nature. Well, well, I ask no questions—quite discreet. But my stars, sir, where are you going? This way to the breakfast-room, for I have three rooms on this floor, besides offices."

"I thank you, sir," said Trevor, "but I must be away to London."

"Well, but one cup of tea—hissing hot—all ready."

"One cup of tea, then—and thank you, sir," said Trevor, whose lips and throat were husky and parched. Having drank it, he was in Vivian's cab; and a few minutes brought him to Old Burlington Street.

The servants were just opening the shutters; and a slip-shod housemaid, in that sooty dishabille in which it is the good pleasure of London housemaids to perform their labours, that dark envelope, from which, at the hour of noon, the future butterfly emerges in all the elegance of lace and ribands; and a lounging, powdered, fine gentleman of a footman, with hose ungartered, and knee straps hanging about his knees, were the only living creatures to be seen.

The master of the house was yet in his bed-room, from which without any unusual signs of hurry, the livened fine gentleman proceeded to dislodge him;—the battered and dusty cab, at the door—the heated horse—and the hurried and disordered air of Trevor, denoting nothing sufficiently aristocratical to warrant extraordinary hurry. Trevor forbore to send up his card; but, becoming impatient, he left the room into which he had been ushered: and finding the man cleaning the splendid lamp in the hall, asked hastily when Mr. X. would be ready.

"Can't take upon myself to say!" said the man.

"Did you tell him it was a most urgent case?"

"Upon my word, we have so many urgent cases; and it is very unpleasant for gentlemen of eminence to be worried up and down at every body's command."

"Did you deliver my message?"

"Can't justly recollect whether I exactly delivered the message. Mr. X. seldom has time to listen to long messages: we find it of little use to attempt to hurry him."

"Where is his dressing-room?" said Trevor, who never wasted time by going into a rage. "I will speak to your master myself."

He knocked at the dressing-room door:—"Mr. X!"

"A voice I know!—God bless my soul—Mr. Trevor, can it be you? Why did you not send up your card?"

"I sent up word it was a most urgent and distressing case," said Trevor; "I fancied that might do as well."

"Damn the fellow; he never said a word of the sort—but what is it?—ah, a mystery. Come in while I finish dressing, and tell me all."

The *all* being explained, Mr. X. was as speedy as he had hitherto been dilatory, and, accompanied by Trevor, was soon on the road to West End. Trevor had at first intended to execute, without delay, his painful task of apprising Mrs. Vivian of what had happened, leaving Mr. X. to proceed alone to Hampstead; but, on second thoughts, he determined first to hear the sentence of that eminent surgeon, before he communicated with the unfortunate Iñez. He wished to spare her the racking alternations of hope and fear which she must endure before fresh intelligence could be procured from Hampstead; and he believed that, if, as he had anticipated, the worst should already be over, she had better hear it at once—certain that little could be added to the agony with which the first intelligence of the accident must be received.

When the gentlemen arrived at Mr. Palmer's, they found the blinds down, the passage laid with green baize, and an air of universal stillness pervading the house. Mr. Palmer opened the door himself; saluted them in a whisper; and, stepping upon his toe, led them into his breakfast-parlour, where the surgeon from Hampstead was waiting, whispering, as he trod softly along:—"Quiet—quiet—quiet is every thing!—we shall do very well with quiet. I have ordered Biddy to get list shoes, and would recommend the same to you gentlemen. Your boots creak, begging your pardon, Mr. Drovor.— Well, sir," to Mr. X., "shall we proceed up stairs?"

"Be pleased, sir, to let me speak to this gentleman alone, first," said Mr. X., looking imploringly at Trevor.

"Come," said Trevor, "Mr. Palmer, let you and I have a walk in your garden, and you can tell me all that has happened while we have been away."

"Yes, sir, most assuredly; but I have not seen the unfortunate young gentleman again—that young captain would not allow it. He is wilful, sir; those young gentlemen are so; but a gentleman of your sense and experience knows better. This way—there are three steps—and now you are in my kitchen-garden, as you perceive, sir— garden *potager*, as I understand the French call it. I shall have plenty of fruit this year, though the March frosts and those vile slugs have done me unknownst mischief—"

The opinion of Mr. X. confirmed that of Mr. Hart, the other surgeon. He pronounced none of the wounds to be of necessity mortal: but the laceration of the muscles had been such that he apprehended the most fatal consequences, unless the circumstances of the case should prove favourable in the extreme. With regard to the eye-sight, he refused to decide as to its absolute destruction or not: he however declared that nothing but a care and attention, almost super-human, could preserve it—indeed, nothing but the most unremitting solicitude and skill could afford even a chance for life. With this sentence, and, having given the most minute directions, Mr. X. entered his carriage, to be whirled away from one picture of intense suffering to another; and with that stoicism of habit, the only stoicism to be depended upon, and that indifference to human anguish, which, under other circumstances, would excite our horror, to pass from scene to scene of misery, impassible as the frozen ice, yet administering the relief within his power with an assiduous attention which genuine feeling might vainly emulate. Such are the advantages and disadvantages of habitual exertion in the remedial science. Trevor, who was no surgeon, and had a heart tenderly alive to sympathy, sat by his side a prey to the most distressing feelings, while Mr. X. chatted carelessly away of politics, scandal, and what not; and, stopping at his own door, having vainly invited Trevor to breakfast, ran in to his comfortable meal, preparatory to an appointment for performing one of the severest of surgical operations.

Trevor alighted, and threaded the streets which led to the Albany. The clocks were ringing ten, as he entered it. He was shown in silence up to the room where Mrs. Vivian still remained.

She had found the billet left by Hervey, and had well understood its meaning—and, reading in it, as she thought, a just and inevitable sentence upon them both, she had endeavoured to compose her mind so as to meet with decency that intelligence, the mere anticipation of which froze her veins with ghastly horrors;—but these were no longer the terrors and anxieties of one who loves, for the dangers of the beloved object—no: that illusion had, as by a charm, vanished from her breast—vanished, the first instant she had read her husband's letter.—As from one fascinated by some strange and unnatural influence to evil, the spell had been suddenly broken, and for ever; and all the warm affection she had ever born her husband had been restored in its first intensity—alas! restored too late.

She had anticipated the death of Laurence, rather with that secret horror with which we should contemplate the execution of some malefactor, of whose crime we had furnished the occasion, than with the softness of a dearer feeling; and, looking upon this catastrophe as her own proper punishment, it was her desire so to meet it, as to add no additional disgrace to that heavy load of infamy, which she had prepared for herself and those she loved.

She had therefore risen from her couch; and having arranged her hair in the closest order, smoothed her dress, and wrapped round herself once more the large decent folds of her cloak, she waited in still and patient expectation the striking of that hour mentioned by Laurence.

About eight, a woman servant appeared with tea; she took some, but attempting to swallow a morsel of bread, was nearly choaked: so she contented herself with that effort, and returned to her posture of expectation.

Nine o'clock rang—half past:—in spite of all her efforts, her heart began to beat with rapidity:—ten—she heard some one enter the apartments—the door opened—and Mr. Trevor appeared.

She looked up, while her pulses seemed to suddenly pause.—She could not speak—she could only, by a violent effort, keep upright, and prevent herself from sliding upon the floor.

Trevor approached with a countenance of which he did not even wish to conceal the deep concern.—He wanted to prepare her. He wanted, by the expression of his face, to foretell the nature of the tragical intelligence of which he was the bearer. He sat down by her, hesitating how to begin, or what to say.

She spoke first.

After one or two sighs, and a gathering of the breath—"I know what I have to hear—I am prepared for it. Great criminals should endure, at least in patience, the consequences they have brought upon themselves. You will relieve me by saying that all ended speedily."

"I am afraid—admirable as is your constancy and composure, that you are *not* prepared for what I have to tell—"

"How—there could be but one termination!"

"Mr. Hervey has escaped unhurt."

No triumphant joy shone in her countenance; but she looked relieved and grateful, and, in a very humble voice said, "Then I thank the mercy of God, which has suffered the consequences of my errors to terminate here—it is a very great relief to my mind."

"Alas!" said Trevor, looking ruefully in her face.

"What?" said she, with a searching look, suddenly recovering her energy, and fixing upon him eyes that sparkled with animation— "no—no—I do him injustice—he could not be so cruel."

"There has been a very unhappy accident. By some strange mismanagement, Mr. Hervey's pistol—"

She looked transfixed, with her mouth and eyes staring open.

"Exploded. He is not to blame;—but Captain Vivian—He is still living," cried Trevor hastily.

But, before he could articulate this, she had sunk down upon her knees—wrapped her head in the folds of her cloak, and, burying her face in the cushion of the couch, remained some time motionless.

By her attitude he saw that she had not fainted: indeed, he heard her low, suppressed groanings, and the heavy breathing as of one struggling with herself. He left nature, in this dread moment, undisturbed—and, in about ten minutes, for so long did that mortal agony last, she rose. No tears were on her cheeks—her eyes were dry and stony—a dark, troubled cloud of despair hung over her brow, but she sat down, and said,—

"Will you be so good as to tell me, as tenderly as you can, all that has happened?"

Trevor related, with as much calmness as he could collect, the dismal story, to which the changing colour and varying expression of his auditor responded. She listened with deep attention. When he had concluded, she sank into a reverie of some minutes, and then a soft beam of comfort gradually diffused itself over her still beautiful countenance. Trevor then, in the kindest manner, made proffers of service.

"Your goodness is extreme," said she, "but I believe what I wish to do can be accomplished by myself.—If, however, you will favour me with your card, I will take the liberty of applying to you—should that asylum to which I propose to fly, be closed against me.—If you hear nothing more of me, I shall be, you may rely upon it, in security, and no person need be under anxiety upon my account."

Trevor, looking upon this most lovely creature in so desolate a situation, was with difficulty to be satisfied with such an assurance as this.

"I would not be presuming—but this great city. Have you well considered what you are about to do?—but, no doubt, you have abundance of friends."

"Even yet?" said she with a sigh; "but where I go I shall be perfectly secure. If I do not find myself so, I will apply to you."

Trevor still lingered, but he so plainly detected an ill-suppressed impatience for his departure, that he felt compelled to take his leave, determining to call again in a few hours. He came accordingly at one o'clock, but Mrs. Vivian was already gone.

All he could learn from Hervey's servant, a stupid sort of fellow, was, that she had left the house, in company with his own wife, but that he had not thought of asking what for—and Trevor was obliged to rest satisfied with the slender consolation that, at least, she had not gone away alone.

XVIII

IÑEZ had remained, after Mr. Trevor left her, lost in reflection—yet she seemed not so much stunned as excited by this climax to her misfortunes, and might have exclaimed, with something of the sentiment of Orestes—

Graces aux dieux, mon malheur passe mon espérance.

The picture of her husband—that tender, faithful, injured husband—in consequence of her frailty cut to the earth, mangled, bleeding, helpless, blind, affected her in a manner which would, no doubt, have driven any one possessing a feebler mind, or less elastic nerves, distracted. With her, it produced a determination, force, and energy, more than natural, perhaps, but free from the slightest tincture of mental disorder. To go to him, to wait upon him, to tend him, to save him, became not so much a resolution, as an irresistible necessity—like that which drives the mother through the roaring flames, to snatch away her perishing child. To be near him—to look upon him—to hear him speak once more—appeared a recompense for all she must risk of humiliation and shame in the endeavour: and the persuasion that, if she attended upon him, she should save him, and that no one on earth could render him services, tender and efficacious as hers, can be compared only to what a mother feels, impelled to the sick bed of her child.

But how to carry her scheme into execution, how, unknown, undetected, to steal to Harry's chamber, to obtain the privilege once her own, now so wretchedly forfeited, and, as a stranger, gain permission to perform those services, which, as a wife, no power on earth could have disputed with her!

After sitting some time considering on the means of effecting her wishes, she began to reflect that, like other difficult objects, it would be accomplished only by one way—by the use of that master charm which opens nailed prison doors—unlocks the secrets of the closest hearts—melts the most determined purposes—levels the most obstinate obstructions—by the all-powerful agency of gold.

She put her hand slowly into her purse, to inquire what was the present amount of the worldly wealth of one, who, yesterday, could have commanded hundreds for the most trifling pleasures. What was now the extent of her means to accomplish the most important object of her life? She counted the gold as she poured it into her hand—ten guineas. Would that bribe? Would that persuade? It might afford the means of providing the necessary disguises; but to tempt cupidity—what was it? Then she called to mind the words of Isabel,—

Hark ye—how I'll bribe you—
Not with rich shekels of the tested gold.

She recollected that Mr. X. was a man above corruption, at least, the vulgar corruption of money; and that if she were to succeed with him, it must be by the effect produced on his feelings by her prayers and entreaties; and, with that sanguine persuasion, under which those new to the struggles of this world imagine their energy and their eloquence will bend all to their purpose, she resolved to set forth, without delay, to go to Mr. X., and, offering herself for employment as a nurse for the sick, endeavour to gain permission to attend upon Captain Vivian. She was sanguine enough to believe that she should be successful;—but if difficulties should arise, she determined, in defiance of shame and humiliation, to declare who she was, throw herself upon his mercy, and entreat permission, in humble garb and as a menial attendant, to superintend her husband's recovery.

The first thing to be done was to disguise herself in the dress of the character she intended to personate; and, for this purpose, it was necessary to have clothes;—but her impatience to quit the abode of Laurence would not allow her to think of sending for them, and clothing herself there and to go out alone, traverse London streets, of which, excepting the larger ones, she was as ignorant as a stranger, and provide herself with what she wanted, appeared, at the very outset, an insurmountable difficulty. She now remembered the young woman who had brought up her breakfast. She had been struck with the decent gravity and compassionate gentleness of her demeanour; and she thought she might rely upon a countenance which bore an expression of goodness and purity that rarely deceives. She rang the bell—a thing she had before shrunk from doing in those apartments— but she was now in no temper to regard refinements of delicacy.

When the man servant entered, she, who before had been unable to look up while he happened to be in the room, addressed him, without hesitation, and asked him whether the young woman, who had brought up her tea, was in the house?

"Not exactly," the man answered. "She sometimes came to do needlework for Mr. Hervey, who had ordered her last night to come to attend upon the lady." He added, "She is my wife."

"Is she still here?—and could I see her again?"

"Certainly," said the man, in a grumbling sort of tone. If she required it—but his wife was not hired to wait—and for his part—"

"I will make it well worth her while," said Iñez.

"Oh! doubtless—but it's not exactly the money—"

The colour was now rising fast to the cheeks of the unhappy Mrs. Vivian; but, faithful to her resolution, she humbled herself to shame, and said,—"I should be very much obliged to you, if you would allow her to come to me for a little while—I will pay her whatever you think right, and will not keep her employed long."

The humility of air with which this was said touched even the vulgar piece of insensibility before her.

He should have no objection, if the lady would be pleased to recollect "that certain sort of folks were used to pay better nor other sorts of folks"—and he left the room to send his wife.

The young woman came in with the same air of gentle reserve that distinguished her before.

"I am very much obliged to you for coming," began Iñez in a faltering voice. "I am in very great distress for assistance; and if you will help me to what I want, I will do any thing to serve you, and be grateful to you for ever."

"What is it, madam, that I can do?—I am sure any thing in my power—"

"Will you go out with me, then?—I cannot go through these streets by myself—I want you to get a coach, and take me where I can get some common clothes, such as would suit a maid-servant, before I go to the place where I am to be at—I'm not coming here again—I want to go to service. Do you understand me?"

"I'm very glad to hear you talk so, madam. I will do all in my power to help you—with my husband's leave."

"Certainly, with his leave.—Will you go and ask whether you may go out with me for a few hours?"

She returned with leave. A coach was procured; and Iñez, wrapping her cloak once more closely around her, and tying her hat as low as possible over her eyes, leaning on Mrs. Bell's arm, left the only roof in the world where she had now a right to ask shelter.

They proceeded first to a ready-made clothes shop, where Iñez, having by the way informed her companion that she wished to hire herself out as a nurse for the sick, was, by her advice and directions, soon equipped in a printed gown and very close cap. On looking at herself in the glass, she found, however, that this did by no means disguise her sufficiently: but recollecting some tricks she had played as a girl, with some of those dyes which are to be found on ladies' toilettes, she sent for a bottle, and stained with it her face and hands till they were as swarthy as those of a gipsy. She then, in spite of all Mrs. Bell could say, began to cut off the long sweeping folds of her beautiful hair.

There is a sacredness in this lovely female ornament; and every woman feels as if there were something votive in the act when she sacrifices it. So feels the widow, as she makes this oblation to the memory of departed love;—so feels the devoted nun, as (separating from a world, perhaps too dear,) she severs it before the shrine for which she has forsaken all;—so feels the unhappy penitent, shorn ere she is received to that abode where she is to learn how slow and mournful are the steps she must tread to return—how painful the steep, so rapidly descended;—so felt Iñez, as Magdalene in heart, her beautiful head bowed down by penetrative shame, she severed tress after tress of those silken waves of lustrous black, and remained shorn of her fairest ornament, that mysterious veil which had added such charms to her beauty. She felt that she was performing an act of humiliation, called for by her crime, and which carried with it a far deeper sense than the other degradations to which she had submitted.

When this was done, and the small, delicate head and remaining hair, cut plain over her forehead, was covered by a muslin cap, she felt that she was so altered as to defy common investigation. Her husband's eyes, alas! which she might have found it hard to deceive, could no longer discern those features, once so fondly dwelt upon.

It was about one or two o'clock, when two respectably dressed women knocked at the door of Mr. X's house, and begged to know whether they could see him on business.

The footman, who was now dressed for the day, and was not, on that account, one whit less indolent or less insolent, than he had been at seven in the morning, begged to know their business, and he would see.

"We want very much to see Mr. X., sir," said Mrs. Bell:—"would you be pleased to tell us whether he is at home, or when he is likely to be at home?"

"Good woman, will you be pleased first to tell me *your* business," said the footman, glancing at Iñez, who, in spite of all her pains, carried that in her air which could not be disguised, "and what that strange gipsy-looking young baggage has to say to *my* master. I fancy, young mistress, you have mistaken the house."

"No," said Mrs. Bell. "This house belongs to Mr. X."

"Right, madam, upon my honour—but what do you want with Mr. X?"

"To speak to him."

"On professional business is it?—Then I must tell you, you're too late;—we don't see patients after twelve o'clock—so be pleased to call again—I've turned dukes from this door before now. Mr. X. will *not* be disturbed at this time o'day."

"It is not exactly professional," said Mrs. Bell. "This young woman wants a place."

"A place!—not your first, I will be sworn.—As if Mr. X. had time for such nonsense. Place—place—a pack of nonsense.—

You'll soon get a place, young woman, I'll be bound, though you have such a queer-coloured skin."

The heart of Iñez first sickened, then fluttered—then faltered—then fired at this insolence. Then humbleness, that blessed virtue, which extracts the sting from insult and contumely, conquered. She came up to Mrs. Bell's relief, and with great composure and dignity said—

"Young man, I wish to see Mr. X., and if you will take the trouble to introduce me at an unusual hour, shall be very much obliged to you. Pray accept of that—" offering a sovereign.

The golden bough of the sybil was not more efficacious—the footman was used to crowns and half crowns, but gold for a single introduction was new. "Humph," said he, "a mystery,—I thought as much—I'll step up, Miss, and inquire. Pray walk in for a moment."

He soon returned. "Mr. X. will see you.—Walk up stairs."

Mrs. Bell remained in the passage.

Iñez entered the drawing-room.—The surgeon was alone. So near the completion of her wishes—the moment of a meeting so dear—her courage forsook her. She turned pale and red, and held by the back of a chair without speaking.

"Well—what is your business?" said Mr. X., in an abrupt, sharp voice.—"I am in haste.—What is it you want?"

"I am come, Sir, to ask a great favour—"

"Well—go on—"

"I want a place as nurse. Would you be so kind as to recommend me?"

"Young woman, you have mistaken …"

"I beg your pardon, Sir, I have not. I wish to be employed as nurse to attend upon the sick. I believe I could promise to give you satisfaction, if you would have the goodness to recommend me where I desire to go."

"Have the goodness to recommend you, and where you desire to go! Young woman, this is a very extraordinary request.—What can you mean?—Where do you desire to go?"

There was something in the appearance of the young woman before him so unusual that it arrested even the attention of Mr. X., otherwise he would not have bestowed so large a share of his golden moments upon her.

"There was a gentleman very badly wounded, I heard, Sir, this morning. I thought you might be able to recommend a nurse to attend him. It would be an act of the most christian charity to recommend me."

"God bless my soul!—I never heard such a request. Why, where did you come from? Do you think we pick up nurses in the street, my good girl?—Have you attended in the hospitals?"

"I have been in the hospitals."

"And where is your recommendation?"

"I have none, Sir,—but only try me, and I will promise you shall be satisfied."

"And in such a case.—Why, my girl, you are asking for the care of a case that all the skill in England may not be able to save.—What can you be thinking of?"

The young woman seemed suddenly affected at this, and grasped by chair. She recovered herself, however, and said—

"Oh, Sir, if you would have the kindness to try me!" Her voice was so soft, her manner of pronunciation so delicate, that, like the white hand in the French story, it betrayed her to be of no vulgar order.

"It is a very strange thing," said Mr. X., rather severely, "what you can mean; and I am at a loss to guess what can bring any one on such a fool's errand to me. You cannot suppose that I lightly engage those to whom I commit the recovery of my patients. This case, with which you desire to be entrusted (for what reason I am at a loss to conceive), is one of the most lamentable I have met with in the whole course of my practice. If the young gentleman live, it will be next to a miracle; if his eyesight be recovered, more than a miracle. What can you intend by this absurd proposal?"

"I throw myself on your mercy alone—I have no plea to urge, but a desire so earnest to be entrusted, a persuasion so intimate, that I can be of service, when no one else could, that my care— my assiduity—my solicitous watchings—my earnest prayers, would effect that miracle—that I implore you, Sir, for the love of God—recommend me—let me attend upon Captain Vivian."

"Captain Vivian!—Who told *you* his name?"

"Alas! I know it too well!"

"You know it too well! Give me leave to ask who you are?"

"Alas! alas!" sinking on her knees before him, "I am his guilty wife."

The crimson which rushed over her face, dyeing it to the very temples, penetrated through the dark tint she had assumed, as she bent herself to the earth, the picture of grief and shame.

"Mrs. Vivian!"

Iñez kneeled.

"Mr. X., you see kneeling at your feet the most unhappy of those wretches whom vice has driven to misery. I am come to implore your mercy—do not deny me.—Let me go to my husband—I will go in secret—stay in secret—he shall never know I am near him—he shall not be agitated by me.—Only let me be his servant while he is ill—only let me tend him—dress his wounds—watch him and soothe him. Do you think I do not know how?—Oh, Harry! Harry! let me smooth your pillow—let me assuage your pain—let me return to you!—In pity, Sir!"

Her hands were clasped and raised, her imploring eyes streaming with tears.

"Mrs. Vivian, you distress me very much. Pray—not in that posture—pray be seated, and let us talk coolly of this matter."

He raised her, and put her in a chair.

"Then you will be so humane—so compassionate," said she, imploringly.

"I am very sorry to say that it would be absolutely impossible at present. When Captain Vivian is better some means may, we will hope, be found of effecting a reconciliation; but to force the subject upon him at this crisis, I would not answer for the consequences."

"A reconciliation!" said she, mournfully. "Alas! I was not thinking of *that*; there is no hope of *that*—*that* is indeed impossible."

"Then on what other grounds can you possibly wish me to allow of this most unusual proceeding? If it might be the means of restoring you to society (pardon me, I speak bluntly,) I might perhaps—but indeed it is utterly out of the question."

"I only wish to be allowed to *serve* him," said Iñez, in a desponding tone. "I had not even hoped for the poor consolation of thus demonstrating to him my duty—my repentance. I never proposed that he should know me, least of all dare I—do I—wish, or hope that which would be his dishonour. Oh, Mr. X.!" again throwing herself upon her knees, "in mercy let me go to him, he may die—he may die—let me be with him." Her hands were wrung, and raised beseechingly above her head in all the agony of prayer—in vain.

The very agitation into which she had been surprised only served to confirm the surgeon in his first opinion, that, under existing circumstances, she was the most improper person in the world with whom Vivian could be entrusted. He therefore very patiently explained to her that, in the present condition of Captain Vivian, the slightest agitation might be fatal; that, therefore, as it was impossible to feel assured that her feelings might not betray her, as they had already in the present instance done, that he should not think himself justified, &c. &c.

Mr. X. was justified by all the laws of common prudence, and yet how greatly was his conduct mistaken. Deficient in that nice penetration which enables its possessor to depart with impunity from common rules, he was denying Captain Vivian the tenderest of attendants, and one whose resolution was at least equal to the task she had imposed upon herself; but he was accustomed to dwell in generals: he was accustomed to disregard, among his medical resources, that solicitous attendance which results from passionate devotion—all those thousand alleviations which the ingenuity of affection can alone supply. He was moreover accustomed to be impenetrable to tears; and he soon showed that he was not to be moved—indeed, that he was beginning to get rather impatient.

When Mrs. Vivian perceived this, she suddenly ceased speaking—remained perfectly silent for a few seconds—then rose from her knees, dried her eyes, and quitted the apartment without speaking another word.

Once more in the coach with the compassionate Mrs. Bell, Iñez, not to be diverted from her purpose, began to consult upon the possibility of introducing herself into the house of Mr. Palmer, without the knowledge of the surgeon, or without betraying her secret.

After a good deal of deliberation, the only plan that seemed to hold out a chance of success was to make out who the nurse might be to whom the charge of Captain Vivian had been committed, and endeavour to persuade her to admit Mrs. Vivian, under the character of an assistant, to a share in her office. By this means an opportunity would be offered to her of assisting in all those cares which she longed to bestow upon her husband, while, by absenting herself whenever Mr. X., or, indeed, any of those who had once seen her, should be visiting Captain Vivian, she might effectually escape discovery.

Mrs. Bell, armed with another sovereign, returned to the house of Mr. X. for information, and, after about an hour, came back with the intelligence that a nurse had been ordered down to West End, and that the servants supposed she must already be gone. Iñez resolved, therefore, to follow to the house of Mr. Palmer, send for the nurse, and see what could be done.

It was now between four and five; but the days were long, and Mrs. Bell promised to accompany her.

"But, indeed, madam," said the kind young woman, who, now in her confidence, entered fully into all her plans and feelings, "you will be quite ill before you get there. If I might presume so far as to offer you my humble room, I would get you a little tea before we leave town again."

"Indeed, I thank you," said Mrs. Vivian, whose aching heart and wearied limbs ill seconded her untired spirits. "I will go to your house, if your husband will not be angry, and rest, and consider a little what we must say and do."

They drove into one of those small narrow streets which may be found appended to our most magnificent places and squares, in one of the houses of which Mrs. Bell inhabited a room, where she pursued her humble occupation of needle-work, and studied to preserve a decent appearance in the midst of those narrow circumstances to which gentlemen valets usually consign their wives.

Up a narrow, dark, dirty stair, the house noisy with the cries of bawling children and the shrill tones of scolding mothers—amid those sounds, smells, and sights which render the habitations of the poor so abhorrent to the senses of the rich and the refined,—under that mysterious system of things by which fellow men, separated, it may be, by but some fifty or a hundred yards from each other, are found—the one, amid all the attractions of elegance and beauty, rioting in an extravagance of wasteful luxury, almost amounting in itself to a vice—the other, after toiling all day to earn his scanty bread, consuming it at night, surrounded by his semi-barbarous companions, amid every privation of sordid, grinding, pitiless poverty.

"Misery makes us acquainted with strange bed-fellows." So thought Iñez, as she made her way up stairs, and entered the little unprovided room of her new and humble friend; while Mrs. Bell covered her small round table with a snow-white cloth, blew up the fire, put on the tea-kettle, brought from her small cupboard her single pair of cups and saucers, spread her bread and butter, and, like the gentle hermit, "pressed, and smiled," and endeavoured to cheer the pensive melancholy of her guest. Iñez, absorbed in reflection, sat in an old moth-eaten chair, the seat of honour of that humble abode, ruminating on the means of effecting a purpose, the desire for which had become only the more intense the more it was reflected upon. To see Harry once more, to be near him, to hear his voice, was contemplated with that excessive longing which triumphs, sooner or later, over every human difficulty.

The only chance that now presented itself was to see the nurse, and bribe her so largely as at once to overcome scruple and resistance: but where should she find the means? Five sovereigns were all that remained in her purse after the expenditure of the morning; and what was that?

She was sitting and drawing that elegant web of silk and silver listlessly through her hands, when Mrs. Bell rose, and presented a small parcel.

"I would not say any thing about it this morning, madam; but what would you wish to be done with this? It is too valuable to be left in such a poor place as mine, near so many lodgers,—all, I am sorry to say, under great temptations from poverty."

And she laid on the table the watch and massive chain which had suspended it round the throat of Iñez. The watch was small, and of great value, set with brilliants.

"Thank you, thank you, dear Mrs. Bell. I had quite forgotten it. Where could I have laid it down?"

"Where you changed you dress, madam, and seemed quite to have forgotten it. I brought it away to give you when you might want it."

"Oh! thank you, I do indeed want it. Where can I dispose of it to the best advantage?"

"Indeed, madam," said Mrs. Bell, "I am afraid that will not be very easy; people are so suspicious in this town. I am afraid, wherever it were taken, people would be for asking questions."

"True; I had not thought of that," said Mrs. Vivian, despondingly. "What can I do?"

"I think, madam," replied Mrs. Bell, "that if you would be pleased to show it to the nurse, with the seals, it would be a warrant like of what you were, and that whatever you should be pleased to promise her she might trust to, because she would know you must be the lady by the watch, madam."

"True again, indeed. Thank you, good Mrs. Bell. It might, indeed, be difficult to prove my identity to a stranger—but what can I promise? I who have nothing," mused she, "and am now penniless, without the means of providing myself even with bread."

"The watch, madam, might be sold by and bye," said Mrs. Bell, "and that would bring a very large sum. I recollect Lady Bligh, where I lived, had a watch just like it, and they all said it was worth two hundred guineas; only just now—" and this naturally delicate and feeling young woman hesitated and blushed, from the fear of giving pain, "just now I thought it might not be so agreeable, may-be, to be offering the watch for sale."

"I see—" said Mrs. Vivian, whose mind readily seized upon an expedient,—"I see, I can let her have the watch in pledge, and redeem it or leave it, as may be. And now, my good Mrs. Bell, if you have quite done tea, will you call another coach, and let us be going?"

A coach was soon procured, and Mrs. Vivian, having directed the man to drive to West End, and inquire for Mr. Palmer, entered it with her companion.

The coach stopped in the narrow retired lane, a little distance from the house, and Iñez, who found it now difficult to articulate, begged Mrs. Bell, as they had agreed, to call out the nurse to be spoken to in the lane.

She got out of the coach to wait, thinking the air might revive her spirits. It was a sweet still evening. The distant sound of the children at play—the cackling of a few geese—and now and then the sharp yelp of a little dog, came softly mingled from the village at a little distance. The place where she stood was shaded with dog-roses and honeysuckles, which waved and struggled in wild sweetness over her head.—The hay was down in a field hard by, and filled the air with its delightful perfume, while a few nightingales were warbling their latest melodies among the bushes and trees of a neighbouring shrubbery. She sat down upon a little bank, and, looking round, endeavoured to fix her attention upon the scene, and soothe her nerves for the coming interview.

She was then, at length, near him. A hundred paces alone separated her from that abode where *he* lay, who had been for so many happy, innocent years as a part of her being, and who still appeared to form a portion of her very self, united by those close, indissoluble ties which bind the wife to the husband of her youth. Vainly she attempts to wrench these ties asunder; she will find them, in most cases, resisting every effort to dissolve them, and asserting their force and their authority at the moment she fancies them severed for ever.

Conjugal love is a sacred thing; and though many have held and do hold cheap its obligations, and undervalue its power, in comparison with the claims of that passion which it inevitably supersedes, it will be found to be more strong, and more devoted, and more enduring, and to make as essential a part of the nature of man as if it were independent of human institutions.

To Iñez it appeared that to Vivian alone she of right belonged, though she had separated herself from him for ever, under the influence of a miserable infatuation: and it would be difficult to describe the complete dislocation of feeling which was the result of the false and criminal position in which she stood. She now in bitterness reflected on the destruction of all her social relations, the annihilation of every plan and hope of life. Then, as her mournful ruminations continued, and she bent in spirit submissively to her fate, like other criminals, she first began to experience what is meant by repentance.—She began to comprehend some of the mysteries of her own moral nature,— she dimly saw that pain, humiliation, sorrow, were not only the natural consequences of her fault, but the means of regeneration, the means of purifying her soul from the pollution into which it had fallen; and she experienced that irresistible desire of the penitent, to fall before the Author of all being—

> To prostrate fall
> Before him reverent, and there confess
> Humbly their faults, and pardon beg with tears,
> Watering the ground, and with their sighs the air
> Frequenting, sent from hearts contrite, in sign
> Of sorrow unfeigned, and humiliation meek.

She felt the power such tears possess to cleanse and wash away the stains of vice, as she covered her face with her hands, and once more ventured to address that God, to whom, in the days of her error, she dared not turn, even in thought; and, as the streams trickled through her fingers, she prayed in the name of

Him who was not without pity for one fallen as herself—prayed for grace to repent as she ought, and, by a life of humiliation, obtain a regeneration of her spirit before her death. She felt, and understood fully, for the first time, what these things mean. Happy are those who arrive at such deep convictions while yet the soul is pure of grievous sin!

"Whatever infidels may vainly talk," a mysterious blessing surely waits upon prayer.—A calm, an earnest of that peace which is a pledge of heaven in this world, began now to steal over the heart of Iñez.—Her fluttering pulses became still.—Strength to perform, with fortitude, whatever might lie before her—the consoling sentiment of atoning, by what she might endure, for what she had done—

> Prevenient grace descending, that removes
> The stony from the heart—

soothed and tranquillised her. She rose from the bank on which she had been praying, and waited with a composure she could scarcely have conceived possible the arrival of the nurse.

XIX

Mrs. Crane, who now made her appearance, was a large, portly woman, of somewhat more than forty-five. Her countenance, decided and rather masculine, was stamped with those lines of strong good sense which much communication with the serious business of life impresses on the face of a woman of clear understanding. It was evident Mrs. Crane was one never led through weakness to deviate from the plain, direct path she had proposed to herself to pursue. Unlike most of her profession, no bland insinuation sat upon her lip, no hypocritical softness modulated her voice, no doubtful expression falsified her physiognomy. Her clear grey eye, her well-set, firm mouth, and well-filled cheek, carried an expression of benevolence, rather than of softness—of kindness, than of flattery—of authority, than of fawning.

Iñez looked up in her face, and, with her usual quickness of perception, understood her character in a moment. Though by far the more sensitive of the two (and sensitiveness is, in the intercourse of the world, almost equivalent to weakness), yet Iñez possessed that ability and penetration which render one human being infallibly the master of others,—a power she, during the smiling sunshine of her summer day, had felt little occasion to exercise. Now, with an important object before her, she seized instinctively on the means of its attainment; and estimating, at once, the force of her with whom she had to deal, she attacked her by a direct appeal to her interest and to her benevolence.

She saw Mrs. Crane was kind-hearted—she saw she was not one to be withheld by trifling scruples from doing what she thought right. She also remarked certain lines in her face which testified that an appeal to self-interest would have its due, though not more than its due effect, upon one who was, after all, paid every day for the exercise of humanity.

Mrs. Crane looked surprised when she was introduced to the rather singular-looking person who stood before her: but Iñez came forward without the smallest hesitation.

"Mrs. Crane, I believe.—Has Mrs. Bell informed you who I—*was*?"

"Mrs. Bell said a lady wanted to speak to me."

"I am Mrs. Vivian; and I am come to make a request to you, which I trust you will not refuse. You know already, no doubt, why I have no right to approach Captain Vivian—why I am obliged to beg for that which I ought to command … I wish to nurse my—Captain Vivian—till his recovery—I would not ask it if I were not sure that in many things I could study his comfort better than any one.—I wish you to introduce me as your assistant—I will never betray you.—The thing shall be buried in silence between us and this good Mrs. Bell. Only make an excuse, and introduce me as your maid—I will give you one hundred pounds. Here is my watch as a pledge—keep it till I redeem it.—Will you oblige me?"

Mrs. Crane stood for some few minutes reflecting, then, with hesitation, began what seemed like a denial; but Iñez, before the words could pass her lips, took her hand, and began again to urge her suit, with so much earnestness, laying open, with a plainness almost approaching to magnanimity, her situation, feelings, and wishes, and urged her bribe with so much sincerity that Mrs. Crane at length gave way and said she would see what could be done.

She was about to propose that Iñez should return to London for the night, and come back in the morning: but this could not be endured—Iñez felt that to go away was the only thing impossible, and she said so. It was at length settled that Mrs. Crane should go to good Mr. Palmer, and, persuading him that Captain Vivian's situation required more than her assistance, ask leave to introduce a friend into the house, to watch with her for a few nights.

Mrs. Crane was not absent long; she soon returned to say that Mr. Palmer was quite satisfied of the propriety of the measure, and begged that Iñez and Mrs. Bell would follow her to the house.

Iñez did not attempt to speak. A sense of choking about the throat rendered that impossible; but anxious to prove her power of resisting emotion, she quietly took Mrs. Bell's arm, and signed to Mrs. Crane to lead the way.

They came to the little green gate, where the busy host was already in waiting to receive this new addition to his family.

"A very pretty young woman, indeed, Mrs. Crane. A mighty pretty figure.—Pray, young woman, walk *this* way—that leads to my front door—this is the back you see—here is the kitchen."

The kitchen!—There was a crowd of servants in what was usually occupied by Mr. Palmer's quiet maid Bridget alone. Among the rest, Captain Vivian's own valet; happily not John— he would have known his mistress, however disguised. The servants were chatting away, with the volubility common to their care-exempted race; a fire was blazing in the grate, and Bridget and another woman busy roasting a joint of meat, and preparing supper for all the gentlemen who, being under orders of inquiry, chose to stay, and share the good things which the busy Mr. Palmer had prepared upon this momentous occasion; for his hospitality extended to the most humble of his numerous guests, and his anxiety and vanity were evidently as much alive to provide for and gratify the grand gentlemen's gentlemen, as the gentlemen themselves: nay, it may be doubted whether these first, with all their second-hand exaggerated airs, did not appear to the simple citizen the most important personages of the two.

Iñez glanced at the wide open door, and seeing what was before her, hesitated.—She feared discovery—far more she yearned for one moment's pause to relieve her full heart. To sit down in the midst of all this noisy vulgarity!—little do those whose sensations have been refined by civilisation comprehend the depth and the breadth of that gulf which separates them from those of a lower condition and ruder habits. Those who only observe the inferior classes of society while under the influence of restraint, such as the presence of their superiors invariably imposes, can form little idea of the grossness and the coarseness of their communications with each other—or how in the very tone of the voice, the forms of expression, even the mode of pronunciation when released from that influence, something may be detected painful and offensive to a purer taste. These things my be thought trifles, but trifles as they may be, are perhaps sufficient to prove that the distinctions of society are not merely arbitrary

Mrs. Crane and Mrs. Bell both felt for Mrs. Vivian—for people in their rank often shew the most delicate sympathy for the sufferings of a refinement in which they do not share.

"You had better come to my room," said Mrs. Crane. "Mr. Palmer, we will go up stairs."

"But won't the young woman take some supper. Supper is just going to be taken up. Do, Miss, take, some supper—a capital piece of meat—and a tart—do, Miss."

"Thank you," said Iñez, "I will go with Mrs. Crane."

The stairs were before her—those stairs—covered with her common-place carpet—bordered by their mean painted bannisters. To her eyes what did they not convey?—Those stairs—the last few steps that lay between her and the object of such earnest wishes. She longed to fly up—to open the door—to fling herself at Harry's feet; but she restrained herself, and pressed her folded hands close against her bosom.

"This way, Miss," said Mr. Palmer, whispering. Tread softly—may be he's asleep, poor young gentleman—hush!—hush!—that's his door—no, there's Mrs. Crane's room—that way."

Mrs. Crane opened the door into her own small apartment, which was nearly filled by a large bed.

Iñez entered—sat down without speaking—and, folding her arms against the side of the bed, laid her forehead silently upon them, and waited till the throbbing of her heart should subside, and voice and motion be restored.—To weep, she refused herself, ignorant, that torrent once set to flow, by what power to staunch its outpourings.

Mrs. Crane respected her silence, and honoured her self-command. Like all those who have to do with the sick, she reverenced an abstinence from tears and weak complaints.—She stood by quietly: in about a quarter of an hour Iñez raised her head.

"Now, good Mrs. Crane, I can see him—may I?"

"We must wait a little. I left Captain Sullivan watching him. I will go in and see whether I am not wanted.—The dressing should be looked to."

Iñez shuddered slightly.

"Is he sensible?" It was the first question she had ventured to ask.

"Yes, he is; but he does not seem inclined to speak, I think."

There was at this moment a knock at a small door placed at one corner of the room. It opened, as soon appeared, into that in which Captain Vivian lay.

"Mrs. Crane!"

It was Sullivan's voice. Iñez hastily tied on the large bonnet which she had removed.

"You are wanted, Mrs. Crane. Will you please to come to Captain Vivian? The bandage is shifted."

"Directly, sir. Will you go down a little now?"

"Yes, I am going to town for a few hours. I shall be back very early in the morning."

He ran down stairs—Mrs. Crane approached the half-opened door—Iñez followed.

"How do you feel yourself now, sir? The bandage has slipped, I see, a little."

"I think so"—in a voice so low and languid, that it was scarcely audible to Iñez, who, pale and cold as marble, stood at the half-opened door, afraid to enter, but finding it impossible to retreat.

The voice told at once the tale of Harry's sufferings. It was faltering, broken, faint; but not with sickness alone; there was in it that tone of pathetic despondency which speaks volumes to the ear. His heart was broken—she felt it was. She stood still, scarcely breathing.—Presently he spoke again.

"What o'clock is it, good Mrs. Crane? This is a weary day."

"It is near upon nine, sir.—Will you take tea?"

"Yes, something to drink," languidly. "My throat is parched and dry."

"I will get you some directly. This young person is my assistant, sir. She will stay in the room while I go. If you want any thing, you will please to ask her."

She signed to Iñez to come in.

Iñez came to the bedside.

There he lay—a ghastly figure—the upper part of his face covered with bandages, still foul with blood—his cheek below pale and haggard—his lips white, yet preserving their expression of ineffable sweetness and candour—his hand faintly supporting his head—there lay the wreck of Harry Vivian.

She stood by his side and gazed.

She neither sighed nor groaned. Two large tears rolled slowly from her eyes—this was all the emotion she showed. At length she slid softly on her knees and bowed her head, as if in acceptance of sorrow; and after remaining some time immovable arose, and with a composure the most extraordinary sat down by the bedside to watch. There is a despair which is calm—there is a misery which mocks expression. Feeble characters perish under it; those of more force live, and move, and think, and act, burying the concealed and festering wound with the heroic self-command of the Roman matron.

It was not long before Captain Vivian felt a light and soft hand (how different from the firm, strong, and not very tender touch of the nurse!) gently arranging the pillows under his head, so as to relieve the uneasy posture in which he was helplessly lying. The bed, all ruffled and heated, was smoothed—the windows of the room softly opened. A fresh breeze played upon his fevered brow—a sense of comfort and rest seemed to steal over his frame. Tired and exhausted with continual suffering, the first moment of relief was inexpressibly grateful; he felt tranquillised by a charm he could not understand, but which seemed to soothe him with a strange sympathy—nature yielded to the gentle sensation—the irritation of mental and bodily suffering subsided, his hands sank languidly from his face, and he fell asleep. She heard him breathe more quietly—she saw by the expression of his countenance that he rested. She for one moment (it was but for the moment) almost felt that her sin was forgiven her.

All that night did she, with the permission of Mrs. Crane, watch by his pillow, administering the little refreshment he was able take, and when he slumbered laying herself down on the floor by his side; while he, too much confused in his sensations by his blindness and pain to attend much to what was going on, never remarked that he heard not once the voice of his guardian, but grateful for her care, and the charm of attentions which seemed to divine all that he wanted, passed the night better than could by possibility have been anticipated.

The morning broke upon her with that calm, cold, mournful stillness with which it visits the watchers of the night. To them it brings no cheering freshness on its wings, but chilly shivers, striking through the veins, and melancholy pressing on the spirits. The candles were expiring in their sockets, as the sun began to make ruddy the eastern clouds, and light dawned upon the earth, though all was as profoundly silent as in the dead midnight. This stillness gives a mournful character to the dawn, well known to those who, sitting by the bed of sickness or of death, have seen its first faint streaks crimsoning the parting clouds.

Iñez was now standing at the window in melancholy reverie. She heard Captain Vivian move and sigh, as if awakening. His sleep had been rather sound than refreshing, and his head was evidently still confused and inclined to wander. The scenes and shadows of the last eight and forty hours were slowly passing before his fancy, as he lay between waking and sleeping. At last he muttered something—she listened with intense attention.

"It was all a dream—a horrid dream!—When shall I be awake?—Where am I?—In my cabin?—What was it?—Where is she?—and my children—and my home—where are they?—What did they tell me?—How was it all?—Why is she not here?—My Iñez—my Iñez, come back to me, my love!—Nay, let us talk it all over.—Why were you not at home to receive me?—My Iñez! where are you? Oh there!—I thought you would come again?"

Once more he slumbered, for the sound ceased.

She had imposed upon herself a task of which she as yet knew but half the bitterness; every faltering accent struck her to the heart. She, too, looked back, as on a hideous dream, upon what had been done. She longed to forget—to press forward at his call, as in the days of her first happy affection—to cover his face with her innocent kisses—to obliterate all that had taken place—to blot out the dreadful past. Alas! alas!—time past—the irreparable, the inexorable past! Sin committed—the dark—the ineffaceable stain! She had done that

Which takes the rose
From the fair forehead of an innocent shame,
And plants a blister there.

She had done that which had rendered her a thing infect, impure, no longer worthy even to touch that hand which once had seemed to grow to hers. She had done that which had severed, by a deep, impassable gulf, herself and him who seemed as half herself, bound to her with a oneness, an exclusiveness, which none but those united in a happy marriage can understand.

His cruelty was great who bound the living body to the cold, inanimate corpse; but the sufferings of the miserable victim scarcely equalled the torments of those who exist, as it were, with half their soul of being bound up with a distant, parted frame. But she was patient, submissive to sufferings too well deserved. She bent her head to the window, and let the tears stream down.

Morning advanced, and the misty twilight was succeeded by the more brilliant radiance of the ascending day. "The sun shone bright on every eye in the village" save hers and those of the unfortunate Captain Vivian—alas! to be visited by those beams no more. The birds were hailing the rising sun, whose golden car, now high above the horizon, gleamed over the sweet landscape which spread before the window of the bedroom. The stir of business was in the house; all those pleasant sounds of awakened life and action that speak so cheeringly to the heart.

She stood by his bedside with Mrs. Crane.—He was restless and full of suffering. It was evident that, now, thoroughly awakened to a clear perception of circumstances, the anguish of his mind rendered the torments of his wound nearly insupportable. Restless, yet scarcely able to move—tears upon his heart, which, alas! could no longer flow from his mangled eyes … The picture is too shocking. She saw and felt it all; and, as at intervals, the deep and heavy sighs burst from his bosom, they seemed to sever hers.

She dared not take that hand—she had lost the privilege to circle in her arms that head, and endeavour to soothe and soften anguish—she dared not speak and bid him take comfort; and, might she so have spoken, alas! what comfort was there to offer? She looked with a glazed, staring expression of helpless sorrow, while Mrs. Crane endeavoured to allay the pain of his wounds, and to ease the bandages.

"Are you better now, sir? Indeed, if you could make yourself a little easy, it would help you. Let me bathe your hands with eau de Cologne," said she, giving the bottle kindly to Iñez, who felt, only when she was employed, as if delivered from the most racking torments.

"Thank you, Mrs. Crane," with another heavy sigh, "I will endeavour to be more quiet"—another heavy sigh—"I will be more patient. Is Sullivan come?"

"No, sir—he said he would be here very early;" and as she spoke, the bell of the gate was heard, and Sullivan might be seen crossing the garden. He soon entered the room, and Iñez retreated to the next apartment, where, resting her aching head against the slender partition, she heard without design all that passed.

"Well, my dear fellow, how do you find yourself?" said Sullivan, in the cheerful accents of his friendly voice. "Have you rested? Are you better? How is your pain?"

"I have slept, I believe, a good part of the night. I feel less stunned and confused than I did yesterday. I am beginning, I hope, to collect myself; but I am a very unfortunate fellow, Sullivan;" and his voice faltered.

"Oh, you must not think of *that*—oblivion. You must return to your profession."

"Sullivan," in a low, hoarse tone; "you will not suspect me of a weakness unworthy of me; but I hope she is safe … I hope she will be treated with honour. If she wishes to come away, I hope she will not want the means. I should be sorry if she had an inclination to retire from—from—his protection, I mean—I should very much desire that she should be provided with the means of rendering herself independent of him. I think, my good friend, it would be a very great consolation to me to know that she depended for subsistence upon one, who—oh, God of Heaven, why did she ever leave him?—one who was her legitimate protector—who has still a right—to—alas!" with a heavy sigh, "to what has he a right?—but who has a title to consider what will be best for her amid the unparalleled misery into which she has plunged us both? Yes, Iñez, misery for both! I know you. Your tortures will equal my own!"

"But," said Sullivan, "surely you do not intend to—. You cannot. The means of redress—. You will have recourse to legal proceedings—to restore you, at least, to your liberty."

"No," said Captain Vivian, "I have no use for liberty. 'Thou wert! thou art!'" he checked himself. "Not unless it be *her* wish. What!

drag her before a court of justice; have my hearth profaned—my secret love blasphemed—my sacred home disgraced, by such an unblushing display of our joys, our griefs, our infirmities, our crimes, and our despair! No, no, Sullivan; Iñez shall not be made a fable for the idle, chattering town through fault of mine. I will not assist to rend asunder that veil which yet may shelter her dishonour. I will not help to sully that name, whose brightness was my pride and glory—to bow that head in shame, whose lofty frankness I adored—no, no!"

"But, Vivian, your own honour—consider—. Things are gone too far; you cannot take her—."

"Back—no," in a hollow tone; "that she has indeed rendered impossible.—I have lost my Iñez.—Honour—love, forbid it.—I have lost my Iñez.—She is no longer the same—she is to me, henceforth, an alien and a stranger: but I need not forget what she has been. Her honour—her reputation—it may not be too late to rescue; but," and he mused painfully, "what if she should refuse to leave him?"

"I have heard," said Sullivan, "that she has already left him."

"She has!—I thank God. Then, Sullivan, will you learn where she has taken shelter? and will you, my good fellow, provide that she has those means necessary to the comfort of one—so tender—and so beloved? I want time to reflect upon the arrangements that ought to be made, if I live. If I die, she will be provided for by dispositions made before our last unhappy parting. Now tell me of my children, for a coldness and faintness is upon me, and the spirit is weak."

"Miss Vivian has taken your two sweet little girls to Roehampton. Mr. X. positively forbids her bringing them here at present, or even visiting you herself; but rest assured they are in good hands."

"I know it—I know it—poor little destitute orphans! Will you go now, and execute the commission that I have given you? and if you could see my little ones, and carry them their poor father's blessing, and bring me word they are well, I think it would do me good. Sullivan, I give you much trouble."

"God bless you, Vivian—how can you imagine such a thing? Send me over the world for you—I will be off this moment, and do what you desire."

And, running down stairs, he left the unhappy husband and tender father once more alone.

Alone, he indulged for a short time, without restraint, the bitter regrets which a sense of honour and dignity forbade him to display, even before the eyes of so close a friend as Sullivan. He yielded to a violent paroxysm of grief, while the name of Iñez, his beloved—his only life, joy, and hope—and of his children—his orphan, motherless children—mingled with his deep and heavy groans. She heard it at first with a distress that seemed so completely overpowering, that she felt rooted to the spot; but she was alone, Mrs. Crane had left the watching to her, and dreading that the violent agitation which she witnessed might seriously injure him, she roused herself, and opening the door of the partition glided gently into the room, kneeled down by his bed, and in a voice distinct, but very low, said—"In the holy name of God, think of your children, and take comfort."

"Who speaks?" said he, suddenly arrested. "Whose voice is that?"

No answer. She dared not speak again: but the interruption had changed the course of his thoughts. Her purpose was effected.

"Who spoke?" he repeated.

"It was only your nurse"—in a low tremulous voice, which she endeavoured to disguise. "I beg your pardon, sir—pray excuse me."

"Ah!—speak again—speak again—that voice!"—for she was silent—"that voice!" Alas! even the faint echo of those tones so fondly loved fell upon his heart with inexpressible sweetness. The colour flew to his faded cheek. "Who *are* you?"

"I am your nurse, sir—a young woman hired to assist Mrs. Crane."

"Ah!" with a deep sigh, "is that all? Let me be quiet then, my dear: I think I may sleep."

Her hands, which were now icy cold, once more arranged his pillows; and then, statue like, she remained by him, trusting that her presence would restrain these dangerous bursts of feeling.

XX

AND what was become of Laurence?—Shall we follow him to a dark, gloomy apartment, in one of the narrowest streets of ancient London, where, devoured by his own thoughts, he remained, his head buried in his hands, the picture of stupid despair? The excess of mental as well as of bodily pain terminates in insensibility, and stupefaction for some time deadened the poignancy of his feelings. Like one in a dream, circumstances present and past hurried through his fancy with a strange rapidity, independent of the slightest act of volition. He saw his friend, in the bloom of youth, hanging on his arm, as they used to walk the parks together, discoursing with animated frankness on his hopes, his prospects, his designs. He saw the colour flash to his cheek, as he spoke of her,—the—as yet unknown to Laurence—the idol, the divinity of his adoration. Then that garden at Middleton Court rose up to his imagination. He saw the lovely, fantastic Miss Thornhaugh indulging her airy caprices—the petulance and insolence of wit, innocence, and beauty—then the second meeting—the softened wife—the complete woman—the graceful, the gentle, the elegant—the happy husband—the confiding friend—Portsmouth—the return. But at those thoughts, Laurence, the philosopher—the temperate—the sage—gnashed his teeth, and tearing off large handfuls of his hair, cursed the demon who had entered that paradise, and ruined the angel of purity once there enshrined. He saw her, as last he had seen her, sitting shamed and miserable upon his hearth—beaten, broken down, and blasted, like a beautiful flower all dabbled with mire; and aloud he cursed his being.

Towards evening Trevor came.

Trevor was one of those rare characters who, educated at a public school, a denizen for three years of a college, a witness of all the disorders which attend unbridled youth, and afterwards circulating freely in that great world of dissipation to which fortune and independence introduced him in London, had preserved, as by the native brightness of his own original temper, his heart pure from dissolution, his habits unstained by sin. A very deep and sincere sense of religion, for which he was indebted to his excellent parents, (parents, for many have pious mothers, but few know what it is to see piety made reverend by the habits of a father,) had been, to a considerable degree, the talisman which had carried him undefiled through all the corruptions which surrounded him, aided by that calmness and well ordering of the passions, the best fruits of a careful and judicious education. The imagination of Trevor had not been enlisted on the side of vice, either by injudicious and scrupulous severity, or by ill-concealed license. He had learned to dislike and despise excess as a weakness and a brutality, and to love virtue and order for their own sakes.

The pain and shrinking of the soul with which he found himself bound up in a tale so abhorrent to all his feelings as this of Laurence may be conceived; and the tenderness with which he persevered in endeavouring to lighten the host of evils which now overwhelmed the unfortunate and guilty victims, proved, in this instance at least, that the most generous benevolence and rigid personal virtue are not so incompatible as some, not remarkable for the latter quality, have wished to make us believe. Still there was a feeling of indignation prevailing in his mind when he looked at Laurence, which, suppressed as it was by a compassion he could not but feel, gave a certain restraint and coldness to his manner which he found it impossible to overcome.

The immediate effect of this on Hervey was, however, so far good, that the want of sympathy he instinctively felt induced him to check the violence of his present agitation, and acting as a powerful sedative, perhaps, preserved his intellects.

The first question was not for Vivian. Two men, loving the same woman, can have neither sympathy, friendship, nor affection. Jealousy is, in man, a master passion, and produces effects so wide and various, that we often overlook the original spring of those effects when witnessed. The husband of Iñez was no object of interest to Laurence. The thought of what had happened was dreadful, and well nigh upset his mind; but his remorse, his tenderness, his anguish, were all for her.

"Where is she? What is become of her?" said he raising his head, but without rising from his chair, as Trevor came in.

"She has left your lodgings," said Trevor.

Laurence sighed. "I thought it would be so. Where is she gone?"

"I hope, indeed, I am sure, that she is safe," said Trevor; "but where she is gone, I have yet to learn."

"You have?—good heavens!—In this town. Who was with her?"

"The wife of your servant accompanied her. They went out in a hackney coach,—where, the man could not tell. I have made fruitless inquiries. I can get no trace of her. The people with whom they lodge say that your servant's wife came in about five o'clock with a young woman, a sort of upper maid-servant— rather an odd-looking person—that then they went out, and she has not been home since. I saw Iñez this morning. She then spoke of some asylum that she should seek; but if that were shut against her, she promised to apply to me. Vivian yet lives."

"And is this all you know?"

He got up, and began looking about the room.

"Where's my hat?"

"You are not going out, Hervey," said Trevor. "Leave it to me; rely upon it I will not rest till I have discovered where Mrs. Vivian is lodged. I came down here hastily, thinking you would suffer so much anxiety to know the state of—; but rely upon it, wherever she is, she is safe. The person she went with is a most respectable young woman."

The sympathies of Trevor were at this moment more engaged by the unfortunate husband than by the erring wife; and the accident by which he had struck the man, once his friend, appeared to him the dreadful climax in Hervey's fate, compared to which, all other circumstances were of trifling account. Satisfied that Mrs. Vivian was in no real danger, he did not, therefore, share the agitation and anxiety of Hervey.

Laurence made no answer, but continued to look about the room. He then rang the bell.

"I want my hat."

"You did not bring one, Sir," said the foot-boy who opened the door.

"Go and fetch me one."

"Sir?"

"Buy me a hat," said Laurence, flinging to him a couple of sovereigns.

Trevor now interfered:—"You had better remain where you are, Hervey.—Vivian is in a most precarious state. Consider what your situation is. Wait till to-morrow. You shall have the earliest intelligence—you may safely leave all this to me!"

Laurence made no answer; he looked doggedly at the window: the moment the door opened, he seized the hat which the boy held, and, without looking at Trevor, left the room, and the house.

Evening was now beginning to fall—he threaded the streets with rapidity, walking at his utmost speed, regardless of every interruption. He passed up the Strand, indifferent whether seen or not, and through the different wide public streets, until he reached the Albany. The first thing he saw was his servant, yawning at his door. The fellow started at the sudden apparition.

"Where's your wife?"

"Lord, Sir—you do startle so?—My wife? I do not exactly know!"

"You scoundrel, where has she been all day?"

"How should I tell, Sir?—I suppose you know she went out with—"

Laurence arrested the name; he shuddered to have it profaned by passing such lips.

"Where did they go?"

"I really can't say; but perhaps home."

"Where does she live?"

The man gave the direction. Laurence turned on his heel; he was, in a few moments, knocking sharply at Mrs. Bell's door. She was within, and opened it.

He came straight into the middle of the room.

"Good heavens!—she is not here! Where is she gone? Woman, tell me instantly."

"Sir," said Mrs. Bell, with some reserve, "I was charged not to tell!"

"But I insist upon knowing, this instant," said Laurence, passionately.

"She is where you cannot go, Sir," said Mrs. Bell, whose habitual awe and respect for Hervey had been much diminished since the morning. She now felt in the situation of one defending Mrs. Vivian from further contamination; and, inspired by the circumstances, the modest, humble young woman became intrepid and firm.

"Good God!—What has she done? How dare you trifle with me?" seizing her by the shoulder, and shaking her with something savage in his manner. "Will you tell me what has become of her?"

"She charged me not to say, Sir."

"She charged you not to say? You don't intend to say, reptile, that she mentioned *me* to *you*."

"Not exactly that, Sir; but she begged me to keep her secret. And oh, Sir!" said the young woman, releasing herself from Laurence's relaxing hand, "oh, Sir! don't try to follow her. She's where she ought to be, Sir!—don't," clasping her hands, "don't ask of her—she's in her duty now, Sir!"

"In her duty! What do you mean by that? What wretched, presumptuous stuff is this?—In her duty—Where is she?"

The woman was silent.

"Do you mean to be murdered?" said Laurence, setting his teeth. "Do you know, woman," in a low tone, "what it is to enrage a desperate man? Tell me, this instant, where she is, or I'll shake you to atoms!"

Mrs. Bell was now really frightened.

"Oh, Sir! let me go! she's at West End."

"At West End?"

"She's gone to nurse her husband as was," said the woman, bursting into tears. "And may God help her, and support her—poor, poor young lady!"

Laurence fell back.

"She has cut off her beautiful hair," continued the young woman, seizing on the circumstance which had most affected her imagination. "And she has put on a cotton gown like mine: and we went first to the doctor, and he would not let us go; and then to the nurse, and she let us in; but he's never to know. They say it would break his heart outright to see her—poor, poor gentleman: but she is to be his nurse by day and by night; and may that be a comfort to her poor heart!"

"Tell me all she did, from the beginning," said Laurence, sitting down.

The young woman did as she was bid, and told the story of the day.

Laurence extracted the minutest particulars relating to the behaviour of Iñez, and then putting five guineas into the woman's hand, and having obtained an exact description of the house, he left her, and proceeded to West End.

With what design? Not with a hope—not with a wish to see Iñez again—but to watch over the house which contained her—to wander round its precincts—to rest his head upon the earth by night—to roam like a restless, unhoustled spirit by day—to glut his heart with a misery, of which the intensity can only be conceived by one, not sinking by slow degrees into depravity, but hurled at once like some bright falling star from excellence to darkness.

Laurence was, in truth, formed to taste the full bitterness of his situation—led, neither by the slow, insensible advance of profligate habits, nor by thoughtless gaiety to vice—the victim of great temptation, and of unsettled principles. With a mind which weighed, examined, and pondered over all the interminable relations between guilt and misery, he conceived the horrors of his situation in their full extent; while his heart, not hardened by long licentiousness, but rather softened by a certain refined self-indulgence, was tempered to endure the most poignant torments of remorse. The dreadful shock he had sustained when he saw Vivian fall had produced the effect of deadening every other sentiment, save one—a sort of dogged, sullen resolution, never to forsake Iñez—a defiance of every law, human and divine—of every propriety, of every danger, which might interfere with the absolute and entire devotion of each thought and feeling to her.

Six days and six nights might his blasted figure be seen wandering round the fields, stretched beneath the hedges, his hair rusted with the wind, his linen defiled, his clothes in disorder, his eyes fixed upon that window which lighted the apartment, where, in fancy, he beheld, stretched, the form of the man he had most loved, while over it hung that penitent and broken Magdalene, that had grovelled on the ground before him, buried in the long folds of her hair, the victim of his passions.

Six long days!

Trevor had ascertained where he harboured, and had made one or two fruitless efforts to draw him from this strange and wild way of passing his time: but he had been repulsed with a harshness, once foreign to the nature of Laurence; and, convinced that there was something almost approaching to insanity in his determination, he had ended by leaving him almost entirely to himself—all interference appearing only to exasperate him, and increase the terrible irritation of his feelings.

XXI

THREE days were passed by Iñez in the faithful discharge of her mournful duties—her heart alternating between hope and fear—if that could be called hope which bore, indeed, no promise of happiness to herself, and only flattered with the prospect of relief from the insupportable idea of having occasioned her husband's death.

On the fourth day, Sullivan, who was unremitting in his attendance, entered the room much earlier than usual, looking annoyed and anxious.

Iñez was holding the cup whence she had been supplying Vivian with tea.

"Mrs. Crane!" said Sullivan.

"Mrs. Crane is not here, Sir," said Iñez, in a low tone of voice.

"How are you, my dear Vivian, to-day?" said Sullivan, going up to the bed-side,—"how have you rested?"

"Better," said Vivian—"I have slept some hours, I believe. My dear," to his nurse, "leave us now."

Iñez obeyed—Sullivan followed her.

"What is to be done?—Has Mr. X. been here to-day?—The Admiral is come to town, and insists upon seeing Captain Vivian.—I don't know what to say or do."

Iñez felt very sick, and turned to the window to conceal her face, and prevent herself from falling.

"What do you think?—May he be allowed to see him?"

"Sir?" repeated Iñez gasping for breath.

Sullivan was too much occupied to perceive her emotion; he merely thought her stupid, and said, "If Mrs. Crane were but here, she would decide this business. Mrs. Crane!"—for the good woman at this moment entered the room,—"here is Admiral Thornhaugh arrived in town, and he wants to see Captain Vivian."

"Good gracious, Sir! does he want to kill him? Mr. X. declares perfect quiet gives the only chance of recovery,—and, poor young gentleman, he does fret so much!" shaking her head; "and the Admiral, you know, of all men in the world, just now, Sir …"

"It must be prevented, at any risk," cried Iñez, coming hastily forwards. "My father!—Good Heavens! such a meeting—and at such a moment.—Oh, Captain Sullivan!—find some means to prevent it—let him not come—alas!—alas!—Harry is utterly incapable of such an exertion."

"You think so," said Sullivan, his anxiety rendering him insensible to the strange manner of this address; "but what must be done? Shall I return to town, and endeavour to stop the carriage?"

"Anything—everything—but, good Heavens! what is here?"

At that moment a carriage stopped at the little gate; two gentlemen alighted from it, and the treble sounds of Mr. Palmer's voice might be heard as he marshalled them across the garden.

"Certainly, my Lord Admiral, undoubtedly this is the place where the young gentleman has been lying, ever since, in my best bed-room; and I have been too happy to do my best: and undoubtedly he is, I am proud to say, very considerably much better. No doubt he will be proud to see you, my lord—shall I step up and see?"

"Good Heavens! it is he," cried Sullivan. "The obstinate old fellow—I told him—but he'll never believe, he says, that Harry will be sorry to see him. God bless me! he's upon the stairs."

The door of Captain Vivian's apartment opened, and Mr. Palmer's voice was heard.

"I beg pardon, Captain Vivian—I believe you are not asleep. A gentleman, by name—Rear-Admiral Thornhaugh, and a Mr. Roper are below, and request to see you."

There was silence for two seconds; then in low broken tones— "I shall be glad to see them."

The tall, rugged Admiral entered the room—his countenance working with emotion, which he vainly endeavoured to suppress. He walked up to the bed with his usual abruptness.

"Harry!—my poor fellow!—My God!"

It was all he could articulate—tears coursed rapidly down his iron-furrowed cheeks, and his mighty frame heaved like that of an infant. Mr. Roper, whose broad square figure and rough weather-beaten face yet bore an air of gentleness and goodness, singularly attractive, wept as he followed his master, with a silent melting of the man within, which contrasted with the more convulsive passion of the Admiral, little used to such a mood.

Captain Vivian stretched out his hand, and grasped that of the father of his Iñez. He could not speak. The Admiral clasped it fervently, and clearing his voice—"Cheer up—cheer up, Harry!" he said at length. "This is a bad business, Vivian. The unworthy creature! Are you so badly wounded? You will have your eyesight again, no doubt; and as for the rest—"

Vivian pressed the hand he held, and groaned.

"Why, as for the rest, you must be a man, and forget her."

"Oh, Admiral!" was all he could say.

"You must forget her, I say, Vivian—forget her as I do. A false, worthless, ungrateful wanton! Don't trouble yourself about her more—discard her from your heart and thoughts as I do. My daughter!—no daughter of mine. My blood in her veins!—never believe it. I disown her—I cast her off—never waste a thought on her, Harry. We all loved her so! You must get well—and be off to your ship—a better bride, I warrant you. A false woman! Pooh! pooh! think no more of her."

Vivian sighed, but made no answer; while the Admiral, exhausted by his own vehemence, sat down and caught his breath his eyes still fixed upon the pride and darling of his heart, whom, it may be truly said, he loved as his own son.

"To leave you, for that long-legged—book-learned—lubberly landsman! you, the pride and delight of her old father's eyes! A wretched Jezebel! You must forget her."

"Admiral," at length, said Vivian, with the appearance of great effort, "let us not speak upon this painful subject. I hope to bear my misfortunes as I ought to do."

"No doubt—no doubt—no fear of that, Harry—no fear of your spirit and honour—But your eyes—your eyes—tell me—tell me, you won't be a poor blind, helpless driveller, or I shall curse her aloud."

"God forbid! God forbid!—don't curse her—no, God forbid!—God forbid!"

"You—and your children—and her children—to leave you all—to shame us, and disgrace us—to dishonour her mother's grave—her father's grey hairs—and blast her husband's honest name and fame! Let me curse her, as she deserves.—Daughter of mine!—Damn her—."

The bed shook under the unfortunate Captain Vivian, struck as he was to the soul by the severity of the justly irritated father, whose rude passion, bursting forth in these rough and violent expressions, seemed to tear in pieces the heart of the tender and affectionate husband. He gasped for breath—he strove to stifle his emotions, but the agony rived his shattered frame.

Mr. Roper perceived the excess of his emotion, and sympathised in its cause. He, too, justly grieved, disappointed, and indignant as he felt, cherished a latent tenderness for the sinner, while he detested the sin.

"Oh, Sir," he cried, "don't say so—God forgive her, and forgive us all! We are all sinners—have pity on your own flesh and blood, Sir! Don't curse your only child."

"Did she remember she was my child," said the stern father, "when she dishonoured him whom I had chosen for my son? Did she remember her father was a seaman, when she shamed and disgraced him? No: but as she forgot me, may I forget her! and may God forget her in the hour of his mercy!"

Inexpressibly shocked at this speech, Captain Vivian sank back upon his pillow. Mr. Roper was silent, and the Admiral went on.

"Harry, my boy—my dear boy! what do you mean to do?"

"I have not thought of what I shall do," said Captain Vivian, now sighing heavily, and quite overcome. "I hope sometimes," with a faint smile, "I shall be spared that trouble."

"Pooh—pooh never be down-hearted. Why, Harry, this is like a child! We shall live to forget all this."

"Never, Sir," said Vivian, faintly.

"Admiral," said Mr. Roper, who perceived by the crimson flushes which passed rapidly over the face of Captain Vivian, how dreadfully he was agitated by this scene, "Admiral," he said, "this is too much for Captain Vivian—we had better leave him now, and come again presently."

"Leave him!" cried the Admiral. "Poor fellow—poor fellow! and this is what he is brought to! he, as brave as a lion—as hard as a rock—now laid out like a puny girl—ruined by a false, ungrateful woman.—God bless you, Harry! Yes, yes—I see you are too ill to speak. Its all over—all over. A vile wanton, why do you waste a thought on her? Whistle her down the wind, as I do—and may the great God punish her as she deserves!"

So saying, in an agony of grief and rage, the stern father rose from the bed-side, and, accompanied by Mr. Roper, left the room.

"Never think of her more!—discard her!—disown her!—Yes, Iñez, he who gave you birth may forget—disown—and curse you;—yes, he may renounce and deny you:—but I—my Iñez!—my Iñez!—my idol!—my love!—my only, only love!—Oh Iñez, cruel, barbarous Iñez—what had I done, that you should abandon me?—my loved one! my wife!—what had your poor Harry done?—alas! I loved too fondly—alas! I was not worthy to fill a heart like yours—my idol!—too fondly loved!—alas!—alas!"

In exclamations like these, which the delirious heat of rising fever seemed to render more vehement and piercing, the long controlled feelings of Vivian, driven almost to madness by the bitterness of the last scene, burst at length the restraints his sense of honour had imposed. Deep groans, amounting, at times, almost to cries, mingled with his wild expressions of grief, while he writhed in agony upon the bed, which trembled with the passion of his frame.

Iñez, in the mean time, now greatly enfeebled by the sufferings and fatigues of the last two days, seemed, like himself, almost annihilated by the scene overheard; she had rolled upon the floor, in anguish that mocked control, at the bitter severity of her father's denunciations: but when his solemn curse struck her ear the violence of her distress was arrested, as by a charm. She sat up, upon the ground, and, listening with a face in which dismay seemed to have effaced every other expression—

"It is done!" she cried. "Mrs. Crane—he has cursed me."

"Alas, madam!" said Mrs. Crane, whose eyes, little used to weep, were running over, "it was only in his passion. He seems a violent old gentleman, and takes things warmly. He'll be sorry for this, some time."

"Did my husband curse me too, Mrs. Crane?'

"No, dear young lady—he says nothing."

"He will never, never curse me," said Iñez, melting into tears; "he is an angel of goodness, he will never curse me."

As she spoke, the cries and groans of Captain Vivian were heard.

"They are gone," said Mrs. Crane. "Poor gentleman! he is crying, alone."

"Does he curse me?"

"No, he's calling for you."

"For me?" and she sprang from the floor, and hurried to his bed-side: "Harry!"

His voice ceased as she entered, but he was too much agitated to hear her words. When she approached the bed, she was thunder-struck at what she saw. His countenance was fallen, his whole frame quivering—his teeth rattled and chattered—blue and livid colours spread over his face. At her cry, Mrs. Crane came in.

"Good mercy, madam!—oh, what a change!"

It is needless to describe it. The shivering fit was succeeded by a violent paroxysm of fever. All the flattering symptoms which had rewarded the excessive care of the preceding days disappeared. The wound, exasperated by fever, assumed an appearance the most alarming. On the evening of the second day Captain Vivian was declared past recovery.

Calmed by that languor which succeeds to the dreadful excitement of fever, his feelings, which, thus irritated, had displayed themselves in the most fearful agonies, softened at the near and certain approach of death. A gentle and melancholy composure once more tranquillized his spirits. He asked to see his children.

They were speedily brought, and, by his desire, came into his chamber unattended.

Iñez, trusting to the power of that disguise which had deceived so many, and indeed almost reckless of consequences, now that the termination of all seemed so fast approaching, remained in the room, partly concealed by the shade of a curtain. Her heart in its desolation yearned after her little ones,—and she resolved to see them once more, at any risk.

They came into the room, like the babes in the wood, holding by each other's hands, but no longer cheerful and prattling. Already Iñez could detect in the air of both the effect of Miss Vivian's notions of education.

Florence, indeed, always soft and gentle, appeared only paler than she was wont: but the joyous, open hearted little Georgy had already wore that broken-down, dull look, which children of an ardent, hasty, affectionate character assume when treated with coldness and severity.

Tutored, repressed, for ever naughty, the poor little child had passed in disgrace and tears the days which had elapsed since,—forsaken by her mother, she had been consigned to the care of a cold, unsympathising stranger.

Iñez, whose penetration, ever acute, was sharpened by a mother's sympathy, read all this with a bleeding heart, as the lovely children entered the room.

"Are you there, my treasures?" said the father's broken voice.

"Papa! Papa!"

"Gently, gently, Georgy," said little Florence, but the child was already pressed to its father's bosom.

"Ah! how glad I am to come to you!—We have been so unhappy," said the little girl.

"Have you, my darlings? Where is Florence?"

"Here, papa, close by—can't you see her?"

"My little ones—I can't see."

Florence wept—Georgy cried! "And you're so ill! Poor, poor papa!—where's mamma to nurse you?"

"Oh, Georgy!" said Florence.

"They won't let me speak of her at Aunt Vivian's—and they say I'm very naughty, 'cause I can't help it—and I will speak of her—I love her best of all the world, and—"

"Hush! hush! my dear," said Iñez, softly, from behind the curtain. She saw that this was more than Captain Vivian could bear.

"That's mamma," said the child, springing joyfully up. "That's mamma—she's behind the curtain—she's hiding herself for play.—Mamma! dearest! sweet mamma!" flinging herself across the bed, and throwing her arms round her neck, "I knew you would come again."

"My child," said Iñez, endeavouring vainly to unclasp the eager arms which embraced her. "I am not your mamma. I am the nurse."

"Oh don't, don't play at that any longer," said Florence, bursting into tears, as she ran towards her and hung upon her gown. "Mamma! Mamma! do kiss me."

"Indeed, you are mistaken," said Iñez, still struggling to preserve her disguise, "I am the nurse."

"Papa, she will say she's the nurse," cried Georgy: "don't let her. You've got an ugly gown, but you are mamma." She covered her face with her kisses.

"Speak," said Captain Vivian, in a hollow tone. "Speak again. The child is not mistaken. Have you been with me all these days?"

"Forgive me!" was all that Iñez could say.

A pause—

At length:—"My children, embrace her!—it is your mother!"

Iñez, thus permitted gave way to all her fondness. She clasped the children alternately to her breast. She covered them with kisses, while her sobs and tears were audible. Captain Vivian understood the scene he was unable to witness, and a tear rolled down his wasted cheek.

At length, having allowed time for their emotion to subside, he desired her to bring the little girls close to him, and, having kissed, and given them his blessing, and exhorted them, in broken accents, to be good children, he told Iñez to take them to their nurse, and "then return," he said, "to me!"

She re-entered the room, alone: but, timid and ashamed, she feared to approach the bed.

"Is it, indeed, you?" said Captain Vivian. "Come nearer to me—time is short—my moments are counted. Have you nothing to say?"

She now came up, and kneeled down by the side of the bed.

"Harry, I had not intended to allow myself this consolation. I had not hoped that, in this world, you would speak to me more. I did not dare to hope it. I came to perform, as I best might, my poor duty of attending you to save, if possible, a life my guilt had destroyed. It has not pleased God to bless endeavours such as mine; but, Harry, you have not cursed me. When my father cursed me, you did not curse me. Forgive me, before you die."

"Too happy so to die," in a deep and broken voice. "The dark curtains of the grave are folding round me—the pride of inexorable honour asks no more. Death sanctifies the affection it cannot interrupt. My Iñez! may God forgive you, as I do!"

He stretched out his wasted hand. She took it reverently, and pressed upon it one long holy kiss.

"May I stay with you?" at last she said, with great humility. "Don't send me away!"

"Alas! you need not fear it; a few brief hours, my Iñez! and I shall be nothing—this heart, that beat too fondly, will be still; but stay with me—we have much to speak of.—Ah!" and a smile of ineffable sweetness played over his pallid lips. "Ah! death is sweet near thee!"

He now lay some time still, holding her hand in his, seeming to forget all that had parted them. "I had much to say!" he kept repeating; but that was all: he seemed to rest in a tranquillity he was unwilling to disturb, his cheek leaning against her arm, his hand locked in hers. But too soon his breath began to thicken; shades of darkness gathered round his features. He agitated his arms.

"Here—here!" he said.

She rose, and stretched out hers—he caught her to his bosom—he was no more!

Surprised at the deep silence of the apartment, Mrs. Crane at last ventured to enter. Every thing was still, except the sound of low, suppressed sobbings, which proceeded from the bed. She ran for a light, and, at a glance, discovered what had happened. Captain Vivian lay lifeless, and Iñez sat in a chair by the bedside, her eyes fixed on the body, with a sort of vacant, unmeaning stare, while a dull, low sob broke at intervals from her breast.

Mrs. Crane spoke to her, but she did not appear to listen; she sat in a stupid manner, sobbing at intervals, as a child does after a long and exhausting fit of crying. From this state it was found impossible to rouse her. When they tried to move her, she stretched her arms, with a faint cry and repulsed the attempt—then suffered them to fall again on her lap with the same expression of unmeaning listlessness.

Many hours were passed in the same manner. Captain Sullivan, Mr. X., and Mr. Trevor called. Mrs. Crane did not attempt to conceal the secret of Iñez any longer, and each of them, affected by her situation, was unwearied in endeavours to relieve her. A physician was sent for, and declared that the only chance of rescuing her from what might prove a permanent state of imbecility of mind, consisted in bringing into her presence what might suddenly awaken her recollections, and call up her tears. He mentioned her children, and Captain Sullivan instantly set off for Roehampton, to beg of Miss Vivian to bring them to her.

He was received coldly enough by Miss Vivian, who could not understand, and secretly felt a little jealous of, the interest excited by Iñez. She declared that it was quite impossible to suffer the children to visit their mother, whom they ought never to see again, &c. &c.: entrenched herself in all the pride of virtue, and all the coldness of her unamiable character, and persisted in a flat refusal.

Sullivan returned to West End to find Iñez in the same state of helpless inanity, sitting by her husband's body, and sobbing, while good Mrs. Crane was crying over her like a child.

It was now midnight, when, affected beyond measure at this scene of helpless distress, Trevor had gone down to Mr. Palmer's little garden. The moon had risen—the stars were glistening in the firmament—the calm magnificence of nature contrasting forcibly with the scene of human ruin and misery within the house.

Trevor, lost in melancholy reflection, leaned against the gate which led from the garden into the fields, when a figure, tall, thin, and wasted, with garments worn and tattered, and dark and troubled countenance, approached him. It was Laurence.

"He is dead!"—said a voice, feeble and hollow—"He is dead!"

"It is all over, indeed," said Trevor. "But why are you here?— we keep it a secret a few hours, as it is impossible to move Mrs. Vivian from the room."

"She lives, then?"

"If that may be called life, which is existence without perception, and without aim! But, indeed, Hervey, this will never do! It is time you should abandon your present strange indifference to your own safety. Be persuaded to take shelter from the pursuits of the law, which must soon overtake you!—and rest—" laying his hand on the wasted arm of his friend, and looking kindly in his face. "I never saw a man so changed."

Well might he remark it. Hervey had more the appearance of a tenant of the grave than of a human being! His cheek was pale and hollow. His eyes, enlarged and glassy, had little power of speculation or expression remaining. His voice was so low and husky, that he could with difficulty make himself heard.

"The law!—the law will not wreak its vengeance upon me!— A few more hours But, Trevor, as you hope for compassion from your Maker, in your darkest moment, have mercy upon me in mine. Open the gate—I must, and I will …"

As he spoke, he feebly pushed at the barrier, and entered the garden.

"What are you about?" said Trevor.

"I will see her—I will see *them*!" He gasped for breath as he spoke; his respiration was evidently becoming very difficult. "I will see her. It is necessary I should once gaze upon the ruin I have made, before I close my weary eyes. Do not, Trevor—do not attempt to prevent me. I am a dying man! Barbarians," with some return of his old bitterness, "even barbarians listen to the prayers of the dying!"

Trevor, shocked, and distressed, offered no further opposition; and Laurence, guided by a sort of instinct, crossed the garden, entered the house, and mounted the stairs. The door of the apartment stood open: he attempted not to cross the threshold; but, leaning against the door-post, contemplated, with a countenance of moody despair, the scene within.

The body of his friend lay stretched upon the bed, composed, and covered with a sheet. The face, however, from which the handkerchief had fallen, was visible, by the faint light, of two or three candles, disposed irregularly about the room. Close by the side of the bed, the unhappy Mrs. Vivian, his miserable victim, was still seated, pale as marble, her hair falling disordered over her face, no longer waving in luxuriant beauty, but tarnished, damp, and heavy: her features, of which even her present helpless situation could not destroy the celestial beauty, fixed, and immovable—her eyes, wide open, but without expression:—she resembled one frozen and arrested—a stony statue, rather than a living being—a statue of despair and dismay.

Mrs. Crane kneeled by her side, chafing her listless and insensible hands—in vain.

Laurence remained some time in contemplation of this picture—his heart, which had nearly ceased to beat, now palpitating with a violence which threatened almost instant destruction of its feeble and wasted powers. He did not attempt to enter the room; and, after having, as it would seem, satiated his soul with bitterness, he slowly turned away, and went silently down stairs. He passed again through the garden, unperceived by Trevor, and went out at the little gate.

It would appear that he wanted strength to go far; indeed, that he had not attempted it—but having reached the field, had laid himself down with his face to the earth, and expired.

The next morning he was found, extended on the grass— his face against the ground, his two hands clasped over his forehead.

But Iñez lived.

Vanquished by the earnest and honest prayers of Mr. Roper, the frozen Miss Vivian at length gave way;—the tears of the children were allowed to water the bosom of the mother—their embraces called back the warm currents to her heart—their innocent voices summoned her back from that world of shadows to which she was fast hastening.

She lived—not to re-appear, restored after due lustration, and rear an unblushing front the heroine of a romantic story:—not after a season of decorous retirement, to resume that place in society which she had so justly forfeited.

She lived—but it was in humiliation and obscurity—offering the daily sacrifice of her repentance and her shame, before the throne of that God whose laws she had broken—at the shrine of that loved being her frailty had destroyed.

Many years after this, a gentleman just arrived at Naples, walking in that lovely garden which, stretching along the shore of the fair bay, forms, with its bowers and groves, the most charming promenade in Europe, was attracted by a very interesting group of English people which passed by him. It consisted of two beautiful girls, about fifteen and sixteen, in the bloom of youth and health. Grace and elegance were in their motions, and their countenances were singularly expressive of modesty, sweetness, and intelligence. A little behind them walked a lady in deep mourning, who appeared to be their governess. She had evidently once been remarkably beautiful, and still preserved more than beauty in the serious, yet tender, character of her face. Her carriage was grave, almost to nunlike steadfastness—her looks calm and thoughtful, more than thoughtful—the deep traces of ineffaceable sorrow and suffering were marked upon her beautiful brow. At her side walked a square, thick-set man, with a rough and ruddy countenance, well bronzed by exposure to wind and weather. His whole appearance would have been common-place and vulgar in the extreme, had not such an air of inexpressible goodness and kindness been diffused over them, as would have served to rescue any face and figure in the world from such an imputation.

"Who are those sweet girls?" said the gentleman to a friend— "I never saw two such lovely creatures."

"Don't you know?—Oh, I forgot—you are but just arrived. Every body knows them—and yet nobody knows them—they are, to be sure, poor girls, in a singularly awkward situation. Do you see that old Trojan there? he seems to be the only person belonging to them—neither father, mother, grandfather, nor grandmother, aunt, uncle, nor cousin, have they. And so, you see, they don't get introduced—and they go nowhere—but not one jot seems the young one to mind—she's as gay as if every day in the year were carnival."

"But you have not told me—who they are."

"Oh! the Miss Vivians."

"Vivian!—Vivian!"

"Captain Vivian's daughters. You recollect an odd—ugly story—years ago—an elopement—a duel—and two murders. Well, then, these are the daughters."

"Charming creatures."

"You may say so—but charming as they are, no one much likes to meddle with them. It's an ugly story to append to one's pedigree. However, some Irish fortune-hunter will, it's to be hoped, have mercy on them, some of these days—for they're well enough off."

"And who's that remarkably beautiful woman who walks behind them?"

"Oh! their governess—yes, we do think her most transcendently beautiful—but cold—cold, as the icicle on Dian's temple. There's no blot on her escutcheon. Every one is at liberty to make up to her—and really, she's so divinely handsome—many of us would do a foolish thing for her. But would you believe it? she's as savage as a she bear—no speaking to her. Always the same grave, cold, distant, distrait, manner—puts a man quite out."

"What's her name?"

"Oh! Madame St. Aulaire—quite a name *à la Genlis*—of which school I conclude she is—a sort of *mélange intéressante of grande dame and institutrice*—like that most illustrious petticoat preceptor of princes."

As they talked, the group passed again—the young ones chatting and smiling; more especially one pretty dimpled sparkler—the youngest. She was less beautiful than her sister, but, perhaps, still more engaging.

"Who will introduce me?" said the gentleman; "I must and will know them." As he spoke, he fixed his eyes on Madame St. Aulaire. "I see it all," said he.

"Who will introduce you?—I'll be hanged if I know they're so deuced proud and shy—as if that was their cue, when they can hardly get noticed at all."

"I think I have seen the old gentleman before—Roper?"

"Ay, that's his most nautical name as if he required *that* to mark him for a purser, or some such thing:—only look at him—did you ever see such a guardian for young ladies?"

"Well, well, he looks good-humoured enough," said the other, now evidently in a hurry to be gone. "Good morning."

"Good morning!—Why, Trevor, I should not wonder, if, in your romance and knight errantry, you should actually fall in love with one of these forlorn ones;—but mind me—that won't do—I tell you nobody knows them."

The sagacious gentleman was right. Trevor actually did fall in love with one of these neglected girls; nay, more, he actually married the sparkling Georgina Vivian, though five-and-twenty years older than she was. And Georgina Vivian was the happiest of wives, and the young Marquis of L., who, though a peer, and a man of the world, was neither a coxcomb nor a *roué*, married the lovely Florence. And Madame St. Aulaire, having resigned her pupils into such guardianship—as though a task for which she had been mechanically wound up was completed—sank very suddenly into one of those anomalous declines for which medicine assigns no cause, and offers no cure. Her life had been one of the most deep and humble repentance; and after the two or three first terrible years had expired, one of strenuous effort, in the endeavour to repair, as far as her children were concerned, the heavy evils her guilt had occasioned. She had, in the character of their governess, laboured unremittingly in their education, and her exertions had been crowned with success: they were amiable and accomplished; and their young minds, early enured to sorrow and mortification, had acquired that firmness of principle, and regulation of feeling, which their mother's, alas! had wanted—a want, of which the consequences had been so inexpressively grievous. Their hearts were as tender as hers had been, but well and rightly disciplined: they were as excellent, as they were lovely and engaging.

But the fatal errors of the mother had blighted their dawning prospects; and the cruel reflection of the irreparable evils she had occasioned to these, the darlings of her heart, had embittered every thought and feeling of the unhappy Iñez. It was now given to her to close her long pilgrimage of expiation, and to see them safe and happy. She bowed her head in deep and reverend thankfulness, and, breathing a "*nunc dimittis*," in the faith and grateful spirit of the ancient Simeon, she sank to rest, and was buried, by her own earnest desire, in the grave where Captain Vivian had been deposited just eleven years before.

Mr. Roper may still be seen, either at Mr. Trevor's, or at Lord L.'s, occupying the place carefully reserved for him by the fire-side, or playing with the little prattlers fast springing up around him.

THE END